THE

THE
BLACK
BAY

MOUNT
GAĪA

THE TRIBES
OF BALDEÍRIK

TOMI ADEYEMI

CHILDREN OF ANGUISH AND ANARCHY

HENRY HOLT AND COMPANY • NEW YORK

Henry Holt and Company, *Publishers since 1866*
Henry Holt® is a registered trademark of Macmillan Publishing Group, LLC
120 Broadway, New York, NY 10271 • fiercereads.com

Our books may be purchased in bulk for promotional, educational, or business use. Please contact your local
bookseller or the Macmillan Corporate and Premium Sales Department at (800) 221-7945 ext. 5442 or by email
at MacmillanSpecialMarkets@macmillan.com.

Library of Congress Cataloging-in-Publication Data is available.

First edition, 2024
Book design by Patrick Collins and Samira Iravani
Map illustration by Keith Thompson
Printed in China

ISBN 978-1-250-17101-6 (hardcover)
1   3   5   7   9   10   8   6   4   2

ISBN 978-1-250-35782-3 (international edition)
1   3   5   7   9   10   8   6   4   2

ISBN 978-1-250-35758-8 (special edition)
1   3   5   7   9   10   8   6   4   2

ISBN 978-1-250-35939-1 (special edition)
1   3   5   7   9   10   8   6   4   2

ISBN 978-1-250-35940-7 (special edition)
1   3   5   7   9   10   8   6   4   2

ISBN 978-1-250-36146-2 (special edition)
1   3   5   7   9   10   8   6   4   2

To The Most High,
Thank you for the mountaintops and the valleys,
and the incredible journey in between.

THE MAJI CLANS

IKÚ CLAN
MAJI OF LIFE AND DEATH
MAJI TITLE: REAPER
DEITY: OYA

....

ÈMÍ CLAN
MAJI OF MIND, SPIRIT, AND DREAMS
MAJI TITLE: CONNECTOR
DEITY: ORÍ

....

OMI CLAN
MAJI OF WATER
MAJI TITLE: TIDER
DEITY: YEMOJA

....

INÁ CLAN
MAJI OF FIRE
MAJI TITLE: BURNER
DEITY: SÀNGÓ

AFÉFÉ CLAN
MAJI OF AIR
MAJI TITLE: WINDER

DEITY: AYAO

....

AIYE CLAN
MAJI OF IRON AND EARTH
MAJI TITLE: GROUNDER + WELDER

DEITY: ÒGÚN

....

ÌMỌ̀LÈ CLAN
MAJI OF DARKNESS AND LIGHT
MAJI TITLE: LIGHTER

DEITY: OCHUMARE

....

ÌWÒSÀN CLAN
MAJI OF HEALTH AND DISEASE
MAJI TITLE: HEALER + CANCER

DEITY: BABALÚAYÉ

....

ARÍRAN CLAN
MAJI OF TIME
MAJI TITLE: SEER

DEITY: ORÚNMILA

....

ẸRANKO CLAN
MAJI OF ANIMALS
MAJI TITLE: TAMER

DEITY: OXOSI

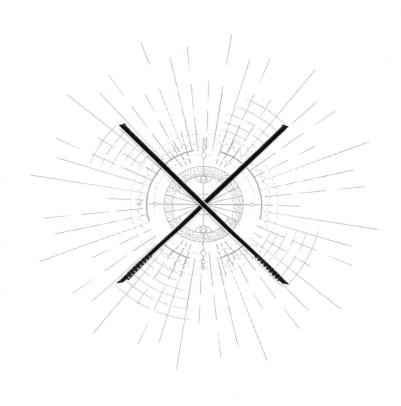

I keep thinking about before . . .

before it all began.

Before the scroll,

and the stone,

and the promise of magic.

Before our war against the monarchy

broke out across the lands.

I think of the divine storm the Iyika brought to Lagos's gates.

The way the palace windows shattered like glittering rain.

I think of Mama and Baba,

of my brother, Tzain.

I think of Mâzeli and my Reapers,

of how we were supposed to reign. . . .

That was before the Skulls threw us onto their ships.

Before they stripped us of all we had.

Before they dragged me away from those I loved,

held me down, and shaved my head.

Before I looked into the eyes of my abductors

and could only see the blood runes carved into their masks.

I think of all the maji who were stolen from their lands.

All the maji who will never feel

Orïsha

again.

PART I

CHAPTER ONE

ZÉLIE

HELP ME.

The quiet prayer waits on my lips—afraid to be spoken aloud, somehow knowing if I reach for help, only silence will follow. Heat hangs like the shackles around my neck. The air churns with the stench of the dead. A thick layer of dirt and grime coats every section of my skin. My bones ache from within.

Thunder rumbles like the pounding of canvased drums, stirring me from my haze. It draws me from my dark corner up to the curved iron bars that create my hanging cage. The metal shackles around my ankles clank together as I press my face as far into the bars as it will go. Fresh rain and sea spray break through the shaft above my cell.

I close my eyes and inhale.

Oya . . .

The name of my goddess fills me. It moves something in my soul. Her brewing storm calls out to me like a song. It holds the promise to make me whole.

For a few moments, the slanted rain washes away my pain. The distant thunder carries me back to better days. The whistling winds take me to the snowcapped mountains of Ibadan, the village I lived in before the Raid. I used to shake in my cot when the thunder roared.

It was Mama who taught me not to fear the rain.

"*You must not be afraid, my love.*" Even after all these years, the memory of Mama's voice wraps around my heart. I feel the warmth of her soft fingers against my cheek. The gentle cadence she used to speak.

"*Oya doesn't just visit us in death,*" Mama whispered into my ear. "*We can feel her presence in the storms and the racing winds.*"

I remember the way Mama coaxed me out of bed, past Baba and Tzain, fast asleep in their hanging cots. It wasn't the first night she brought me to the mountaintop, but it was the first time she brought me to meet the storm.

She took my hand and led me up a winding trail. I could hardly see beyond the tangle the winds made of my white hair. Our bare feet slid along the gravel-lined path. Every time I tried to turn back, Mama forced me to go on.

By the time we reached the flattened mountain peak, the huts of our sleeping village looked like anthills hundreds of meters below. Jagged silhouettes flickered around us every time a lightning bolt lit up the sky. I felt like I could reach over the peak's edge and touch the clouds.

"*Feel her, Zélie.*"

My tiny frame shivered in the pounding rain, but the violent downpour only made Mama feel more alive. She stretched her long arms wide and raised her head to the chaos above.

When the lightning crackled around her, she looked like a god.

"*That's it, little Zél.*" Mama nodded. I closed my eyes and lifted my hands to the raging skies. "*Oya's storms don't just bring the rain. They're our harbinger of her sacred change.*"

I hold on to the memory of Mama's words until my eyes begin to sting. Every time I think I can't lose anything else, I lose everything.

I've lost count of how many times over the past moon I've called out to my gods. How many times nothing but sorrow has answered in return. I cannot bear to hope anymore.

The more I hope, the further I fall.

"No! No, please!"

Sharp screams break through the wooden floorboards above. I wince as the girl's shrieks grow. I don't know what hurts more—the sound of the maji's screams, or the haunting silence that follows when they stop.

There have always been enemies to fight. Always those who wished the maji harm. I knew our battles might never end. But I never thought those battles would stretch beyond Orïsha's borders.

It's been almost a full moon since the Skulls descended upon Orïsha's shores. A full moon since my fellow maji and I were ripped away from our home. After we awoke on the ship, they separated the boys from the girls.

That was the last time I saw my brother, Tzain.

At first, I had the other female elders—the captured members of the resurrected maji clans. But for the past half-moon, I've been locked in this hold alone, left to face the Skulls' torture on my own.

I still don't know why they've taken us. I don't know to where we sail. All I know is that before the Skulls abducted us, the maji were closer to victory than we'd ever been before.

We were moments away from winning the war. . . .

"Attack!"

Tattoos ignite along my skin, covering my body in a twisting light.

Gravel and dirt float around our feet.

Bark splits in the surrounding trees.

The legion of tîtáns run forward in droves, all glimmering in their golden armor. When I raise my hand, every tîtán freezes in place.

They seize as I close my fist. . . .

When I shut my eyes, I can still see it—the battle for Lagos runs through my mind. When we brought magic back to Orïsha, it didn't just return to the maji. The sacred ritual gave birth to the tîtáns, granting Queen Nehanda and her military followers devastating power.

Before our final attack, Mama Agba sacrificed her life, allowing me to connect my heart to the hearts of the other nine maji elders. Together, we created a force the tîtáns couldn't withstand. As a united front, the maji elders commanded the earth and raised the winds.

That night was supposed to be the end of the monarchy's reign. The night the maji joined together to rule our kingdom again. After centuries of oppression, our fight was at an end.

We had retribution for all of our pain.

But now . . .

I stare at my shackled hands. At my bare brown skin. The tattoos that used to glow are gone. My white mane has been ripped away. The magic I fought so hard to restore is dead. My Orïsha is farther away than it's ever been.

I don't know how to carry on.

I don't know how to hold on to the will to live.

"Oya, please . . ." I whisper the words, risking the heartbreak of another unanswered call. But thunder still rumbles through the ventilation shaft. I have to believe that even this far from Orïsha's shores, the thunder means Oya is here at last.

"Please." I think of all the times she's answered me before. The glimpses I've caught of her hurricane spirit, raging like the storms. "Please free us from these Skulls. Please bring your people back home—"

"*Bindið hendr honum!*" a shout rings out.

My stomach drops at the harsh, guttural sound of the Skulls' tongue. Heavy boots thunder over the floorboards above, and lines of sawdust rain into my eyes. Feeling drains from my fingertips as I prepare for the Skull's cold grip. My neck burns in anticipation of the thick needle they'll jam into my throat, the venomous majacite they'll pump into my blood. Every night, the Skulls return like clockwork, injecting the poison into my body to keep me numb.

"Oya, please!"

I reach for the magic my goddess once granted me—the power to raise the spirits of those who have passed. I can't bear another night of the Skulls' beastly palms holding me down. Of pain so great, I can hardly make a sound.

There were days when entire armies of animations fought at my command, days when my spirit soldiers ripped through my enemies like the wind. If I could raise just one, I could hold the Skulls back.

With one animation, I would have a fighting chance.

"Please!" I beg. But no matter how hard I push, no power comes forth. I'm left staring at my open palms. I haven't felt the touch of my magic since we sailed from Orïsha's shores—

The wooden door to my hold shudders open. I scramble to the farthest corner of my cage. Fear slams my mouth shut. The Skulls beat us whenever they hear my tongue.

Torchlight dances into the hold as the first Skull enters. Flames light the same mask they all wear—skeleton heads smelted together in bronze and blood. The crushed bones come together in jagged pieces, creating one large, tarnished skull.

Braids run through the Skull's auburn curls. Unruly scars cover his bare chest. Bloodstains coat his beastly hands and his wool pants. A crimson axe hangs from his animal-skin belt.

I brace myself against the bars of my cage as the Skull leers at me, an animal closing in. His snarl is apparent despite the bronze mask fixed over the bridge of his nose and hooked underneath his chin.

In his eyes, I see the gaze of every enemy I've had to face. Every oppo-nent who's ever stood in my way. The way the Skull stares at me now . . .

I ball my fists.

King Saran's beady eyes held the same hate.

Do your worst. I meet his stare. I won't cower. I won't show fear. But more boots follow overhead. Instead of opening my cage, the Skull uses his ring of brass keys to unlock another.

"Let me go!"

I crane my neck as the familiar sound of Orïshan travels down the stairs. Two Skulls enter with a struggling prisoner between their burly arms. A canvas bag covers the boy's head. Fresh blood is splattered across his bruised chest.

The boy thrashes as the Skulls throw him into the second cage. The men struggle to shackle the prisoner's wrists. With a sudden wrench, the boy slips free and kicks, sending a hard heel into a Skull's nose.

"*Náðu hann!*" the injured Skull calls.

I watch in awe as the boy puts up a valiant fight. He drives his other foot into the second Skull's chest. He throws a wild punch, colliding with another Skull's mask. Though blinded, he strikes in all directions, doing everything he can to attack.

"*Þú lítill skítr!*" the third Skull shouts. His ferocity makes me curl. He seizes the boy's hand and holds it in the cage's doorframe. I turn away as the bronze Skull slams the door shut.

"*Agh!*" The crack of breaking bones echoes through the cell. The boy writhes on the floor. Phantom pain shoots through my own fingers. I hold them as they shake.

New shackles clamp shut around the boy's wrists. The Skulls lock him inside and retreat. A padlock clicks behind the hold's door. I don't dare speak until the thundering boots fade.

"Are you alright?" I lean forward. I don't know what to do. What to say. A string of curses flies from the boy's lips. Blood leaks from his broken hand.

His chest heaves with shuddering breaths. But after a long moment, he pulls the canvas bag off his head.

It can't be. . . .

My mouth falls open. My heart sinks into my chest. The damp walls around me close in. My cage starts to spin.

"Inan?" Rage grips me as I dare to whisper the name.

The boy shifts, and a thin ray of moonlight illuminates the amber eyes I know far too well.

CHAPTER TWO

ZÉLIE

MY GODS.

Blood pounds between my ears. I don't know what to think. What to feel. A part of me wants to wrap a chain around Inan's neck. Another part of me can't believe that he's here.

The last time I saw Inan, we were in the palace cellars. The *Iyika* razed the royal throne to the ground. As the palace fell, I chased Inan down. He was my final target.

I went in for the kill.

"You're alive." The familiar scratch of his voice is like a chain pulling me back in time. In an instant, I'm thrown back into our fight.

The moment before we were knocked unconscious by the thick cloud of white . . .

There are nights when you visit my dreams. Nights where I can forget. When I wake, I drive myself insane thinking of what could've been.

I don't know what comes next, but I know it's time for this reign to end. But should our paths collide again, I will not raise my sword.

I am ready to end my life at your hand.

My own hands shake as I stare at him, remembering that fateful night. Inan vowed to dissolve the monarchy. He vowed to destroy his own birthright.

After every broken promise between us, I didn't allow myself to believe another lie. From the moment we met, the crown was everything to Inan—worthy of every sacrifice. Orïsha's throne was the very thing he lived to protect.

It didn't matter who else had to die.

But that night, Inan went through with his plan. Despite everything against him, he ended his family's long reign. When I faced him in the underground cellars, he never put up a fight.

He shared the monarchy's secrets with me as I ripped away his life.

Staring at Inan now, my mind races. A full moon at sea has taken its toll on his sturdy frame. This long below deck, his cinnamon skin has gone pale, creating a stark canvas for the fresh and faded bruises traveling down his back. His movements are sharp. Almost feral. Something about him feels more animal than man.

But entire oceans span between our past and our present. Old fury wars with relief. I feel the guarded divîner I was when we first met. The sting of the venom from the brooding little prince. The force of his sword against my staff. The brush of his lips against my neck.

I see the boy who told me we could build a new Orïsha.

The boy who tore my heart in half.

But what does that mean when we're both trapped in here?

What does that mean when the Skulls are closing in?

"Your hair," Inan croaks.

I lift my fingers to my bare scalp, and my cheeks burn. I've been alone for so long.

No one else has seen what the Skulls have done.

"There was a man. . . ." My voice trails off as I remember his shadowy figure. "His mask gleamed in silver."

"The captain of the ship?" Inan asks.

I nod. "The other Skulls listened to him. He must have been."

I try to continue, but the words disappear. The memories strike like the tides. Slowly, I'm brought back to the way the Silver Skull loomed over me. I feel the sweat that dripped down my skin.

Two Skulls held me down the first night they locked me in here. Another took hot shears to my scalp. The Silver Skull raised the twisted majacite crown in his hands.

The world darkened when I realized his plan.

I thrashed as the Silver Skull shoved the poisonous metal into my temple. The searing alloy steamed as it merged with my skin. When I passed out on the rusted floor, tears streamed down my face.

I begged for death's embrace.

With the majacite welded to my temple, I don't know if I'll be able to access my gifts again.

"I'll kill them," Inan almost growls. Nothing soft lies in his amber eyes. His conviction makes my throat tight. It stirs the feelings I've tried to bury deep inside.

"I know I've hurt you." Inan averts his gaze. "I know I've let you down more times than I can count. But I need you to trust me."

"*Trust* you?" I scoff.

"If the two of us can bring down a kingdom, we have to be capable of bringing down a single ship."

Though everything in me wants to keep Inan at bay, the threat of the Skulls takes that choice away. For the first time since being locked in this hold, I have an ally.

I have a chance to escape.

I force myself to reach deep down, past every single betrayal, past every fallen tear. I have to trust him.

At least until we're out of here.

"What can we do?" I ask.

Inan rips a strip of cloth from his dirt-stained pants and ties the strip around his bleeding hand. His swinging cage creaks as he paces the small perimeter. He tests the iron bars' strength.

"How long have you been locked in this hold?" he questions.

"Half a moon."

"Do you still have your magic?"

I shake my head. "Every night . . ."

Inan extends his neck to the rays of moonlight, illuminating the puncture wounds along his throat that mirror my own.

"I know about the liquid majacite," Inan says. "If we could stop it somehow . . . disrupt their supply——"

"There's no guarantee our magic would return." I look down at my empty palms, wishing I could stir the ashê that used to lie within my blood. "Our powers come from our land. We might not be able to restore them unless we return home."

"Then we need to overwhelm them." Inan grabs the iron bars as he thinks. "Break free at once. The others have been working on a plan."

"What do they need to escape?"

"A distraction. A way to get close to the Skulls without them realizing what's going on. But we can't think about that now. We need to get you out of this hold."

The seas push against our damp walls, making our hanging cages creak. Inan runs his hands up and down the bars, likely searching for a place where the metal is weak.

"Why'd they take you?" he continues. "Why'd they separate you from the others?"

I stop and think back to the day. So much of my time in this cage has passed in a haze. Moments spent waiting for the Skulls to descend. Hours spent in agony after they inject the majacite into my neck.

"They lined us all up. Every girl, one level above." I close my eyes until I see it—the Silver Skull fills the blackness of my mind. I hear the creaking floorboards under his approaching boots. I feel the warmth of the girls' shaking bodies, pressed tight against mine. "The Silver Skull separated us with some kind of compass—"

"What did it look like?" Inan asks.

I focus, trying to remember exactly what I saw. "Bronze. Hexagon-shaped. A triple arrowhead painted in blood . . ."

The terror that gripped me that day returns like the rain. I see the compass's thick red dial. I hear the way it hummed as it spun. I could barely survive waiting with the others in chains. I didn't realize how much worse it'd be to be taken away.

"Did it react to others?" Inan continues.

"A few." I nod. "They took me and three other girls. A Lighter from Ibadan. A girl from Zaria's coast. A Healer from the sand huts of Ibeji."

I think of the Healer's round face, the lilt in her voice, her kind beauty, her grace. I recall the ways she collected rainwater and instructed us to dress our wounds, caring for us all, despite the pain she faced.

"Where are they now?" Inan pushes. A crease forms above his thick brows and I look down at the rusted floor. The empty cages answer in my silence.

"We have to get you off this ship." Inan's pacing quickens. His eyes dart around the hold. "We don't have time to wait for the others. We need to find a new way to escape."

The way Inan moves makes my stomach clench. There's something he holds back.

"What is it?" I press. "What do you know?"

Inan stops and holds my gaze.

"These men aren't just searching for maji, Zélie. They're searching for you."

CHAPTER THREE

INAN

"ME?" ZÉLIE WHISPERS.

Her delicate face falls.

Locked behind the curved bars of her cage, she looks so weak.

Weak and small.

Dried blood rains from the black crown embedded into her temple. Her mane of white coils is no more. Moonlight catches a ring of black and purple bruises around her neck. It makes me want to drive a blade through every Skull's mask.

"I don't understand." Zélie looks to me. "How would they even know who I am?"

Even in the dark, I see the terror that snakes around her throat.

I felt that terror myself those first hollow nights on this boat.

I thought it was all over—the war between the maji and the tîtáns. The line of bodies left in my family's wake. I sedated my own mother to dissolve Orïsha's throne. I thought the plague brought on by my family was at its end.

When Zélie and her maji attacked, I felt relief. I awaited my final release. She laid her hands on my chest, and tendrils of white hair floated past her sharp cheeks. I thanked the gods that it was her, that I had one final chance to see her face.

But a thick gas billowed as it traveled down the hall. Zélie couldn't see the approaching wall of white. One by one, maji fell unconscious. Masked mercenaries descended upon their bodies like vultures.

We were all lost in the fight. The Skulls didn't hesitate to strike. There was nothing we could do.

My people were stolen in the dead of night.

"There are always enemies, Inan. . . ."

Father's ghost joins me in my cage, bleeding through my scars. I brush my good hand against the leathery skin where he stabbed me after seeing my magic and learning who I truly was.

The damp hold starts to fade. Father's voice brings me back to earlier days. Suddenly I'm twelve years old, surrounded by old books, burgundy walls, yellowed maps. Father sipped from his goblet of wine, watching intently as I moved my sênet pawn.

"They lie in wait." He stared at the decorated game board. *"Inside your kingdom and beyond. The moment you show weakness is the moment they strike."*

Father shifted his final sênet piece to capture mine.

"Remember, Inan—an entire empire can crumble in one night."

I wonder what he'd say now that real enemies have invaded our shores. If he were still alive, would the Skulls have had a chance?

If I'd been a better king, could I have held their invasion back?

There's no time for regret.

I force myself to wipe the memories of Father from my mind. The Skulls invaded under my rule. Crown or no crown, it's my duty to protect my people. I have to find a way to defeat the Skulls and expel them from our borders.

"These men hail from a land to the far east," I explain, recalling what I've seen. What I've heard. They used a few prisoners across the ship. Working on their deck was the only way for me to learn. "They call themselves the Tribes of Baldeírik. They sail under one king, a man named Baldyr. Whoever they're searching for, they're searching on his behalf."

Zélie's feet falter. She has to grab the bars of her cage to stay upright.

"What is it?" I ask.

"Something one of Roën's mercenaries once said . . ." Zélie's fingers lift to her lips. "We were back in Jimeta, the moon after magic returned. Harun cornered me and spoke of a bounty. Do you think he was talking about the Skulls?"

"He must have been." I can't count the number of times the night we were taken has played in my mind. "It was the mercenaries who abducted us from the palace. If Roën sold us out—"

"No." Zélie cuts me off. "He wouldn't. He *couldn't*. He parted with his men. He fought by our side! He wouldn't do this to me. To the maji—"

"But would his crew?" I push. "Cities of maji have been disappearing from Orïsha for moons."

Zélie hesitates and her fingers fall to her side. "We got reports during the war, but the elders and I thought it was you."

"Mother and I thought it was you."

An entire empire can crumble in one night.

Father's old teachings swim in my head as guilt rises like bile up my throat. We made it so easy for the Skulls. They've been raiding our lands for moons.

But if our empire can crumble in one night, theirs can, too. If we escape this ship, we have a chance.

We can obliterate their forces in one fair fight.

"The Skulls keep saying one thing," I continue. "'*Stúlkan með blóðið sólarinnar.*'"

Zélie shudders at the sound of the enemy's tongue.

"What does that mean?" she asks.

"A girl with the blood of the sun."

Zélie's silver gaze grows distant. I've never seen the empty look in her eyes. The weight of my words seems to hit her like a boulder. She fights not to cry.

"Do you really think it's me?"

I tread gently. I don't know how much more she can take. "They need someone with great power . . . that's why I think—"

Zélie's chest starts to heave. She claws at her own skin, as if struggling to breathe. I push against the front of my cage.

I would give anything to take her terror away.

"There's a way off this ship," I talk quickly. "Three levels up. They have lifeboats on the deck. If we can board just one, we can head to land. Get you back to Orïsha. Figure out a plan!"

Though Zélie fights her own haggard breaths, she shakes her head, rejecting my idea.

"The others," she manages to gasp. "Amari. Tzain. The elders—"

"If we can get you off this ship, I'll find a way to free the rest. But you're the one these Skulls are after. You're the one we have to protect."

Zélie wraps her arms around herself. I yearn to wrap my arms around her instead. Staring at her now brings me back to another time, back to those nights in the dreamscape when I was hers and she was mine.

The abyss grows in her silver eyes. The little light I feel inside of her dies. For a long while, the waves crash in our silence. Then Zélie lifts her head.

"Tell me it's going to be alright."

Her whispers hit me like a spear to the chest. I think of my vow to protect her. To fight for her with every last beat of my heart.

"It's going to be alright." I speak the words without a shadow of a doubt. "I don't care what it takes. I don't care who we have to face. We're going to get you out of here. We're going to get you back home."

"Promise me."

For an instant, I don't feel the cages between us. I don't carry the toll of the countless battles we've fought. The strain of the parents we've taken away. The weight of the broken kingdom that tore us apart.

For a single breath, we are together—connected, just like that first day in Lagos's marketplace. I run my fingers through the jagged white streak that appeared in my hair after that fateful moment, remembering the jolt like lightning that passed through my skin. It's like our very spirits wove together. My heart thrums with the bond neither of us has ever been able to break, despite every wound and every mistake.

"I *promise*," I whisper. I reach out my good hand. Though I can't bridge the entire space, Zélie reaches back. Her breaths start to relax.

"We'll get through this," I assure her. "I just need time—"

Boots thunder above. Too fast for me to prepare. With a click of the padlock, the door to the hold flies open. A wall of torchlight floods in.

The captain . . .

The Silver Skull enters, distinguished from every other bronze Skull on this ship. Tall and stocky, the captain towers above the rest. Crude tattoos cover the shaved sides of his head.

The Silver Skull mutters something to his men as he holds a torchlight to our faces. It passes over mine with disdain before stopping in front of Zélie's. My heart constricts when the Silver Skull raises a leather-clad finger and points.

It's happening, I realize.

We've run out of time.

"No!" I bang against the iron bars. I don't know what to fear more. If they take Zélie now, she'll never return. And what will happen to Orïsha if the Skulls find what they're searching for?

Zélie throws herself to the back of her cage. The other Skulls open her cell door. Though she struggles, they unlock the shackles around her neck, waist, and ankles. Two Skulls lift her up, and Zélie thrashes in their arms.

"Inan!" Zélie cries out.

A new set of shackles clamps shut around her wrists. I rage against the bars as they drag her away.

But the door to the hold swings shut, keeping me locked in this cage.

CHAPTER FOUR

ZÉLIE

Gods help me.

My insides freeze. Inan's shouts die in the hold below. The Silver Skull yells orders at his men, and we follow close behind, ascending the wooden steps in the cramped stairwell.

The Skulls' meaty palms dig into my arms. Their hooded eyes gleam in the dark. A sulfur scent rises from the pouch bombs strapped to their animal-skin belts. Brine coats their fair skin and their chestnut hair.

Where is he taking me?

The human bones embedded in the Skulls' masks glower in the flickering torchlight. Even without my magic, I sense the torment soaked into the crushed skeletons. I hear the cries of their dead.

The fight that started to light in me before withers away. The hope of escape strangles me, restraining me like my chains. Everything Inan shared with me swirls in my mind.

If I'm the one they're after, I die tonight.

They're searching for a girl. I hear Inan's voice. *A girl with the blood of the sun.*

I think back to the sunstone that shattered in my hands the moment I brought magic back. I remember the power that surged through my form, the force that crashed through my very being, threading deep into my heart. In that instant creation swirled before my eyes, the birth of man, the origin of the gods. Is that power what these beasts hunt now?

Do I even hold that power if I can't feel my magic at all?

I have to break free.

I ball my fists. Escape is my only hope. But what can I do with my hands in chains? How can I fight when I can't even move my legs?

As we move past yards of rope and tarp-covered cannons, I search for a weapon, anything I can use to escape. The broken shards of wood that hang overhead, the rusted harpoons mounted on the walls. I look down at the Skulls' waists and shift, wondering what it would take to snatch one of their knives. A few daggers hang from each of their belts, but they pale in comparison to the crimson hammers and axes strapped to each Skull's back.

Something about their weapons feels alive. . . .

When we reach the top of the stairs, I'm hit with a familiar stench. The cells I shared with the others when the Skulls first locked me on to their ship hang with the bite of death. Flames pass over rows of cages, revealing broken bones and gaunt brown faces. There are nearly a dozen young girls per cage. They cower as the Skulls near.

"Zélie?"

I hear Amari's hushed whisper before I see her emaciated frame. The sight of my former ally takes me by surprise—her hollowed cheeks, her sunken eyes. A ripped kaftan hangs over her skeletal shoulders. Her bones protrude from her copper skin. Grime and dirt mat the curls in her hair. She withers from within.

Hold on. I mouth the words. Instinct to protect overpowers our former war. I can't bear the sight of her in enemy chains. Her slender face, twisted in pain.

Across from Amari I spot Nâo, the elder of the Tider clan. Always one of the most powerful fighters in our group, I hardly recognize the scrawny figure who stares back.

Cropped white coils pepper her formerly shaved head. She looks at me like she's crawled back from the dead. Nâo reaches her tattooed arm through the bars of her cell as we pass. The Silver Skull is quick to react.

"*Farðu!*" The captain bangs on the bars of her cage. Nâo and the girls back up at once, staring after me as the Skulls carry me away.

But they're alive. We're still alive.

I attempt to let the news spark hope. But pairs of empty shackles lie between the lines of girls. Every maji I was captured with isn't onboard.

I note the open chains where Imani, the leader of the Cancers, once was. The freckled face of her twin sister, Khani, fills my mind. Grief tears at me from inside.

If I lost my brother to this horrid ship, I would die.

Flames dance over the faces of eight maji chained to a corpse, a body they've yet to throw overboard. The young girl's round eyes hang open, and a tattered rag doll lies in her clenched hand.

She can't be more than twelve.

How could this happen?

The girl's body haunts me as the Skulls drag me through the long, damp hall. My body aches with the pain she must have felt. The utter misery her final hours of life held.

I take in the captured faces of my people, the festering lesions where the Skulls' shackles meet their skin. The cramped quarters echo with their unspoken fears, their questions of whether or not they'll ever escape from here.

I think back to Inan's plan, his insistence that I need to escape. Despite what the Skulls may be after, this can't just be about me. We are all locked in these cages.

We all need to break free.

Push, Zélie.

The heat of determination flares in my core. I try to move, though panic seizes every limb. My legs start to shift as the Silver Skull opens the door to the next level. We rise up another narrow stairwell.

When we reach the next hall, the sight of the boys sparks a new thought—I consider how many maji sit before me now, how many Skulls might lie above deck. What chance might we have if the maji on the ship outnumber the Skulls?

How many of us would need to break free to overwhelm them all?

Seven . . . nineteen . . . My head swivels from side to side as I try to keep count. Hatred burns through me with each protruding rib cage and hollowed face I pass.

If I could just get the keys . . .

I glance to the Skull on my left; a ring of brass keys jangles against his hip. The Skull jostles me, and my majacite crown pricks at my forehead.

Its blackened thorns hang just beneath his chin. . . .

This is it. I brace myself. One shot is all I'll have. I rear my head back. My body quivers with my impending attack.

But before I can strike, we pass another cage. Everything changes when I see a familiar frame.

A boy with sturdy shoulders and cropped black hair.

My brother, Tzain.

CHAPTER FIVE

ZÉLIE

"Tzain?"

For the first time since they locked me on to this ship, a smile spreads across my lips. Feeling returns to my legs in a rush. The sight of my brother hardens something in my gut.

Tzain sits in the corner of a cage, face buried in his hands. When I speak, his body goes rigid. He lifts his head, and his dark brown eyes meet mine.

What do they need to escape? The question I asked Inan back in the hold runs through my mind.

A distraction. A way to get close to the Skulls without them realizing what's going on.

Time slows down as I soak in Inan's words. I can give my brother that.

If a distraction is what he needs, I won't hold back!

"*Hah!*" I ram my head into the Skull to my left. The thorns of my crown break through his mask, impaling his right eye. The Skull cries out as hot blood spurts between his fingertips. It coats my chin as we fall to the floor.

The other Skull reaches for me as I scramble forward. With another roar, I kick out, and my heel connects with the Skull's jaw. He hits the wooden floor with a heavy thud. His ring of brass keys goes flying down the hall.

There! I move for the keys, but the Silver Skull cuts me off. The captain lunges at me, a frenzy filling his hazel eyes.

Before the captain can strike, a maji named Udo comes to my defense. I recognize the skilled Welder though they've shaved his full beard. Metal burns cover his large hands. He shouts after me as I pass.

Udo whips out a pair of empty shackles, catching the Silver Skull by his feet. The captain crashes into the bars of a cage. A small dagger in his belt slides free.

This must be it. I extend my leg and kick, sending the dagger into Udo's cell. As the ship shifts, the maji turn rabid. The long hall echoes with the power of their rage.

But in the chaos, the maji claw at the fallen Skulls. They snap weapons and tools from their belts. Bits of rusted metal and dropped knives disappear into their cells.

As they work, my eyes return to the ring of brass keys sitting down the hall. The Skulls are still down.

There's a chance I can set these maji free right now!

I launch myself up, closing the distance between me and Tzain. My brother throws himself against the bars of his cell. The five maji he's chained to are dragged forward by his strength.

I leap over the Silver Skull. Even with his mask, I see the anger our rebellion brings. The captain's fingers graze my ankle, but I don't slow down. My heartbeat spikes as I snatch up the keys.

"Hurry!" Tzain yells. The ship jostles me from side to side as I fight my way back to his cell. My muscles burn with the strain, yet I run as fast as I can.

When I reach his cage, Tzain grabs my shoulders. I don't know how long it's been since I felt anything but the enemy's cold hands. Tears well in my eyes as I struggle to fit the first brass key into his lock. When the gears don't shift, Tzain steadies my shaking hands.

"Breathe," he whispers. "*Breathe.*"

With a large exhale, I force myself to calm down. I pull out the first key and move to the next. I jam in the third. The fourth. The fifth.

The floors creak as the Skulls rise behind me. The hairs lift on the nape of my neck.

"Go!" Tzain tries to push me away.

"I won't leave you!" I shout back. I jam the sixth key into the lock. With a click, the gears start to shift. I twist to pull him out—

All at once, Tzain shoves me to the floor. A knife meant for my shoulder lodges into his right arm. Tzain roars and stumbles back. The brass keys are yanked from my hands.

The Skull I impaled hovers over me, baring his bloodstained teeth. Crimson droplets fall onto my neck. He removes the hammer in his sheathe.

"*Nei!*" the Silver Skull shouts. I crawl away as the bronze Skull transforms. His blood soaks into the rectangular runes carved into the oak shaft of his hammer. The same runes carve themselves down the Skull's chest.

The bronze Skull cries out as the hammerhead glows red. The very air around him shakes. Veins bulge against his fair skin. His muscles swell with new strength.

My eyes widen as the bronze Skull grows so tall he eclipses the captain's height. The entire hall freezes at his display.

I didn't know the Skulls could fight this way.

"*Hættu!*" The captain lunges. It takes all of him to tackle the bronze Skull. With great force, the captain shoves his warrior against the cells. The bronze Skull dents the iron bars.

27

My pulse races as heated words pass between them. The Silver Skull points to the majacite crown on my head.

"*Hún tilheyrar Baldyri!*" he declares.

Did he just say Baldyr?

The bronze Skull resheathes his hammer, and the effects of his bloodmetal fade. He stumbles back as he returns to his normal strength. Though a monster of a man moments ago, now he struggles to catch his breath.

The Silver Skull grabs me. He yanks the knife from my brother's arm and holds the blade to my neck. The edge digs into my throat, forcing me to stay still.

"Hold on!" Tzain shouts as the captain marches me down the hall. "I'm coming! Zélie, I'm coming—"

I don't hear what my brother says next.

The arched door at the end of the hall flies open. Whipping winds swallow all sound. We pass through the gateway, and the entire world spins. I struggle to take it all in.

Mighty waves crash against the ship's side. Sea spray stings the open cuts on my head. The yellow moon shines above, and its delicate light spills across my face. I gasp at the sight.

The deck . . .

A second is all I have to savor the fresh sea air. I lift my head to the open sky. A hard rain falls into my eyes. An endless expanse of clouds swirls overhead, forming a blanket over the glittering stars.

Everywhere I turn, Skulls cover the ship—all brawn and menace and grit. Paint is smeared across their fair skin. They shout in their brutish tongue as they man the colossal ship.

Over a hundred meters long, the vessel has seven mastheads spread across the deck. Each square sail ripples with the image of a man formed from storm clouds, the emblem of the Tribes of Baldeírik. Rows of mounted cannons line both sides of the deck, each positioned to shoot out of the circular gunport. Iron plates reinforce the massive hull, topped with the figurehead of a tarnished silver skull.

The captain sends a Skull back through the arched door before pointing to the opposite end of the ship. Above the deck, living quarters rise three levels high. At the top level, a tower sits. Its walls are marked with white.

That has to be where they're taking me now. . . .

My throat dries as we move. I stare at the place the other girls in my hold disappeared to, never to return. But as we walk, I catch the lifeboats Inan spoke of. Our only way off the ship. Enough for the dozens of Skulls above deck.

Enough for the dozens of maji locked in their cells.

Let it be enough. I think of my brother and the maji, of everything they snatched in the frenzy. If they got what they needed, they still have a chance.

The maji can be free at last.

But when the captain marches me up the stairs, the thoughts of the others vanish. I come face-to-face with a crimson door.

I look up to the sky as they push me inside, praying I'll live to see the yellow moon again.

CHAPTER SIX

TZAIN

"Zélie!" I shout. "Zélie!"

I yell my voice hoarse. I yell long after they take my little sister. Long after she disappears through the arched door.

For so many nights, all I wanted was to see her face. To know that she was okay. But now that's not enough.

They're dragging my sister away.

"Mama! Mama!"

I slam my eyes shut. My body turns to lead. I squeeze the bars of my cage as it all comes rushing back. The night I've lived to forget.

They took Mama just like this. They beat her down. They dragged her by her neck.

I was too afraid to fight.

I let my mother die that night.

"Mama!"

Something breaks inside me at the memory of my own cries. The entire world ripped in half that day. I thought the sun would never rise.

And now it's happening again. Right before my eyes. The only family I have left is slipping through my hands.

I have to do something before my sister dies——

The arched door to our hold rips open. Instinctively, every boy moves to the back of his cell. One Skull re-enters the cargo hold, brass keys jangling in his hand.

As he leers through the iron bars, blood drips from the open gash in my arm. The wound burns like a fire under my skin. The Skull has to be coming for me.

Retaliation for almost breaking free.

But instead of opening my cell door, he opens another down the hall. The maji scramble as the Skull reaches for Udo, the boy who used his chains to trip the Silver Skull.

Fight! I will Udo on. The maji tries to escape the Skull's grasp. But the Skull grabs his head.

An angry crack echoes through the hall as the Skull snaps his neck.

No.

My hatred flares. The others look away, but I force myself to stare. Udo's chains rattle as he falls to the floor.

Another maji stolen, lost to this war.

All of us stay silent as the Skull leaves. The Skull doesn't even bother to take Udo's body from the hold. We're left with Udo's fresh corpse, a warning of what will happen if we attempt another escape.

But staring at Udo's body, I see Mama's feet hanging overhead. I see Zélie bleeding out on the floor.

I'll save you, I vow to myself.

I won't allow myself to lose anymore.

I reach into the back of my pants. The animal-skin pouch I managed to grab is warm in my hands. Tar-like liquid leaks from a tear in the pouch's skin. The rope that ignites its fuse is split and frayed.

I move to the front of my cell, sticking my hand out to wave the other maji forward. The threat of the Skulls forces us to keep our voices low. The wooden ship creaks as we gather.

"Hold out what you managed to grab," I instruct.

One by one, maji extend what they stole: bits of metal, sulfur pouches; a maji in Udo's cell even brandishes a dagger. Gathered over the past moon, almost every cage has a tool, a way to pick at our chains and break the locks on our doors. With Zélie's distraction, we have a chance.

We finally have enough to break free of these cells.

"Listen to me," I whisper to the others. "We have to strike. *Now.* Udo was just the first. The Skulls will return to kill us all."

"It's too dangerous." Taiwo, the maji chained to my left, speaks up. He points to the blood soaked into the wooden floor. "You saw what happened after Zélie attacked that Skull!"

At the thought of the Skull who transformed, a shiver runs down my spine. When his blood fed into his crimson hammer, he became someone else.

It was like he lost his mind.

"That was just one." Taiwo shakes his head. "How are we supposed to take them all?"

"Together." I dare to raise my voice. I offer the maji a show of strength. "If we swarm them at once, we can take them down. We can keep them from using their weapons."

"We should wait till we make land," another maji offers. "Surprise them when they take us off the ship."

"Even if we survive the trek, who knows how much worse it will be when we reach their lands? How many we'll have to attack? I know you're scared," I continue. "I know we're taking a risk. But we have to *try.* This is our best chance!"

I look around my cell, searching for an ally. Anyone who will help. But no one joins in.

Everyone in the ship's hold stays still.

"Come on!" I scan the desperate faces beyond my cage. "If we work together, I know we can break out. We can even take the ship!"

Across the way, Kenyon, my old agbön mate, meets my eye. The elder of the Burner clan, he's barely recognizable without his white locs. Dirt covers the tattoos on both his arms.

"We're not meant to die in these cages." I shake my head. "The Skulls think they've broken us, but they're wrong. I *know* we're strong enough!"

Kenyon rises to his feet. I recognize the familiar flame that ignites in his eye.

"Tzain's right." The Burner looks to Udo's corpse. "We fight or we die."

With the order of an elder on my side, the rest of the maji fall in line. The hold begins to ring with the sounds of maji tinkering. My heart pounds as we work to pick our locks.

I take the animal-skin pouch and let the tar run over the padlock on my cell. I cover my nose as its sulfur scent reeks. Though there's little left in the pouch, the metal starts to bubble and steam.

Smoke builds in the hall as the others use what they have of the enemy's corrosive tar. When every lock is weakened, we prepare to charge. As soon as the Skulls hear what we're doing, they'll return.

It'll take everything we have to break out before they swarm.

"On the count of three!" I look to the maji in my cell. To the others down the hall. "Give it all you've got!" I demand. "Don't hold back!"

I cling to the image of Zélie's face in my mind, to the feel of her trembling shoulders in my hands. I don't have time for fear.

I have to escape from here.

"Three!"

I'll become strong, I vow to her spirit.

"Two!"

I won't let anyone hurt you again.

"One!"

The moment I count down, we all break forward. The hall erupts as we hurtle our bodies against the weakened iron.

CHAPTER SEVEN

ZÉLIE

THE MOMENT THE SILVER SKULL pushes me forward, my bare toes slide through something sticky and warm. A fresh pool of blood surrounds my feet. I follow the trail with my eyes to the young girl lying in a crumpled heap.

My insides curl at the blood smeared across her forehead; it spills from her mouth and from her round nose. Though pale, her skin carries deep red undertones. They must have taken her from the Warri coast.

I can't look away from the gaping hole that lies in her chest. The scent of burning flesh hangs in the air. Tendrils of black smoke curl up, rising from the hole where her heart used to be.

If this is my fate . . .

I turn away. My hands start to shake. My throat closes up at the thought of Tzain.

What if that was the last time I ever get to see his face?

A lock clicks and I snap my head up. In the back of the room, a heavy door creaks open. The Silver Skull releases his firm grip, and each Skull bows. I'm left staring ahead.

I hold my breath as a new man enters the room. Deliberate. Slow. Unlike the other Skulls, his mask isn't smelted in silver or bronze.

It blinds in gold.

Baldyr . . .

The man I feel to be their king walks with a commanding gait. The Skulls stiffen with his approach. Power reverberates through his every step. The captain's quarters seem to shrink in his presence.

Instead of a fur cloak, Baldyr sports an entire wolf's pelt. The fanged creature's immortalized snarl hangs over his chestnut curls like a hood. Rectangular runes are carved into Baldyr's fair skin. The sharp black marks travel from the left side of his head to the hard lines cut into his abdomen.

"*Rísið upp,*" Baldyr commands the men, a low growl behind every word. The Silver Skull holds me once more. His grip tightens on both of my arms.

No one speaks as King Baldyr moves through the room. He unclasps his pelt and throws it on the bed. My lips part as he removes his mask.

I see the face of the enemy for the first time.

King Baldyr is young. Far younger than I expected him to be. Though he commands men twice his age, he can't be more than twenty-three.

I take in his high cheekbones and crooked nose. The wild beard that coats his jaw. His chestnut waves gather in a messy bun, loose strands falling onto his bare shoulders.

Three black marks are painted across his left eye, accenting the stormy look in his hazel gaze. His eyes darken when they settle on me.

I itch to break free.

"*Er þetta sú?*" King Baldyr gestures to me.

"*Já.*" The Silver Skull nods.

King Baldyr studies me from a distance, and the little that remains of my kaftan sticks to my frame. I shiver under his gaze.

He approaches and I stiffen; his dirt-stained fingers graze the maja-cite crown embedded into my skull. Sharp ripples shoot across my scalp. I clench my teeth to keep from crying out.

Baldyr's touch reminds me of where I am. Of what I must do. Tzain and the others are still trapped below deck. I have to find a way to escape.

I look beyond Baldyr to scan the Silver Skull's room. Marble walls block out the building storm. If it wasn't for the way the floor swayed under our feet, I wouldn't even know we were still on the ship.

A grand wooden carving covers the back wall, depicting the colos-sal man made of raging storm clouds. A raised bed holds a mattress stuffed with feathers. When King Baldyr catches me looking, I stare at the floor.

"*Merle*," he appears to name me. I flinch as he reaches forward, grab-bing my chin. I expect a rough grip, but his touch is soft, almost gentle as his fingers rest against my skin. He turns my head back and forth in the torchlight, as if inspecting a ripe papaya in the sun.

"It means 'blackbird,'" he whispers in Orïshan.

I don't believe my own ears.

"You are surprised I speak your tongue?" Baldyr unhands my cheek to raise the bloodmetal strapped to his palm. He reaches down and presses his hand into the slain maji's chest. The crimson metal steams as it soaks in the maji's essence, allowing me to see the translation at work.

"I like hearing your people call out to your gods." Baldyr looks back to me. "They never seem to come."

Ice crawls down my neck like a spider as the king steps away, turning toward the back of the room. A wooden table is set with a rich, half-eaten spread. The warm smell of bread punches my empty stomach. Baldyr goes for a bronze goblet of mead, at ease despite the corpse lying on the floor.

To my right, a desk lies in the corner of the room, covered with maps and parchments and different reading tools. Beside it, I spot a shelf, lined with unfamiliar weapons—animal claws, wooden clubs, and curved sabers. A collection of crystal daggers catches the light, shining right above a sleek black rod.

My staff!

I almost cry out. A piece of home I still have. Given to me by Mama Agba, the ornate staff shines. Its black neck still glimmers with the symbols my mentor etched into its spine.

I comb over each mark, eyes settling on the crossed blades of war. The familiar crack of colliding staffs echoes between my ears. I feel the touch of Mama Agba's wrinkled hands.

I teach you to be warriors in the garden so you will never be gardeners in the war.

Words Mama Agba shared with me all those moons ago ripple through my mind. They reach for me through the darkness, traveling through her spirit, through time.

In this world, there will always be men who wish you harm. That is why we train.

I always thought she was speaking of the guards. The monarchy and King Saran. Could she have known what enemies would invade our shores? As a gifted Seer, did she see the battles our future held?

The sight of my staff reignites something the Skulls stole when they abducted me from my land. Something I thought was taken when they held me down and shaved my head. I lost my magic once before, yet despite everything that was against us, I managed to win it back.

Despite everything, I found a new way to attack.

We brought King Saran to his knees. When Queen Nehanda stood against us, we razed Lagos to the ground. I won't allow myself to cower now.

I won't bow to any other crown.

"*Be vigilant*," I hear Mama Agba hiss. "*Wait for your moment to strike.*"

I fix my eyes on King Baldyr, soaking the instruction in.

This is the man who hunts my people.

Tonight he dies.

CHAPTER EIGHT

ZÉLIE

But how?

I close my eyes. I try to block everything out of my mind. I think of every weapon at my disposal. The edge I'll need to attack. To kill.

When I first started training with Mama Agba, I was one of the smallest. My arms were weak. I could barely hold up a staff. But with her training, I managed to find a way.

If I push, I know I can fight today.

Baldyr motions to the maji on the floor with a hole in her chest, and the two Skulls grab the girl by the ankles. They drag her corpse across the marble floor with no regard. The door closes behind them, leaving me alone with Baldyr and the Silver Skull.

Something dark claws at my heart as I stare at the trail of blood that follows the maji's retreat. The pain she must have felt.

How will her spirit ever sleep?

"How many of my people have you tossed in the sea?" The bite in my voice steadies me. My muscles begin to hum. I think of the way he's treated my people. Every innocent soul ripped from our lands.

A curious smile spreads across Baldyr's lips. He mutters something in his tongue and the Silver Skull chuckles. He nods his head toward me.

"Finally, one of you speaks."

I watch as Baldyr settles in his chair. His ease spikes my fear. He grabs a chicken thigh and sucks off the meat. The entire time he keeps his stormy gaze on me.

I glance at the knife to his left. The Silver Skull still holds my arms tight. But I imagine the feel of the wooden hilt in my hands, the satisfaction of driving the blade straight through Baldyr's forehead.

"Your people seem to like the sea." The bloodmetal strapped to his palm glows as he continues to speak in my tongue. "On one of our first expeditions, every captive escaped. Instead of revolting, they walked into the sea in chains."

His words hit me like shards of glass. The weight of every skeleton pulls me under the sea.

All those people . . .

Those maji were taken because of me.

"*Veikt fólk,*" the Silver Skull remarks. Even without a translation rune, I understand his words.

"It's not *weak* to choose our waters over your chains."

My anger pulls King Baldyr back to me. He gets so close, I inhale the scent of mead on his breath. He brushes my cheek with his dirt-stained nail, inspecting me again.

"Such rage," he mutters. "More anger than fear."

My eyes drift back to my staff. He follows my gaze to the wall of weapons.

"And a warrior." Baldyr steps back. He studies me once more. "*Merle,* I think you are the one I have been looking for. . . ."

Before I can strike, the Silver Skull grabs my shackled wrists. He holds me tight against his muscular frame. King Baldyr moves to the back room. He returns with an ornate chest, setting it down in front of the wood carving on the back wall. A golden key hangs from Baldyr's throat. It glimmers in the candlelight as he nears.

"Years ago, my people were nothing." Baldyr's voice darkens. A sharp hatred coats his tongue. "We were battle worn. Starving. Worse than the worms crawling out of the mud. But one day I heard a promise." Baldyr takes in the man made of storm clouds as he reaches for the golden key around his neck. "A promise that my people could be more than the mere mortals we were born as. A promise that we could become gods."

I think of the Skull I impaled, the way the hammer fed on his blood. Though he was mighty to begin with, the crimson alloy magnified his strength. His entire being transformed.

"Then that's what you think you are?" I challenge Baldyr. "Gods because of the weapons you wield?"

"It takes more than a weapon to be a god."

My pulse spikes as the chest creaks opens. Whatever's inside casts the king's face in a warm glow. Baldyr steps back to reveal a trio of ancient medallions. Carved into different shapes, the bloodmetal is sculpted from antique gold.

"Our blood grants us strength, but it doesn't come close to giving me the power I was promised. But your blood is different." Baldyr glances back at me. "Your blood carries the power of the gods."

Ashê. My eyes widen as I realize what he seeks. The divine power of the gods that runs through our blood. The reason maji can do magic at all.

Baldyr removes one of the medallions, and it shines in his palm. Even from a distance, I can feel the golden metal buzz. My eyes trail over the same triple arrowhead I saw in the compass of the Silver Skull.

"Legend says there is one of your kind who carries the blood of the sun."

Thunder rumbles outside the captain's quarters, and my throat dries.

These men aren't just searching for maji, Zélie. Inan's words return. *They're searching for you.*

"If someone like that existed, she would never fight for you," I declare.

Baldyr steps closer. Hunger drips from his form like sweat.

"I don't need her to fight." His eyes comb down to my chest. "I need her heart."

CHAPTER NINE

ZÉLIE

No!

The moment I feared rushes at me. There's no place for me to run. Blood pounds between my ears. The little time I had to strategize is gone.

I try to escape, but the Silver Skull holds me tight. He mutters a curse against my ear. Baldyr raises his palm and aligns the golden medallion with my heart. As he moves, the gaping hole in the maji's chest flashes into my mind.

Her blood still coats my feet. The stench of charred skin still taints the air. In an instant, I understand how she died. Her and every other maji they've tried.

I can't let that medallion touch me.

If it does, I won't survive.

"Strike, Zélie!" Mama Agba's voice rings through my head, and I force myself to act. I drive my elbow into the Silver Skull's groin. With a sharp grunt, the captain keels over.

The swaying ship makes him lose his footing. I pivot and kick back. My heel collides with his stomach, sending the Silver Skull flying into the back door.

Baldyr reaches for me as I scramble forward. I launch myself across the bloodstained floor. I head for the table, reaching for the knife I spotted before. Baldyr's goblet of mead crashes to the floor as my fingers graze the knife's wooden hilt—

"*Nei!*" King Baldyr roars like a wild beast. He grabs the shackles around my wrists, yanking me back. My feet slip out from under me as he throws me to the right. I hit the marble walls with a powerful thud.

The impact ignites the majacite crown on my head. It burns with a new wrath. Its matte-black thorns dig into my temple. Hot blood drips into my eyes and rains down my neck.

Fight, Zélie.

Though I can hardly see, I reach for everything in sight. My fingers grasp at a fallen chicken bone. When Baldyr comes for me, I swing wildly, stabbing through his cheek.

A brass candleholder falls to the left. I grab it and beat Baldyr over the head. I swing the candleholder again, clocking the king across the jaw.

But before I strike once more, the Silver Skull grabs me from behind and throws me against the back wall. Another sharp crack rings as my head collides with the marble. With another shove, the candleholder falls from my hands.

King Baldyr rips the chicken bone out from his cheek and releases a mighty laugh. Blood mixes with the black paint on his face. It travels down his chest, staining the golden medallion he holds in his hands.

The Silver Skull uses my shackles to hold my arms back. Baldyr's eyes home in on my chest. The medallion in his hand starts to glow.

There's nowhere to run as Baldyr drives the medallion into my breastbone.

"*AGH!*" I shout. Pain unlike anything I've ever experienced drowns everything out. I seize on the floor as the medallion digs into my sternum like a branding iron. It goes so deep, its metal melts around my bones.

The sharp heat burns through my heart. Tendrils of smoke start to flare around its rim. Despite how hard I push, I can't breathe. My lungs sear from within.

"*Það er hón!*" King Baldyr shouts. My skin burns red as my blood begins to glow. A blinding gold light fills the room. It bounces against the marble walls. It cascades in brilliant arcs, blocking everything else out.

"*Oya, please . . .*" I whisper the prayer. I call for her to take my soul. I don't want to die out at sea in the hands of these foreign beasts. So far away from home.

Please . . .

My seizing body stills. My heartbeat slows, tasting the bitter end.

A deafening boom of thunder is the last thing I hear before everything fades to black.

CHAPTER TEN

TZAIN

"AGAIN!"

My command travels down the long hall. All the boys hurtle forward, united as one. The iron bars screech with each charge, struggling to hold back our combined force.

"More!" I shout. Our chains rattle against the bars of our cell. Metal bolts fly from the lock. Our cage door starts to give. The rusted iron groans against its hinges.

Zélie, I'm coming.

I keep my sister's face in my mind with every charge. I see every time Zélie's needed me to be strong. Every person who's caused her harm. The guards. King Saran. Nehanda and her tîtáns. Even Inan. Every enemy falls, leaving me face-to-face with the Silver Skull.

I didn't always know my place. Without magic of my own, I didn't know how to keep my sister safe. But in this moment, it all feels so clear.

Rescuing Zélie is the only thing I can make sense of in here.

"More!" I rally the boys. Blood drips down my knuckles as I throw my body against the lock. The cage door starts to squeal. Our freedom begins to feel real.

"It's working!" I spur them on. Adrenaline pumps through my veins. "Don't stop! We're close! We just have to push—"

A monstrous bolt of lightning shudders down from the sky, flickering through the ventilation shaft. Pure white light crackles through the cargo hold. It illuminates swirling storm clouds above.

"What was that?" Taiwo whispers. One by one, the maji are drawn to the sight. Though the view is limited, I feel the power that gathers in the air. High in the sky, thunder roars. Below the ship, the waters pick up force.

An ache burns through my chest, digging deep into my ribs. My fingers grow numb when I slide my hand over the spot.

Something's wrong. . . .

Somehow I know Zélie is the cause.

What have they done? For a moment, terror traps me. I don't know if I'm too late. But I don't allow myself to give up.

I can't stop until I see Zélie's face.

"Keep going!" I order the maji. We all return to the charge. The halls echo with our cries. The boys fight with new resolve.

The maji bleed against their cages. They push so hard, they break their own bones. They fight with their fury. With their sorrow.

For every life we've lost to the Skulls.

"Incoming!" Kenyon warns.

Heavy boots move overhead. There's no hiding our attempt to break free now.

The Skulls are here.

Our time has run out.

"*Make them pay!*" I scratch my voice raw. "*Make them feel what they've done!*"

With one final charge, my cage flies open.

We spill into the hall as the Skulls open the arched door.

CHAPTER ELEVEN

TZAIN

"Attack!" Kenyon screams. More maji start to break free. A flash of rain cascades down the wooden steps. The Skulls slip as they fall down the stairs.

I try to lunge forward, but shackles still bind me to the maji. My chains hold me back. I won't be able to fight like this.

I have to find a way to separate myself from the others.

One Skull charges down the hall. He bites into his hand and removes his crimson hammer. Blood leaks from his broken skin, feeding straight into the runes on his sculpted hilt.

As the same runes carve themselves into the Skull's chest, the warrior transforms before my eyes. His muscles bulge with new strength. The very ground rumbles under his feet. His neck thickens. His bones crack. He releases a guttural roar as he runs to attack.

Six maji swarm the Skull at once, but the Skull swings with inhuman force. All six maji are blown away. They fly back into their cells, bones crushed.

Another Skull runs toward us. He raises his glowing axe in the air. Blood drips from his hand as the Skull swells, growing so large he fills the space between the cages.

I duck as the Skull swings at my neck. The force of his axe cuts through the iron bars of our cell. The Skull rears back and swings again. I throw myself to the floor as the glowing axe passes above my head.

But on the floor, I see my chance. A dagger hangs from the Skull's belt. With a powerful wrench, the dagger flies free. I don't waste a second before slicing through the tendons at the Skull's heel.

The Skull shouts as he goes down. The crimson axe falls from his hand. Taiwo tries to grab the glowing weapon, but touching the foreign metal burns his skin.

"Buy Tzain time!" a maji screams. They hold the Skull down as I strike. I stab again and again, cutting through the Skull's thigh, through his chest. I dig the dagger into his gut and pull, carving through his abdomen. His blood flies into the air, coating our dark skin.

When the Skull's body lies still, the glow of his axe fades away, draining with the warrior's lifeforce. His blood pools around me as my cellmates raid his animal-skin pouches. They use the sulfur-scented tar to break through our chains.

As they slip free, they flood into the hall, aiding the other maji as we struggle to take down the rest of the Skulls. I move to help them, but something pulls at me.

I turn to see the axe lying on the floor.

A sharp heat prickles through my fingers, daring me to get close. Though Taiwo wasn't able to wield the weapon, after killing its owner, my hands are drawn to it. A magnetic force I can't fight. I look to the dead Skull as I bend down.

When I grab the sculpted hilt, a quiet force erases all sound.

Blóðseiðr.

The foreign words fill my head. The sound of chanting men rings between my ears. My eyes go blank. My heart pounds in my chest. A new power surges through my body as my very muscles expand.

The blood from the wound in my arm leaks into the hilt. The crimson metal starts to warm.

I raise the weapon above my head as my axe glows with red.

"*Argh!*" I swing. The blade cuts straight through a Skull's chest. Another Skull comes at me with his glowing hammer. I strike first, slicing through his neck.

The axe releases the rage buried deep inside. Crimson splatters in every direction as I fight. It coats my hands. My face. My tongue. But I can't control the animal that awakens in me.

The more blood that spills, the more I need to see.

"The cells!" Kenyon points. Through the wild haze, I see the maji who've yet to break out. With a roar, I cut through the iron bars that have caged them for a moon. I slice through their chains, setting them free.

It's working.

I stand in the center of the hall as the frenzy builds. With the axe, we have enough power. With this weapon, the Skulls have to cower.

"Get to the deck!" Kenyon roars over the maji. "Throw every Skull into the seas!"

I bring Zélie's face back into my mind and head for the arched door.

I race to set my sister free.

CHAPTER TWELVE

ZÉLIE

RAIN.

Falling rain. It's the first thing that finds me in the dark. Its steady patter rings through my ears. It drags my mind out of the abyss.

Sharp light breaks into my eyes, filling my vision with red. My muscles shake against the cold marble floor. I struggle to lift my hands.

Something warm glows above my heart. It burns every time I breathe in. I reach up and my fingers scrape gold.

Baldyr's medallion is welded into my skin.

No.

My breath shrivels. I can't believe what I feel. The triple arrowhead carved into the gold medallion pulses with light, synced to my heart like a breathing organ. My fingers shake as I pull them back. The sight makes my head spin. Something sharp pulses through my being, but it's not the magic I know.

"*Finally.*" My ears ring as Baldyr approaches me, a zealous fervor alight in his eyes. His hands hover over my frame. In mere moments, I've become too valuable to touch.

But Baldyr speaks in his tongue. Why can I recognize the words? The foreign tongue keeps building in my head.

It's as if the medallion changes me from within.

"*Awaken.*" Baldyr whispers the command. He smears the blood from his cheek across the medallion. In an instant, the captain's quarters fade away. My eyes flash red as Baldyr's memories hold me hostage, trapping me back in time. . . .

The land of Baldeírik comes alive. I run through its barren plains; I look up to its darkened skies. Navy flags whip through the air, each patterned with a seal of one of the land's six tribes.

I see the round-faced child Baldyr once was. The turf-lined walls and thatched hut that formed his home. I hear his screams as warriors rip him from his mother's shaking arms. I stare up at the maskless tribe leader who takes him in, counting the scars that fill the man's freckled skin.

My arms strain under the boulders and tree trunks Baldyr lifts. My instincts sharpen with every captive boy he fights. My knuckles bruise as his fists fly.

Baldyr doesn't stop until another boy dies.

The ground shakes under the mighty paws of the armor-plated bears he and his fellow tribesmen ride into battle. Timber-lined fortresses fall before him in flames. Hammer strikes against hammer. Blade cuts against blade. Brutal raid follows raid.

But as the six tribes of Baldeírik battle, their nation falls to waste. Corpses line the muddy streets. Torches light fields of barley ablaze. The people don't eat for days.

In the chaos, I hear the promise—the constant whisper that fills Baldyr's ears. The claim that he can bring his splintered people together, that they can build a nation no other kingdom could eclipse.

The voice guides Baldyr to climb the rocky mountains that arc around the heart-shaped land. Heat licks Baldyr's face as he stands before the well of molten metal oozing from the mountain's core. Baldyr takes a bone knife across his hand. When his blood drips into the well, the sacred metal turns red.

The crimson bloodmetal is born. . . .

"*Ugh!*" I wheeze as Baldyr steps back. My mind spins with the memories of his life—the bloodmetal he created, the first warriors he rallied, the invention of the Skulls' very masks.

"*Blackbird.*" Baldyr shakes his head, and I see the man who united the six tribes of his land. "*I have been searching for you for years.*"

The growl in Baldyr's voice takes on a new form. The small smirk he held before is gone. Blood still drips down his cheek from my attack. When it falls onto my face, Baldyr moves to the table, wiping it with a rag.

Behind Baldyr, the Silver Skull shakes. He no longer meets my gaze. It's as if he's afraid to misstep. To do something that will bring an end to his fate.

"*I have to depart.*" Baldyr rises.

He returns to the heavy chest. Now only two medallions are left. Baldyr locks up the chest with care and hangs the golden key around his neck. A new purpose charges his gait.

"*Where will you sail?*" the Silver Skull asks.

"*To find the other. The Blood Moon is near.*"

The Blood Moon? I think back to the yellow moon that shone above the deck. I've never heard of such an event. But the way Baldyr speaks, it's as if he's been waiting for this moon all of his life.

"*What should I do with the girl?*"

"*Keep her in here,*" he orders. "*The medallion is still transforming her blood. When her new power is ready for the harvest, I want her brought to the fortress in Iarlaith.*"

"*And the others?*" the Silver Skull asks.

"*Drop them at the trading port.*"

King Baldyr dons his golden mask. The pressure makes more blood drip from his face. He takes the wolf's pelt from the captain's bed and looks to me. I turn away as he lays the white fur over my back.

"I will see you again," he speaks in Orïshan.

The Silver Skull takes a knee as Baldyr prepares to leave. A hardness enters Baldyr's hazel eyes when he looks down at his captain.

"Return her to me."

CHAPTER THIRTEEN

ZÉLIE

THE RED DOOR SHUDDERS behind King Baldyr as he leaves. Boots follow his retreat. With Baldyr gone, I'm left with the Silver Skull. Ripped away from what I was before.

I have to fight to move my feet. My body doesn't feel like my own. I dare to touch the charred and blackened skin on my chest. The ancient medallion that's ripped through so many of my people's hearts hums under my fingertips.

What has he done to me?

The sound of thunder erupts between my ears. Something inside me swells like the building tides. It rushes through every limb. It makes the room around me spin.

When I close my eyes, a new vision fills my mind. I see rectangular runes carved into my skin. Wiry women wearing horned animal skulls surround me. A giant moon burns red in the sky. . . .

"*Strike, Zélie.*" Mama Agba's whispers return. Her voice breaks through the swelling storm. I feel the echo of her wrinkled hands press over my own, reminding me I'm not alone.

I fight past the part of me that yearns to break. The way every breath I take aches.

Think of the others, I push myself. *Think of Tzain!*

In the back of the room, the Silver Skull rises. His shoulders seem to slump with relief. He lifts his mask and returns to the table with another pitcher of mead. He drinks straight from the rim, taking generous swigs.

With his back to me, I force myself up, rising to my unsteady feet. Baldyr's wolf pelt falls to the floor. Blood stains the white fur red.

I grip the chain between my shackles, preparing for war. *For the maji.* I brace myself against the marble wall. *For every girl this medallion has burned.*

I won't let him drain my people of their blood.

I won't allow the Skulls to get away with what they have done.

"*Die!*" I launch myself forward, yanking my chain tight around the Silver Skull's throat. The brass pitcher drops from his hand and mead spills across our feet. I have to hold tight as the Silver Skull slips.

I brace myself against his back and pull. The foreign chants keep ringing in my ears. The ancient medallion warms in my chest. It stings as I fight to kill.

The Silver Skull releases a strangled shout and charges backward. The wooden table falls to the floor in his surge. The captain drives my body into the wall. The copper taste of blood fills my mouth as I fight to hold on.

He rams me again and again, and my hold finally loosens. He rips the shackles from his throat, and I collapse to the floor.

"*You are not to be harmed!*" he shouts in his tongue, but I don't listen. My fingers close around a broken shard of glass. Its sharp edges cut into my hand.

With a roar, I dive forward, slashing the glass across the Silver Skull's leg. The Silver Skull curses as I bring him to his knees. I try to strike again, but the Silver Skull grabs me by the neck.

Blood shines through his teeth. It drips from the gashes in his neck. The Silver Skull squeezes my throat as I wheeze for air. The glass shard falls from my hand while I choke.

The Silver Skull throws me into the wall of weapons. Swords and machetes clatter to the ground. Mama Agba's face fills my blurry vision as my staff rolls across the floor.

"*Come on, Zélie,*" her spirit urges me. I drag myself across the blood-stained marble. The Silver Skull barrels toward me, and I catch the glint of a chain.

I don't know if I have the strength to fight him off again.

"*You are close, my child.*" Mama Agba speaks to me. "*You are almost there.*"

My fingers wrap around the crossed swords etched into my staff. I press the button that extends its serrated blades.

The Silver Skull grabs me as I whip around, shoving the blade into his gut.

Finally.

My arms shake. The Silver Skull is stopped in his tracks. The iron chains fall from his hands. Blood drips from beneath his mask.

My serrated blades dig beneath the Silver Skull's rib cage, impaling him like a hyenaire. The Silver Skull curses at me before stumbling back. He takes my staff with him as he falls to the floor.

Though my bones feel like they might break, I force myself to my feet. I push my shaking legs and limp, dragging myself forward until I stand over the captain.

I stare at the man who's stuck my people in cages. The man who's thrown my people to the seas. I watch how he strains for breath. How he shakes.

How he bleeds.

"*He will find you,*" the Silver Skull croaks at me. "*There is no place you can run.*"

I grab my staff and wrench it free. The Silver Skull groans with pain. His unsteady gaze follows me as I reposition the blade above his chest.

His words make my hands shake, but I won't allow him to stop my escape.

"Say hello to my gods."

The Silver Skull's eyes widen as I speak in his tongue.

Then I drive my staff into his heart.

CHAPTER FOURTEEN

AMARI

I USED TO DREAM OF MONSTERS.

Long before the Raid.

The years when I looked up at Father and still saw a radiant king.

The man who would chase every monster away.

One night, I dreamed I was walking through a forest. I had finally made it beyond Lagos's walls. Rich green trees danced around me. Blue-whisked bee-eaters flew by my cheek. I lay in soft moss and stared up at the open sky. The clearing filled with brilliant butterflies.

But then the skies turned black. The towering trees twisted into harsh shadows. A pack of wild hyenaires slithered out of the ground. With sharp yelps, they hunted me down.

I shouted for help as I ran through the dark forest. The hyenaires seemed to cackle at my fear. The beasts cornered me into a den and pounced at once. Their fangs ripped through my flesh, drowning out my cries.

When I awoke, I was covered with sweat. My cheeks were damp from the tears I had shed. My legs shook as I crawled out of my sheets.

It was as if I'd died right there on that bed.

I went to Inan's quarters, but he was nowhere to be found. I tried to crawl onto Mother's mattress, but she insisted I return to my own. I found Father alone in the throne room. He opened his arms, and I nuzzled into his robes.

"*There are walls for a reason, Amari.*" He was gentle, running his hand over my hair as I shook. "*You would do well to stay inside them, even in your dreams. They were built to keep every monster out.*"

"*Even the hyenaires?*" I asked.

"*Especially the hyenaires.*" He almost smiled, but something weighed him down. "*And those who wish us harm.*"

I always thought Father spoke of scheming nobles. Of the maji he seemed to hate so much. But in all my time locked on this ship, I've wondered what he knew of the monsters beyond Orïsha's borders.

I wonder what he knew of the Skulls.

It was my sword that sent Father to his death. It was my vow to protect the people of Orïsha and defeat Mother that led to chaos and bloodshed. I fought for the maji elders to accept me and betrayed their trust. I sacrificed an entire village and still failed to win our war.

When Mama Agba gave up her life to help us overthrow the monarchy, she told me I was more than that moment. That I was more than all my mistakes. If I'd survived, it had to be for a reason.

With the threat of the Skulls, that reason is clear.

A new monster is here.

"Something's happening," I call, pointing to the floorboards above. A clamor builds over our heads. The frenzy grows like the ocean storm beating against the ship's hull.

My chest tightens as I draw closer to the iron bars. Shouts mix with the groans of breaking metal.

It has to be Zélie, I think to myself. *She must have found a way to fight.*

I yearn to peek through the floorboards. To see where Zélie is now. In spite of our turbulent past, she told me to hold on.

What if she has a plan to get us out?

If the others have found a way to fight, this could be it. We could take over the ship. End the Skulls' torture once and for all. We could finally escape.

Escape.

I close my eyes. In the past moon, the hope is all I've had. It's satiated my hollow stomach and dried every tear. The thought of escape has mended every wound I've sustained since being locked up in here.

To go home, back to Orïsha, no matter the price. To be buried in my own land.

Not to die at the hands of these beastly men.

"Prepare yourself!" Nâo instructs the others as voices build outside our door. "Go for their weapons!" She rattles the bars of her cage. "Claw out their throats! Tear out their eyes!"

Nâo rallies a strength I try to summon deep inside. Still the elder of the Tiders, her voice causes the maji to rise. My heart thunders in my chest as I reach for a broken shard of wood in the walls. I raise the shard with shaking hands as the door to our hold shudders open.

A tangle of bodies flies down the wooden steps. Through the darkness, I make out a group of maji fighting against three Skulls. With a lurch, the boat makes a violent turn, and the mess of bodies slides down the hall. I stick out the wooden shard, flinching as it catches a Skull in the throat.

"Help me!" Nâo shouts. The heaviest of the three Skulls falls in front of her cell. One girl digs her thumbs into the Skull's eyes, and blood oozes from behind his mask. Another girl catches the Skull by the ear. He screams as she tears.

I brace myself as the maji rip the Skull apart. They claw at his face. His hair. His skin. The Skull flails against the cage, and his mask falls off. I'm paralyzed by the sight of his crazed beard and braided hair.

"*Deyið!*" the Skull shouts. He reaches for the animal-skin pouch tied to his belt. The smell of tar hits me like a cannon. In an instant, I realize his plans.

"Get back!" I pull the maji I'm chained to into the farthest corner of our cage, shielding their bodies with my own. Behind me, the Skull frees the bomb from his belt. He pulls the rope that ignites its flame—

All of a sudden, brown hands grab the Skull's face.

With a sharp snap, the Skull's neck breaks.

What in the skies?

The bomb rolls across the floor. Its flame goes out in a puddle of stormwater. For a moment, my body relaxes. I turn to find our savior.

"Kenyon?" Nâo breathes.

Blood and grime cover every centimeter of the Burner's skin. A barbaric rage contorts his face, but at the sight of his fellow elder, all Kenyon's rage seems to wash away.

"*O seun, Sàngó.*" Kenyon's voice cracks. He holds on to the iron of the cage.

Nâo reaches through the bars and grabs the sides of her friend's face. Tears swell in her deep brown eyes.

"Tell me this is the end," she whispers.

"It's over." Kenyon nods. "We're taking the ship. Tzain's leading the charge."

Tzain's alive? My heart skips a beat. The last time I saw Tzain, he couldn't bear the sight of me. *But if he's alive . . .*

I'm surprised at the part of me that dares to dream.

If Tzain's alive, then there's a chance.

One day he could forgive me.

Kenyon calls to a group of maji down the hall. They throw him a ring of keys. The Burner breaks open Nâo's cell, and she practically leaps into his arms. I'm struck by the way Kenyon kisses her forehead, holding his friend as she trembles.

"You're safe," Kenyon whispers. The words send a shiver through my skin. After all we've endured, it's too good to be true. Half the maji in this hall are still chained to the dead.

Kenyon sets Nâo down and unlocks her shackles. Nâo passes the ring of keys down the line. I watch as Nâo cracks her neck. The fighter I know reemerges, gathering herself.

"Where are we needed?" she asks.

"The deck. The boys are fighting there."

With a nod, Nâo takes off. The maji in her cell follow her up the stairs.

When Kenyon turns to my cell, I freeze. The last time we were face-to-face, I was his enemy. If it weren't for Mama Agba, he and the other elders would've killed me.

Kenyon stares and something flashes across his face. I prepare myself for how he'll retaliate. He frees the rest of the maji in my cell, leaving the two of us alone.

"Do it." I lower my head.

Kenyon grabs my shackles and I ready myself for his strike. I don't know what to think when the shackles drop to my sides.

"Really?" I look up at him, rubbing my bruised wrists.

"You're not the enemy." Kenyon steps away. "Not right now."

His words wash over me like a wave. I feel the chance to atone for my mistakes.

"I won't let you down." I move for the deck, but Kenyon grabs my arm, stopping me before I can travel up the stairs.

"Your brother attacked a Skull tonight. They locked him on the lower deck."

I think of the struggling boy the Skulls carried past us before. The canvas bag tied over his head.

"That was Inan?" My eyes go wide as Kenyon places the ring of keys in my hand.

"Go after him." He nudges me forward. "Before it's too late."

I take off, bracing myself against the sliding walls of the ship. I picture my brother locked below, isolated in the Skulls' hold.

"Wait!" I turn back to Kenyon as I reach the next stairwell. I hold the Burner's gaze. "Thank you."

Kenyon almost smiles.

"Kill every Skull in your way."

CHAPTER FIFTEEN

INAN

I FAILED HER.

The thought of Zélie with the Silver Skull makes my blood run cold. The places they might have taken her. The things they must have done.

When they locked me down here, I thought we had a chance. With time, I could break her out. Get her back to Orïsha and make up for every single time I've hurt her. Every time I've let her down.

The Skulls have been searching for her heart. I knew it the moment I made sense of their words. Whatever their plans, they needed her enough to invade another kingdom. Enough to haul ships of my people across the seas. What will happen once they discover it's her?

What will Baldyr do to the rest of Orïsha?

I have to stop them. The realization settles in my core. *All of them. Every single Skull.* For the first time in centuries, Orïsha can't battle against itself. We have to unite.

Our kingdom is at war.

Outside the vessel, the ocean's storm picks up force. The entire ship quakes with the deafening thunder that booms from above. The reverberations shake through my bones. Waves slam against the ship's side like battering rams. Sheets of water crash into the hold.

My hanging cage swings wildly in the flooding prison. The gears groan above my head, rusted from the damp sea air. At any moment, the attachment will break. The force of the fall might give me a chance to escape.

But these shackles . . .

The shackles the Skulls clamped tight around my wrists make it impossible to leave. Even when my cage falls, I'll be trapped. If I can't break the chains, I won't be able to make it to the deck.

I whip the chains binding me to the rusted floor back and forth. I brace myself against the iron bars of the cage and pull. My feet struggle to get a firm grip, and I slip. I hit the floor with a heavy thud. Pain rakes through my body. I fight through it to drag myself up.

I take my shackled wrists and smash them against the iron bars. I hit them again and again. Above me, the gears holding my cage continue to creak. One of the attachments weakens. A bolt flies free.

Water continues to fill the ship's hold. It rises so high, it nearly hits the bottom of my cage. My time is running out. If I can't break these chains, I'll drown.

Despite how hard I thrash, the shackles around my wrist don't give. I pull against the chains with everything I have. I pull though the metal tears at my skin.

"Come on!" I try to yank my wrists free. The old metal burns as it cuts through my flesh. I roar with the agony that rips through me. My skin begins to peel, revealing gleaming white bone.

Nausea rises inside me. Sweat pools down my skin. My vision starts to blur, but I don't see another way. I need to keep going.

I have to do whatever it takes to escape—

"Inan?" a voice calls, and I stop. I don't believe my ears.

Who would even know to look for me in here?

"Inan, are you down there?" the voice calls out again, and this time I recognize its cadence. Its speaker's heart.

"Amari?" I shout back.

"I'm coming!" she calls. "I'll break you out!"

My heart pounds as footsteps travel down the stairs. Something collides with the padlocked door. The jangle of keys rings. With a click, the door flies open.

Amari . . .

My sister bounds into the hold, nearly tripping over herself in her fervor. Relief mixes with rage at the sight of what the Skulls have done. The shell of the warrior she's become.

Amari's bones protrude from her shriveled kaftan. Bruises cover her neck and delicate wrists. Thick layers of dirt coat her copper skin. Grime runs through her dark curls.

But despite her weakened condition, she fights, stomping through the flooding hold. When she reaches my cage, our hands link. I stare at the sister who shares my amber eyes.

For a moment, neither of us can speak. The years we've spent at odds seem to dissipate. My eyes sting at the thought of Father. Mother. Orïsha. The throne that constantly got in our way. I think of all the ways I could have been a better brother.

All the ways I should have kept her safe.

"I'm sorry." I whisper the words, though I know they're not enough. But Amari shakes her head.

"We didn't get here on our own."

My sister holds me, and I feel it—the dedication we both share. Now that the Skulls have landed on our shores, we can't afford to be at odds. Orïsha needs us together, fighting on the same side.

"The Skulls are after Zélie," I explain. "They've been raiding our shores for moons. They plan to—"

"We'll find a way to stop them," Amari assures me. "Together, I know we can."

In her voice, I find a new conviction. A reason to believe we can win. In this moment, we're bonded together.

The way we always should have been.

"Your hands . . ." Amari grimaces at my broken bones and my peeling skin. The fight I've been waging alone returns. My cage continues to creak.

"I'll be alright." I nod. "Just get me out!"

Amari removes the ring of keys around her wrist. Key after key goes into my lock until she finds one that fits. She grits her teeth when she meets resistance. Finally, the padlock opens with a sharp click.

A smile spreads across my sister's narrow face, but her forehead creases when she touches the shackles around my wrists. She attempts to find the right match, but the keys are too big.

"These won't fit. . . ."

I brace myself to pull my wrists free, but Amari stops me.

"I'll find a blade." She leaves the key in the cage door. "I'll cut you out! Just wait!"

"Be careful!" I call.

I watch, helpless, as Amari pushes herself through the water-filled hold. But heavy footsteps thunder down the stairs. Amari freezes as a bulky silhouette fills the doorframe.

A flicker of lightning illuminates the mighty Skull's mask.

He looks between the two of us, glowing axe in hand.

CHAPTER SIXTEEN

ZÉLIE

I DON'T KNOW HOW long I stand there, staring at the Silver Skull's corpse.

The room sways as his blood pools at my feet. His horrid mask falls to the floor.

My hands are like rocks around the neck of my staff. Its blade is still carved into the beast's heart. Finally, I unclench my staff with a shuddered breath.

Everything hits at once.

Oya, help me.

My throat grows tight. The room starts to spin. My vision blurs white. It's like the entire ship is collapsing in.

My hands fly to my sternum, and a sob I've fought so hard to cage breaks free. I feel myself collapse.

The battle has taken all of me.

I hit the marble floor with a thud. I itch to wash away the enemy's touch. I snap my eyes shut, trying to force air into my lungs.

The golden medallion still pulses in my chest, a constant reminder of whatever I've become. A foreign force shakes through my arms, pouring through my bleeding palms.

I have to get out of here.

I try to fight through the noise. Through every wound. Through every ache. My brother is still trapped on this ship.

The other maji need my help to escape.

Despite how hard I push, I can't summon any more strength. My legs won't move. My arms only shake. I don't know how I'll go on, but then I see it.

The first glimpse of hope I've had since being locked up in chains.

Home . . .

I push myself onto my shaking elbows, trying to focus on the elusive sight. A mess of fallen parchments lies on the floor with overturned tables and fractured weapons; pools of mead and puddles of blood.

One scroll pulls my focus, calling out to me with its familiar lines. My bloodstained fingers close over the yellowed parchment. I can hardly believe the sight.

Thick black lines create the borders of my Orïsha. More strokes illustrate the western coast, with figures circling the port of Lagos. My eyes find Ilorin on the map, and I suck in a strangled breath.

Baba's face breaks into my mind.

Baba . . .

At the thought of my father, sorrow leaks from the well inside. My memories come alive with the gentle tide that rang through the floating village of Ilorin at all times.

I feel the woven reeds that formed our ahéré. I hear the way Nailah, my lionaire, used to snore. I hold the map to my heart as if it were a doll. Despite all I've endured within its borders, seeing my motherland is like seeing a piece of my heart.

I push myself to my shaking feet as new life moves through my brutalized form. The sight of Orïsha fortifies my resolve. My lungs start to expand. Slowly, my full vision returns. I rip off my tattered rags and throw them to the bloodied floor.

I won't let myself wither on this ship.

I won't stop until my feet touch the soil of my homeland again.

Thunder rumbles from beyond the door. The sway of the ship grows with every passing second. I search the room until I find the Silver Skull's wardrobe. I pull on a pair of his wool pants, cutting away the extra fabric and wrapping it tight around my waist and my chest.

I find two machetes on the floor, and my hands mold to their beaded hilts. I remember the images of Oya I saw when I was young. The machetes she'd wield as she rode into war.

"*Fún mi lágbára.*" I pray to my goddess again. *Grant me strength.*

The current of the storm buzzes beneath my skin. I feel its power deep within.

I remove my staff from the slain Silver Skull and strap it to my back. I search the fallen captain's pockets and find the hexagon-shaped compass that he used to separate me from the rest. I open it and catch my reflection in the glass face. With the majacite crown on my head, I look like the princess of death.

I hook the compass to my belt and face the crimson door.

Rage rises in me like a volcano ready to erupt as I walk past the Silver Skull.

CHAPTER SEVENTEEN

ZÉLIE

Stepping outside the Silver Skull's quarters is like stepping into another world. Gone are the thick marble walls that caged us in. Nothing hides me from nature's rampage.

Rain pelts like arrows from above. Brilliant bolts of lightning crackle through the clouds. Thunder roars like a beast in the sky. Its booms shudder through my bones.

Mama was right. I brace myself against the door, in awe of the raging sea and racing winds. I see the way Mama lifted her head to the chaos on that mountaintop. I see the way the lightning illuminated the bright smile against her dark skin. I lift my own head and open my arms, remembering that sacred night. When I close my eyes, I hear Oya's cry in the tempest.

I *feel* Oya's power in the storm.

The golden medallion pulses in my chest as I embrace the pouring skies. A wild force races through my blood as the triple arrowhead etched into the medallion's surface starts to flash.

I scan for King Baldyr's hulking frame, but his golden skull is nowhere in sight. Another ship sails in the distance, nearly triple the size of the Silver Skull's.

Baldyr.

A shudder runs through me as I watch his golden banners flutter in the winds. What will it take to track him down?

How can I destroy him and his people before the Blood Moon?

But when bodies move below, I don't have time to stop and think. Skulls spill out of their quarters in droves. A heavy bell starts to ring.

Across the ship, the skies flash against the fighting silhouettes. Maji battle across the deck, taking over the vessel. My people fight with broken iron bars and stolen daggers, overwhelming the Skulls before they can activate their weapons.

My heart flutters when I see Nâo leading a group of girls. They push two Skulls over the edge of the ship. Kenyon leads others to tackle another Skull to the ground. They use their fists to keep the enemy down.

"*Wake the captain!*" a Skull yells from the levels below. Movement rises, traveling up the stairs. I charge down the steps, gripping the beaded machetes tight. A Skull approaches and I run forward before he can strike.

"*Hah!*" I slice my machetes across his throat. Hot blood spills across the wooden steps. The Skull grabs his neck and falls back. Lightning crackles as he hits the ground.

A second Skull swings his axe. I duck and kick, sending him down the stairs. With a running start, I leap from the captain's floor. I raise both machetes over my head. Lightning illuminates the needles of rain as I arc through the air.

"*Awaken, Zélie. . . .*"

Time starts to slow. The whispered chant shivers through my ears. But I don't know who speaks the words. I don't know how I can hear.

I feel the voice from within as the medallion warms in my sternum. A swell of power surges in my skin. With a roar, I land on the Skull's chest. I drive both machetes through his abdomen.

"*Awaken, Zélie. . . .*"

The whisper builds. Blood coats my hands as I'm hypnotized by the chant. The triple arrowhead on the medallion starts to burn.

Behind my eyes, a red moon shines. . . .

Again, the world starts to spin, but I don't have time to sit still. Footsteps pound down the stairs. I turn to find a group of Skulls. Curses ring as they bite through their hands and reach for their weapons.

Dammit!

I scramble to my feet and charge forward as the Skulls transform behind me. The deck shakes with their every step. Heat flares from their glowing hammers and axes.

I start to run for the other maji, but they're too far away to help. The Skulls close the distance between us. I scan the deck for a place to escape.

There!

The skies flash above a flapping doorway in the middle of the ship. With no other place to turn, I run in. I nearly slip down the winding stairs.

The stench of feces and fur hits me like a wall. When I reach the bottom, a withered beast starts to growl. I skid to a halt, coming face-to-face with sharp, black-lined eyes.

A trio of cheetanaires glares at me from behind the bars of a cage. They look like they haven't been fed in days. The spotted beasts are only a few of the dozens of ryders locked away. I pass red-tailed antelopentai, blue-butt baboonems, and black-horned rhinomes. In one cage, I even find a rare baby elephantaire. Yellow pus oozes from a horrible gash in its left ear.

At once, I think of Nailah, my beloved lionaire. She was with us when we stormed the palace.

Is it possible the Skulls locked her in here?

"Nailah?" I spin around. I don't know which way to turn. Commotion builds outside the door. I crouch behind the cages as I search.

"Nailah?" I drop my voice to a hiss. For a moment, nothing calls back. Then I hear a groan.

My ears perk up as a weak roar greets me in return.

Nailah!

Torches charge through the door. I drop to the dirtied floor. I crawl across the ground as the Skulls' orange light spills into the pen, illuminating the wild maze of cages.

I move past wounded panthenaires and a white-chested gorillion. A fifteen-meter black mamba snake rises in its cage as I approach. The snake pulls one Skull's attention. My muscles tense as he points.

"Nailah!" I scream my ryder's name. This time, Nailah roars in return. Her call draws me to the corner of the room. My eyes widen at her wounds.

"Oh my gods, Nailah!"

My lionaire rises in a cage far too small for her hulking frame. Ugly red gashes mark her golden skin. Like me, her mighty mane has been shaved.

I press my forehead to hers, and she purrs in return. But I turn as the torchlight draws near. Three Skulls round the corner, menacing in their stares.

My pulse races as I strike my machetes against the lock on Nailah's cage. Sparks fly as the metal meets my blade. But no matter how many times I strike, the machetes aren't strong enough to break through the heavy iron.

Behind me, the Skulls' boots near. Blood pounds so hard in my head I can't hear. But then everything goes dark.

I freeze as the torchlight disappears.

What's happening?

I drop to the floor and brace myself against Nailah's cage. Out of the black, two axes glow red. They face each other, going head-to-head.

I turn away as glowing axes crash together. The weapons collide again and again. With a wild cry, a heavy body is thrown into the wall of ryders. A clamor erupts from the cages that crash to the floor.

Wounded animals shriek and roar. A few cages spring open, and ryders run free. I pull myself closer to Nailah's cage to avoid the frenzy.

A long silence follows before heavy steps approach. I grab my machetes, not knowing who I'll have to fight. My heart thunders as the figure nears.

Then someone picks up a fallen torchlight.

"Tzain?"

I blink. I don't believe the sight. The brother I saw before is nowhere to be found. A strange haze fills his mahogany eyes. His skin drips with the enemies' blood. One of the Skull's weapons glows red in his palm. He raises the weapon to fight.

It's like he doesn't know who I am.

"Tzain . . ." I step up tentatively. I let my machetes fall by my sides.

My brother does the same, and all at once, the life returns to his eyes. He stares at his own hands. I feel the weight of his surprise.

"It's alright." I touch his shoulder.

Tzain falls to his knees, and we collapse into each other's arms.

CHAPTER EIGHTEEN

AMARI

PANELS FLY AS THE mighty Skull breaks through the doorframe. He charges at me like a ryder on the hunt. Blood drips from his hand. Runes flicker on his glowing axe.

"Amari, run!" Inan demands, but I ignore what he says. I glance back at my brother, homing in on the shackles that bind his wrists.

If I can find a way to draw his swing . . .

The blade I wanted is right before my eyes. I have to take the chance. I won't leave Inan to die.

The Skull swings his glowing axe, and I drop to the floor. My skin stings as it hits the ice-cold water. The blade passes over my head, cutting straight through the metal of one of the hanging cages.

The hold rings with the violent clash. The bottom half of the cage falls to the hold's floor. As water splashes around me, I struggle to rise. The water chills me to the bone. My teeth chatter as I finally manage to throw myself against the wall of the hold.

But the rising waters do nothing to slow the massive Skull. The air reverberates around us as he raises his axe once more.

Skies!

I throw myself to the side just as the Skull swings. He attacks with no regard. Instead of cutting through me, his blade blows through the wooden wall.

Shards whip through the air. More water spills into the hold. The collapsed wall reveals a room full of barrels with thick black liquid. Blast oil leaks into the water as the barrels start to float.

"Amari, go!" Inan points to the open pathway.

"I'm not leaving you behind!"

I fight through the sloshing water, dragging myself to my brother's cage. Behind me, the Skull closes in. His boots splash through the water at my back. But I need him to get close.

This is the moment to draw his attack.

"Hold out your shackles!" I shout to my brother.

Inan stretches as far as the chains will allow. The Skull's blade will have to be precise. With the right blow, Inan and I can fight.

"Hurry!" Inan's amber eyes grow wide. I feel the heat of the Skull's glowing axe. I reach Inan's chained hands and turn as the Skull's blade barrels down.

"Now!" Inan orders. I dive to the side. The Skull's axe strikes through Inan's chains. His glowing axe cuts my brother free.

Inan leaps from his cage, driving his elbow into the Skull's temple. His attack catches the Skull off guard. But before he can strike again, a giant wave rams into the ship's side.

With a violent lurch, the entire floor tilts. Our feet fly out from under us. The Skull crashes into the wall, and his axe drops to the floor. The Skull's frame begins to shrink as seawater slides over his axe's tarnished brass.

I lunge for the hilt, but the glowing metal burns my hands. Tendrils of smoke rise from my palms.

It's as if the weapon is bonded to its owner.

"Don't touch it!" Inan tries to warn me. He goes for the axe instead. But before he can try to pick it up, the Skull clubs him over the head.

"Inan!" I cry out as my brother falls to the floor. I try to reach for him, but the Skull doesn't give me the chance. His meaty palm grabs me by the hair. Another wraps around my neck. The Skull lifts me up, squeezing the air from my lungs.

My eyes sting as I fight for breath. I kick. I thrash. I claw. But no matter what I do, I can't break free. My throat burns as death wraps around me.

Not like this, I think to myself. *Not when we're so close.*

That's when I see it—the animal-skin pouch with a rope strapped to the Skull's belt.

I think back to the Skull who attacked Nâo's cell. When he pulled the rope, flames erupted in a single breath. If Kenyon hadn't stopped him, the bomb would have gone off. It would have blown through our cell.

As white spots fill my vision, I don't give myself time to think. With the last of my strength, I reach down, ripping the rope free.

"*Nei!*" the Skull roars at my attack. Sparks start to fly. Flames erupt down the rope. The Skull drops me, reaching for the bomb.

Inan rises from the water. With an unsteady start, he shoves the Skull forward. The warrior falls into Inan's open cage. Inan works fast, using the right key to lock the man inside.

"Hurry!" I say.

Inan grabs my arm. A burning scent fills the hold. My heartbeat spikes as we run up the stairs.

We push to make it to the deck before the bomb ignites.

CHAPTER NINETEEN

※ —— ⨯ · • › ● ◎ ● ‹ • ⨯ —— ※

TZAIN

HOLDING ZÉLIE IN MY arms, I don't ever want to let go. For an instant, the ship fades away. The fallen Skulls and freed ryders vanish into thin air.

I feel every time my sister's been ripped away from me. Every time I thought I would never see her again. When she ran after Mama. When she was tortured by King Saran. When she disappeared in the caves of Ibadan, forced to survive the toxic clouds of gas.

Never again. My body shakes with the words I hold back. *No more mistakes. Whatever it takes to keep her safe.*

"You're *here*," Zélie finally whispers. Her soft words bring me back. Outside the ship, the storm rages around us. The cries of the fighting maji travel through the ryder pen.

Zélie's hot tears spill onto my neck, and I tighten my grip.

"I'm not going anywhere," I whisper back. "I promise."

Behind us, Nailah roars. Despite everything, I smile. I reach through the cage and lay my hand on her golden head. I never thought I'd see our lionaire again.

A crude muzzle is tied around her snout. Patches of fur have withered away where her body meets the bars. Her rib cage protrudes from her skin. She looks like she's suffered just as much as we have.

"Can you break her out?" Zélie asks. I glance back at the foreign axe.

I think of the way its power surged through me before. All the Skulls I cut out of my path.

A part of me doesn't ever want to feel what I feel when I grab on to its hilt. But its power is the only reason I got to Zélie in time. It's the only thing that will keep her safe.

"Get back," I instruct my sister. She moves away as I pick up my fallen axe. Again, my blood feeds into the hilt. The foreign chants fill my head.

I breathe in as fresh anger rips through me. My muscles grow taut. The red glow surrounds the crimson blade. I lift it up, almost in a daze.

With one smash, Nailah's padlock breaks. Our lionaire leaps out of her cage. She topples me to the floor, knocking the axe out of my hand before I feel anything more.

Nailah coats my face with her pink tongue in thanks before running to my sister. Zélie throws her arms around the lionaire's neck and releases a sob. A moment is all I give them before returning to the fight.

"We need to go." I raid a fallen Skull, removing the sheath attached to his back. Though I fear the power of the axe, I slide it into the leather handle. I won't leave the only true power I have to attack.

"Back to the deck." I grab the rope around Nailah's snout and help Zélie up. "The ship is almost ours!"

We push past fallen Skulls and fallen cages as we make our way out of the ryder pen. The ship's sway has increased threefold. It's a struggle to stay upright.

We pull ourselves up the spiraling steps. With a powerful lurch, we make it back to the deck. Lightning dances above, illuminating the final battle that rages across the ship.

I hold Zélie back, watching as the maji attack. Our people strike with a vengeance. Blood pours like the rain that pounds from above. To our right, a towering Skull takes a sword to the gut.

To our left, a group of maji use a cannon like a battering ram. They knock a pair of charging Skulls overboard. The howling winds steal our enemies' yells.

We've done it. . . .

I can't believe it. Our victory draws near. One by one, every Skull falls to the deck. The masks of our enemies crack in half.

When the last Skull falls, Kenyon raises his fists to the flashing sky and roars. The other maji join his battle cry. I think of every maji we lost in this fight. The bodies tossed into the seas. Tears fill my eyes as I lift my hand and shout for them.

I pray they feel our victory.

"It's really over?" Zélie squeezes my arm, and I nod.

We've survived this terror.

We have a chance to go home—

BOOM!

An explosion rings from below the deck. The entire ship quakes. The wooden panels at our feet are blown apart. Debris shoots into the air.

"What was that?" I turn toward the sound as a sharp crack reverberates through the boat. Two silhouettes rise from the lower levels, running onto the deck.

Lightning flashes against a girl's terror-stricken face and I freeze. My hands fall numb.

Amari . . .

The sight of the princess I once loved still makes my heart stop.

She clings on to her brother, both soaking wet.

"We have to go!" Amari screams. "The ship's going down!"

CHAPTER TWENTY

ZÉLIE

"GET TO THE LIFEBOATS!" Inan roars like the thunder above. All at once, everything shifts. Tzain launches into action, pulling Nailah and me to the other side of the ship.

The elements fight against us as we run. The rain cuts. The winds howl. The deck is slick with the blood of the slain Skulls. We slip and fall across the floor more than we're able to run.

The other maji stampede across the deck. They trip over one another in their trek. We all race to escape the damaged ship, running toward the wide boats covered with animal skins.

"Your blade!" Tzain snatches a dagger from another boy's hand. He cuts through the ropes tying one of the boats to the deck. Together we turn the boat right side up. A dozen maji pile in as Tzain and I inspect the boat's mechanisms, trying to figure out how it works. Though more complex than the coconut boats we sailed in Ilorin, some of the foreign parts are familiar.

Tzain snaps the wooden mast into place. I tug on a rope, and the mainsail flows free. Tzain points to the lever in the center.

"Who can steer?" He searches the group.

Two lean boys with matching birthmarks step forward. Tzain positions their hands over the lever, showing them how to control the sails.

"Where do we go?" one of the boys asks.

Inan pushes to the front, pointing to a chain of islands on the flashing horizon.

"There!" he shouts over the howling winds. "Head north until you hit sand!"

"Everyone move!" Kenyon orders. Maji back out of his way. The elder of the Burners loads a giant cannon and lights the torch. We cover our ears as the cannon explodes. The ball shoots through the ship's railing, creating an opening big enough for the lifeboats to escape.

Tzain and Inan don't waste a second. They push the first lifeboat across the slippery deck. The twelve maji scream as they go over the ship's edge.

Their lifeboat falls more than twenty meters through the air.

I grab our ship's railing as the lifeboat lands nose first. The thrashing waters drench the maji in seconds. But the lifeboat stabilizes on the sea's surface. The wind-powered propeller attached to the boat's back roars to life.

I hold my breath as the maji fly across the waves, clinging to the sides of the boat. They almost tip over more than once, but they make their way through the choppy waters. Lightning illuminates their trek toward the island chain.

"Again!" Tzain cuts another boat free. "Come forward if you can steer!"

Everyone starts to work together. We find an order through the growing chaos. One by one, Tzain cuts the boats free and maji pile in. Levers snap into place. Sails blow in the wind.

Storm clouds spiral in the raging skies. The sea thrashes from side to side. The ship groans with its pain. Wooden panels crack under the strain.

We push boat after boat over the edge as the ship's bow starts to rise. As the deck tilts, Skulls' corpses slide past us. We have to fight our way through the dead.

The trio of cheetanaires sprints across the rising deck, fresh blood matted into the spotted fur around their snouts. One cheetanaire leaps, and Tzain pulls me back. It misses me by a hair, tumbling off the broken ship.

"Let's go!" Tzain yells. Only one lifeboat remains. I pull Nailah on, and Amari follows.

I keep my hands on the lever. Amari pulls our sails free. Tzain and Inan take position behind the boat. I brace myself as they push.

But as we make our way to the ship's edge, the medallion glows in my chest. My skin starts to hum with a new force. Fresh bolts of lightning erupt above, each so bright they illuminate the entire horizon.

"What in the gods' names," I whisper. The brilliant blaze of color stops time. For a moment, we're caught under deep oranges and turquoise greens, blazing reds and shocking purples. The lightning forms a crackling circle around our heads.

Somehow I know the medallion is the cause. . . .

The black waters flash under the brilliant light. More bolts dance across the entire width of the seas. The lightning gathers in one lethal swell.

Then the Skulls' mighty ship snaps in half.

CHAPTER TWENTY-ONE

ZÉLIE

IN ONE SINGLE INSTANCE, the entire world shifts. Our lifeboat doesn't make it over the railing. The capsized ship lurches in the seas. Tzain and Inan manage to pull themselves into the lifeboat just in time.

We're left staring at the open sky as our craft flies down the raised deck.

"Hold on!" Tzain screams. All around us, the massive ship breaks. Giant masts whip past our heads. Cannons tumble from their gunports. The Skulls' bodies fall through the air.

With a violent lurch, we shoot from the deck and our boat careens. Pain radiates through my being as we crash into the ocean. The remains of the Skull's ship fall overhead.

No!

The moment we hit the black waters, the five of us are torn apart. The thrashing waves pummel me in an instant. The ocean wraps me in its icy claws.

I open my mouth to scream. Only the blackness answers my call. Salt water burns down my throat. My eyes bulge as I choke.

Oya, please . . .

The bright bolts of lightning still crackle above, illuminating how far below the water's surface I am. With nowhere left to turn, I reach for my magic with the little that I have left. I pray for its heat to surge through my blood. I pray for the magic of life and death.

Please . . .

I mouth the words as my eyes flutter to a close. My chest tightens, wheezing for air. Feeling fades from my toes. But as my body turns to ice, the medallion burns in my chest.

A new hum fills my ears.

Oya?

I blink my eyes open. The waters around me start to glow. It begins with small beads of light. They surround me like a spiderweb. I marvel at the vibrant orbs—deep purples and bleeding reds. The web of light spreads beneath the sea, illuminating the shipwreck around me.

Bronze masks fall like snow. Crimson hammers and axes sink like anchors. The entire captain's quarters goes down, twisting as it falls past my head.

As the light travels, I spot Amari and Tzain. The two float unconscious, nearly a full kilometer away. I reach my arms out toward them as the familiar whisper breaks back into my head.

"Awaken, Zélie."

A pulse of golden light breaks free from the medallion, traveling through the ocean in waves. It captures Tzain and Amari like a current, pushing them toward the island chains.

I reach for my magic again, and another golden pulse shoots free. The waters around me swirl. The triple arrowhead in the medallion radiates as the same golden light fills my bones.

Above the glowing sea, the storm flashes with wild rage. It's like the entire sky is ripped open at the seams. Lightning strikes down from every cloud, somehow traveling into the ocean waters. Brilliant bolts crackle toward me like snakes, predators closing in on their prey.

Before I can shift, the bolts of lightning hit the medallion in my chest.

My arms flail back with the force. A golden light surrounds my entire body, coating my skin as a new power swirls through my blood.

"*Find her.*" The voice that fills my ears seems to travel beyond time. As it speaks, my wounds knit together. My scars begin to heal. My bare scalp heats, and long white tendrils of hair push free.

When the golden light shines through my eyes, my vision transforms. My irises start to sparkle. The sea disappears, replaced with one blurry form.

"*Find her.*"

I see a girl. Her skin is a rich russet brown. Diamonds glitter in her angular eyes. A patterned scarf of vibrant jewels wraps around her night-black hair.

"*Find her.*" The ancient voice thunders through my soul. "*Before it's too late.*"

"*I will.*" I whisper the promise back to the sea.

The medallion's golden light fades as everything disappears around me.

PART II

CHAPTER TWENTY-TWO

TZAIN

"WE FOUND THE LAST ONE!"

The moment Nâo's call rings through the palm trees, I jump to my feet. My heart beats in anticipation of the face I need to see.

I slide down the cliff that houses our makeshift shelter. Nailah follows me, pouncing onto the sandy bank. Though unsteady on her feet, the lionaire stays by my side as we make our way through the dense greens.

"Be here," I whisper to myself. My legs don't carry me fast enough. Sharp rocks shift under my hardened feet, and thinning branches nick my skin. So much swirls inside me, I can barely feel the pain.

The moment our ship hit the water, everything went black. There was no way to keep Zélie in my grasp. The raging ocean tore us apart. I couldn't save her or myself.

I gave in to the dark.

When I awoke on the sandy shores, it didn't feel real. I couldn't understand how we'd made it to the island chains. But only Nailah and Amari were by my side.

Zélie and Inan were gone.

Nâo was the first to find us. I couldn't speak as she walked us to the nascent maji camp. When we arrived, I spotted all the maji who had made it off the ship. I looked for Zélie in every tent. With every new lifeboat that's been discovered, I've waited to see her face. Every single time I've been left waiting in the sand.

"Be *here*." I repeat the prayer. The palm trees give way to the open shore. Jagged bluffs fill the white sands, and tangles of seaweed line the beach. A group of yellow crabs skitters by my feet.

The hot sun blinds from above. I shield my eyes as Nâo leads another boat of rescued maji down the coastline. I scan the twelve maji for my sister's face, and something deflates inside.

Despite how hard I search, Zélie is nowhere to be found.

Where are you? I close my eyes, fighting back the swell that wants to burst. We were finally free of the Skulls. I held her in my arms.

I look out to the ocean waters. A steady tide laps the beach. I refuse to believe she's gone.

After all we endured to escape, Zélie can't be lost to the seas.

But as the maji make their way toward me, I don't have time to sit still. The maji's limbs drag through the wet sand. They're all so weak they can barely stand.

"Here." I run forward to meet them. I extend my arms to the two maji who struggle the most. The young girls hold on to me as I lead them away from the beach. When one of them falls, I stop, taking her off her feet and into my arms.

"Thank you." She squeezes my hand. I offer her a smile in return. I see Zélie in her scars. The thought of this girl in chains makes my stomach turn.

Her small voice brings me back to what we've done, reminding me of the magnitude of our escape from the Skulls. I take great care as I hike back up the cliff. I lift the maji over the edge one at a time, watching as the new arrivals disperse through the modest shelter we've built.

Eight tents surround our signal fire, each crafted from the strongest branches we could find on this side of the island. Gathered moss binds our shelters together. Woven banana leaves form our blankets. Stone pots sit under the trees, collecting the rainwater that falls at night. Fresh catch fries over the open flame. It's more than any of us has had in days.

The strongest in our camp come to meet us. The new arrivals seem taken aback by the nourishment they bring. One maji offers large seashells full of rainwater. Another maji follows with fried swordfish and oysters.

Khani, one of my old agbön mates, rushes forward. A pit forms in my chest as I watch her work. From the day I first met her, she was always a part of a matched set. I've never seen her without Imani, her twin.

The sunlight warms Khani's freckled skin, but I sense the emptiness she holds within. She approaches a maji cradling his arm. She's focused and gentle, taking great care as she inspects the broken limb.

"Come with me," Khani soothes. "I don't have my magic, but I can set your bones."

Despite the death of her own sister, the elder of the Healers helps everyone she can.

I don't know if I could be that strong.

I gaze over the camp, taking everything in. Though we've found a moment of respite, the toll of those we've lost hangs in the air. When I'm still, I feel the weight of my old chains. I'm choked with the stench of our cell. Though my feet grip the sand, I feel myself being pulled under the ocean, pulled back into the pain. Those Skulls locked me up.

But someone else broke out of that cage.

"Come on." I nod to Nailah. I place my hand on her neck as we make our way back to the coastline. The faint echo of foreign chants fills my ears. I squeeze my eyes shut to keep them at bay.

We walk to an isolated part of the beach and climb over moss-covered reefs. I wade into the warm waters, and Nailah follows me in. She plunges her massive head below the surface, returning with a mouthful of fish.

As she feeds, I pull myself through the tangled roots of a mangrove tree. I push the branches away, revealing the Skull's crimson axe.

Blóðseiðr . . .

My skin prickles at the words that run through my head. It's as if the axe calls to me, daring me to wield it again. In the sunlight, the blood-metal shines. Crimson stains the rectangular runes carved into its rose-wood hilt. My fingers drift toward the handle, and I remember the way I lost control. I see the bodies of the fallen Skulls. With a drop of blood, I know the axe would awaken once more.

I'd feel the power of its red glow——

"Tzain!" The sound of Amari's voice snaps me out of my haze. Water splashes at my back as she makes her way through the tides. I rush to move the branches and cover the axe's hiding place.

"It's Kenyon!" she speaks through her pants. "He's gathering the others. . . ." Amari's voice trails off, and I follow her gaze. Despite the branches, the sun reflects off the axe's crimson blade. Her brown cheeks flush, reminding me why I hid the axe so far from camp. The way the others look at me with it, I might as well be wearing one of the Skull's horrid masks.

Amari eyes me for a moment before reaching out and touching the hilt. A sharp hiss sounds and she draws her hand back. She gazes at my palms.

"Doesn't it burn when you touch it?" she asks.

I think back to the Skull I killed. To the sharp heat that prickled through my skin. It was like the axe called out to me in its former own-er's death. Is that why I'm able to wield his weapon when the others can't?

"I couldn't leave it behind." I fill the silence. "If something happens——"

"You don't have to explain." Amari speaks too quickly to mean what she says. But in her voice, I feel something gentle. A part of her that wants to understand.

I almost want to tell her what the axe does to me. The strange words I hear in my head. Being this close to her now, I remember the warmth of her embrace. The way she used to fit inside my arms. I think of the Tzain I was when all I wanted was for us to be together.

That Tzain thought our love would last forever.

But in her attempt to defeat her mother, Amari almost killed Zélie and an entire village. Even with the threat of the Skulls, I don't know how I can forgive her for everything she's done.

What future can we have when she was willing to destroy everything I loved?

"I didn't know where to go." Amari crosses her arms over her chest. She stares out at the endless sea. "Kenyon's gathering the others. They're preparing the boats for the journey home."

"Back to Orïsha?" My brows arch. We haven't even been on the island for two days. I hadn't dared to think that far.

"There are maji at the camp," Amari explains. "Sailors who know how to chart the stars. By the time night falls, they'll be able to point us back home."

I look out over the horizon. Again, my hands itch for the glinting axe. More Skulls could appear any second. If another ship landed on our shores, we wouldn't stand a chance.

"When does he want to leave?" I ask.

"Dawn." Amari closes her eyes, and her shoulders slump. "Talk to him. Please. We have to make them wait."

"We can't."

"We don't have a choice!" Amari's voice turns shrill. "Inan and Zélie haven't returned!"

"We can't hold the rest of the maji hostage waiting for ghosts."

Amari's lips part. She looks at me like I've struck her with the axe. "You don't mean that."

I turn away. I don't know what she wants me to say. I think of Khani back at the camp, caring for the others despite everything she's lost. Zélie wouldn't want me to wait.

She'd want to make sure the rest of the maji were safe.

"The others had boats," I say. "They got off the ship. They had a real chance to get away."

"So did we." Amari doesn't allow my words to shake her faith. "They're alive, Tzain. I know it. I *feel* it in my gut. If you won't help me stop the others, I'll do it by myself."

CHAPTER TWENTY-THREE

ZÉLIE

CRASHING SURF ROLLS THROUGH MY EARS. The soft chirps of birds follows next. Sensation crawls up my skin in waves. It feels like I've been knocked out for days.

I blink my eyes open to blinding rays of sun. It beats down on me from above. It's been so long since I've seen blue skies.

I marvel at the sight.

"Where am I?" My throat is so dry, the words practically scratch themselves free. I push myself onto my elbows. All I see before me are endless stretches of turquoise seas.

There's no sign of the raging ocean. No remnants of the Skulls' ship or King Baldyr's golden mask. Waves and forested bluffs surround me. Sunlight catches the edge of the medallion in my chest.

It's still here. . . .

I reach under my wrap. Touching the tarnished metal brings every memory flooding back. I see the way the ocean lit up. I feel the golden glow that surrounded my skin. I remember the bolts of lightning that charged through my being.

I move toward the tides, bending down till the waters catch my reflection. The majacite crown is still welded into my temple, but a new mane of white hair sprouts around the black metal. The thick tufts fall to the small of my back.

I touch my neck, but there are no puncture wounds. The bruises and cuts I sustained on the ship have healed. I run my hands up and down my spine, and I can't believe it.

Even the MAGGOT King Saran had carved into my back is gone.

What is this?

I return to the lightning that struck my core. Whatever Baldyr's done to me has transformed more than my magic. I don't feel like the Reaper I've always been.

It's like I've been born again.

I run my hand over the medallion again, and I see the girl from my vision. Thick curls run through the dark hair that falls down her slender back. Her eyes sparkle like diamonds, and yellow silks cover her brown skin. Emerald plants lean into her as she passes.

"*Find her.*" I hear the ancient voice. I hear the promise I made back. In that moment, I felt a bond form. It was like a contract weaving itself through my soul.

I think back to the chest Baldyr carried out of the captain's quarters. There were two medallions left. The Silver Skull's compass still hangs from my wool belt. I open the lid and stare at the spinning dial.

I have to find that girl. Somehow I know she's the one King Baldyr needs next.

But how am I supposed to find her when I don't even know where I am?

I rise to my feet, taking in the island's shores. The cresting waves lick my knees as I search for signs of the others. Far down the coast, a body lies facedown in the sand. The tides push the half-conscious boy onto the beach, and sand dirties his white streak.

"Inan?" My heart lurches and I break into a sprint. Inan's arms shake as he tries to rise. He chokes up seawater and algae, collapsing back into the tides.

"What's going on?" he croaks. His skin is red with burns. I reach down to help him up, but the moment our bodies touch, the medallion warms in my chest. A blue light I haven't seen in over a moon erupts under Inan's skin.

Magic.

The dark blue wisps lick my hands, taking me from the coastline all the way back to my homeland. The sunlight shifts as our world transforms. Lush green valleys take shape, surrounding us on all sides.

In a rush, I'm brought back to the day I sat with Inan on the riverbank, the day I started teaching him how to control his gifts. The old memory comes alive, trapping us back in time. . . .

"How does it work?" I ask. "There are times when it feels like you're reading a book inside my head."

"More like a puzzle than a book," Inan corrects me. "It's not always clear, but when your thoughts and emotions are intense, I feel them, too."

"You get that with everyone?"

He shakes his head. "Not to the same degree. Everyone else feels like being caught in the rain. You're the whole tsunami."

When the memory disappears, I struggle to breathe. Inan lifts his glowing palms. His brows crease as the blue light fades. He looks back up at me.

"How did you do that?"

I raise my hands as the medallion's heat cools. I reach for my own Reaper magic, but a foreign force rises to the surface. Instead of the power of life and death, thunder rumbles through my veins.

The medallion is still transforming her blood. The growl in King Baldyr's voice haunts me. The hard look in his stormy gaze. *When her new power is ready for the harvest, I want her brought to the fortress in Iarlaith.*

I don't know how to explain to Inan what I'm just beginning to understand myself. I'm not ready for him or anyone else to see the grotesque metal in my chest. How would he even help?

Instead, I ignore Inan's question. I hook my arms under his.

"What're you doing?" he asks.

"Getting you out of the sun."

I grit my teeth and pull. My head spins in the heat. Inan continues to choke as I drag his body across the white sands. Salt water spills down his bare chest.

I lay his body against a palm tree, and he leans against the ridged bark, reveling in the shade. His hands are still mangled from everything he had to do to escape. A new bruise colors the right side of his face.

"Do you see that?" Inan points to the skies. Far to the north, a chain of black smoke rises over the dense forest.

"Tzain!" I whisper to myself. A smile spreads across my lips. It has to be him and the others. They're safe. They made it back to land.

"We can get to them." I walk forward, calculating how long the trek will take. But as I walk, my steps falter. Something crackles beneath my skin. Baldyr's memories swell within me, rising as the medallion burns my chest. . . .

A soft rain pours as Baldyr tends to his tribe's stable of white bears. More than two dozen ryders lie in an open pen. They gather around as Baldyr fills their troughs.

Crates of freshly butchered meat fall one by one. The kill is so fresh it still oozes with blood. As the bears feast, Baldyr uses a stiff brush to tend to each ryder's fur. He keeps his face stern in concentration, removing the dirt and debris.

No runes mark Baldyr's skin. Though still muscular, he carries a leaner frame. A brown tunic covers his typically bare chest. He can't be more than nineteen.

Lanterns illuminate the longhouse behind him where his fellow tribesmen gather for a measly supper. Their gentle chatter fills the night. Baldyr glances over as the wooden door opens.

His tribe leader walks into the dark.

Done already?

Baldyr watches Egil stroll through the barren fields. The fur-clad warrior stops before a round clearing to stare up at the yellow moon.

Baldyr drops his brush and walks over, joining Egil to take in the sight. Egil always carries a stern gaze, but for once his freckled face is lost in thought.

"My mother used to tell me stories." Egil breaks the silence, a far-off look in his dark eyes. "She told me one day I would rule over the lands. That I would command the strength of over ten men."

"I heard your mother was a witch."

"The galdrasmiðar *are not witches." The scars along Egil's cheeks strain as his jaw pulls taut. "They are connected to the hidden forces of this land. They have the power to turn the very moon red."*

"That is but a myth," Baldyr scoffs. "No one believes that."

But Egil reaches into his pocket and removes the ancient medallion that now lies in my chest.

"One day, you will see." Egil looks up at the yellow moon once more. "When I find what I need, I won't just be king of this nation. I'll be more than the mortal I am now. I'll have the strength to be the god of this new world."

"You believe you can become a god?" Baldyr's eyes flash and he homes in on the medallion in his leader's hand.

"I don't just believe it." Egil winks. "I have a plan."

I close my eyes, and the sound of pounding rain fills my ears. The heat sticking to my back chills like ice. The gentle breeze rises to a gale-force wind. Baldyr's calling out to me.

I feel the pull from within.

"What's wrong?" Inan calls.

I don't know how to explain the new power that moves through my blood.

"Another storm," I whisper instead. "A big one."

Like clockwork, thunderclouds gather on the far horizon. They glimmer like black pearls. Inan rises to his feet and stares at the flashing masses.

"How did you know?" he asks.

I place my hand over the medallion, praying it doesn't glow under my wrap. The fear I haven't allowed myself to feel crawls back in as the storm draws near. Lightning starts to crackle, and I see the blood-red moon behind my eyes. I feel it in my bones.

I'm running out of time.

"We need to get to higher ground," Inan says. I don't fight him as he helps me back onto my feet. I hook his injured arm over my shoulder, and we take off.

Hours pass in silence as we make our way through the bamboo trees. The green stalks grow high above our heads, disappearing as we reach a steep incline. The trickle of a waterfall guides us as the first rain falls. I set Inan down by the bank and he drops to the fresh pool, inhaling the water like air.

As I join him, my muscles tense. It's been so long since the two of us have been like this. The trickling waterfall brings me back to the dreamscape, the world Inan and I created in our minds. Suspended between our conscious and unconscious states, together we made the dreamscape come alive.

Thinking of the plane now, I see the white dress I'd always wear. I feel the delicate reeds our bodies tangled through. In the dreamscape, I let my guard down.

I fell under his spell.

"There's a cave." Inan points up the waterfall. "We might as well wait out the rain."

My stomach clenches tight as we hike.

I try to erase the memories of the last time we were alone all night.

CHAPTER TWENTY-FOUR

INAN

Day turns to night.

The storm rages beyond our cave.

I sit at the mouth, silent as I watch the falling rain.

Everything it took to escape the Skulls plays through my mind. Their brutal fists. Their bronze smiles. I wonder what it will take to defeat them for good.

I wonder how to keep Zélie alive.

I glance over my shoulder to find her sitting by the fire. She hasn't moved since we entered the cave. She clutches the wool wrapped tight around her chest, staring at the dancing flames.

Despite how many times I've asked, she won't tell me what happened after they took her. I don't have a clue what she knows. But the girl who was taken from the cage is not the one who sits here now.

Her white hair spills over her dark shoulders like a cloud. Every wound she had before has disappeared. The way she walked onto the beach, it was as if she called forth the storm. She squeezes her eyes shut whenever light-ning cracks from above.

And then there's my magic. . . .

I lift my own scarred hands. With a push, the blue wisps of my old powers come forward again. A curse I reached for every night on that horrid ship, reignited the moment Zélie's fingers met my skin.

Everything I wanted to protect Zélie from on that vessel already feels like it's come to pass. There's not one scar on her body, yet I've never seen her look so afraid. The way she stares at the fire, it's as if something inside her has died.

The Skulls have done something to her. She's changing, right before my eyes. How can I keep her out of Baldyr's hands if she won't tell me what she knows? How can I protect Orïsha from the Skulls' attack?

If she won't talk, then I'll find out for myself.

My magic burns as it pushes free from my wounded hand, gathering around my fingers in a turquoise cloud. For so long magic has been the only way for me to get through Zélie's walls. The only time she's been forced to let me in. If I can just peek inside her mind, then I'll have another clue.

I may discover what King Baldyr's planning to do.

I hold my breath as I release the turquoise cloud. It travels across the cave floor like a snake. I follow the trail as it closes the space between Zélie and me, crawling toward her back.

"—*he will find you*—"

"—*there is no place you can run*—"

The voices cycling through Zélie's mind begin to bleed into mine. But the moment before my magic connects, Zélie whips around. Her eyes go wide at the turquoise cloud.

"What're you doing?" Her nostrils flare. She pushes herself against the cave wall. My magic disappears into thin air. Shame colors my cheeks as I rise to my feet.

"I can help," I offer. "I want to help—"

"By breaking into my head?" Zélie charges at me like a black-horned rhinome. She gets so close I feel the heat of her breath. "I don't care about the Skulls. I will never let you back in."

Her words hold the weight of all my failures. I feel every single time I've betrayed her. If I'd stayed loyal to our plans, would we be in this mess? Would the Skulls have ever had a chance to attack our homeland?

Bring her home. I turn away. *That's all I can expect.* She'll never look at me the way she once did.

I can't expect her to ever give me another chance.

But the dreamscape we once shared fills my mind. Our connection, beyond space, beyond time. I tumble through the memories of when she was mine. The way her bare skin felt in my arms. The gentle touch of her soft lips against my own. There's nothing I wouldn't give to return to the blowing reeds now. To be with her in the world of my dreams, far beyond King Baldyr's reach.

"You don't have to let me in." I choose my words with care, trying to find a crack. I can't protect her if she won't tell me what we're really up against. "But you can't shut me out. Not now. Something's happening to you, Zélie. I can see it. I *feel* it."

Zélie opens her mouth to speak, but the words don't come out. She glances down at the hexagon-shaped compass hooked to her belt. Even without my magic, the wave of terror that rises in her rises through me as well.

"Let me in." I dare to step forward. "Whatever you know, help me understand. You're not alone in this fight. I'm prepared to stay by your side—"

"You're dead to me." Zélie comes alive. Her words cut like knives. "You were supposed to die that night in Lagos. You might as well be dead now!"

"You really want me dead?" I rip the dagger from my own belt and force it into her palms. Zélie's brows furrow as I wrap her fingers around the hilt.

"What're you doing?"

"Giving you exactly what you want." I raise her hand to my neck, lifting my chin to expose the flesh. "You want me dead? Go ahead."

Zélie's eyes flash. A slight tremble rocks her hand. With one swipe, she could slit my throat. I'd bleed out on the cave floor. No one would ever know.

"What're you waiting for?" I whisper. I release her shaking wrist. Tears brim in her eyes, at war with the hatred I feel burning deep inside.

With a cry, she shoves me back. She throws the dagger to the floor. Before I can touch her shoulder, Zélie takes off. She exits the cave, disappearing into the rain.

"Zélie!"

Though every muscle in my body aches, I push myself beyond the pain. I throw myself after her, sprinting from the cave.

Zélie runs like a gazelle. Lightning flashes against her dark limbs. The sky seems to crackle with her every step. She races through the jungle, fighting through the howling winds.

"Zélie, wait!" I call out her name. The storm swallows my every shout. I spot a cliff before she can stop. I reach for Zélie as she careens over the edge.

Her body rolls through thick vines and large green ferns, twisting all the way down the steep incline. She comes to a stop at the bank of the waterfall. I follow after her, meeting her in the mud.

"Are you alright?" I extend my hand as her wrap falls away. Zélie grasps the wool fabric to her chest, but not before I see the tarnished gold fused into her rib cage.

"What in the skies . . ."

Zélie shuts her eyes. She doesn't fight me as I approach. I peel her wrap back with care. The sight of the ancient medallion welded into her chest turns my body to stone.

"Who did this to you?" I breathe.

Tears stream down Zélie's heart-shaped face. "King Baldyr," she finally whispers.

"You saw their king?" I tilt my head.

"They were supposed to take me back to their land." Zélie crosses her arms over her chest. "A place called Iarlaith."

Zélie turns her head away. It's as if it's too painful to speak.

"Please." I draw closer to her. "Just let me see."

This time when my magic sparks at my fingertips, Zélie doesn't run away. I breathe in as the turquoise cloud connects us. The storm and jungle disappear as I join her in the Silver Skull's quarters. . . .

King Baldyr roars like a wild beast. He grabs the shackles around her wrists, yanking her back. Her feet slip out from under her as he throws her to the right. She hits the marble walls with a powerful thud.

The impact ignites the majacite crown on her head. It burns with a new wrath. Its matte-black thorns dig into her temple. Hot blood drips into her eyes and rains down her neck.

With my magic, I feel every part of Zélie in a new way. I taste the bite of her rage. A dark pit twists in my chest at the way King Baldyr inspects her face, calling her *Merle*. I see her valiant fight. I sustain every cut and every single bruise. I feel the agony of the moment King Baldyr forces the medallion into her chest. I hear the way she wishes for death.

By the time my magic fades, I find myself shaking with her in my arms. Guilt tears me apart from inside.

Why couldn't I have gotten her out in time?

"It's starting to eat at me." Zélie reaches up her hand, clawing at the tarnished metal. "What if I lose control? What if I can't stop him in time?"

"We won't let that happen." I grab the sides of her face. Determination fills my chest as I force her to look in my eyes. "I wasn't fast enough on that ship, but I won't make the same mistakes. We'll reunite with the others and form a plan. We'll defeat the Skulls and keep you safe."

Zélie brings her forehead to mine, and I shudder at her touch. For a moment, there are no Skulls. There is no hunt for her heart. There is only this.

There is only us.

"I promise," I say. Her body softens at my words. "We'll find a way. Whatever it takes."

CHAPTER TWENTY-FIVE

TZAIN

"KENYON, DON'T DO THIS!" Amari's pleas travel down the beach. She chases the elder of the Burners across the white sands, at odds with the rest of the maji preparing to leave.

A maji named Deji carves out hollowed logs to store fresh water. A boy named Oye wraps piles of cooked fish in dried leaves. Another group of maji ties four surviving lifeboats together to create a unified ship.

All I can do is stand still.

All night, I waited along the coast, praying Zélie would show. There were times when the sky raged and I felt it in my chest.

I was *sure* the raging storm was her.

When dawn broke and she didn't return, I knew we were out of time. There was nothing I could say or do to convince the others to stay behind. But as our departure nears, Amari refuses to give up her fight. I watch with the others as she cuts off Kenyon's path, forcing the Burner to wait.

"One more night." Amari grabs his hand. "I'm begging you. Please!"

"We don't have time to waste." Kenyon shakes his head. "Another ship could show up at any moment."

"You would abandon another elder?" Amari challenges. "You would strand the fiercest among us on this beach?"

"She's *gone*." I'm surprised by the way Kenyon's voice strains. For an instant, hurt flashes across his bruised face. "I know she wouldn't want us to waste our chance to escape!"

"Tzain, tell him what you felt!" Amari says.

At the mention of my name, Kenyon turns my way. He drops the supplies he's carrying in the sand.

"Enough of this." Kenyon marches over. "It's time for us to leave."

"I'm not standing in your way," I say.

"You're not helping us, either." Kenyon drops his voice at the gathering crowd. "The maji are looking at you, too. I need you on my side."

I look past him to the faces scattered across the beach. I see the girl I picked up in my arms. She stares at me with hope in her eyes. I try to smile at her, but all I can do is frown.

"We broke out on *your* call," Kenyon presses. "We all risked our lives. Don't abandon us now. We need you to get home."

I grip Nailah's side as the weight of the maji's expectations closes in. I don't have a single sign that my sister's survived. But if Amari and I washed up on the beach, why couldn't she?

"*They're alive, Tzain.*" Amari's conviction returns to me as I stare at the open waters. The answers I've been searching for hit me like the ocean breeze. If Zélie's alive, I can't abandon her on this beach.

Even if that means watching the rest of the maji leave.

"I'm staying," I decide, planting my feet deeper into the sand.

"You can't be serious!"

"If you want me to talk to the others, I can explain—"

"And if the Skulls show up?" Kenyon challenges me. "What then? You'll fight them all by yourself?"

I think of the axe still strapped to the mangrove trees. "If that's what it takes."

Kenyon steps back. He pulls at his own hair. For a moment, his anger breaks and I feel his fear.

"She wouldn't want you to stay." Kenyon tries one last time. "Staying here won't bring her back."

"I understand why you have to go." I put a hand on his shoulder. "Try to understand why I can't."

Kenyon clenches his fist, and I prepare for him to hit me, knock me out, force me to come along. But with a sigh, he drops his hands. My shoulders slump as he pulls me into a hug.

I fight the tightness in my chest. I don't know how to prepare to never see him again. A new swell of terror rises in my throat, but I hold on to the image of Zélie in my mind.

I won't leave you. I close my eyes. As long as there's a chance, I'll keep fighting. I'll do whatever it takes—

Nailah releases a mighty roar, breaking Kenyon and me apart. Far down the coast, two silhouettes make their way down the white sands.

"Zélie?" I step forward. The entire beach seems to hold its breath. One silhouette sports a thick head of white coils. When I last saw my sister, her head was bare.

But when the girl nears, the sun highlights her silver eyes. A weight releases from my chest. I take off, sprinting so fast I nearly collapse into the sand.

Nailah runs by my side. She joins me as we splash through the tides. My greatest fears dissolve the moment I pick up my sister and sweep her into my arms.

"You made it!"

Zélie laughs, and this time I can't hold my tears back. Everything I was afraid to face fades at once. It feels like we spend an eternity in the shores, reuniting under the sun.

"Thank the seas!" Nâo is the first to break away from the group. She throws her arms around Zélie's neck, but when their chests meet, Nâo cries out.

A teal-blue light sparks at the Tider's fingertips, traveling through her ancestral lines. Nâo raises her palms to her face in disbelief as the teal glow lights her up from within. Her eyes roll back as something reawakens deep inside.

"*O ṣeun Yemọja.*" Nâo whispers the words. The Tider stretches out her fingers and wriggles them above the ocean. The shallows start to spread around Nâo's feet, radiating around her in circles. Her hands seem to shake with the weight of what she feels. She shuts her eyes and takes a long, slow breath before reciting an incantation.

"*Òrìṣà òkun, jọwọ́ gbọ́ tèmi báyìí—*" Nâo whispers the incantation, and her fingers glow with new force. The light travels up her tattooed arms. The ocean water lifts into the air and rises up to her hands, glistening under the hot sun.

I don't believe it. . . .

Somehow, Zélie's touch has reawakened her magic.

Kenyon wades into the shore, brows furrowed at Nâo's gift. He looks to Zélie, and my sister nods, beckoning him to come close. Zélie raises her hand to his heart. Red light sparks at the ends of his fingertips the moment they connect. The surge catches Kenyon by surprise.

I almost see the flames light in his eyes.

"*Òrìṣà iná, fún mi ní iná!*" Kenyon roars. Two streams of fire shoot from his fists, heating the white sands. The grains fuse together. The ground beneath his feet turns to glass.

"How are you doing this?" Kenyon asks. Every maji on the beach stares. They gather in a circle around my sister, waiting for her to return their gifts.

Zélie pulls down the wrap around her chest. The taste of iron hits my tongue when I see the glowing metal fused into her rib cage.

"We may have escaped the Skulls." Zélie's face falls. "But our freedom is far from won."

CHAPTER TWENTY-SIX

ZÉLIE

As THE SUN ARCS in the sky, the rest of the maji on the beach form a long line. One by one, they join me in the tides. Each time I lay my hands on their shoulders, the medallion pulses in my chest, and their magic comes alive.

One Tamer summons a pod of yellow-finned dolphins to the shores. A Grounder erects a line of small sand huts. Khani breaks down when the orange light reignites around her palms. Tears fall from her eyes as she uses the power to heal again.

Despite the way the medallion feeds on me, it's given me the ability to make my people whole. The return of our magic transforms our fates. In just a few hours' time, the small settlement turns into a functioning port.

"As many as you can get!" Nâo calls. She works with Kenyon to lead the others as they prepare to make the long trip home. Under their command, Tamers lure schools of fish into Grounder-made barrels. Khani and the Healers tend to every maji's wounds. Tiders and Winders harness their reawakened gifts, combining their magic to boost the refashioned lifeboats.

By the time night falls, everyone gathers around the bonfire. A gentle chatter joins the nocturnal chorus of crickets. The seconds wind down as I prepare to brief the others on what I've learned.

Across from me, Khani lies against Nâo's hip. Kenyon leaves his Burners to join the pair. Beside the trio, Amari sits with Inan. The two of us haven't spoken since we left Orïsha's shores.

Since we were torn apart by the maji-tîtán war.

Looking at Amari now, I don't know what to say. After she damned me and an entire village to die, I never wanted to speak to her again. I didn't think anything could make up for her betrayal. I thought our friendship had come to an end.

But with the threat of the Skulls, I see the girl who's wiped my tears. The girl who braided my hair, holding me close when no one else was there. Amari catches me staring, and her lips part. The question hangs in her amber eyes—*are we still allies?*

Despite myself, I reach out my hand. A small smile spreads across her narrow face. She laces her fingers with mine, and it feels right.

I can't imagine facing the Skulls without her by my side.

But when Tzain joins our small circle, Amari drops my hand. She seems to shrink in his presence. I look back and forth between them, wondering where they stand.

"Here." Tzain hands me another cut of swordfish, though I'm still picking at my first.

"Tzain—"

"You're thin." He forces me to eat. When I finish, he rises back to his feet. "I'll get more water—"

"I'm fine." I pull my brother's hand. "Sit. It's time to begin."

With Tzain settled, the conversation around the bonfire begins to die down. I feel every maji's eye on me. When Kenyon gives me a nod, I start to speak.

"We weren't the first to be stolen." I look around the crowd. "The Skulls took advantage of our war. They worked with the mercenaries and started raiding our shores moons ago."

At the mention of the mercenaries, my mind flashes to Roën and my chest grows tight. I wonder where he is. If he survived the betrayal of Harun and the rest of his men.

A grief I don't want to face rises inside me like a tidal wave. I take a deep breath to fight it back. After everything we endured at the hands of the Skulls, I pray he's alright.

I pray he's still alive.

"What're the Skulls after?" Nâo asks. Like this morning, I reveal the medallion in my chest.

"They were searching for a maji with the blood of the sun. A maji who could take this and survive. The medallion's transforming my blood. It's awakened a new power inside."

The others drink in my every word as I explain what happened in the Silver Skull's quarters. I describe King Baldyr's golden mask. I share the way we battled before he shoved the bloodmetal into my sternum.

When I describe the maji lying dead on the floor, Khani shifts. I give her a moment as Nâo guides her to the edge of the camp. I imagine the hole the same medallion left in her twin's chest. The careless way the Skulls must've thrown Imani's body to the seas. A flood of guilt hits me at the thought of every maji the medallion's touched.

Every maji King Baldyr's killed in his hunt.

"I don't know what their king is after." I stare into the open flames. "But I'm only one part of his plan. He had two more medallions. One for another girl, and one for him."

"Another maji?" Kenyon asks.

"Not a maji." I shake my head. "A girl from another land."

I start to explain the girl from my vision—her long black hair, her russet-brown skin. I speak of the way her eyes sparkle like diamonds. I tell them of the ancient voice under the glowing seas that told me to find her.

"I don't know where the girl is," I continue. "But I think I can find her using this."

I unclip the Silver Skull's compass from my waist. The others take turns inspecting the hexagon-shaped device. I wait as it passes through the circle. Most maji are too afraid to touch.

"What does it point to?" Nâo asks. The thick red dial lies dormant in her hands. But when I take the bronze compass back, the metal hums. The medallion flickers beneath my wrap. The red dial starts to shift, pointing to my heart.

"It points to me," I explain. "I think I can make it point to her."

"But that would mean . . ." Nâo's voice trails off. She looks away from our camp, toward the crashing tides. I picture the lifeboats anchored to the sands, waiting to set sail.

"We have to split up." I finish her thought. I can almost see the hope deflate in the air. We just reunited. It feels wrong to go our separate ways.

But Tzain slings his arm around my shoulders. Once again, Amari grabs my hand. Their touch warms something deep in my core. It's been so long since the three of us were truly on the same side.

"Orïsha must be warned." Inan breaks the silence. "They won't understand what's to come. It's been centuries since we've been attacked by a foreign nation. Without a king, they won't know how to respond."

"You mean without your father?" Kenyon pushes back. "Or are you referring to yourself?"

"I didn't mean—" Inan starts.

"If Orïsha still had its king, there'd be no maji for the Skulls to take," Kenyon continues. "If Orïsha still had its king, we'd all be dead!"

With Kenyon's words, the air around the fire changes. I tense as the tides shift. A line is drawn in the sand, breaking the fragile unity we just had.

"I wasn't trying to . . ." Inan looks around the camp. "There is no excuse for what the monarchy's done—"

But the maji drown him out. Amari rises as a few begin to swarm. My head spins as the discussion spirals out of control.

How is it we can still fight like this when we know of the Skulls?

"Enough!" I yell.

Tzain grabs my arm. "Don't defend him. Not here."

"This isn't about him!" I rip my arm free and step forward. "We can't keep doing this. We can't keep *fighting* like this. We've brought our kingdom to its knees, and now their fiercest are at our door. How many of our fiercest lie in the ground?"

My voice cracks as I think of all the blood that's been spilled—Mama Agba's, Mâzeli's, Lekan's. If the maji and the monarchy hadn't been at war for centuries, would we even be here now?

"We are it." I look around the circle. "We are the only true defense Orïsha has left. Whatever we've done to hurt each other, whatever scores we have to settle, it ends now. We can't afford to be at each other's throats."

The bonfire crackles in our silence as my words ripple through the camp. Some of the maji hang their heads. But the crowd building against Amari and Inan begins to disperse.

"And if I can't?" Tzain says, staring directly at the royal siblings.

"Then you're dooming our kingdom to die." I return to my brother and grab his hand.

"Please," I whisper.

Tzain breathes deep. He still glares daggers through Inan. But he looks down at me and nods.

"For you. Not for them."

I squeeze his palm, and he squeezes mine back.

"So what do we do?" Nâo voices the question on everyone's minds. "How do we fight?"

"We need to raise a defense," Inan offers, tentative in his approach. "The Skulls may have come for Zélie, but they won't stop until they've conquered all of us."

"Is there even an Orïsha to go back to?" Amari asks. "We left Lagos in ruins. It's been over a moon since we were taken from our homeland."

Amari's question ushers in a wave of doubt. I have to fight the fear that wants to come out. If Orïsha has fallen, we're done.

What chance will we have against the Skulls?

"Our kingdom has stood for over a thousand years." Inan rises to his feet. "Someone will be there to fight."

"We can find the surviving elders." Nâo looks to Kenyon. "Rally the maji for a defense."

"You'll need more than the maji," Inan says. "The tîtáns, what's left of the soldiers. Even the kosidán. We'll all need to work together to mount a defense."

"You should go with them." I'm surprised at the way the words make my heart fall. But out of any of us, Inan is our best chance to unite them all. "Show the people what's coming. Tell them what we've endured. It'll take every single fighter to keep the Skulls from raiding our shores."

Inan stares at me, and I feel how much he wants to stay. But he nods in agreement.

"And the three of you?" he asks.

I look down at the compass in my palm, staring at the triple arrow-head painted in blood.

"We'll find the other girl." I touch the glass face. "Before King Baldyr does."

CHAPTER TWENTY-SEVEN

◆ ⋯✕⋯ ◉ ◉ ◎ ◉ ◉ ✕⋯ ◆

AMARI

THE WEIGHT OF EVERYTHING we're up against doesn't hit me until my eyes blink open the next morning. Our makeshift camp is bare. There are hardly any maji here.

I grab the remnants of a roasted fish and make my way down the cliff, following the noise beyond the palm trees. As my feet move through the rocky sand, I remind myself of Zélie's plan—find the other girl King Baldyr hunts.

The thought of Baldyr and his men doing to others what he did to us twists my stomach into knots. I imagine the operations they set up back when Orïsha was supposed to be under my watch, back when I was fighting to be queen. I failed to bring peace to my kingdom. I failed to keep the maji safe.

I can't afford to fail at this.

I reach the edge of the trees as dawn crackles on the horizon, lighting up the sky with bands of pink beneath the clear stretch of blue. Steady winds blow through the open skies. There isn't a cloud in sight. Waves lap ashore with the promise of a gentle sail. Their crash softens the squawks of seabirds above.

The majority of the camp moves along the shores, preparing for the trek back home. Maji load up their final supplies. They board the ships in lines.

I watch as Nâo stands with the other Tiders in the shallows, leading them in practiced chants. They move into position behind the repurposed lifeboats, now three powerful ships.

"Once more!" Nâo calls. The twelve Tiders stretch out their hands.

"*Òrìṣà òkun, jọ̀wọ́ gbọ́ tèmi báyìí*—" Their voices ring in unison, creating a powerful melody. The blue light of their magic travels up their brown skin. The waters around them begin to move. The seas sway back and forth with the rhythm of their hands, lifting the ships from the sand.

In each ship, one Winder sits up high in the crow's nest built from bamboo trees. As the ships take to the waters, the Winders release the newly woven sails. Each blows in the air, ready to carry the maji across the ocean. They haven't even left, yet they already feel leagues away.

Don't go, I want to whisper. I'm surprised at the silent pleas that well in my throat. There's no hiding from the truth now.

The moment they set sail, we'll be on our own.

Farther down the beach, Tzain stands in the tides with the only remaining lifeboat, fortified by the Grounders to aid our trip. Dakarai, the elder of the Seers, hands Tzain a map made of woven bay leaves and inked with ash from the fire. Dotted lines mark the path he, Zélie, and I are expected to follow on our own if we ever get a chance to return. But watching the others, the map feels like a futile effort.

Will we even survive if we separate from the others?

"Having second thoughts?"

I glance over my shoulder. I didn't even notice my brother's approach. Inan joins me by the trees, hands in his pockets. After all we went through to reunite, the thought of him leaving hits me like a fist to the gut. Entire oceans will stand between us.

What if we never see each other again?

"I didn't say that."

"You didn't have to." Inan gestures at the boats with his chin. "You're staring at the ships like you can keep them stuck in the tides."

I lay my head on his shoulder, something I haven't done since we were young. Inan wraps his arm around me, and I think of how far we've come. How much has gone wrong.

"I keep thinking this is my chance," I release the words inside. "A way to make things right. I want to stand behind Zélie, but . . ."

My gaze drifts to her—she sits alone, on the farthest corner of the beach. She stares transfixed at the horizon, arms hugged around herself. The medallion pulses above her heart. Storm clouds gather above her head. A charge circles her in the sand. The white hairs that rest along her back start to lift into the air.

Though Zélie puts on a brave face in front of the others, I can see the doubts she tries to hide. We don't know what we're walking into, and we're an army of three, thousands of kilometers away from the only home we've ever known.

"What if she's wrong?" I turn to my brother. "What if we're not meant to go at it alone? Right now we have each other. We have Tiders and Winders. We have enough food and fresh water to make the sail. If the three of us don't go with you now—"

"You may never make it home." Inan's grip on me tightens, but he stares at Zélie's back. If I can convince my brother, I know we can convince Zélie and Tzain.

"The safest place for her is back home," I press. "Where *we* know the land. Even if she can lead us to the other girl Baldyr seeks to harvest, that leads us *right* back to him and the Skulls. If they need Zélie's heart, we shouldn't be running toward them. We should be running away." I pull back and search my brother's face. "Think of everything we're up against and tell me I'm wrong."

Inan stays silent for a long moment. He touches the scar left by Father's sword.

"If we had followed her before, even when it didn't make sense . . . Things would be better. Orïsha would be better."

"You don't know that."

"I do." A sad smile sits on his face. "We both had our chances to lead, and all we did was follow in Father's and Mother's footsteps. The Skulls only got this far because the two of us failed. Whatever she's become, whatever she's feeling—following her is the only way forward."

I stare at my brother. I don't recognize the person he's become. The way he speaks. The way he stands. The conviction behind his words.

"Without you we're *three* people . . . ," I breathe. "Three people against an entire empire."

"You won't be without me for long." Inan holds out his pinky. It's a gesture I haven't seen in years. The last time he offered me his pinky, we were sneaking into the palace kitchens, stuffing our faces with sweet cakes and evading the night guards. "Find the girl and keep Zélie safe. I'll make sure that army of three turns into thousands."

I stare at his finger, wanting to take hold.

"This isn't the end," he says. "I promise, I'll see you again."

"You cannot promise that."

"You're my *sister*." The skin around his amber eyes crinkles. "Yes I can."

Despite the fear inside, I hook my pinky with his. We stay, linked together, until the maji call for him to board.

CHAPTER TWENTY-EIGHT

ZÉLIE

It's hard to speak when the other maji set sail. Tzain, Amari, and I stand at the shores. All at once, everything is too quiet. The only sounds among the three of us are the lapping tides.

We watch as the ships disappear over the horizon. When they leave our sight for good, a lump rises in my throat. The only thing that kept me fighting on that ship was the thought of home.

Without the others, I feel so alone.

"Find her. . . ."

I exhale, wrapping my resolve around the command. With the Skulls closing in, there's no time to waste.

I have to stick to the plan.

"Let's move," I say. I'm the first to break away. Tzain follows my lead, axe strapped to his back. Amari trails after him.

With no Winders or Tiders at our disposal, we have to work the boat ourselves. Amari opens up the sails as Tzain pushes us through the cresting waves. I take position behind the steering lever and open the bronze compass in my hands. I run my finger over the glass face, staring at the triple arrowhead painted in blood.

"Are you ready?" Amari asks, and I nod. The medallion warms in my chest as I reach for the girl, pulling on whatever thread we share. When

I close my eyes, different images start to swirl through the blackness of my mind. . . .

Rich green trees. Ripe papayas. Banana leaves.
Thick vines crawling over emerald stone.
Ceramic bowls of black beans and warm rice.
Fried plantain baking under the hot sun.

I breathe in as I sink into the girl's world, and I smell thick plumes of volcanic ash. I hear the chant of women's voices joined in song. The jingle of bangles against brown skin. The trickle of turquoise waters.

The compass starts to hum, and I open my eyes. The red dial spins away from my chest. Its needle points to the south, directly opposite from where the other maji set sail.

"I think this is the way." I grab hold of the steering lever. Tzain and Amari don't question the path I take. The sun arcs in the sky as we sail away from the island chains.

Time passes, and I hang my fingers over the side of the boat, allowing them to drift through the ocean waves. I relish the chill against my skin, but in the peace of sailing the open waters, the horrors of the Skulls' ship return.

Though sea-salt air hits my face, I choke on the putrid stench of death. I feel the weight of the shackles they closed around my neck. The face of the young girl in the Silver Skull's quarters returns to me. I wonder where her body lies.

Please stay with her. I lift up the silent prayer to Oya, though the skies are clear. *Be with her spirit. Save every maji who fell.*

By the time night comes, the three of us prepare for a long rest. Tzain's snores mix with Nailah's. Swatches of stars sparkle above our heads. In their twinkle, I see the faces of those I've lost.

Mama's smile returns to me first. Baba's warm hug follows next. Mama Agba's entire form seems to dazzle, just like the cosmos she was able to draw between her palms. Their faces blur together around me as I drift off. . . .

Pale hands come at me from all directions. They drag me into their caves. I can't fight as they throw me against a stone slab. Corded ropes tie me into place.

Baldyr appears before me, his golden skull glimmering in the torchlight. His galdrasmiðar *gather in a circle around us, each magicworker hidden by the heavy furs and the horned animal skulls they wear. Bloodmetal covers their frail bodies like garments, stretching from the collars on their necks to the round medallions hanging from their leather belts. The* galdrasmiðar *move as one, closing in with a menacing step.*

"For the Father of the Storms——" the galdrasmiðar *chant.*

Rocks fall away as the ground opens up. The sacred well of their bloodmetal burns beneath me, fiery lines traveling through the molten ore. Its heat sears my skin. The well echoes with the screeches of the dead. The ropes pull tight as I struggle to break free.

Then their torture begins.

"Drain her." Baldyr gives the order. The galdrasmiðar *raise their bloodstained hands. I cry out as cuts rip through my skin. An angry gash spreads across my chest. Another splits down my abdomen. The* galdrasmiðar *attack me from within. Their cuts cover my face, my arms, my legs.*

The runes of their people spread across the cave walls as my blood leaks into the well. The molten ore lifts into the air. There's nothing I can do as it covers my body like a cast.

It tears through my flesh, burning straight through my bones. Baldyr smiles as the molten ore reaches past my throat, covering the top of my skull——

"Zélie!"

I wake with a sharp flinch. A thick coat of sweat drenches my wrap. Amari sits before me, hands pressed to my chest.

I breathe deep as I look up at the open skies. It takes me a moment to gather myself. I reach up to my neck and my head, feeling the undamaged flesh.

"Are you alright?" Amari asks.

I nod, fighting the part of me that wants to cry. The animal-horned skulls of King Baldyr's *galdrasmiðar* haunt my eyes. I run my hands over my body, feeling every place they cut up from inside.

"Did I wake you?" I ask.

Amari shakes her head. She looks out over the black waters and hugs her knees to her chest. I can't imagine how she must feel away from her brother, out here with just me and Tzain. I glance at his sleeping frame—we share less than ten meters of space, yet he hasn't looked her way.

"Do you want to talk about it?" she asks.

I don't answer. I wouldn't know how to talk about it if I tried. The dream felt real.

Too real to just be in my head.

I have to stop him.

I pick up the compass, once again focusing on the metal in my chest. This time the tangle of vines spreads through my mind. The thick vegetation curls to life over stretches of black rock.

"When you close your eyes, what do you see?" Amari asks.

"It's different every time," I explain. "Small flashes of her people, the foods they eat, the things she must see."

Amari nods at my words, but from the way she stares at the compass, I can tell they're not what she truly wants to hear. I offer to hand her the compass, but she shakes her head.

"Does seeing make it any easier?" she asks. "Handling the fear?"

"Do I look like I'm handling anything?" I raise my sweat-soaked wrap. "We're sailing into a new world. I'm terrified of what's next."

Our fingers lace together once more. Instead of Nailah, I rest my head against Amari's shoulder. I miss the days when we were able to sit like this. The days before magic flared between us.

"You should've seen him," I speak quietly. "You should've smelled the mead on his breath."

The golden skull of my nightmares glimmers behind my eyes, and the medallion starts to pulse. Amari tenses as the winds increase. I reach for the steering lever to keep us on course.

Once again, the sound of falling rain bleeds into my ears. The skies start to crackle above. I think back to the wooden carving on the Silver Skull's wall—the man built from storm clouds. What will I become if I can't stop Baldyr in time?

If he finds me again, what will he do with my heart?

"I won't let him get you." Something shifts in Amari's tone. She steadies her shoulders, removing her fear to take on my own.

"You can be so sure?"

"We've taken down kings before." Amari smiles, and I see the girl in the marketplace. The princess who was brave enough to steal the ancient scroll. Her words make me think of all we've faced together. Every enemy who's fallen at our hands.

"We follow this compass." She looks back down at the red dial. "We'll sail it to the ends of the earth if that's what it takes. We can do this, Zélie. We'll find a way to keep you safe."

I wrap her words around me like a blanket, allowing it to grant me ease.

The waning moon smiles down on us as we fall asleep under the open stars.

CHAPTER TWENTY-NINE

INAN

THE MAJI MAKE STEADY progress in our trek across the seas. With Nâo leading the Tiders, the currents work in our favor. The very waters propel us forward. Above us, the rotating Winders grant our ships great speed. The large sail billows with their powerful gusts of air. We fly through the ocean waves, traveling closer and closer to our shores.

As we sail, I'm reminded of the potential of my kingdom. Of all the things we could be. If we can unite the people of Orïsha, we can do more than protect ourselves from the Skulls. We can rebuild our great nation, create the Orïsha I always dreamed we could become. But the thought of what awaits us at home haunts me. My mind spins with the wreckage of our war.

How am I supposed to reunite my kingdom when I couldn't do it before?

I scan the ship from my position by the supplies in the far back. The majority of the maji rest under a bamboo pavilion in the center, leaves woven together to block out the sun. The rest of the maji wait by Kenyon at the front of the ship, following the Burner's every command.

The few times I've attempted to pull him aside and strategize, he's ignored my every word. Without Zélie's presence, the maji only tolerate my existence. I know they don't need me to rally their own, but if I can't get them to respect me, what hope will I have with the monarchy that I dissolved?

There has to be a way to make them see. . . .

With a push, I ignite the turquoise cloud in my palms, considering what role my magic might play. I think of the Skull Amari and I took on. Of what Zélie suffered in the arms of the Silver Skull. If the people could understand what was coming, we might have a chance. I have to make the threat of the Skulls real.

I have to find a way to make them *feel*.

"Kenyon!" Dakarai calls out. The elder of the Seers has an edge in his voice that makes me rise. Round with a thick head of white curls, Dakarai draws attention as he holds out his hands.

"Orúnmila, bá mi sòrò. Orúnmila, bá mi sòrò——"

As Dakarai chants, the night sky bleeds into the space between his palms. My lips part in awe as the stars spiral, opening up to reveal the ocean waters. The moment I see the Skulls' ship, my blood runs cold. Another mighty vessel cuts through the waves, nearly identical to the one we escaped.

Countless Skulls man the deck. Dakarai's image is so clear, I can see the individual bones welded into their masks. The sight of the enemy shifts the mood of the ship in an instant. It's like the sun darkens above.

"How far out are they?" Kenyon asks.

The elder of the Seers closes his eyes, pushing for the answer to Kenyon's question. With a lurch, Dakarai's eyes shoot open.

"Just over the horizon," he says.

Kenyon's nostrils flare. He leaves the circle and walks to the very edge of the ship. He raises his open palm, and a flame comes to light.

"Prepare to fight," he orders. "We're taking the ship."

Dread hits me like a cannonball. All around me, the maji start to move. Though I can summon my magic, I know it's not enough. We can't take the risk.

Right now we're Orïsha's only hope.

"Kenyon, wait," I call. "This isn't the time to attack."

"You're not an elder." Kenyon glares down at me. "You don't get a say."

"That doesn't mean I'm wrong." I push myself to his side, keeping my voice firm. "Think of what it took to escape."

"We didn't have our magic before," Nâo joins in. "This time we have the strength to fight!"

"But what if we're captured?" I push. "What if we're killed? Right now we're the only ones who know what's out there. We are the only ones who know what's coming to invade our lands. We can't afford to risk that knowledge battling one ship. Our people need us to stay safe. They need us to live."

"And what of our people on the ship?" Nâo's voice cracks. She speaks the fears I hold myself. The thought of the maji who might be locked inside twists my insides into knots. But it doesn't change everything we face.

I look back to Dakarai, observing the Skull's ship between his palms.

"Are you able to track the ship?" I ask. "See where it sails?"

Dakarai nods, and I rub my fingers together as a new plan begins to take shape. With Dakarai's knowledge, we could have an advantage. One that gives us a greater chance to survive.

"Then we hide," I decide. "For now, we don't engage. If we can track where the Skulls are sailing, we'll have the upper hand. We can gather forces in Orïsha and mount a proper attack."

Nâo's gaze drifts from me to the flame in Kenyon's hands. The Burner's face is unreadable.

"Think of your people," I beg. "*All* of them."

The flame disappears from Kenyon's hands.

"How do we hide?" the Burner asks.

The maji stand back as Nâo coordinates with the Tiders and Winders on each ship. The boats slow as they redirect their magic, keeping us still. A group of Lighters steps forward on each boat. Silence falls as the maji join hands. They whisper among themselves as the Skulls' sails appear on the far horizon.

"Quickly!" Dakarai shouts.

"*Ìmọ́lẹ̀ tẹ̀, ìmọ́lẹ̀ kán, ìmọ́lẹ̀ dárijọ síbíyìí*—" The Lighters begin their chant. As they work, a yellow light ignites around their hands, traveling until it covers their entire bodies. The soft glow continues its trek, spreading across all three ships in a steady wave.

I lift my hands to my face as the light surrounds me. The yellow glow bends and refracts, twisting until my very fingers disappear before my eyes. My arms fade next, followed by my chest and my legs.

I inhale a sharp breath as the Lighters work, erasing all trace of us from the seas. Below my hidden feet, the ocean waters dance. Above my head, the giant sail and towering mast vanish into thin air. The Lighters' magic covers each boat, completely hiding us from view.

"Incoming," Dakarai warns, his large frame no longer visible to any of our eyes. The concealed Lighters drop their voices, continuing their chant so quietly the ocean waves swallow their incantation. But faint glimmers break their spell, creating sporadic flashes of yellow light where our ship reappears. I hold my breath as the Skulls' ship nears.

Come on.

My pulse thunders between my ears as I wait for the ship to go by. Their cannons pass directly overhead. Bronze masks glint over the railing. The sound of the Skulls' tongue sends a familiar ache up my spine. For a moment, the crow's nest of our boat flashes, revealing a Winder's wide-set eyes.

But when the Skulls' ship sails past our boat, I know the Lighters have covered us in time. The Lighters continue their incantation until the enemy's ship disappears in the distance.

All at once, the yellow light breaks, revealing every maji and all three ships. The Lighters collapse over one another in a heap. A shared pool of sweat spreads beneath them.

"Perfect job," Kenyon commends them. The maji rally around each Lighter, bringing them under the bamboo pavilions. Countless hands offer them food and fresh water, thanking them for their protection.

As our boats begin to sail away, Nâo walks to the back of the ship. Her forehead creases with despair. I can feel the strain of what she's sacrificed like a weight in the air.

Dakarai joins from the front, the window into the Skulls' location still stark between his palms.

"We'll find them," I promise. "Just give it time."

CHAPTER THIRTY

ZÉLIE

TIME PASSES IN A gentle flow as we follow the compass's red dial south. As the days bleed into dusks, Amari, Tzain, and I slip into a silent rhythm. We each take turns steering the lifeboat as the waning moon disappears in the starry night.

Tzain transforms a dagger into a spearhead to refurnish our dwindling fish supply. Amari mends a rip in the sails. On the twelfth dawn, I awaken to find the three of us asleep on Nailah's coat. Amari and Tzain lie side by side. I smile as their fingertips brush.

"*Find her. . . .*" The ancient voice comes back to me, louder than it's ever been. Nailah shifts as I brace myself against her golden paw. The voice quivers against my skin.

"What's going on?" Tzain stirs.

The currents pushing us shift. The wind leaves our sails. Our boat begins to drift.

A twisting fog crawls in from both sides. Its icy touch causes goosebumps to rise on my arms. In a moment, we're caught in a haze.

The sunlight disappears. . . .

I lift up the Silver Skull's compass. The red dial spins in rapid circles. Amari grabs my arm tight. I brace myself as we pass through the fog. A long beach of black sand stretches before us. My nostrils flare around a familiar scent—fresh soil and volcanic ash.

"Is this it?" Tzain asks.

"I think so." I squeeze the compass shut. "We've reached the girl's land."

Tzain jumps from the boat, wading into the dark waters to push us to the shores. He has to use all his strength. It's like the waters fight to resist us.

The moment I step onto the black sands, a ripple spreads through the land. I blink, not sure if I can trust my eyes. The pulse seems to travel outward, disappearing behind the twisting fog.

Amari joins me on the beach. She reaches down and grabs a handful of sand.

"Skies," Amari breathes. Each black grain is shaped like a crescent moon.

Tzain inspects a large skeleton submerged in the shallows. The bones look like those of a fish, but the curved ivory frame matches the size of Nailah. Vines weave through the skeleton like the threads of a loom. I run my fingers through the cracked bones. The fish's head is severed from its tail.

It's like the vines have snapped the fish in two.

An emerald forest stretches in the distance, so dense it feels like it would take Tzain's axe to cut us through. The plants seem to sway back and forth like ocean waves, blowing though no breeze passes through the air.

I dare to step forward, but something about the island makes me want to retreat. With the compass spinning out of control, I close my eyes and inhale. This time when I reach for the girl, it's as if she's close enough to touch. I smell her honeyed scent. My fingers start to spark—

"Do you hear that?" Amari whispers. She turns to the emerald forest.

A steady hiss rises behind the trees. Tzain's face falls, and he reaches for his axe. I grab my staff and extend the blades.

Amari steps back. Something slithers toward us in droves. The black sands begin to rumble. . . .

"Back in the boat!" Tzain yells. "Now!"

We splash through the dark waters, and I pull myself back onto the boat. Amari lands on top of Nailah. Tzain grits his teeth, pushing us through the shores.

Deep green vines lurch out of the black sands like spears. They launch themselves around our boat. One vine wraps itself around my arm. I cry out as it squeezes the staff from my hand.

Amari snaps into action. She grabs my fallen staff. With a grunt, she stabs the vine. The plant squeals as it writhes. Tzain pulls my arm free as the vines take over the boat. They wrap around the mast, squeezing so tight it snaps in half.

"Come on!" Tzain drags me back into the waters. Amari follows with Nailah. Tzain throws me onto my lionaire's neck, and the others mount. We dig our hands into her golden fur.

"Nailah, run!" I shout. My lionaire takes off. She releases a mighty roar as she races across the black sands. The fog blinds our path as we try to escape. Vines lunge from all directions. They slither toward us like snakes.

One vine shoots up, snapping around my ankle. I hold on to Nailah with all of my strength. My brother twists, hacking at the vine with his axe. I lurch free as the tail whips back into the fog.

"Hurry!" Tzain yells.

The vines seem to triple by the second. They close in from all sides. Tzain's gaze darts back and forth, trying to find the next vine before it attacks.

"Head toward the forest!" Tzain points. "They're rounding us into the sea!"

I steer Nailah up the only trail I see, pressing my head to Nailah's neck as we charge into the forest. Heavy branches pass over our heads. The little light there was on the beach vanishes. The symphony of hissing vines crescendoes.

Then undulating cries shoot through the air.

I snap my head up as silhouettes soar. The islanders move in ways I've never seen. They don't just fly.

They careen.

Thick vines wrap around the forest branches, catapulting the islanders through the air. They twist and spiral through the trees. Their howls echo as they near.

More vines shoot toward us like arrows. One catches Nailah's ankle. My lionaire yelps as she falls. The three of us fly across the soft soil.

The islanders descend from the trees like giant spiders. Their vines lower their taut frames to the ground. Each woman sports kohl-lined eyes. A wide band of emerald pigment stretches from temple to temple. Like the girl in my vision, they share russet-brown skin. Each wears her dark hair in a long singular braid.

Behind them, heavy paws thunder toward us. Tzain pulls me close. Six brawny men break through the trees, each riding a giant beast.

Black tigenaires . . .

The legendary ryders circle us in droves. Jagged white stripes cut through their silky coats. A line of serrated horns circles around each tigenaire's neck like a mane, primed to pierce through any person they oppose.

The leader comes to a stop, a man built like a tree trunk. Thick muscles ripple under a thick layer of sweat. The ground shakes as he drops to the dirt from his black tigenaire.

His brown skin is inked with a series of different weapons. The inked armory travels up both his arms and down his chest. His fingers glow and he goes for the cleaver tattooed on his left shoulder. With his emerald touch, the inked cleaver ripples to life. My eyes grow wide as the man reaches through his skin, pulling the weapon straight from his being.

Tzain lunges for his axe, but a vine wraps around it, snatching it from his grasp.

The leader steps forward and raises the cleaver above his head.

I throw myself in front of my brother, falling to my knees.

"*Misericórdia!*" I shout. The medallion glows as the foreign tongue spills out. I hear the word again in my head, but this time I understand.

Mercy.

"*O que foi que ela disse?*" a vineweaver questions. I don't dare lift my eyes as the woman circles me. The medallion deciphers her words.

What did she just say?

"*Misericórdia,*" I whisper. I raise my trembling hands. The medallion's glow strengthens as it continues to feed me words.

"*Viemos em paz.*" My voice shakes. How do I explain? I glance at the bronze compass tied to my belt. I flinch as the warrior rips it off.

The leader turns the compass over in his hands before opening it up. He stares at the spinning red dial.

"An enemy—" I clear my throat. "*Um inimigo . . . se aproxima.*"

The leader's face wrinkles. He bends down, inspecting me with his startling green gaze. I take in the features he shares with his men—thick, muscular frames; round noses; and square faces.

"*Mate ela, Köa!*" a vineweaver shouts at the leader. The man they call Köa grunts in response.

"*Você fala como nós?*" he asks.

The medallion hums in my skin, taking the new language in.

You speak like us?

I try to respond, but my throat is so dry, it's like I am swallowing shards of glass. I force myself to nod. The entire forest seems to hold its breath.

Köa's gaze beats down on me. The cleaver glints above my head. The medallion translates his order.

"Take them in."

CHAPTER THIRTY-ONE

AMARI

AT KÖA'S ORDER, THE VINEWEAVERS DESCEND. The women are rough with their grips. I gasp as they yank my hands back. Vines wrap around my torso with a hiss, binding my arms to my sides.

The islanders shout at me in their tongue. Someone pushes me to walk, but my legs are so numb they feel like cement. Before I can even attempt to explain, vines lift me into the air.

What's happening?

Beads of sweat drip down my neck. I wheeze as the vines tighten around my chest. I hang suspended until the vegetation sets me down on one of the warrior's tigenaires. More vines slither under me. They create a saddle that weaves me in place and locks me on to the mighty beast. A warrior hops on behind me, and I quiver as we touch. All muscle and brawn, his body is built like a wall.

The male warriors all share russet-brown skin, bare chests, and cropped black hair. Fanged necklaces hang from their wide necks. The arsenals inked onto their skin travel from beneath their ears to the thick belts on their ornately beaded pants.

In front of me, Tzain yells for his axe. One of the warriors goes to pick it up. His square face twists into a grimace when the foreign metal burns his hand. He walks back to Tzain and shouts before punching him in the stomach.

I flinch as Tzain doubles over. My terror rises to new heights. Though my magic burns at my fingertips, I force it back down.

They're more likely to kill us all before I land a proper attack.

Ahead of us both, Zélie stays perfectly still. The medallion pulses beneath her wrap as they bind her arms in vines. The weavers lift her onto Köa's black tigenaire.

Has she negotiated something with them? I crane my neck. *Do they understand why we're here?*

"Zélie—" The moment I call out to her, a new vine wraps around my mouth. The most she can do is glance back at me as I'm forced to stay quiet.

Beyond the warriors, I catch Tzain's gaze. Like me, they've covered his mouth in vines. But the way he looks at me, it's like he speaks through his big brown eyes. I feel the silent question—*are you alright?*

I want to shake my head. To ask him what we've done. But something about his concern touches me. I force myself to nod.

"*Passeio!*" Köa gives the order.

The vineweavers take to the trees. I stare, awestruck, as the women twist through the air. They disappear over the brush, flying far ahead.

The male warriors slap the sides of their ryders. The heavy beasts rear onto their hind legs. I choke on my screams as I lurch backward. Behind us, Nailah roars, trapped in a tangle of vines.

We race far away from the black shores. The warriors yelp as they ride through the jungles. Unseen creatures howl back. The men ride up a trail not visible to our naked eyes, turning past fallen branches and moss-covered logs. They navigate the dense jungles like the roads of a city. After a while, we reach a wall of woven vines.

The natural net stretches far higher than the trees. One by one, the vines start to unfold, creating a hole for the warriors to enter. The sound of trickling grows as the ryders jump through. My brows lift at the sight of the glistening turquoise river hidden behind the woven net.

Giant lily pads float down the waterways, each almost as large as the lifeboat we sailed in on. They bump against each other, swirling as they travel downstream. The warriors leave their ryders to jump onto the lily pads, traveling farther into the jungle.

The vines weaving me to the tigenaire unbind, and the warrior behind me sets me on the ground. Feeling returns to my legs as I approach the bank of flowing waters. One of the warriors lifts me up, pushing me onto his lily pad. I tense as the water around it begins to bubble and steam. The lily pad takes off, zooming through the water like an eel.

Skies.

Despite my fear, I'm floored at the sights. We float past lush plains, past the green terraces of endless rice fields. Farmers ride on the backs of massive elephantaires, using the beasts' enormous strength to toil the land. Thin sheets of fog lick the hills.

We approach black mountains covered in green foliage. They reach far past the clouds. A thick waterfall roars at the end of the river. I brace myself as the foaming wall of white crashes overhead. The icy column drenches me in an instant, but the city that lies behind the waterfall steals my heart.

I expected a tribe. A village at most.

Their entire civilization floats.

The city rests in a mountain lake, stretching far beyond where my eyes can see. Giant webs of floating vines fill the water before us, each organizing the city into different rings. Carved canals take the place of streets. A grid system weaves itself through the entire city.

Woven huts and floating plots of farmland line the outer rings. Long schoolhouses lie inside them. Merchant huts stand with legislator buildings. Vineweaver fortresses rise through the city.

Villagers move between gorgeous temples with offerings of candles and jasmine flowers. Their people circle open bathhouses filled with steaming waters and decorated pillars. One entire plot of woven vines holds a vibrant marketplace. Each stall is built from the hard skin of their large lily pads. The people mill from stand to stand, trading dried meats and hanging fish for crafted bangles and colorful silks.

Behind the city, a giant sculpture rises. A goddess with emeralds in place of her eyes. Vines grow around her carved face like hair, stretching all the way down into the waters. I look below the lily pad I'm riding—the same vines spread across the canal floors. More carvings continue beneath the long green stems, surrounding us with the goddess's story.

"*Veja! Veja!*" a child shouts in their tongue. The boy stares, mouth open wide as we pass. His brown finger points to me the moment our lily pad joins the city's main canal. He stands at the edge of a floating plot housing lines of woven domes, each decorated with different wildflowers.

The shouts continue to build as we sail down the canal. Dozens of spectators turn to hundreds. In mere moments, hundreds become thousands. People gather along the edges of their floating plots and the roofs of their square huts. They climb the columns of bathhouses. They scale the statues of their goddess to get close.

The people point at our dark skin. Others marvel at Zélie's white hair. Villagers try to enter the canals, but before they can approach, vineweavers descend from the skies. Thick vines writhe around the canal's edges, creating a moving wall that sections us off. Two men try to scramble over the woven walls. Large warriors yank them back.

I try to keep calm as the chaos builds. Köa all but ignores the crowds. He keeps his green gaze on our destination: a vast temple floats in the city's center like a crown jewel, surrounded by floating gardens. It extends over acres of woven vines. Emerald-green steps ascend like a pyramid, leading to the temple's gilded doors.

Warriors surround the grounds. A new army of vineweavers keeps the masses out. Our lily pads come to a stop. One at a time, Köa pulls us off. The three of us are brought to our knees before the steps.

Everything goes silent when the emperor walks out.

CHAPTER THIRTY-TWO

INAN

WHEN I SEE THE shores of my homeland, the sight breaks something inside. It locks me in chains, taking me back to the horrid nights on the Skulls' ship. I feel the crack of the bones they broke. My neck prickles with the memory of the majacite they forced into my veins. Even when I thought I could escape, I didn't know if I could make it back.

At times I thought I'd never see my homeland again.

The ships are silent as we pull into the remains of Lagos's port. Nâo lifts her hands, moving the waters to bring us to land. She's the first to jump from the boat. She reaches down, digging her hands into the dirt. Silent tears streak down her face. Khani joins her, falling to her knees. The Healer puts her arms around Nâo's shoulders. I give them space as they grieve.

The moment I touch down to Orïsha's soil, my entire body thrums. The force of my magic expands like a breath in my lungs. It leaks from my hands in turquoise wisps as voices fill my head.

"—I can't believe it—"

"—thank the gods—"

"—I pray the clans still live—"

The swell becomes too much to bear. I leave the maji to embark, exploring the damaged docks on my own.

I remember the days when the docks teemed with life, long before magic's return. An endless stream of boats moved in and out of the harbor on the hour. Sailors carted crates filled with livestock and foreign spices. Prosperity filled the air. I used to ride through with Admiral Kaea on Lula, my snow leopanaire.

The port I walk through now is a mere shadow of what once stood. With the exception of the wrecked ships peeking below the water's surface, the entire harbor is bare. The storage houses that line the port lie in shambles.

In the distance, what's left of the royal palace sits on a hill. Even from here, I see its broken walls, its smashed windows, its fallen towers. Clouds of smoke rise from the only home I've ever known. Staring at the palace, I feel the weight of my fallen crown.

Something crunches under my feet, and I bend down. Broken bones fall away, revealing the mask of a bronze Skull.

There are always enemies, Inan.

Father's warning returns. A new flash of shame hits me like a battering ram. I look out at the deserted port, wondering how many ships the Skulls were able to fill while we were at war.

The sight of the mask fortifies my resolve. We have to change the tides in our fight. I fix my gaze on the palace once more, erasing any trepidation I felt before—

"*Ògún, fún mi lágbára!*" a voice calls.

All at once, the ground shifts around me. I step back as mounds of dirt shoot through busted planks. The risen earth cages me in, hardening around my arms and legs.

A large maji comes out of hiding. Dark green energy glows around his hands. He walks forward slowly, limping with one metal leg.

As more maji peek their heads out from damaged storage houses, I recognize their leader's face—Kâmarū, the elder of the Grounders. He was one of the maji who laid the palace to waste.

"I'm not here to fight—"

Before I can finish speaking, the Grounder grabs my neck. I choke as he bends down, bringing his face to mine. One maji whispers my name, and calls travel of the returned king.

"What have you done with the maji?" Kâmarū growls.

"Kâmarū, wait!" Nâo's call pulls the Grounder's focus. At the sight of the lost elder, the anger falls from his face. He stares, confused, as Kenyon and the rest of the maji make their way through the port.

Kâmarū releases my neck to greet the others. Slowly, the maji reunite. Word starts to spread, and their numbers multiply.

Maji spill out of the destroyed ruins of the merchant quarter. They pour through the alleys of the marketplace. A line of maji even travels down from the ruins of the royal palace. White hair shines from kilometers away.

The way the maji swarm, realization strikes. The *Iyika* have a hold on the city. They must have won the war. There isn't one noble, tîtán, or soldier in sight—

BOOM!

I whip my head to the north. An explosion shudders through the air. Black smoke rises from beyond Lagos's walls. Shouts ring from the jackalberry trees surrounding the city.

Inside Lagos, horns blare. Teams of maji gather at the city's perimeter. Incantations ring as they summon their power, preparing to attack. Clouds of black majacite gas meet the orange plumes of Cancers' poisonous gas.

They're still fighting. . . .

My stomach drops as the realization takes hold. Nothing has changed in our time away.

Orïsha is just as divided as before.

All at once, the earth caging me in falls away. I tumble to the ground and rub my neck. Kâmarū stands over me, Nâo at his back.

"He won't kill you." Nâo bends down. "Not yet. But you can't stay. Only maji are allowed in the city."

"Where is everyone else?" I ask.

"They've fled." Kâmarū points beyond Lagos's borders, into the jackalberry trees. "Those who want to live stay outside the city walls."

I shake my head. We can't afford to fight among ourselves anymore. If we don't unify soon, we invite our own end.

"I'm not the one who took the maji." I pick up the Skull's fallen mask. I try to hand it to the Grounder, but he pushes me back.

"Beyond the wall." Kâmarū stands firm. "I won't give you another chance."

I look to Nâo. There are still maji who need our help. But the Tider ushers me off the port, bringing me back to the deserted lifeboats. Her presence shields me as we move through crowds of maji. Each glares with the hatred of their Grounder.

"What about everything Zélie said?" I lower my voice. "What about all the progress we made?"

"Zélie isn't here," Nâo replies. "We have to find a better way."

Nâo cuts through the vines tying the different lifeboats together until one comes free. We work to reposition its mast and steering lever. With no other choice, I board, preparing to sail it down the coast.

"I can rally the maji." Nâo points to the battle beyond Lagos's walls. "But you need to rally them."

CHAPTER THIRTY-THREE

ZÉLIE

THE VERY SIGHT OF the emperor quiets all sound. He moves with the might of a mountain. His footsteps thunder across the emerald brick.

The emperor shares the brown skin of his people. His dark hair sits in a low bun. A gold chest plate rests on his bare shoulders, decorating his body with rays like the sun.

"*O que é isto?*" His deep voice rumbles through the medallion.

What is this? The words fill my head. The emperor examines us from the top of the stairs, square face set into a frown.

I force my breaths to still, tuning into the medallion as Köa explains what happened in the jungle. Köa hands the emperor the bronze compass. I watch as he inspects the glass face. The moment Köa points to me, blood rushes into my ears.

Think, Zélie. The moment I've been waiting for races at me. But I'm not prepared to respond. How do I explain what we've escaped?

Why would this man believe a single word I say?

The emperor walks forward, and the entire city echoes with his descent. When he makes it to the bottom, I stare at the cracks in the emerald steps, unable to meet his face. My throat constricts when the emperor stops in front of where I am kneeling.

"*Look at me,*" he orders.

I struggle to follow the simple command. The thought of looking into the emperor's face feels like looking straight into the sun.

"Look at me if you can understand."

I clench my fists and force myself to look up. The emperor's pale green gaze burns straight through my soul. Anger radiates off him like heat.

"You speak our tongue?" he challenges me. Somehow I know that no response will suffice. Even still, I pull from the medallion, allowing it to feed me their words.

"There is a girl," I start slowly. The emperor's jaw sets at the sound of his own tongue. *"An enemy approaches—"*

The emperor holds up his hand.

"Kill the outsiders."

The emperor's order comes so quick, I don't have a chance to react. He turns on his heel, traveling up the stairs. The people roar at my back. Two warriors come forward, holding my arms. Köa stands at the top of the stairs.

He removes the obsidian cleaver from his skin.

"Please! Mercy!" I shout at the emperor's back. Tzain's muffled screams ring as Köa descends. The warrior raises his cleaver in the air. The world around me spins. I smell the sharp cut of ash.

Then I see *her*.

The girl runs down the stairs, orange skirts swirling behind her long legs. Golden bangles jingle around her brown ankles. A jewel-studded scarf wraps over her long black braid.

Her eyes are so luminescent, they sparkle like diamonds, so much brighter than what I saw in my visions. Determination fills her as she lunges forward. She grabs Köa's cleaver with her bare hands before he can strike me down.

"Mae'e!" the emperor shouts. The entire crowd gasps as the girl's blood spills, but she doesn't let go of the blade.

The ancient medallion boils in my skin.

"*Men are coming,*" I shout at the emperor. "*They're coming to take her.*"

BLOOD POUNDS IN MY EARS. I wait in their town circle. The moment I declared the Skulls were coming for the girl they call Mae'e, the whole of the city broke out in a frenzy.

Now the entire civilization watches in the seats above, hundreds of thousands forming new mountains around me. The emperor sits on a dais, surrounded by Köa and his warriors. Tzain and Amari are forced to watch from a cell carved into the mountain's side.

Vines bind me to the stone seat in the center. Dried blood soaks the rock floor. The seconds of life I have left feel like they're slowly ticking away. With nowhere else to turn, I close my eyes and pray.

I followed the ancient voice's command. I turned down the opportunity to sail back to my homeland. I found the girl I saw in the seas.

If they kill me now, what will it all mean?

The crowds roar from the stands. I don't need the medallion to decipher the calls for my head. The way they react to us makes me believe we're the first outsiders to enter their woven walls. I want to shout at them about the Skulls, make them understand that we're here to help. I can only imagine what will happen to their people if King Baldyr lands on their black shores.

Across the circle, a boulder rolls away. My thoughts still as a silence falls over the masses. An elderly woman stands in the cave entrance, wrinkles woven through her brown skin.

"*Yéva is here. . . .*"

The woman's name travels in whispers through the crowd. Gold pigment covers her neck and the curve of her jaw. Her hair forms a river of silver, falling to the small of her back. Shrouded faces reach out from the emerald cloak that adorns her frail shoulders. The entire earth hums in her presence.

I don't speak as Yéva glides toward me. Mae'e follows her into the circle like a faithful servant, dressed in new emerald robes. She keeps her sparkling gaze fixed on the ground. No one makes a sound.

Yéva opens her palm, and the vines around me fall. Cool air rushes into my lungs. I lurch forward, hitting the hard rock. Yéva waves her hand again, and my stone seat slides away, revealing a crystal bath.

Yéva takes a stick of lavender from behind her ear and crushes it in her fingers. When she drops it into the bath, the water begins to steam. She fixes her gaze on me.

"Enter."

Yéva's lips don't move, yet her voice whispers through my soul. My fingernails dig into the stone floor.

This voice . . .

She's the woman I heard before.

I rise to my shaking feet. I feel every single eye on me as I remove the wool pants of the enemy and undo the wrap around my chest. Mae'e gasps at the sight of the gold medallion, but Yéva isn't fazed.

The mystic gestures to the bath. The warm water burns where the vines rubbed my skin raw. Yéva raises Mae'e's hand over the steaming waters. She pricks her palm with an obsidian dagger, and a single drop of blood falls.

The moment it hits the water, everything transforms.

Yéva starts to wail. The crowd above us cries out. Her diamond eyes sparkle. Her silver hair flies with a sudden gust of wind. Something deep possesses the mystic's form. It's like twelve different people yell at once. The medallion buzzes in my chest, more powerful than it's ever been.

"Uma filha das tempestades da Grande Mãe . . ."
A daughter of the Great Mother's storms . . .
"Uma filha da forja da Grande Mãe . . ."
A daughter of the Great Mother's forge . . .
"Um pai criado com sangue . . ."
A father formed from blood . . .

The triple arrowhead ignites as words rip from Yéva's throat. Storm clouds circle above my head. A hard rain fills my ringing ears. Screams ripple through the stands as golden lightning crackles free from my hands.

"Before the Blood Moon, all three will unite.
On the Old Stone, the bodies shall be sacrificed.
He will feel the touch of the Great Mother again.
The skies will open once more,
And a new god will be born."

CHAPTER THIRTY-FOUR

ZÉLIE

A NEW STORM IS UNLEASHED the moment Yéva collapses. An uproar spreads through the crowd like smoke. All at once villagers rise, pushing to break into the town circle.

"*Keep them back!*" Köa orders.

Vineweavers descend from the stands by the dozens, long green stems whirring around them like the tentacles of an octopus. Scores of vines crawl above, creating a dome over the town circle that keeps the villagers sectioned off.

A thick black blade cuts through the new net of vines, creating a hole big enough for someone to pass through. A villager starts to descend, but the vineweavers react in an instant. Long vines wrap the villager up like a fly caught in a spiderweb.

Beneath the chaos, girls in matching silk kaftans run across the stone floor. Their petite frames move in perfect unison. Each sports a long dark braid wrapped tight atop her head like a rose. Like Yéva, golden pigment coats their throats and their jawlines.

Two of the girls reach Yéva first. They lift her body into a woven stretcher. Another pair help me out of the crystal bath. They take my hands with a delicate touch, wrapping my shaking body in soft robes.

More villagers attempt to cut through the new dome of vines. A group of warriors flanks me on both sides. The girls lead me through the opening Yéva appeared in as the town circle devolves.

This can't be happening.

I stare at my trembling hands. They still spark with remnants of the golden lightning. When the brilliant bolts pulsed through the skies, I couldn't believe my eyes. My entire body shook with the force that broke free.

A grief I wasn't prepared to face hits me like one of the Skull's bombs. Deep down, I prayed my magic would return. If not like the other maji, then at least when I returned to Orïsha.

But with the golden lightning's presence, I feel the truth. The magic of life and death, my connection to Mama and the other Reapers—this means it's really gone.

King Baldyr's stolen it with his medallion.

The skies will open once more, Yéva's prophecy echoes through my ears. *And a new god will be born.*

I stare at the glowing metal. It's already transformed from before. New veins spread out around the rim, digging into my skin.

With Yéva's words, I finally understand what Baldyr's after. I know where the last two medallions must go. If he catches Mae'e, he'll plunge it through her chest. Whatever magic she wields naturally will mutate, twisting to King Baldyr's will. He'll harvest both our powers, using the last medallion to transform himself.

But if he does that . . .

I think of the Skulls' own magic—the superior strength granted by the bloodmetal they all wield. It's hard enough to stop Baldyr now. With our combined powers, he'd be impossible to kill.

Baldyr's plans hang over my head as we exit the passageway and find ourselves on a stone dock. Glowing waters stretch before us, branching out in a dozen different directions. Giant lily pads float down an underground canal, riding the steady current. At the edge of the docks, Tzain stands with Amari. I gasp at the sight.

"Tzain!" I break free of the girls in silk, running straight into my brother's arms. I pull back to examine the bruises from where the warrior struck him before. "Are you alright?"

"I'm fine." He pushes my hands away. "What's going on? What did that woman say?"

I do my best to recall all the words of Yéva's prophecy. I show them the growing medallion. I explain what it's done to me.

"He's after power," I say. "The might that would rival a god. The medallion's preparing me for his harvest. If he gets Mae'e, too . . ."

My voice trails off as Yéva passes by the three of us on a woven stretcher. Her russet skin has lost all its color. Her breaths escape in haggard spurts. A wave of guilt hits as the girls in silk set her down on a lily pad. Though the mystic stood tall before, calling forth the prophecy has ravaged her form.

Mae'e emerges from the tunnels. She moves to Yéva's side, kneeling by the water.

"*Nafre.*" Mae'e whispers the blessing. She kisses Yéva's hands. The girls in silk depart, leading Yéva down one of the canals.

The moment Yéva leaves, Köa enters the underground tunnels. The emperor follows behind him, surrounded by warriors and a legion of vineweavers. Their presence adds a charge in the air. I tense as they near.

"*Bind her hands.*" Köa points to me. "*Immediately.*"

As the vineweavers move, Mae'e rises to her feet. She steps in front of me.

"*Mae'e——*" the emperor starts.

"*You will do no such thing!*" Mae'e replies.

"*You heard what Yéva said,*" Köa pushes. "*The danger we risk by letting outsiders in——*"

"*This girl is not our enemy!*" Mae'e turns to me, and I'm hypnotized by her diamond gaze. A flattened vine wraps tight around her hand, covering the gash from the blade she grabbed to keep me alive.

"*They are our allies.*" Mae'e extends her injured hand to me, and I take it. "*Allies in great pain. They must be taken to my temples. Please, Emperor Jörah, allow me to restore them.*"

I dare to glance at Emperor Jörah. He twists the thick gold ring on his pointer finger. It's hard to read the lines in his face. The glowing rivers lap in his silence as he decides our fate.

"*The girls can go,*" he declares. Mae'e's shoulders slump in relief. She motions to the lily pads, preparing to leave.

"*What about my brother?*" I ask. "*Where will he be?*"

The emperor looks at Tzain, considering his place. He nods to his warriors.

"*He will reside with Köa and the Lâminas.*"

CHAPTER THIRTY-FIVE

TZAIN

The Lâminas.

Emperor Jörah's personal guard. Their very steps thunder in unison. I feel like a prisoner as I march among them.

The Lâminas occupy the quartet of temples surrounding the imperial palace. Each temple sports the symbol of an ivory barong. The leaf-shaped blade matches the ones inked onto every Lâmina's arm.

Warriors stand at attention as Köa approaches the stone gate. At the sight of me, they bristle. One eyes the curved blade inked into his skin. But when Köa gives the order, they have no choice but to open the gate and let me in.

Beyond the gate, young boys train in painted squares. The temples ring with the sounds of their matches. Unlike the graduated warriors, each trainee sports a shaved head and plain brown pants. No weapons mark their brown skin.

I stare as Köa marches me through. The boys spar with no regard, faces scrunched and teeth bared. Bones break. Blood spills. But no matter what, the boys don't stop.

They fight to kill.

In one square, the young warriors wield throwing knives made from black glass. They stand in a row across from a line of targets. When an overseeing Lâmina gives a call, they release. Each weapon lands with precision, hitting the exact mark.

In another square, a member of the Lâminas inspects the different trainees. A thick scar runs through the right side of the warrior's head. Unlike the young boys, his bare chest is covered with weapons. I take in the inked swords crossed over his abdomen.

When one of the young warriors fails to land an attack, the Lâmina steps in. He grabs the trainee at the knees, showing him how to throw an enemy onto his back.

In the central court, a Lâmina and a trainee face off. The Lâmina sports a boomerang around his neck and heavy clubs on his muscular arms. A circle of boys gathers as the Lâmina's fingers glow green. Bones crack as he pulls one of the clubs free.

He winds up the ivory weapon to strike. Though weaponless, the trainee dives forward, giving everything he has to the fight. The way their trainees battle, I don't know who to fear more—them, or the Skulls.

Behind the training squares, the warriors' barracks stand. Crafted from hardened vines, each woven structure rises almost fifteen levels high. Winding ladders run from the bottom floors all the way to the top. I have no choice but to follow Köa as he climbs.

When we reach the third floor, two dozen men rise from their cots. Most are double my age; all but one are twice my size. The warriors protest at my presence, and Köa shouts back in their tongue.

My pulse spikes when the path to the ladders is blocked off. The warriors' startling green eyes dig into me like knives. It's like being trapped in another cage.

I need to get out of here.

I stiffen as the men close in like dogs. I feel naked among them. But as they corner me against the back wall, I don't back down.

I don't allow the warriors to see the sweat that gathers at my brow.

Each of the Lâminas sports an armory on his skin: uniquely shaped swords, bone whips, throwing knives. My fingers itch for the hilt of my axe.

Without it, I don't stand a chance.

"My axe," I say.

Köa blinks at me. The breeze from the window blows in our silence. I point to the blade on his arm and make a swinging motion.

"My axe. I want it back."

Köa cracks his neck. He nods to one of his men. The warrior disappears to another room. After a moment he returns with the only weapon I have. They've wrapped the hilt in an animal skin to keep it from burning their hands.

The warrior gives the axe to Köa, and I reach for it, but Köa holds it out of my grasp. His taunt brings me back to being a child, all alone on the agbön court. I was a lowly fisherman's son against the sons of Orïsha's guard. They said I'd lose every match.

"Give it to me," I growl.

My eyes widen when Köa speaks my tongue in a broken cadence.

"Or—what?" He arches his brow. "What—are you—going to do?"

With a hard shove, he throws me back. I tumble out of the window of the barracks. Air rushes past me as I fall. Shouts ring as I land on the hard rock.

Pain shoots through every part of my being. Sharp spasms travel up my spine. Köa practically glides down the vines, cornering me as I writhe.

"You want—your axe?" Köa dangles the weapon over my head. Unlike the other warriors, his hand doesn't burn in contact with the metal. All around us the Lâminas gather.

"Take it."

My jaw sets as Köa hands the axe to one of his men. The monster that awoke in the Skulls' cage rises in my abdomen. I think of all I've had to endure. What it took to make it to these foreign shores.

With a grunt, I rise to my feet. I don't care about all the eyes on me. I shake through the pain and attack, launching myself at Köa's hips.

In the span of a breath, Köa beats me to the ground. He slides, hooking his knee between my legs. With a twist, the world spins. My head smacks against the hard stone.

The other men laugh at my fall. They cheer Köa on in their tongue. Their leader stares at me like I am an ant.

Like I'm not worth the rock I lie on.

I scramble back to my feet. A trail of blood drips from my right ear. It falls from my neck, adding to the bloodstains on the emerald rock.

Do better. Be better. I push myself on. I won't let Köa defeat me.

I won't let him win.

I swing my leg at his ribs. Köa doesn't even shift to hook my heel. With a sweep of his foot, he catches my ankle. I stifle my shouts as I hit the ground again.

I don't know how many times I charge.

How many times I'm thrown to the ground.

My fury builds with every failed attack. I strike with everything I have.

But when I can't bring myself to rise, Köa bends down. The warrior barely sweats. He stares like he can see straight through me.

Like he can feel how powerless I really am.

"Your axe—does not—make you strong." Köa pushes through every word. "It shows—how weak—you really are."

Köa takes the axe back from his men.

Shame rips through me as he drops the weapon by my head.

CHAPTER THIRTY-SIX

INAN

My bare feet drag across the hard soil.

The night winds bite at my skin.

Walking through the forest outside of Lagos, I've never felt more exposed. More helpless. More alone.

Though I was able to sail around the front lines, the battle rages behind me at Lagos's broken walls. The ravages of war surround my every step. Destruction meets me at every turn.

More than half the towering jackalberry trees have fallen. Giant caverns litter the earth. Severed limbs mark my hike. The corpses of tîtáns, soldiers, and maji lie intertwined.

A fallen soldier still grasps his sword. A tîtán lies with a twisted spine. My stomach churns at two children caught in an attack. The trunk of a snapped tree pins their lifeless bodies to the ground.

Guilt eats at me from within. Every body I pass reminds me of everything Orïsha's lost. All I see are my mistakes. The failures that allowed the Skulls to succeed in their raids.

If the Skulls invaded our shores today, nothing would stand in their way. With our infighting, their forces would be unopposed. Their slaughter could travel from coast to coast—

A whistle blows through the air, growing with every passing second.

I barely have a chance to hit the ground before a metal blade passes over-head. It collides with the trees at my back, cutting the old wood in half.

My heart thunders as I scurry across the ground. The treetops come crashing down with a vengeance. A trio of Welders appears ahead, their golden armor glistening under the sliver of moonlight. White streaks pass through their hair. Scraps of metal float around their glowing hands.

"I come in peace!" I shout, raising my arms in surrender. I pray for the words to be enough, but when one tîtán lifts his palm to attack, my fingers grow numb.

Dammit.

I scramble to my feet and take off. The air whistles as more blades launch. I zigzag through what remains of the standing trees. Metal blades fly through the air like arrows.

One blade nicks my cheek as it zips past my face. Another misses my side by a breath. I dive behind a thick trunk for cover. A series of thunks ring as the blades strike tree bark. Nausea rises in my throat as I climb over a pile of corpses. The rotting bodies shield me as more metal blades strike.

"Close him in!" a Welder yells.

My legs strain as I push. I dodge every blade that flies. But when one cuts through my thigh, I stumble forward. Nothing breaks my fall. Air rushes past me as I plummet headfirst into an empty cavern.

"Ah!" I grit my teeth, pressing my hands to the open wound. The metal boots of the Welders clank as they approach. Words of surrender choke in my throat.

Before I can speak, iron restraints wrap around my mouth. They bind my ankles and my wrists. The shortest of the Welders jumps into the cavern, inspecting my white streak.

"We got another." The Welder grabs me by the hair, turning me from side to side. His square brows furrow when he pulls me into the moon-light. Recognition fills his dark brown eyes.

"Do you know who this is?" He turns to the others.

They shake their heads.

"Send word back to camp," the Welder instructs. "We've found the fallen king."

THEY'VE BEEN LOOKING FOR ME.

I don't know whether the realization should spike fear or relief. The Welders don't speak as they carry me through the forest, following the worn trail back to their camp.

Chatter builds through the thinning trees. As we near the edge of the forest, I recognize our path—we head for the only military fortress on the outskirts of Lagos. I used to visit it all the time before magic came back.

Maybe this is a good thing, I try to reassure myself. *This could be my chance.* If some noble or fallen general has put a bounty on my head, that means they want me alive. It means I may be able to convince them of what's to come.

As we reach the end of the trail, teams of Grounders work to bury their dead. A dark green glow spreads from their fingertips. They dig their hands into the earth, and grave plots erupt by the dozens. The fresh mounds ripple as they spread across the land.

I prepare to meet the fortress, but the military's stronghold is no more. Piles of rubble cover the clearing. The tarnished snow leopanaire seal that hung over the entrance lies twisted in the dirt.

In the fortress's place a new iron dome rises, only a fraction of the garrison that stood before. A team of tîtán Burners stands guard in front of the dome's only gate. The blast marks and charred skeletons around them warn of what happens to any maji who attempts to get close.

At the sight of the Welders, the tîtáns exchange nods. With a call, the gate slides up. The Welders are quick to enter the dome. I flinch as the gates slam shut behind us.

This is it? Though restrained, I do my best to take stock of what's left. A few dozen tents lie behind the dome's walls, all that remains of the tîtáns' former forces. A makeshift infirmary sits at the eastern edge of the camp. Across the way, a large tent serves eba and stew to the line of tîtáns who wait. A small group spars in the center of the camp. Blasts ring from other tîtáns training behind the dome's iron walls. Most tîtáns lie in their tents, taking the gift of sleep before the next battle commences.

As the Welders carry me through their army, all eyes fall to me. My presence quiets all conversation. Some tîtáns stare in shock. Others look on with bitter contempt.

"—at last—"

"—I thought he was dead—"

"—he dares to show his face—"

Their voices ring inside my head as we go, making our way to the largest tent at the southern edge of the dome. Wide enough to house six people, the tent stands tall, surrounded by a line of golden armor.

The trio sets me down and takes position, each standing at attention. A crowd of tîtáns gathers around us, eager to see what will happen next.

"General! We found him!" the head Welder calls.

My mind races as I try to think of who lies behind the tent's walls. Last I remember, Lieutenant Okeke was next in line. The stout officer became a Tamer when magic returned. But Okeke resented my every command.

If he's had his soldiers looking for me, it's only to take my head.

My heart spikes as someone stirs. A rustle builds as the silhouette nears the entrance. I prepare to make my case, but all the words leave my mind when I see a familiar face.

Mother . . .

The former queen exits her tent with the aid of a staff. A bandage covers her right eye. More bandages wrap tight around her abdomen. The color's drained from her soft copper complexion. Only ice fills her amber eyes.

The last time we were together, I tricked her into drinking her own sedatives. I knocked her out to dissolve Orïsha's throne. I knew she'd never forgive me for moving against her.

When the *Iyika* attacked the palace, I was certain she died.

But now Mother bends down to meet me. The breath shrivels in my chest. The Welders back away as she finally speaks.

"Give me one reason I shouldn't kill you now."

CHAPTER THIRTY-SEVEN

INAN

Sitting inside Mother's tent, I don't know what to say. I still can't believe she let me in.

The way she stared at me, I thought she would end me where I stood.

She limps under the crimson flaps, anger hardening the creases above her brow. I think of the lavender walls that surrounded her palace quarters. The rich velvets of her bed. Her collection of jewel-studded geles was large enough to fill its own wing. Her wardrobe overflowed with beautiful gowns and colorful silks.

Now her tent houses little more than rolls of bandages, her tîtán armor, a small table, and one metal cot. I never thought I'd see the day.

I can hardly believe the queen I know is living this way.

Mother winces as she sits on her cot. Bloodstains cover the bandages around her abdomen. She reaches for a new roll, and I rise in an attempt to help.

"Let me—"

Mother slaps my hand away with her staff. I grit my teeth against the sting.

"You're just as likely to wrap the bandages around my throat."

I watch her as she struggles to remove the soaked cloth around her stomach. Lantern light reveals a brutal gash. Yellow and blue skin surrounds the wound. Her hands shake as she replaces the dressing.

"Don't you have Healers?" I ask.

"Our Healers were the first to die." Mother's voice drips with bitterness. "I commend your people for damning ours."

I shut my eyes and turn my head away. I think of all the fresh plots outside the tîtán dome. The loss of their Healers doesn't just hurt the tîtáns.

It hurts anyone the Skulls might harm.

The need to unify presses down on me once more. My shoulders threaten to buckle under the weight. We can't afford to take one more Orïshan life. If we keep going like this, we'll destroy ourselves long before the Skulls invade.

"I know you must hate me."

"Hate you?" Mother breathes. "Do you have any idea what you've done? We were at the end of the war! We crushed the *Iyika*! You've brought our kingdom to its knees—"

"Even if I hadn't dissolved the throne, they would have attacked. You would still have these wounds—"

"I would have an entire nation behind me!" Mother roars. But when shadows move outside the tent, she lowers her voice. "I would command a unified army. Not this measly dome!"

"And then what?" I dare to step forward. "More bodies to bury? More endless guilt? The wars we've waged against the maji have destroyed our kingdom! That fighting is what's brought us here!"

"You're just as foolish as the night you disappeared." Mother's amber eyes narrow. "You and your wretched love for the maji—"

"These aren't just ideals, Mother!" I cut her off. "We can't afford to fight anymore. An enemy is coming. A foreign king is already raiding our shores!"

"Do you think I would believe a word from your treacherous mouth?" Mother raises her hand to slap me. I grab her before she can strike.

"Don't believe me," I say. "See it for yourself!"

A turquoise cloud ignites around my hand before Mother can pull away. My magic rips us from the tent. In the span of a breath, we're back on the Skulls' ship. . . .

"Ugh!" I keel over as a Skull rams his fist into my gut. My mouth fills with the copper taste of my own blood. The Skull hits me again, and I fall to the floor, landing on top of a maji's corpse.

The Skull drags me back to my feet. He brings his beady eyes to mine. It's all I can do to spit on his mask. The Skull grabs me by the head, crushing it against the iron bars.

In the hall, another Skull removes his axe. The runes along its hilt turn red as it feeds on his blood. The hallway shrinks in the Skull's bulging presence. Tremors pass through the wood planks as he walks.

He raises his glowing axe in front of my cell, a warning of what will come. Its heat burns my face as I shake in the Skull's arms. . . .

When Mother pulls away, the sensation is so strong she falls to her knees. She presses a hand to her chest. From the way her nose wrinkles, I can tell she still smells the stench of the dead.

"That is where you've been this whole time?" she asks, and I nod.

"They've spent moons mounting raids and attacks. They've taken Amari, too."

At Amari's name, Mother's lips tighten. Her hands travel to the bandages around her abdomen.

"How did you escape?" Mother asks.

"With the maji. I couldn't have gotten back to Orïsha without them."

Mother finally takes my hand as I join her on the cot. Her fury still radiates off her like heat. But with the knowledge of the Skulls, a new enemy has entered her battlefield.

One she might hate more than me.

"Invaders." She shakes her head. "I never thought I'd see the day. If your father were here . . ." Mother shuts her eyes. I don't know if it's out of missing him or out of fear.

"If you're fighting for the Orïsha he reigned over, your efforts are in vain," I declare. "That kingdom is gone forever. But the chance for a better Orïsha is still here. We need the maji, Mother." I kneel by her side. "Whatever remains of the soldiers, too. Our only chance at stopping the Skulls is to oppose their attack together, united as one."

"It will never work," Mother says. "The fighting will never stop."

"Can you call an armistice?" I ask. "Can we put the battle to rest, just for one night?"

Mother stares at her tîtán armor for a long moment before turning to me.

"Give me a few days," she reluctantly agrees. "I will see what I can do."

CHAPTER THIRTY-EIGHT

ZÉLIE

AFTER SEPARATING FROM THE others, we ride through the canals underneath the town circle. Amari and I hold each other as we sail the glowing waters. We follow behind Mae'e, seated on a giant lily pad.

Paintings of their goddess cover the walls and the arches overhead, the bright pigments weathered with time. Some depict the goddess being born of fire on the mountaintop. Others depict her entire body spreading into tangles of vines.

When we leave the central network and exit the city center, the collection of lanterns behind us blurs. Vineweavers patrol the canals, keeping them clear for our approach.

We flow through vast stretches of water, moving past the floating temples and open marketplace surrounding the imperial palace. As we head for the ring of mountains on the outskirts of the city, I'm mesmerized by the faces carved into the black stone. Instead of a rocky terrain, the faces of sleeping women reach up into the sky. Their intertwined bodies surround the floating village like giants.

The carving of their goddess looms above them all, her curved figure watching over the city of vines with vibrant jewels in the place of her eyes. Amari stares up with me as the goddess passes overhead. Mae'e bows her chin in prayer.

When our lily pads dock at the base of the mountains, the weight of the air shifts. Something buzzes in my skin. The winds blow with whispers of the past. It's as if the entire mountain range lives.

A collection of temples sits above us, their gilded rooms jutting out of the mountain rock. A boulder rolls away, and the girls in matching silk kaftans return, each with a glowing lantern in hand. When Mae'e gives a nod, the girls descend as one.

Though Amari and I try to stay together, the girls pull us apart. Amari calls out to me as they lead her through an entrance in the mountain's side. Her voice disappears behind the black stone.

Before I can ask where she's going, a drink like honey is poured down my throat. Within moments, the world blurs. My limbs become weights I can't lift. I find myself carried into the base of the mountain.

What is this?

More candles than I've ever seen flicker against the pale green walls. Their light dances through intricately carved columns and mosaic-covered arches. Vines cover every inch of the temple like spiderwebs. They knit themselves down the long halls, disappearing behind emerald fountains and statues of the goddess carved from obsidian glass.

"*Just breathe,*" one of the girls coos. She presses her hibiscus-scented palms to my temple, attempting to dislodge the majacite crown. The poisonous metal stings at her touch. She draws back her hands with a gasp as tendrils of smoke twist into the air. Though she calls to the others for help, it doesn't matter what they try, the metal won't budge. When I cry out in pain, they all give up.

After hushed whispers, the girls lead me into warm waters. Their gentle hands move through the steam-filled space. The girls wash the dirt and sand from my skin. They run combs carved from coral through my white hair. They grab a ribbon of golden silk, tying my long white coils into a high braid.

When I am clean, the girls lead me to a room filled to the brim with burgundy pillows and deep green blankets. Heat rises through the ceramic floor. Nailah lies asleep in a bed of her own, no sign of the vines that kept her at bay. From the new sheen in her golden mane, I can tell someone's tended to her as well.

Mae'e waits on the balcony, staring out at her city. After all the time spent seeing her in my mind, it's strange to see her in real life. The flashes couldn't capture the grace with which she stands. The way the winds seem to sing as they blow through her raven hair.

I dare to walk over to her, resting my arms along the balcony's railing. The girls in pale green kaftans pass meters below, tending to the mountain's countless gardens. Across the waterway, thousands of temples and woven huts shine in the distance like fireflies in the night. I inhale the sight.

"You look wonderful." Mae'e smiles at the golden kaftan her maidens have dressed me in. "Like the yellow moon."

It takes me a moment to realize I understand her words without the aid of the medallion.

"You speak my tongue?" I ask.

Mae'e nods. "All tongues stem from the same tree. To understand the Mother Tongue is to understand them all."

"Where are we?"

"New Gaīa." Mae'e gestures to her lands. Pride radiates behind her dazzling smile. I take in the floating civilization once more. In the far distance, the sculpture of their goddess stands tall, its silhouette stark against the galaxy of stars. Behind it, I spot the imperial palace, where Tzain is supposed to be. I think of him trapped with Köa and the rest of the Lâminas. All the New Gaīans who called for our heads.

"Will we be safe?" I ask.

"You are under Emperor Jörah's protection. No one in this city will lay a hand on your head."

"But what about my brother?" I push.

"My people need time to understand." Mae'e touches my shoulder. "Every time outsiders have landed on our shores, they have only brought despair. And after what Yéva said, they are more than afraid. They worry you bring the enemy here."

At the mention of the enemy, I see King Baldyr's golden skull. The medallion pulses in my chest. I grit my teeth as new veins scratch themselves free from the tarnished metal, spreading across my skin. The toll of the day hits me like a crashing wave. I grab the railing of the balcony as my feet give way.

"*Garotas!*" Mae'e rushes to my aid. She shouts for the eight girls she calls the Green Maidens, but I shake my head. The fear I feel is not something they can heal.

Instead, Mae'e takes my hand and leads me to the bed of pillows. She strokes my hair with her delicate touch. Though we have just met, I melt into her arms.

She starts to hum an ancient song. Even the medallion doesn't understand the words. The flickering candles pop around us. It's like the flames cry out at her voice.

"Is Yéva ever wrong?" I whisper.

"Never," Mae'e sighs. "She channels straight from the Great Mother herself."

"Then why aren't you scared?" I ask. I allow her to see the medallion embedded in my chest. "The man she speaks of isn't just coming for your people. He's coming for you."

"You doubt our strength." Mae'e returns to her balcony and gazes out at her lands. Something hard enters her diamond gaze. "By attacking New Gaīa, those you call the Skulls have not chosen war. They have chosen annihilation."

PART III

CHAPTER THIRTY-NINE

AMARI

WHATEVER SALVE THE Green Maidens give me keeps me unconscious for the next half-moon. At times I think I'm back in Lagos, safe in the pampered comforts of my old quarters. In the brief moments I stir, Mae'e's maidens surround me, feeding me spiced meats and freshly picked fruits. At times they draw me baths and rebraid my dark curls. If it weren't for the flashes of the Skulls' ship, I would think I'd passed into a new life.

By the time I pull myself from the sea of satin pillows and woven blankets, the crescent moon hangs in the starry sky. The ground beneath me quakes. The mountain rumbles with a sudden force before the tremble quietly fades away.

A bronze table to my right withstands the quake. Welded to the mosaic floor, it holds a full spread with jasmine tea. The candles that never seem to go out flicker against the vine-covered walls. A warm bath steams in the other room, calling to me with its floating lilies and bright sunflowers.

But as I sip the tea, my gaze shifts to the wooden entrance of my room. I set the ceramic saucer down. Soft pink silks glide across my skin as I slide the gilded doors apart.

A melodic voice echoes from down the hall. I follow the sound to find Mae'e kneeling before a magnificent portrait carved out of the entire stone wall. More candles dance across the intricate sculpture, bringing it to life. The work of art captures every detail of New Gaīa, from the rice fields to the underground canals. Children gather in front of the floating schoolhouses. Chiseled villagers stand before the imperial palace, heads bowed for a coronation.

At the top of the stone sculpture, I see the goddess of their statues, the largest of the majestic faces carved into their mountains. The goddess opens her arms to the cloud-filled skies and vines made of emeralds shoot from her hands. Lava crafted from shattered rubies erupts around her in waves.

Something about the sculpture captures me. I'm surprised at the way I drift near. It's as if the goddess looks right at me, seeing me for who I truly am.

"*Obrigada.*" Mae'e kisses her fingertips and offers them up to her goddess before bowing her head. Free of her usual braid, her raven hair cascades down her back in waves. Orange skirts shift around her russet skin.

I step back as she moves to her feet. The air seems to shimmer in her presence. Her eyes widen in surprise when she turns and spots me. My cheeks flush as I take in the sacred space. *What was I thinking?* I shake my head. I am a stranger in a foreign land.

"I apologize——" I start, but Mae'e smiles and presses a hand to her heart.

"You are up!" The melody of her voice tickles my ear.

"I didn't mean to interrupt."

"You are my guest." Mae'e waves her hand. "You could never interrupt." She speaks as if she were hosting a royal envoy, instead of escaped prisoners from King Baldyr's ship. Mae'e beckons me over, and I dare to answer her call. Her honeyed scent wraps around me as the scent of ash travels through the halls.

"This is Mama Gaīa." Mae'e's face radiates with light as she speaks the sacred name. She gazes at the sculpture as if she hasn't seen the goddess's image every day of her life.

"You have to see it from here," Mae'e insists. A shiver runs down my skin as Mae'e takes me by the arms. She brings me to the sculpture, placing me exactly where she knelt. Despite the goddess above me, I find myself staring at Mae'e instead.

Mae'e chews on her bottom lip. Mischief fills her sparkling gaze.

"We are not supposed to leave. . . ." She looks down the hallways. "But do you wish to see more?"

RUNNING THROUGH THE TEMPLES at night brings back memories long since forgotten. I hear my old handmaiden's laughter. I see the white tendrils that would fall around her angular eyes.

We used to dream of traveling to all the corners of Orïsha. We spoke of journeying from the port of Lagos and making it all the way to the white sands of Zaria. There were days I never thought I'd leave the palace.

Binta was convinced I'd see the world.

I wish you were here, I think to her spirit. I'm brought to tears at the beauty that surrounds me. Brilliant vines cover stone columns. Jewel-encrusted arches hang above our heads. Emerald-green tiles fill the walls, accented with golden flowers.

Two Green Maidens herd a litter of baby tigenaires onto an open lawn. Dozens of the young ryders tangle together in an open field. One black tigenaire stumbles into our path, and Mae'e scoops it into her arms. She plants a kiss on its striped forehead before sending it back to its pack.

I watch Mae'e as she runs, enraptured by the way her black hair swishes behind her. Though the Green Maidens move through all levels of the temples, Mae'e knows how to evade them. The vines squeal and hiss in her presence, instructing Mae'e on when she can move.

"Wait, wait!" Mae'e whispers when a vine unfurls before us. She squeezes my shoulder as more Green Maidens pass.

"*Obrigada.*" Mae'e grazes the vine's stem. It curls back into the wall.

Mae'e pulls me down a long hall filled with emerald fountains. When she leads me out of a tunnel, my hands fly to my heart. Another world unfolds before me.

The hanging gardens are endless.

A vast forest in the center of the temple, vibrant flowers shine from every bush—purple alliums, fuchsia angelonias, and azaleas in full bloom. Deep red plums hang over our heads. Mae'e grabs one and takes a bite. A trail of juice drips from her full lips down her chin.

Mosaic tiles create paths throughout the greenery. They circle around countless fires that burn inside sculptures of Mama Gaïa. A river runs through the vast forest, sliding over smooth basalt.

Mae'e takes a lantern in her hand, leading me through the gardens. As we walk, I see Mama Gaïa's face everywhere I look—she stares from the statues and the faces behind trickling waterfalls. Her figurehead rises in the sparkling fountains. I see her in the birds that sing. I feel her life pulsing inside of the leaves.

"This is my favorite part of the island." Mae'e closes her eyes and inhales. I follow her lead, taking in the sweet scent for myself. "You can feel her spirit everywhere. You can hear her in the air."

"She's in everything?" I ask.

Mae'e nods. "She is the Mother Root. All of New Gaïa stems from her."

Mae'e drifts to a sculpture of Mama Gaïa cut from black glass. Her shoulders fall in awe. I consider all that surrounds us: the hanging gardens, the temples, the city of vines. I can hardly believe all of New Gaīa grew from one being.

"Right now, Yéva maintains our connection to our civilization's source. As the sacred hierophant, Yéva has connected my people to the Mother Root for almost two hundred years."

"*Two hundred* years?" I marvel, and Mae'e smiles.

"As a direct descendant of Mama Gaīa, Yéva grows like the trees. But her time is nearing its end. Soon, her sacred duties will fall to me."

For the first time all night, the serenity leaves Mae'e's eyes. For a moment, I feel what she must mean to her people, the sacred being King Baldyr threatens to take away. Of course her people feared our arrival.

What will become of New Gaīa if Baldyr harvests her heart?

"My people are looking to me to see them through this. It is my duty to keep them safe. When you first arrived, I felt so sure we would prevail. But the mountain has started to shake." Mae'e turns to me, and her eyes break into my soul. "Over the past few nights, I've had dreams," she whispers. "I have seen the Blood Moon."

The vines slither near us as Mae'e sits back. They wrap themselves around her, almost taking the future hierophant into their arms. The scent of lavender leaks from the garden in waves. Mae'e softens as she inhales the sweet aroma.

"Tell me." Her lightness fades. "Should we be afraid?"

"You should be terrified." I am surprised at the honesty she pulls from my throat. But a few weeks spent in the safety of her mountains doesn't erase all we've had to face. Every maji who didn't make it out of the Skulls' chains.

"He hunted my friend across the earth. He didn't care how many of our people he hurt. And with what Yéva said . . ." My voice trails off. "I don't know how he can be stopped."

Mae'e returns to her knees. She continues to pray before Mama Gaīa.

"What do you pray for?" I whisper.

"Protection," she answers softly.

Though the action is foreign, I join her on the floor. I think of all those I love and bow my head, praying for the same.

CHAPTER FORTY

INAN

WAITING IN THE FOREST outside Lagos, I prepare myself for what's to come.

A still breeze blows through the jackalberry trees.

The crescent moon shines down on our clearing from above.

The maji gather in a ring around my back. Though we've agreed to lay down arms for one night, my palms start to sweat. I feel it in my bones.

Everyone is still ready to fight.

This will work. I steady myself. *This has to work.* I prepare for the words I'll need to share. The fatal warning the people of Orïsha must hear.

With each passing day, I feel the Skulls' imminent attack. I picture their mighty ships cutting through the twisting waters. Their monstrous forms storm through the port of Lagos. Their glowing axes cut through every Orïshan in their way.

We need to start preparing our defenses, combining our forces to gather intelligence. There's no more time to waste. Either we come together to unify, or we leave the Skulls free rein.

It feels like we wait for hours. I worry no other Orïshans will show.

But then a flickering torch appears through the dark trees. Slowly, people trickle in.

I hold on to the Skull's mask as the trail of torches travels into the clearing. The flames light what remains of the Orïshan guard. The very men I used to command march in broken lines, staring at me with a hatred that burns like a branding iron.

Their forces have dwindled over the past few moons. Their shoulders slump with the weight of the battles they've waged. Soldiers sport wooden splints and bloodstained bandages. Ash coats the Orïshan seals on their breastplates.

On the other side of the clearing, the first tîtáns arrive, their golden armor and white streaks glistening under the crescent moon. Though their numbers are small, they move with a different confidence. Mother makes it to the front of the tîtáns with the aid of her staff, regal in the absence of her crown.

The tîtáns' presence is like a barrel of blastpowder. I sense how easy it would be to light the spark. With a snap of Mother's fingers, the tîtáns could attack. Behind me, the maji step forward, ready to charge.

Despite the risk, I take my place at the center of the clearing. I glance up to the skies and pray for the right words to leave my lips. I have to act before this armistice devolves into a battle nobody can win.

"The last time I stood before a crowd like this, I renounced my crown," I declare. "I failed as your king. I failed because I couldn't bring Orïsha the unified front it's always needed. But now . . ." I glance down at the Skull's mask, remembering what's at stake. "Now we don't have a choice. Either we unify, or we lose everything."

I hold the mask up high, walking it around the circle so everyone can see. One soldier reaches for the mask, and I hand it to her. Her brows furrow as she touches the broken bones.

"An enemy is coming." I point at the mask. "An enemy is already here. We've allowed our once-great nation to be ripped apart by war. While we've battled each other, they've raided our lands, searching for the power locked inside one maji."

"Why should we care what happens to the maji?" Mother voices the question that must be on every tîtán's and soldier's mind. Behind me, a Burner's hands light with a flame. I hold up my hand to stop her, pleading with my eyes.

"They won't stop at the maji." I turn to the tîtáns. "They intend to rule over us all. Our best chance to stop them is together. Right now, we need each other."

"We can stop them on our own," another tîtán shouts. "We can round the maji up ourselves!"

"You threaten us after all we've endured?" Nâo pushes forward.

"Better you than us!" a soldier shouts back.

The fragile peace shatters like glass. The armistice devolves before my eyes. All at once, everyone moves to attack. The maji push in from the west. The tîtáns charge from the east.

"Ìpè inú igbó, ẹ yí mi ká báyìí—"

Tamer-summoned hyenaires surround us on all sides.

"Babalúayé, a ké pè ọ́ báyìí—"

Clouds of orange gas swirl in the Cancers' hands.

A trio of purple-clad maji moves to the front.

As they chant, animations rise.

"Hit them!" Mother yells. The ground shakes as she summons her power. Green light surrounds her body like a blaze.

The Orïshan guard takes up arms as everyone runs for the center of the clearing.

"Stop!" A force rises inside me. A wave about to crest. If even one drop of blood spills, it's over. The Skulls might as well declare victory over these lands.

"I said *stop!*" my voice booms. I shut my eyes and extend my hands. Magic pours out of me like a river. Turquoise clouds flood through the earth, catching every Orïshan like flies in a spiderweb——

Drums beat through the air. A rumble travels beneath our feet. All at once, we turn to the east. Something shakes the remaining trees.

"What is that?" Mother calls. Terror grips me in its arms.

My hands fall to my sides as a wild band of Skulls swarms.

"Run!" I shout.

Three dozen Skulls fill the clearing at once, the scars stark on their swollen chests. Their bronze masks glimmer in the moonlight. Their colossal forms tear across the grounds.

The men roar as they attack, their crimson weapons primed and ready to strike. One Skull swings his glowing axe, cutting through an entire troop of soldiers at once. Another Skull raises his hammer. The maji who charge are crushed in an instant.

"*Òrìṣà iná, fún mi ní iná*——" Kenyon runs forward, streams of fire swirling in his hands. His flames shoot toward one Skull like a cannonball. The Skull cries out as his skin sears and he's burned alive.

But before Kenyon can strike again, another Skull attacks. Kenyon's eyes bulge as he takes the hammer to the chest. The sheer force cracks through every bone. His body flies into a tree and he hits the bark so hard the trunk explodes.

"Inan!" Mother roars.

I whip my head to the left. The ground quakes as Mother rips caverns through the earth. She tries to bury the Skulls that charge, but with their mighty strength, they leap over the gaping holes. One Skull grabs her by the neck. With a snap, Mother falls to the ground.

Her eyes hang open as she joins the dead.

I watch as the Skulls rain down hell, attacking every soul in the clearing. The soldiers who try to fight have their blades ripped in half. The maji who attempt to flee can't outrun the transformed Skulls.

Body after body falls to the ground, bleeding into the earth. It's only when the Skulls give their victory cry that I close my eyes, recalling the turquoise clouds.

"What in the skies?" Mother wheezes, coming back to life from the magic of my mind. Her confusion matches the rest of the clearing as the turquoise clouds return to me, bringing everyone back to the moment before the Skulls attacked.

All at once, the band of Skulls disappears. My hallucinations vanish into thin air. By the time my magic fades, I can hardly stand. Veins bulge against my skin. Sweat soaks through my tunic.

"That is what you are up against," I pant. "That is the enemy you face. The Skulls are a ruthless, unified force and they serve their king with one purpose. For him, they've hunted our people with no remorse."

In seeing the full face of the enemy, I sense the break in the air. My words take on new power.

The chance for real unification is here.

"This isn't the time for us to be divided." I walk the circle, meeting every fighter's eye. "We cannot look at each other and see maji, soldier, and tîtán. We have to be Orïshans now, united as one. Are you with me?"

Nâo is the first to step forward. I catch her eye and we share a nod. A line of maji follow after her, and the soldiers step forward next. But the tîtáns don't move.

They all look to Mother.

A heavy silence hangs in the air as we wait to see which way she'll go.

Despite what's coming, she has no reason to fight by my side. But even she steps forward, bringing the tîtáns in line.

I take in our new coalition, smiling as battle plans fill my mind. There's no time to waste.

"Let's get to work," I call.

CHAPTER FORTY-ONE

ZÉLIE

"YÉVA TOLD US TO meet her at the top of the mountain," Mae'e calls down to me from the ledge above. The two of us continue our spiral ascent up Mount Gaïa's black rock, traveling up a well-worn trail. A tangle of vines reaches up from the mountain's base. I hold on to them every time the mountain starts to shake. The city of New Gaïa glitters kilometers below. Its waters gleam white in the burning sun.

It's been a half-moon since our arrival, but crowds are still protesting outside Emperor Jörah's palace. They call for us to be thrown out. The fear of Yéva's prophecy hangs over our heads like a cloud.

Every time I reunite with my brother, new scars and bruises cover his skin. Tzain won't tell me who he is fighting day in and day out, but I see the way he stares at Köa and the rest of his men. Mae'e insists her people will come around, but the longer we stay, the more their hatred rises.

At my request, Mae'e's sent emissaries to Orïsha to recover Inan. Every day I await their word. I don't know if he was able to unify a fighting force. I don't even know if he and the others made it back to Lagos's port.

Outside these shores, King Baldyr still hunts for my heart. And I don't know when the Blood Moon will rise. I glance at the waxing silver crescent hanging in the sky, and Baldyr's golden skull fills my mind.

I will see you again. His promise returns to me, making my stomach clench. The medallion's veins have spread throughout my chest, digging over my rib cage and reaching the base of my neck.

I escaped the Skulls. I found the girl. Yet I feel no closer to their defeat or returning home. Time is slipping through my hands.

I have to find a way to change the tides in our war.

"We need to hurry," Mae'e calls down when I reach a gap in the stone. "Yéva grows weary. She will not be out for long." She opens up her palm, and the vines around the mountain come to life, knitting themselves into a ladder.

"You can tell from here?" I ask as I climb.

"I see many things." Mae'e gestures to her sparkling eyes. "But Yéva feels all. Her connection to the Mother Root allows her to sense the entire island all at once. It was she who alerted Emperor Jörah and the Lâminas when your boat landed on our shores."

I stop, remembering the shudder that passed through the bottoms of my feet when I stepped onto the black sands. The vineweavers were there in an instant. Yéva must have sent them there.

More questions rise as we near the mountaintop. My pulse starts to spike. I haven't seen Yéva since that day in the town circle.

What does she want with me now?

Mae'e pulls me over the final ledge, and my feet warm across the black stone. Yéva stands in the center of the volcanic crater, staring straight into the blinding sun.

The very mountain seems to still beneath her. The shrouded faces that reach out from her emerald cloak whisper as they shift in the wind. A circle of vines slithers at her feet.

In her presence, I struggle to speak.

"What do I do?" I whisper to Mae'e.

Yéva doesn't turn from the sun. She doesn't even acknowledge our arrival.

"Do nothing," Mae'e breathes. "You just have to wait."

Mae'e leaves me in the crater, returning to the mountain's edge. I hold on to her instructions as the sun arcs above, ignoring the strain in my legs.

All the while, Yéva doesn't move. The air dances through her silver hair. My shoulders start to relax when I hear the slither of approaching vines. I look down as the vines weave into a circle around me, connecting me to the circle Yéva stands in.

In a breath, the weight of the air shifts. Yéva remains still, yet I feel the faint brush of her fingertips. My skeleton turns to lead. The medallion pulses through my skin.

"What did you feel when it chose you?"

The mountain rumbles. Yéva's ancient voice pulls me in like the tides. Before I know it, I'm standing next to her. Her all-consuming aura wraps around me, strangling me like vines.

"What did you feel when it chose you?"

Her unspoken question rumbles through the ground once more. She forces me to my knees. I look to the medallion in my chest.

"Did it choose me?" I whisper back.

"Their metal lives." Yéva keeps her eyes on the sun. *"It has a spirit. A soul. It feeds off your being. It is feeding on you now."*

Yéva waves her hands, and the ancient medallion heats. New veins sprout from its golden metal, spreading across my dark skin like the roots of a tree. I scratch like I can tear the medallion from my chest, but the veins continue to spread.

"Their bloodmetal prepares you for the harvest. Its roots will grow until they've overtaken your soul. You will be his greatest weapon. With the power of the storms, he will end civilizations."

All at once, I see my kingdom ablaze. From the vast grain fields of Minna to the stone huts of Ibadan. Our temples. Our people. Our language.

Everything I've ever known disappears in the flames.

There are no maji. No títáns. No nobles and no kosidán. My motherland lies barren, destroyed by the power I hold within.

"How can I stop it?" I gasp through the pain. "Tell me how to stop it!"

My chest heaves up and down at the sight. I close my eyes, trying to shut the images out.

"*You must fight.*" Yéva finally looks at me. The world stills in the center of her gaze. "*You must take the power he seeks to harvest from your soul and use it yourself. Rise!*"

Yéva circles me, sharp like a red-breasted firehawk. I hold my breath as she walks. Her stride could draw blood.

"*Tell me what you hear.*"

My body starts to shake. Thunder booms between my ears.

"*Tell me what you hear!*" The mountain quakes with Yéva's voice.

"Thunder!" I shout back.

Yéva sweeps out her hands. All at once, the mountain disappears. Everything darkens in an instant. It's like she blocks out the entire sun.

"*Now breathe.*"

Yéva presses two fingers below my diaphragm, and the medallion lights in my chest. A surge like lightning pulses through my skin. I stare at my buzzing hands, suspended in a black haze.

"*Feel it.*" Yéva's voice shudders through my soul. "*Draw it deep inside.*"

My bones shake with the power King Baldyr hunts. The storm he's awakened in my blood.

"*When you face their king, you must release that surge. Harvesting that power is our only hope.*"

Yéva claps her hands, and I blink. In an instant, I break from my trance. The sun reappears in a brilliant glow. Blue skies look down on me from above.

I find myself on my knees in the center of the crater, clawing at the ground. The golden veins around the medallion buzz in my chest, still pulsing with the power of Yéva's command.

Yéva stands with Mae'e on the mountain's edge. Though fierce moments ago, now she has to hold on to Mae'e to stay upright. Slowly, I realize nobody else knows what she's shared.

The weight of what's to come stays with me alone.

I lift my hand and push—no power comes forth. How am I supposed to defeat their king when I can't summon the golden lightning myself?

"Please." I rise to my feet as Yéva turns to leave. "Show me how to fight."

Despite her exhaustion, Yéva sweeps her hands out. I brace myself, allowing her to bring me back to the black.

CHAPTER FORTY-TWO

INAN

IN THE WEEKS FOLLOWING the cease-fire, Orïsha transforms before my eyes. Word of the Skulls' impending arrival spreads throughout the lands. Orïshans travel from all over the kingdom, bringing their talents to the battlefront.

With the power of the maji and tîtáns combined, we fortify Lagos on all sides. Tamers call in wild animals to create a legion of trained ryders. A large pen is erected to hold the endless hordes of sleek cheetanaires, hulking panthenaires, and rare black-tusked elephantaires. The elder they call Na'imah shows the tîtáns how to enlarge the wild beasts, creating ryders large enough to charge through an entire legion of Skulls.

Out in the port, Nâo leads the Tiders, pushing back the waters so others can erect defenses. Kâmarū and the Grounders mold sand into hardened spikes large enough to rip through the bottom of an approaching Skull ship. Behind them, a legion of soldiers works diligently to lay down a path of floating bombs.

On the shores, Welders create special cannons for the Burners to shoot long-range attacks. With gathered blastpowder, the Burners generate lethal blows. The very air sears with the power of their flames.

Outside of Lagos, Mother works with her troop of tîtáns. I watch as they lift the earth. By working day in and day out, they've created a new mountain range, closing the city off. A single passageway allows fighters to make their way to the front, while leaving a way for the most vulnerable villagers to get out.

"And if the Skulls manage to pass our defenses?" I ask.

Mother clears everyone out of the way. Her hands glow with green light. With a clench of her fist, the earth rumbles. Rocks rise, closing off the passage.

"If we have to, we can bring the mountain down. They won't be able to get away."

I put my palm on Mother's shoulder. She still bristles at my touch. But after a moment she grabs my hand, allowing her fingers to rest above my own.

"You've done well," she says. "You should be proud."

"It's not me." I shake my head. "It's all of us."

After fighting for a unified Orïsha for so long, I can hardly believe we've come so far. No longer a kingdom at war, I see the dreams I used to have for my people come to life. All the hopes I thought had died.

With our new partnership, we have something that might outlast the Skulls' attack. The beginning of a new nation, one where the people are true allies. But to become that Orïsha, first we must survive.

If the Skulls land on our shores, they must be destroyed.

On instinct, I reach for the weathered parchment in my back pocket, bringing it out into the light. When the New Gaïan emissaries sailed into Lagos's port with a vessel woven from vines, I didn't know what to expect. For a moment, I thought we were under attack.

Instead, the russet-skin beauties emerged in orange silks, calling for me with this parchment in hand. Immediately, I recognized Amari's script. I pored over her words detailing everything the others had discovered.

As I finish my rounds around Lagos, I look to the words of Yéva's prophecy again.

A daughter of the Great Mother's storms . . .
A daughter of the Great Mother's forge . . .
A father formed from blood . . .
Before the Blood Moon, all three will unite.
On the Old Stone, the bodies shall be sacrificed.
He will feel the touch of the Great Mother again.
The skies will open once more,
And a new god will be born.

I look back out over all the defenses we've raised. With everything at our disposal now, I know we can put up a good fight. Yet I still don't know if it will be enough.

If Baldyr gets what he's after, how powerful will he become?

"Where is your mind?" Mother searches me with the amber eyes we share.

"Lagos is defended." I look back at the city. "With this mountain pass, Orïsha stands a chance."

"Then what's next?"

I roll up the parchment, making my way back to Lagos's port.

"It's time to go on the attack."

BY THE TIME NIGHT falls, Nâo, Dakarai, and I are already far out at sea. From the moment we joined forces again, there wasn't one day when the Tider didn't beg me to leave and go after the Skulls.

The weeks at home have taken Nâo to new form. The lean muscles she carried before the Skulls' capture have returned. Though her magic was already strong, she wields her gifts with a new rage.

A fresh coat of sweat glistens over her tattoos as she commands the waters around our vessel, alight with the teal-blue glow. Crafted by a Welder to grant us speed, the thin ship allows us to cut through the ocean like a knife. With our skeleton crew, we practically fly.

Dakarai sits at the head of the boat, using a drawn map to chart our path. According to his vision, the Skulls' ship docked at an island a few days' sail from where our own ship went down. At the moment, it's our only clue to where the Skulls are based.

If we can defeat them before the Blood Moon . . .

Though I don't know when the Blood Moon will rise, my mind races with the thought of what we might find. From the moment we encountered the Skulls, they've had the upper hand. Who knows how long they were working with the mercenaries, searching for Zélie and raiding our lands.

With information, we have an opening. With the right knowledge, we can bring the fight to them. Orïsha has a chance to thrive.

Zélie has a chance to live.

I squeeze the side of the boat as the thought of Zélie overwhelms me, remembering the unbearable weight of the terror she held inside. I think of my promise to keep her safe. The opportunity I have now to atone for my mistakes.

I have to find a way to be worthy of her. Her and the crown I once held. I have to be more.

I have to be the king I couldn't be before.

"We're here." Dakarai's words knock me out of my head. Nâo brings her hands down with a sharp wave, and the teal light surrounding her fades. Our vessel stops at once. I grab the iron masthead to keep from going overboard. The New Gaīan emissaries come to a stop beside us, eager to see the Skulls for themselves.

A chain of islands sits a few kilometers ahead, dotted with caves and thick vegetation. Three Skull ships sit in the crescent-shaped bay. The sight makes my stomach twist. Phantom pain spasms through the hand they broke. I hide my shaking fist.

Long ramps extend from each vessel, creating pathways to the island's rocky shores. Skulls move freely up and down the wooden planks. The black waters crash under their feet as they unload a long line of barrels and crates.

"Can you bring us in closer?" I whisper.

A softer teal light encompasses Nâo's hands as she guides us toward the shores. We stay far enough away to avoid being spotted, sailing around the island's borders.

Different bonfires line the coast. Skulls gather around the dancing flames. They toast to one another with glass bottles, their mead flowing like water. Other Skulls pass out in shoddy tents, facedown in the sand.

"What do we do?" Nâo looks at me. I study the island, reaching for a plan. One of the Skulls' ships prepares to depart the trading port. Its crimson sails billow, sporting the ornate seals that mark the Tribes of Baldeírik.

"Can you show me what ships will pass through the bay?" I ask Dakarai.

The elder of the Seers opens his palms.

"*Orúnmila, bá mi sòrò. Orúnmila, bá mi sòrò*—" As Dakarai chants, silver light surrounds his hands. It swirls in a vibrant spiral until the trading port before us appears between his palms.

We watch as time accelerates through Dakarai's magic. The sun rises and falls in the sky. Different ships sail in and out of the trading ports, revealing the Skulls' sailing patterns.

The full moon disappears into blackness. Countless chests and containers move from the ships to the sands. I worry I won't find what I'm looking for when I see it, a ship mightier than all the rest.

I found you.

I bend down, getting as close to Dakarai's magic as I can. Triple the size of any of the other Skulls' ships, King Baldyr's vessel moves like a fortress in the sea. Its golden sails flutter in the wind. Countless multicolored shields decorate the ship's sides, glistening over the crashing waves like scales.

"What does this mean?" Nâo asks. I study the night sky—the full moon hangs above.

"We know when King Baldyr's coming," I answer. "That means we have a chance to annihilate him."

"But are we ready?" Dakarai asks. I look back to the New Gaīan emissaries; one sketches a portrait of the island and the Skulls.

"We aren't," I answer. "But they are."

CHAPTER FORTY-THREE

AMARI

"ARE YOU SURE ABOUT THIS?"

Mae'e ignores my question as she dresses me in the pale ivy kaftan of one of her Green Maidens. She drapes a beaded veil over my face, hiding me in plain sight.

"You have to see it," she insists. "And there is no better time than this. The Maidens have just tended to her roots. Trust me, this will work."

I follow close behind as Mae'e leads us from her temples, passing under the endless archways. When we make it to the base, thunder booms above. I look up to the dark clouds.

Zélie and Yéva continue to train. They fight despite the way the mountain shakes. Though we both reside in Mae'e's temples, I haven't seen her for weeks.

I don't even know if she sleeps.

It feels foolish to sneak around with the danger that awaits, but I don't have the heart to take away Mae'e's smile. As the weeks continue, I feel the weight of the coming fight. It hangs over her shoulders, heavy as the night.

Though Emperor Jörah ordered Zélie and me to remain in Mae'e's temples, no one stops me as we board a floating lily pad. Mae'e presses her hand to its bottom, and the water steams underneath. Smoke rises into the air as we sail from the mountain's base.

My pulse quickens as we make our way back to New Gaīa's city center. The civilization glitters in the morning light. When we join the central network of canals, villagers bow as Mae'e floats past.

"I told you," Mae'e whispers. "All you need to do is sit still."

I press my hands together and straighten my spine the way I've seen the Green Maidens do before. We move through the floating vines, making our way to the inner ring. Lively music fills the air as we sail past the tail end of the marketplace. I watch as a quartet plays agogô bells and double-headed bass drums. People clap in rhythm with the tune, joining along in song.

The scents of cinnamon and black pepper envelop me. We sail past food stalls filled with ripe mangoes and fresh papayas. Jars of açai berries sit alongside tropical caju fruits. My mouth waters at the plates of rice and black bean stew.

Past the market, women walk with baskets full of wildflowers. I watch as they dump them into a vibrant pile. Perfume makers sit in circles as they work, pressing individual petals into their brightly painted bottles.

The imperial palace looms behind us as we sail beyond the marketplace, reaching the temples and bustling bathhouses. I don't want the trip to end.

Then we arrive at the Mother Root.

"Skies . . . ," I breathe. Our lily pad comes to a stop before a tree unlike any I've ever seen. Several meters wide, thick roots pass over one another by the hundreds. They form the body of a woman with her arms stretched wide and her head pointed to the sky.

Roots create a vast dome around her. As I follow their path, the connection becomes clear—every single vine in the city originates from here.

Candles spread throughout the sacred space. New Gaīans lay woven wreaths at the Mother Root's feet. At Mae'e's presence, her people clear the area, allowing the future hierophant to commune with the Mother Root in private.

I look up at the woven sculpture, thinking of all Mae'e's shared. Mae'e stands before the woman of vines. Candles flicker against her brown skin as she stares into the Mother Root's eyes.

"She was born of the mountain." Mae'e speaks softly. "The only time it ever erupted. A daughter of the earth, she broke free of the lava. Molten rock dripped from her blackened form. But she was born with the Sight." Mae'e glances at me, and her diamond irises flash. "She could see what our civilization would be. She knew it was up to her to bring it to fruition."

"How did she do it?" I ask.

Mae'e turns away from the sculpture and scoops up a handful of dirt. She takes a deep breath and then exhales. Green light shines behind her fluttering lids as more light fills the space between the soil.

Slowly, a fresh bud rises, unfurling until it becomes a full vine. The vine sways back and forth. I smile as it taps me on the shoulder.

"It's called the 'breath of life,'" Mae'e explains. "Mama Gaīa grew every vine with love. She transformed lava fields into fertile soil. She carved out her own bones, imbuing them with the life needed to grow our first warriors."

"The Lâminas?" I ask, and Mae'e nods.

"Our entire civilization. It all started with her."

Mae'e removes a necklace with a glittering emerald at its center. She uses her new vine to clasp it around the Mother Root's neck. I give her space as she gets on her knees, lips quick in a quiet prayer.

"What of your magic?" Mae'e asks when she's done. But at the mention of my magic, I freeze. The mistakes of my past play before my eyes, strangling me like one of the New Gaīan's vines.

I see the moment I destroyed Ramaya to become the elder of the Connectors; the way I used my magic to paralyze Tzain when he tried to save his own sister from the attack I ordered on Ibadan. There's still so much I have to make up for.

I don't know how to atone for all of my mistakes.

"Did I say something wrong?" Mae'e asks.

"No." I shake my head. "It's just . . . my magic causes pain. It doesn't come from such a beautiful place."

"I will be the judge of that." Mae'e guides her vine to nudge me forward.

"Mae'e—"

"You cannot scare me off," she insists. "Please, I wish to see!"

I start to push back, but the thought of Inan comes to mind. I remember the dreamscape that we once shared. The words of the incantation start to tickle my ear.

"There's one thing we can try. . . ." I tread with care. "But I've never attempted to do this with another person."

I sit down on the warm soil and stretch out both my hands. Mae'e's brown lips twist into a smile. She sets down her vine and comes close. The scents of honey and ash wrap around my nose.

My skin shivers as Mae'e puts her palms in mine. She moves to lift my veil.

"It's still too dangerous!" I rush to stop her, but Mae'e swats at my hand.

"It's only us here!"

My face flushes as her fingers brush against my cheeks. She hooks the veil over my ears, turning me to face the Mother Root so no one else can see. I look up at the sacred being, the very heart of New Gaīa.

Power radiates from the Mother Root like heat. I close my eyes, letting the connection wash over me. I hold on to the beauty of her magic as my own breaks free.

Power I haven't called on in moons stirs within me, a tingle traveling through my skin. The familiar surge takes me back, reminding me of the great power I used to wield.

Mae'e gasps as the dark blue cloud engulfs our hands. It chills like ice as it travels up our arms. When it reaches our heads, everything disappears. Mae'e squeezes me tight as the entire civilization of New Gaïa fades.

I LOOK DOWN AT my own hands—there are no scars, no sign of the blood I've spilled. A gentle breeze blows through my white streak. I inhale the cinnamon-scented air, and it's like I can truly breathe.

Fields of blue flowers surround us. I smile at the familiar sea. I run my fingers through the velvety petals, reminding myself of when my magic ran free.

"My goodness!" Mae'e exclaims. Her diamond gaze shines bright. Her colorful silks have been replaced with soft whites. She skips through the vast field.

Her melodic laughter echoes through the air. She runs back for me, hooking her arm in mine. We spin around and around until we fall into the soft bed.

"This is your gift?" Mae'e asks. Her cheeks flush as she extends her hands. Thick clouds envelop us like mountains. We lie in the flowers, suspended in a haze. Time stretches beyond the horizon. It's like I stay with her for days.

"A part of it," I explain. "There's a chance we can do more." I bite my lip, remembering the times Inan's told me how Zélie affected his dreamscape. When Zélie entered, she was able to build forests and waterfalls. Could Mae'e and I have the same?

"Close your eyes," I instruct the future hierophant. "Imagine what you most want to see."

"Anything?" Mae'e questions, and I nod.

"Anything at all."

Mae'e shuts her eyes and breathes deep. The breeze shifts, parting the clouds. The field of blue flowers disappears. Everything clears to reveal the full night sky.

I marvel at the arrangement of stars that surrounds us, each glittering with light. Dense clusters radiate a powerful glow. Shooting comets pass far below.

Mae'e's diamond gaze sparkles as she takes in the impossible. Clouds of deep purple gas spread far and wide. A galaxy spirals through the deep expanse. It pulls everything into its orbit, disappearing in a swirling black hole.

The stars spin around us, faster and faster, gathering speed. Mae'e reaches for my hand as the night sky begins to bleed.

"*UGH!*" MAE'E GASPS. She squeezes my hands. She whips around as we find ourselves sitting below the Mother Root, exactly where we were before we took off.

"That was incredible!" Mae'e struggles to keep her voice down. "That was the most beautiful thing I've ever seen! I've always dreamed of sailing with the stars, but I never imagined it could be a real thing!"

All of a sudden, Mae'e releases my hands. My eyes widen as she grabs my cheeks. The way she stares at me, all thought scrambles in my head.

I don't know what to think.

"Thank you," she whispers. My heart thrums in my chest.

"You're welcome." I choke out the words.

Mae'e starts to lean in—

"Mae'e!"

We turn to see the real Green Maidens gathered at the sanctuary's dock. Mae'e rises as they speak quickly, the New Gaīan passing too fast for me to follow.

When they're done, Mae'e returns to me. My heart still flutters like a hummingbird trying to escape its cage.

"What is it?" I ask.

"It's your brother." Mae'e's brows rise. "He's here!"

CHAPTER FORTY-FOUR

INAN

GROWING UP IN THE royal palace, Father's war room was a constant. He kept me right by his side. I made my way through every map in his study until I memorized the location of every single city, every fortress, every port, and every grain field.

I studied my kingdom like the lines on my hand. There were moons I slept under his desk more than I lay in my own bed. I thought if I could feel its vastness in my core, I could never fail.

That knowledge of Orïsha was all it took to prevail.

In all those nights, we never spoke of King Baldyr and the Tribes of Baldeírik. There were no maps of the hidden city of vines. All those years spent preparing, yet I don't think Father ever could've envisioned this.

Despite Amari's letter, my head still spins at the vastness of New Gaïa. Sitting in Emperor Jörah's throne room brings me to my knees. Woven tapestries surround us, showing the stories of Mama Gaïa and the birth of their great nation.

The ceiling holds a golden crypt of emperors past. A towering statue of Emperor Jörah holding up the sun rises in the back of the room. Light filters through the stained glass windows. Incense smoke fills the air with the sweet scents of jasmine and mandarin.

Emissaries and vassals mill around Jörah's obsidian glass throne, accented with thick emeralds and golden carvings of their black tigenaires. The tattooed warriors they call the Lâminas stand guard. Outside the palace, the power of the city's vineweavers stuns.

The marks of the New Gaïan's gifts are everywhere. I marvel at all the strength at their command. Their entire civilization stands together, already prepared to defend themselves against the Skulls.

The thought of what I must protect back home fortifies me. Orïsha has just begun to thrive again. I have to get Emperor Jörah on my side.

I need him to give my nation a fighting chance.

"Inan!" Amari's voice rings out. She runs, a blur through the gold grandeur. She hooks her arms around my neck with so much force we almost fall to the floor.

"I don't believe it." Tears of joy rise to my sister's eyes. "I thought—I was sure—" She hiccups and I smile.

"You didn't even cry this much when I left."

"You don't understand." Amari shakes her head. She wipes her eyes on her green-colored kaftan and takes a deep breath. "You made it here. That means we can really go home."

"We're going home." I squeeze her arm. "We just need to break a few Skulls."

I turn to meet Tzain's imposing frame. I'm taken aback at the way he's grown. He's always been large, but his muscles carry new definition and tone. His arms are covered in scars.

"You're back," he says.

"How have you fared?" I ask.

His dark gaze scans the throne room, landing on the Lâminas.

"I never thought I'd say it, but I'm glad you're here."

Tzain and Amari sit as I explain everything that occurred after we set sail. The speedy journey home. The cease-fire in the war. The fact that Mother lives.

"She's on our side?" Amari's brows crease. "Even after all that's passed?"

"Everyone is unified." I nod. "They grow stronger every day. If the Skulls attack, we'll be ready. But we have a chance to strike first—"

All at once, everyone rises to their feet. I turn toward the door. Their future hierophant enters the room: the stunning girl they call Mae'e.

Tall and lean, her vibrant yellow silks swish around her as she walks. A line of girls in green follow in attendance. Their dress matches Amari's.

But when Zélie glides in, I go blind. Dressed in shimmering emerald silks, she's luminescent. The sight of her brings the room to a stop. The silks drape over her head, creating a soft veil around her dark skin.

"Inan . . ." The way she speaks my name makes my heart stop. I'm surprised when she actually smiles. Zélie starts toward us, but Mae'e redirects her path, motioning for the seat on the emperor's right. When Mae'e takes the seat on his left, the assembly begins.

Emperor Jörah looks at me for the first time all day. I stiffen under his pale green gaze. He speaks to me in their tongue.

"What have you come to share?" Mae'e translates.

I rise from my seat and bow my head in respect. "Our people have located King Baldyr."

The life leaves Zélie's eyes. It's like a pit opens up inside. Her fingers drift to the medallion as she waits for me to continue.

"They've occupied a chain of islands due south of their borders. We expect him to dock tomorrow night."

I roll out the large map across the floor. It unfurls to show the island nation of New Gaīa, the vast lands of Orïsha, and the borders of Baldeírik. I point to the island chain, nearly in the center of our nations' shared waters.

"They use it as a shipping port," I explain. "A place for the Skulls to complete inventory for King Baldyr."

Emperor Jörah is steady as Mae'e translates. He takes in every word like a sponge. I talk for nearly a half hour before he finally replies.

"The king will be there tomorrow night?" Mae'e translates his first question.

"Our Seers have checked. His ship docks after midnight."

I prepare myself to ask for what I need. The real reason I traveled all this way. The speed of their vessels. The power of their vineweavers. The might of the Lâminas.

"We are both equipped to defend our lands. We know King Baldyr seeks to harvest Zélie's and Mae'e's power on the Blood Moon. But now we have a chance to attack before King Baldyr has a chance to invade."

My gaze drifts from Emperor Jörah to Zélie as Mae'e translates.

This is our one hope.

The only way to keep her safe.

"Raise an army, Emperor Jörah," I continue. "A brutal force King Baldyr can't withstand. With an army, we protect all of your people and both of our lands."

"An entire army?" Mae'e translates the emperor's words. "Just to eliminate one king?"

"The king's forces are great." I nod. "And we still don't know the extent of the power he's hunting, or the power he now wields. If we want to take them out for good, then an army is what we need."

Moments pass as Emperor Jörah deliberates with his soldiers. I'm forced to wait in silence. Zélie remains by the emperor's side. From the way her gaze moves between each speaker, I can tell she understands their tongue.

When the bright day falls to dusk, Emperor Jörah finally stands. My gut clenches as I wait for his response.

"I have made a decision," Mae'e translates. "We will take our best and return with King Baldyr's head."

"Wait." I try to step forward, but the Lâminas force me back. "A small tactical team won't work. If we're going to attack, it has to be a battle they can't possibly withstand!"

Emperor Jörah frowns. Behind Mae'e, Jörah shakes his head.

"My people have not survived for millennia by showing our hand. We will take a small team. All we need is her."

When Jörah's finger points to Zélie, the entire hall stills. Zélie's silver eyes widen. She rises from her knees.

"Why me?" she asks.

"It cannot be helped." Mae'e looks among the four of us. "She is the only one who has seen his face. She is the only one Emperor Jörah trusts to identify the king——"

"You're not taking my sister." Tzain reaches for his axe. In a second, the Lâminas surround us.

"No!" Zélie throws herself from the brick dais. She forces herself between her brother and Emperor Jörah's greatest warriors.

"I'll go." Her eyes flutter with the reality of what she has just said. "Yéva prepared me for this. I'm ready to face him again."

CHAPTER FORTY-FIVE

TZAIN

"We went from one cage to another."

I pace the waiting room they've placed us in, unable to sit still. The walls of the holding chamber drip with emeralds and pearls. Golden lanterns swing above our heads.

Vines travel through the open windows, twisting in crisscrossed patterns across the floor. I fight the part of me that wants to rip through them all.

"Maybe it will work?" Amari looks between me and her brother. "He said they're taking their best—"

"We need more than their best." Inan rises from his chair. I can almost hear the gears ticking in his head. "If we can't get him to send an army, we should at least be there. Emperor Jörah doesn't know what he's up against."

As Inan speaks, I can't stop thinking of my sister. I can't erase the empty look in her eyes as they took her away. There was so much we didn't get to say.

It was like they were leading my sister to her grave.

"We need a boat," I speak up. "One strong enough to take us there."

"They'll never grant us one," Amari replies.

"Then we steal," I say.

"The New Gaīans don't trust us as it is!" Amari pushes back. "If we disobey them now, we could lose the little favor we have. They could kick us out of their lands!"

"We have one chance." Inan walks over to us. "*One* chance to end this on our terms. If we don't stop them now . . ." His voice trails off and he gazes at the open sky. Right now, the waxing crescent hangs above. We still don't know when the Blood Moon will come. If it rises—

No. I shake my head. I can't allow myself to think like that.

I don't care what it takes.

I won't let Zélie fall into King Baldyr's hands.

"The Lâminas have boats." I think back to the square armories that sit behind the soldiers' barracks. "There are always guards outside the gates, but with your magic, we might be able to get in."

"You want to attack the Lâminas?" Amari's brows rise. "You won't get out alive!"

"They have my sister!" I exclaim. "What am I supposed to do?"

"Tzain, even if we could get a boat, what does it matter if we're not—" Amari struggles. "If we're not—"

"Not what?" For the first time since the massacre at Ibadan, I really take Amari in and I'm struck by the way she blends in. Since landing in New Gaīa, she's completely transformed. With her braided hair and green silks, she looks just like one of Mae'e's maidens.

Amari drops her gaze to the floor. Her lip quivers as her truth breaks free.

"What if we're not strong enough to help?"

Amari voices the question I have refused to face. The insult Köa hurtles at me every time he throws me onto the ground. I don't have a choice.

If I can't be strong enough, my little sister dies.

"The thought of facing the Skulls . . ." Amari puts a hand on her throat, and I squeeze my eyes shut. My jaw sets with the memories of the long, lonely nights before we staged our attack.

"I felt like we were trapped in those cages forever," Amari exhales. "It felt like it would never end. We barely escaped with our lives. What do we have to add to Emperor Jörah's best?"

"Don't let this place make you think you're weak."

Amari looks up at me. Her amber eyes shine. Despite how hard I want to hold her at bay, I can't fight the way she still makes me feel. The love I've buried inside.

"You're still a fighter, Amari. You're still her *friend*. Zélie needs you." I look to Inan. "She needs us all."

Amari lays her hand on my chest, and my shoulders soften at her touch. It feels right to be with her again. If not in love, a true friend.

"Alright." Amari tilts her head. She chews on her lower lip with the start of an idea. "Forget the Lâminas. Attacking them isn't the way."

Amari crosses the gilded room and places her hand on the brass doors. With a heavy push, they slide open.

"Come on." Amari pulls down her veil. "As of now, we're guests. Not prisoners."

DESPITE OUR FREEDOM, EVERY step we take through the imperial palace feels like walking on glass. Everywhere we go, attendants stare. I don't know if I've ever felt so out of place.

"Eyes ahead," Amari coaches me under her breath. She keeps her chin lifted and shoulders raised, confidence woven through her regal gait.

I watch in awe as she greets attendants in their native tongue. She even moves like the New Gaïans, swaying like she's spent her entire life under the safety of the city's vines. She's never looked more at peace. I start to wonder if she'll ever leave.

"This way."

We follow Orïsha's former princess through thick stone pillars, past crystal pools and servants' quarters. We walk across an entire field filled with grazing elephantaires. We travel through banquet halls set with ceramic bowls of rice and seafood stew.

When we clear the back gardens, Amari points to a boathouse on the canal waters. Sleek vessels woven from vines sit tied to the dock, ready to embark.

"They call them videiras," Amari explains. "They take over half a year to create. The vines are pulled from the hierophant's hanging gardens. They're supposed to fly across the waters."

"How do we steer them?" I ask.

"You can't." We freeze at the sound of our tongue colored with the melody of the New Gaïan accent. "They can only be steered by vineweavers."

Mae'e appears behind us, long arms crossed. Amari's face falls. My muscles tense as Mae'e stares at the three of us.

"Jörah could have your heads," she hisses. "Or worse!" She grabs Amari's wrist. "You know how my people fear you! You could have been killed!"

"Mae'e, please." Amari reaches for Mae'e's hands. "I have seen the Skulls with my own eyes. If Jörah won't send an army, then we need to be there to protect Zélie."

"Help us," Inan joins in. "If not for Zélie, then for your people. For yourself. A small force can't take on the Skulls alone. We need every fighter we can get."

Mae'e looks over her shoulders. A group of patrolling vineweavers nears. She twists the bangles on her wrist as she thinks of what to do.

"Please," I beg. "Don't send my sister out there on her own."

Mae'e exhales a deep breath. The vines start to slither around Mae'e as she boards.

"Quick." She looks back at the approaching vineweavers. "Get on!"

CHAPTER FORTY-SIX

ZÉLIE

SEA AIR WHIPS THROUGH my white braids. The crescent moon glows above. We fly through choppy waters, riding one of the New Gaïans' videiras.

Two vineweavers work the shifting vessel we sail across the sea. One weaves the dark vines into sails of different sizes, while another works to shape the craft we ride. Her brows knit in concentration as she plays the vines like the keys of a balafon. One moment, the videira's hull expands to face a mighty wave. The next, it narrows, allowing us to pick up speed. I press my hand to the medallion as we race across the seas.

This is it. I ready myself for what it will take to end this. The secrets Yéva shared with me on the mountaintop return, rumbling inside me like the stone we stood on.

I see the destruction of Orïsha. I count the skeletons of all my obliterated people. King Baldyr will be there tonight.

This might be the only chance I have to end our war.

You must fight. Yéva's ancient voice rings in my ears. *You must take the power he seeks to harvest from your soul and use it yourself!*

I look to the bow of the ship, where Jörah stands with Köa and five other Lâminas. The emperor's wide arms are crossed over his chest. Jörah promised me he would bring his best.

Each warrior is built like an ox. They wait, unfazed by the mission they sail into. They follow their emperor with no hesitation. Their conviction makes me want to believe there is nothing to fear.

But the veins of the medallion buzz in my chest. Yéva didn't mince her words. I can't rely on the others.

King Baldyr's defeat is up to me.

I close my eyes and try to summon the sound of thunder between my ears. Only silence answers my call. I attempt to draw forth the golden lightning that broke free in the town circle, but nothing comes out.

Though I've practiced, I've yet to summon my power without Yéva's touch. A wave of panic rises inside.

If I could just use an incantation . . .

I look up at the crescent moon. There's nothing I wouldn't give to feel my old magic again. All of this would be so much different if I had the power of my animations, the ability to raise spirits of the dead.

When my magic first returned, animations were the Reaper incantation I mastered. The spirits of the dead always answered my call.

Now I struggle to use any power at all.

"Zélie." Emperor Jörah calls me by name. I turn away from the waters to face him. It's strange to see him out of the imperial palace. Free of his golden mantle, the emperor is stripped of all but his black pants.

Jörah extends me my staff. I wrap my fingers around the crossed blades. The weapon grants me comfort, but I know it won't be enough to take King Baldyr down.

"Do not worry." Jörah seems to read my mind. "You are only here to confirm the identity of their king. You will stay behind me."

I arch my brow. Orïshan floats from his lips with surprising precision. "You've learned our tongue?" I ask.

"Would you let foreigners into your kingdom without understanding their words?"

"My kingdom?" I almost laugh. "I don't think you understand. The boy who delivered the maps—*he* is the closest thing to a king our nation has."

"A king without a crown or an army?" Jörah tilts his head. "I know what I see. You are the one who leads."

I look back out over the waters and think of Orïsha, remembering all the different people who used to mill through the village of Ilorin. For the first time, the fight I must wage is not only about the maji.

I see the tîtáns with their white streaks. The black-haired kosidán I always used to resent. Even the very soldiers who hunted me for years are the people I now must find the strength to defend.

"After tonight, you will be able to return victorious." Jörah stands firm. "Your people will be proud."

I want to believe his words. But the closer we sail to the trading port, the more something gnaws at my core.

"What if it's not enough?" I dare to speak my fears. "What if we should be launching a greater attack?"

"Point out their king." Jörah bends down, allowing me to see the fervor in his pale green gaze. "I assure you—I will bring you back his golden skull."

WHEN WE FINALLY ARRIVE at the chain of islands, my chest turns cold. It's as if the ship we sank in the seas has been resurrected from the dead. A new monster sprouting multiple heads.

Seven vessels sit in the small island's bay. Their crimson banners wave through the night. More Skulls than I've ever seen travel along the decks, unloading their ships.

Warriors just like the ones who tormented us walk the rocky shores. They mill through bonfires and shoddy tents. My skin crawls at the sight of their bronze masks.

Being forced to face the enemy again, I see red. I taste the blood they spilled. My majacite crown prickles against my temple, reminding me of all the ways I suffered on their ship.

Use it. I clutch my staff. Yéva's words rattle within me once more. I reach for the rage Oya granted me on the ship. I remember every one of the maji who didn't get to escape. I think of every single one of my people tossed into the seas. The way the Skulls watched us starve and bleed.

A heavy hand comes down over my own. My fingers crackle at Jörah's touch.

"*Do not fear,*" he speaks in his tongue. "*This ends here.*"

Half the night burns as we wait for King Baldyr to dock. Without his presence, his men run rampant. They treat the island like their own isle of sins. They gamble. They feast. They drink.

The Skulls get so inebriated most can barely stand. I wring the neck of my staff. Just as I start to worry Inan's information was wrong, a loud horn rings out.

HA-WOOOOOO!

The familiar sound twists my stomach into knots. The last time I heard that horn, it was ringing to alert the Skulls of our escape.

I rise to my feet, joining the men at the bow of the ship. The metal in my chest vibrates.

I feel King Baldyr before I see his face.

He sails in on a ship triple the size of the others. Hundreds of colored shields glisten along the ship's sides, making it look like the scales of a magnificent ryder. The ship's many sails flicker in gold, decorated with images of Baldyr's golden mask.

Jörah's lips part at the fortress that floats in the ocean. The mighty vessel moves through the water like one of the Skulls' axes, cutting through the very seas. Its multiple levels burn with the torchlights of an army. A carving of a man made of thunderclouds serves as the ship's figurehead, sculpted out of their crimson bloodmetal.

At the arrival of their king, the Skulls on the beach end their debauchery. Men who were passed out in the sands now stand at attention. Others stumble out from their tents. Everyone rushes to re-don their masks.

When Baldyr's ship docks, a creaking drawbridge falls into the sand.

Every Skull takes a knee as King Baldyr appears.

You.

King Baldyr stands at the head of the drawbridge, bare chested and head raised. His presence is like a whip cracking through the air. He commands power over his men with a simple look.

As he walks, the majacite crown burns through my skin. The scent of mead fills my nostrils. Suddenly, I'm locked back in the Silver Skull's quarters, fighting to get away from him.

"That's him," I say.

"You are sure?" Jörah asks. "Even with the mask?"

I can't explain that I will never be able to forget the shift of Baldyr's gait. The slant of the black runes carved into his fair skin.

"I'm sure." I nod.

King Baldyr makes his way down the ramp. His heavy boots thunder with every step. Blood drips from his large hands. I pray it's not the blood of any captured maji.

Baldyr convenes with a few Skulls on the sands, exchanging words we can't hear. With a torch, he moves into the forest. His torchlight disappears down a dirt trail, heading for a cave on the far side of the island.

Jörah pulls a black mask over his head, and gathers his best men.

I brace myself as he gives the final command.

"Move in."

CHAPTER FORTY-SEVEN

TZAIN

MAE'E'S VIDEIRA HURTLES THROUGH the thrashing seas. I brace myself as we sail. The future hierophant does the work of at least two of her weavers. Her muscles strain as she commands the wild vines.

A ribbon of light cascades across the stars. They glimmer above our heads as we sail under the crescent moon. I stare up at each twinkling dot, fighting to stay calm.

I know Mae'e carries us as fast as she can, but every second that passes fills me with dread. King Baldyr lies ahead.

I have to reach Zélie before he does.

"Are you sure it's this way?" Inan shouts over the roar of the whipping winds.

"Our vines have a signature," Mae'e calls back. "It's like a heartbeat in my ears. The videiras they sailed are near."

I'm coming, I think to Zélie's spirit. I pray she can feel me, even this far away. All the emotions I felt on the Skulls' ship rush forward again. I can't believe how close she is to falling back into their hands.

I grip the hilt of my axe. Holding it now, I can't help but think of how the Lâminas fight. All their strength comes from within, from their sparring prowess to the very weapons they pull from their skin.

I still hate the way the Skull's axe feels in my hand. I know all it will

223

take is my blood for the weapon to reawaken the monster I became on that ship. Yet I don't know what choice I have.

To save my sister, I have to do whatever it takes.

"We're here." Mae'e lets her hands rest. The whipping vines of the videira fall into the sea as we drift before an island chain.

Eight Skull ships float in dark waters. The monster in my heart exhales again. For the first time I see the power of King Baldyr's ship. I think of what it would take to cut straight through him.

Away from the beach, torches march through the dark woods like fire ants. They disappear under the roof of a cave.

"There." I point them out to Mae'e. "Bring us in."

Though sweat plasters Mae'e's robes to her brown skin, she pushes herself forward. With a lift of her slender hands, the vines of the videira twist through the waters, dragging our vessel to the shore.

I jump from the boat, bare feet landing in the cold sand.

"Where are you going?" Inan calls.

I look back to the roof of the cave. "Following a hunch. I think Zélie's there."

"I'm coming with you!" Amari tries to rise, but Inan stops her from leaving the floating boat.

"King Baldyr is close." Inan shakes his head. "We can't afford to leave Mae'e alone."

Though Mae'e's chest heaves from the long journey, the future hiero-phant narrows her diamond gaze.

"*I* brought you here," she starts. "I can protect myself—"

"He's right," Amari interrupts. "We can't risk you getting caught. Besides, you need to rest." Amari raises the back of her palm to Mae'e's forehead. Something unspoken passes between them.

I turn back to the forest as Inan disembarks, attempting to ignore the fracture that travels through my heart.

"Stay off the coast," Inan says. "If all goes well, we'll meet back here."

With that, Inan and I take off. The two of us walk in silence, traversing the deserted beach. Clouds cover the thin rays of moonlight above. Wicked trees reach up to the stars.

As our feet crunch through the sand, I think back—I don't know if the two of us have ever been alone. I always thought if I got him this close, I'd wring my fingers around his neck.

Baba's blood is still on his hands.

From the way Inan glances at me, he seems to feel what's inside. I don't know if it's from his magic or if he can read the hard look in my eyes.

"I made your sister a promise." He breaks our silence. "Back when we were stranded in the Skulls' hold. I swore she'd get back to Orïsha. I want to promise you the same."

I glance at the former king. "You think that makes up for what we've lost?"

"I know I can't make up for my mistakes," Inan sighs. "I can't ever make things right. But fighting the Skulls has brought the people together. The Orïsha you'll return to might be better than the one you left."

Inan extends me his hand, and I hesitate to shake. All those moons as my enemy, only to end up as my ally? But between the Skulls and the Lâminas, I know I don't have a choice.

He's one of the people who will protect Zélie with his life—

"Get down!" Inan hisses. He pushes me into the sand. We wait, perfectly still, as a group of Skulls exits the cave. When they pass, Inan eyes the trail their torchlights walk. It looks like it leads all the way back to the shores where their boats are docked.

We rise back to our feet, but Inan doesn't continue toward the cave.

"Where are you going?" I ask as he follows after the Skulls.

"To stop King Baldyr's ship!"

CHAPTER FORTY-EIGHT

ZÉLIE

THE VINEWEAVERS MOVE LIKE EELS. In mere breaths, they bring our videira to the far tip of the island. New vines extend like threads, anchoring us to the rocky coast.

As I step onto the sands, I do my best to prepare for what lies ahead. The medallion warms in my chest as Yéva's ancient voice rings through my ears.

Feel it, she whispers. *Draw it deep inside. When you face their king, you must release that surge. Harvesting that power is our only hope.*

A tremble rises in my hand. I try to hide it by clenching my fists. The medallion continues to heat as I try to reach for the golden spark.

"It will not come to that." Emperor Jörah speaks in my tongue. I don't know if he can feel what I'm trying to do.

"Yéva said—"

"Trust us." Jörah's thick fingers graze my chin as he pulls a black mask over my head. The Lâminas don their masks as well. "And do not fall behind."

The New Gaïans move like wolves. A silent pack on the hunt. Their strides are long and powerful. I struggle to keep up.

We move under the cover of black trees. Their twisting shadows cloak our approach. We make it a good way through the forest before we meet any interruption.

In the middle of a beaten trail, a trio of Skulls stands guard. They gaze through the trees, talking among themselves. One passes around a bottle of mead. The others are nearly asleep.

I extend the serrated blades of my staff. They haven't seen us yet.

But before I can think of striking, the Lâminas attack.

One warrior pulls throwing knives from beneath his ear. With a sharp flick, he sends them through the Skulls' throats. The other warriors press forward, catching the falling bodies and gently laying them to the ground.

Two more torchlights make their way toward us. Köa pulls a thorn-covered mace from the back of his neck. The moment the Skulls round the corner, Köa swings. With one vicious arc, he smashes through each Skull's head.

I watch, breathless, as the New Gaīans continue their silent onslaught. The next Skull we meet goes for his hammer and tries to activate its full strength. Before he can strike, Jörah snaps his neck.

The Lâminas eliminate every Skull we come across. Their momentum only builds as we near the cave. The seven men work in a steady rhythm, dragging bodies off the forest trail to keep from being discovered.

It's working. . . .

I keep my grip on my staff, though I don't get the chance to attack. After everything Yéva said, I was sure this fight would come down to me. But the Lâminas are blades in the wind. Nothing stands in their path.

Despite myself, I start to believe Jörah and the Lâminas can defeat the Skulls. I picture Köa smashing through King Baldyr's golden mask with his mace. With Baldyr's death, my people will be safe.

I can finally return to my homeland.

We make it to the cave and Köa dispatches the three Skulls on watch. When their bodies are hidden, the emperor holds up his hand. The

Lâminas close in, taking a V-shaped formation with their emperor at the head.

From inside the cave, torchlights flicker against gray rock. King Baldyr's voice echoes from within. I prepare to face the man who hunts my heart.

Jörah's men enter the cave.

Then the slaughter begins.

CHAPTER FORTY-NINE

INAN

THOUGH I SAW KING BALDYR's battleship in Dakarai's vision, seeing it up close fills me with awe. The vessel is like a mountain docked in the crescent-shaped bay. Countless Skulls man the endless rigs.

Watching the Skulls move, I see my way onto the ship. But I can't go on like this. I scan the coast for a disguise.

I have to find a way to blend in.

I tiptoe through the sand, making my way to the outskirts of the forest. Drunken Skulls mill around the coast. A hulking warrior stops meters away, grumbling as he drops his pants.

I lunge forward, driving a blade across his throat before he has a chance to cry for help. The Skull's hazel eyes bulge as blood rains down his bare chest.

He falls headfirst into the sand.

With no time to waste, I drag the warrior's body into the trees. I rip off his mask and fix the human skull over my nose. The cold metal shudders against my skin. The sensation makes me want to vomit. I force myself to keep the bile in.

I steal the Skull's heavy leather coat, and it drowns out my frame. Its tail drags through the sand as I walk with an unsteady gait, making my way out of the trees.

The Skull's scent suffocates me. I try to wipe his blood from my hands. Walking on the open shores, I'm surrounded by the enemy. *Blend in*, I remind myself.

I feign a stumble as I make my way up the drawbridge to King Baldyr's ship. Tremors pass through my body with every step. I can hardly believe it when I make it onto the upper deck. I fight the urge to look over my shoulder at every Skull who passes.

Focus, Inan. As I move, some parts of Baldyr's ship look familiar. I walk down the line of lifeboats strapped to the deck. A pair of Skulls leads foreign ryders from the animal den. They walk chained beasts I've never seen. I gawk at a yellow bird large enough to ride. Another Skull cages a pair of snow-white foxes, each with nine swishing tails.

I do my best to keep to the sides, passing by gleaming cannons until I find a door leading below deck. When I'm sure no one's looking, I slip through the archway, descending into the lower levels of the ship.

Instantly, I'm hit with the stench of death. My jaw sets with every cage I pass. Though the cells are empty, fresh bloods sinks into the wood floors. With every open shackle, I see Baldyr's armies descending onto Orïsha's shores.

But if we can stop him here . . .

I march forward, searching for what I need. If Jörah's men can't defeat Baldyr's forces, I can at least destroy his ship.

I move deeper into the vessel, traveling all the way down to the fourth level. I turn a corner when I smell it—the sulfur scent of their blast oil.

I push open the door to find the precious black oil sitting in barrels. Dozens fill the wooden hold. I walk between the neat lines, stabbing through each drum I find. The sulfur scent stings my nose as the black oil spills across the floor.

That's it. I step back, looking at the foundation of my attack. There's more than enough oil to take down the ship. I just need a way to ignite the fuse.

I slip out of the room and search the halls. My footsteps echo against the old floorboards. I keep my eyes peeled for a torch, but before I can find one, a pair of chattering Skulls nears.

With no other choice, I round the corner. Blood pounds between my ears as I sprint up the steps. The coat and mask are enough to cloak me, but they won't hold up under a Skull's steady gaze.

When I make it back onto the deck, sweat loosens the bronze mask's grip. It threatens to slip from my face. I stiffen as another pair of Skulls passes. One stares at me far too long for comfort.

Get to the forest. I push myself past the minefield of Skulls waiting between me and the drawbridge. From the forest, I can wait for King Baldyr to board. I can find a way to light the fuse. But as I near the drawbridge, my feet come to a stop. I can't bring myself to move as the ship's captain crosses my path.

Another one.

The new Silver Skull walks across the ship, moving to the vessel's upper levels. He carries rolls of parchments in his hand, disappearing into a room with marble walls and a crimson door.

Though the drawbridge is in sight, I can't fight the pull inside. I never made it to the captain's quarters on the ship we escaped. I can only imagine what information the captain of King Baldyr's ship might have.

I keep my head down as I walk up the stairs. When I reach the top level, I busy myself with crates that line the deck. It takes a few moments for the Silver Skull to emerge. When he leaves the room, I move forward, catching the handle before the door locks.

The captain's room is like a war library. Scrolls line every wall. I mill around the room, surrounded by more maps than I can count.

Some maps show the six different territories of their tribal kingdom.

Others show their trade routes. One scroll illustrates their vast naval fleets. I snatch it from the desk, rolling it up and sticking it into the waistband of my pants.

But when I find their largest map, my fingers fall numb. Hanging on the far wall, the map holds nations of our world that I've never seen. The Isles of Samæra. The Straits of Palantar. The joined villages of a land called Sutōrī. Dark red lines mark the Skulls' plans of conquest. I drift to the wall, following their path with my hand.

Horror dawns as I see the nations circled in red. The places King Baldyr's onslaught will begin after the Blood Moon.

The island of New Gaīa.

And the fallen kingdom of Orïsha.

CHAPTER FIFTY

ZÉLIE

THE MOMENT THE LÂMINAS enter the cave, the shouts of battle ring.

A line of blood spills from the mouth of the den.

My heart rattles against the medallion as I look in.

Though caught off guard, the Skulls are quick to react. As their weapons glow red, their muscles swell. Their broad frames expand. Runes carve down the Skulls' chests as their bodies transform. The ground shakes as the bronze Skulls charge.

The Lâminas move with a speed the Skulls can't pin down. One Lâmina dodges as a Skull swings his hammer. The weapon blasts through the cave wall. Stone and debris fly as the Lâmina pivots, driving his white blade through the Skull's heart.

Another Skull charges Köa with his axe. Köa pulls an ivory barong from the side of his abdomen. He cuts straight through a Skull's core before whipping around to stab another. Body by body, he rips through the Skulls. The leader of the Lâminas summons a vicious rage, but even he doesn't compare to the ferocity Jörah wields.

Jörah moves like a mountain. He overpowers every Skull in his path. Green light sparks from the emperor's fingers as he draws out a shark-tooth blade the size of his head. He grabs the weapon's golden handle. A Skull raises his axe to attack and swings.

Before he can strike, Jörah guts him like a pig.

We're winning. . . .

Warm blood spills under my feet as I dare to walk into the cave. The way the Lâminas move, I don't see what can stop them. But Yéva's warning still rings through my ears.

"Protect the king!" a Skull shouts in their tongue. That's when I finally see him. King Baldyr sits on a boulder at the back of the cave, hands cupped over the knob of his battle-axe. Though his men are being slaughtered before him, King Baldyr doesn't react.

Being this close to him again, my blood runs cold. My hands shake beyond my control. My chest aches with the memory of the medallion he shoved into my skin. The very metal changing me from within.

For the first time since arriving to New Gaïa, the sound of thunder pulses through my ears. The veins of the medallion begin to heat. The winds whip around me, blowing my mask away.

At the sight of me, King Baldyr's eyes widen. He rises in the back of the cave.

"Merle . . ." He mutters the words, yet his voice shivers through my spine. Despite his golden mask, I feel his smile. A hunger enters his hazel gaze.

"You have returned!" Baldyr roars.

In front of me, Jörah dispatches the final Skull. The Lâminas regroup around their emperor, resuming the V formation they held before. They move forward as one unit, preparing to take King Baldyr's golden skull.

Jörah rips off his mask. With a curse, the emperor bares his teeth. He raises his shark-tooth blade—

"Blóðseiðr," King Baldyr commands.

Paralysis strikes me the moment King Baldyr utters the words. A chill like ice passes up my legs. It runs down my arms. The staff drops from my hand, echoing as it rolls across the stone floor.

What's happening?

The golden medallion sears my skin. I grit my teeth against the burning flesh. Red light twists from my skin like smoke. A familiar power surges to my fingertips.

My hands rise beyond my control. My feet lift from the stone as my neck falls back. Magic I haven't felt since I was in Orïsha shakes through my bones.

Crimson light spills from my fingertips, reanimating the fallen Skulls.

My magic.

He's using it.

He's in control.

"Jörah, run!" I scream. I can't fight the power that breaks free.

Jörah and the Lâminas gather together. They stand back-to-back as the slain Skulls rise around them, dragging their bodies from the floor. Necks reset. Bones bend. Red light leaks from behind their bronze masks.

"*Run!*" I shriek.

The risen Skulls attack at once. The move like no human can. They lunge like rabid ryders. The Lâminas struggle to defend.

One Lâmina cries out as a Skull rips out his heart.

Another Lâmina takes a curved blade to the throat.

The risen Skulls rain down hell. They tear through Jörah's best with no regard.

No! I try to resist, but my magic tears from my skin in a never-ending flood.

King Baldyr moves from the back of the cave. He marches through the chaos, completely unharmed.

"Zélie!" Jörah shouts my name.

But there's nothing the emperor can do when Baldyr takes me by the arm and drags me away.

CHAPTER FIFTY-ONE

TZAIN

SHOUTS ECHO AS I charge through the forest. All at once, the air stills. Something dark passes over the barren soil.

The black trees begin to twist.

All around me, slain Skulls rise. Their bones crack as they reset. They look at me with lopsided heads. One Skull unhooks his axe, raising it to strike.

Nothing stops me as I dive into the battle. I roll under the first Skull's blade. I slice my axe through his neck before he has a chance to turn around. His head rolls across the ground.

Two more risen Skulls charge at me from behind. With a roar, I cut through both of them at once. Their glowing hammers fall from their hands. Their blood coats the twisting trees.

As the Skulls swarm, I feel all the time spent sparring with Köa and the Lâminas in their training squares. The scars along my arms ripple with newfound strength. My body moves with deadly precision.

But memories of the ship reawaken as I fight through the risen Skulls. They crawl out of me from the void. I see every severed limb.

I feel the blood that fell like rain.

I don't want to draw on the enemy's power again. I'm not ready to lose control. But more Skulls emerge from the forest. Too many for me to fight alone.

"*No!*"

I hear my sister's scream. I whip my head toward the cave.

"Zélie?" I call. My heart lurches as her screams grow. I look to the axe, and I don't see another way. I slice my hand along the blade and grab on to the hilt.

Blóðseiðr.

A shiver runs through me as the foreign words ring between my ears. The hilt of the axe heats, feeding on my blood. A new power surges from within. A red glow surrounds my axe as it comes back to life.

The monster I became on the ship rears its ugly head again.

"*Hargh!*" I barrel forward. I open my heart to wrath. I feel the axe's power like a fire in my blood. I cut through every risen Skull in my path.

The strength of my swing throws their colossal bodies into the trees. Their bronze masks fly as they fall. With the awakened axe, I'm unstoppable.

Nothing can cut me down.

But as I fly down the forest trail, my vision starts to blur. I struggle to keep my mind clear. The frenzy I can't control builds. The axe's bloodlust overpowers my will.

When I make it into the cave, Zélie is nowhere to be found. Köa, Jörah, and a masked Lâmina fight with all they have. More than two dozen risen Skulls wreak havoc. They move like rabid beasts, almost leaping across the cave.

Jörah fights in the back. Blood leaks from the wounded emperor's teeth as he wields his shark-tooth blade.

Ahead of him, Köa swipes his ivory barong across a risen Skull's throat. He pivots to attack another, but the risen Skull sends an axe through the side of his thigh. Köa bares his teeth as he crashes to the ground. The masked Lâmina rushes to Köa's defense.

"*Demônio!*" the masked Lâmina calls. He raises his ivory club. But when he goes to attack, he takes a hammer to the head. Crimson flies as it obliterates his skull.

Though everything in me wants to run after Zélie, I rush into the fight, axe raised. One risen Skull jumps at me and I swing, catching the abomination in midair. I pin him down to the ground before chopping off his head.

Another risen Skull swings at me with his hammer. I meet the weapon straight on. With a powerful arc, I slice through the risen Skull's arms before cutting through his gut.

As I take down every Skull, foreign chants fill my head. My vision blurs once more. I blink, and I see red.

I lose myself in the frenzy. I can't tell friend from foe.

When the final Skull falls, I lose all control.

"*Hah!*" I swing at Köa with the power of twelve men. The leader of the Lâminas throws himself across the ground. A fracture splits through the hard rock as my blade collides with the stone.

"*Parada!*" Köa shouts. "No more!"

My hands shake, but I can't stop. The axe swings beyond my command. Köa barely has a chance to dive before my axe cuts through the wall.

Emperor Jörah runs at me. With a cry, our weapons clash. The shark-tooth blade falls from his hands as he flies into the back of the cave. The emperor falls to a crumpled heap, hand wrapped around his ribs.

Köa drags his wounded body across the cave. He positions himself between me and the emperor, and raises his ivory blade. Though something inside me screams to stop, my feet charge at both of them.

The axe compels me forward. Its crimson metal *screams* for more blood. More death. More carnage. Its red glow expands as I raise it over my head—

"Tzain, no!" Amari's shout rings at my back.

Blue light flies from her hand, freezing me in place. Every single muscle stiffens at once. A sharp pain racks my brain.

With a lurch, I stumble to the ground. The axe falls to the ground as my hands fly to my temples. The red light leaves my eyes. My vision focuses again.

Horror dawns as I take in the scene. Countless bodies surround me. Across the cave, Köa stares, his green gaze wide. Jörah's hand is still wrapped around his gut. He struggles to help Köa up.

"We have to go!" Amari comes to my side. Her magic releases, and sensation returns. She helps me as I stumble to my feet. Köa's nostrils flare when I strap the axe to my back.

Guilt weighs on me like an anchor as the four of us flee the cave.

CHAPTER FIFTY-TWO

ZÉLIE

"Let go of me!" I scream.

King Baldyr drags me down the coast. Skulls rise from their fires as I pass. They stare at me like I'm a myth come to life.

The magic King Baldyr commands twists inside me. It's like knives running through my blood. I grieve the gift of my people, tainted by Baldyr's wretched bloodmetal.

"*I knew I would see you again*," Baldyr mutters in his tongue. His breath stinks of blood. "*It does not matter where you run. With that medallion, you are destined to end up back in my arms.*"

The very medallion he speaks of vibrates in my chest. It's like it senses its owner's presence. Storm clouds start to gather above. Sparks of lightning flash through the clouds. Baldyr looks up at the sight. A dangerous zeal fills his hazel gaze.

Fight, Zélie.

I will myself to kick. To writhe, to thrash, to punch. With no other weapon, I drive my elbow into the back of his neck. I claw at his golden mask.

Baldyr releases my arm, and I attempt to run, but he picks me up instead. I struggle as he throws me over his shoulder, undeterred from my attacks.

"You escaped me once, *Merle*," he speaks in Orïshan. "You will not escape again."

His every word consumes me. His insistence that I belong to him. All around us the Skulls move. They race aboard their ships. I won't be headed to the capital city of Iarlaith with Baldyr alone.

I'll be surrounded by his men.

Feel it.

Yéva's words return to me in the chaos. I'm brought back to our training on the summit of Mount Gaīa. When I close my eyes, the volcanic stone warms my bare feet. The circle of vines closes around me.

Yéva knew it would come to this. She knew no one else would be able to save me no matter what they did. Baldyr's used my magic against my allies.

I have to use his own magic against him.

Feel it!

With my Reaper magic twisting inside me, I sense a pathway I couldn't summon before. The medallion pulses in my chest as I call for the surge. The rumble deep in my core.

Use it, Zélie!

Thunder booms above. It echoes through my ears. A hard rain begins to fall. I grit my teeth as a sharp heat courses through my rib cage before traveling up my neck.

King Baldyr stops his ascent in the middle of the drawbridge. His eyes widen as he realizes what's to come.

"*No!*" Baldyr roars.

With a final push, the golden lightning breaks free. It crackles from my throat in brilliant bolts. King Baldyr shouts, blown back by the blast.

I fall to the ground as my lightning shoots through the vessel like a spear. The smell of sulfur leaks through the air. My lightning ignites a flame below deck. In a rush, the blaze expands.

Then the whole world explodes.

CHAPTER FIFTY-THREE

INAN

THE MOMENT ZÉLIE'S LIGHTNING HITS the lower deck, the trap I laid ignites. A brilliant blaze catches the ship. The bottom of King Baldyr's vessel is blown apart.

Bodies fly in the chaos. Black smoke fills the air. The floor beneath me careens. The bronze mask falls from my face as I fly to the edge of the ship.

"*Þjófr!*" The Silver Skull points at me. He eyes the maps in my waistband. He tries to lunge at me, but the panels snap beneath his feet. He falls to the bottom of the ship, tumbling into the blaze.

"Zélie!" I shout over the railing. She lies unconscious, facedown in the shallows. Algae tangles through her white braids. A fluttering light pulses through the water around her.

With a running start, I leap from the ship. King Baldyr's ship collapses as I fly. Air rushes past me in my fall. My body crashes into the thrashing seas.

The Skull's leather coat drags me under the current. I push the garment away to break free. I surface and inhale a deep breath, before diving back under to swim.

Come on. I will my arms to arc faster. My legs to kick harder. I swim past struggling Skulls and burning debris, pushing to get back to Zélie.

When I reach her, I scoop her into my arms. Her head lolls as she slides in and out of consciousness. The medallion flickers in her chest. Golden lightning sparks at her fingertips.

Shouts build behind us as I reach the shores. Skulls start to disembark from their ship to run to their injured king. He lies half-conscious on the fractured drawbridge. Flames engulf his left arm, searing through his skin.

Others chase us to the forest. I hold Zélie tight as we run through the twisting trees. Dismembered bodies litter the sandy trail. The path to the southern tip of the island looms in the distance.

I push myself to go faster, but the Skulls still close the space between us. One lunges at me, and I fall to the ground. Zélie's body skitters across the sand. The vicious warrior raises a poleaxe above my head.

Then I hear a scream.

"*Não!*" Mae'e runs in from the coast, arms outstretched. Thick vines twist from the sand, strangling the Skull before he can strike.

On the opposite end of the forest, Amari races forward. My sister extends her palms. My lips part as the blue light of her Connector magic rages again.

"Ha!" Amari bares her teeth and her magic shoots free. Turquoise clouds hit the band of Skulls in the face. They grab their temples as she forces them to their knees.

But more Skulls approach from the distance. Far too many for us to fight. Glowing red axes flicker like torches as the weapons come to life.

The transformed Skulls ram straight through the bending trees. It's as if all eight crews charge us at once. If we don't get away now, our hope of escape is gone.

"Let's go!" I shout.

I pick Zélie back up as we run. My heart hammers against my chest. Our feet pound through the sand. The ground rumbles behind us.

Tzain runs in from behind Amari, carrying a wounded Köa with Emperor Jörah. We join forces with them as we race to the beach. When Jörah spots Mae'e, his russet skin burns red.

"*O que você está fazendo aqui?!*" the emperor roars at Mae'e. Even without understanding their tongue, I understand his fear. But Mae'e doesn't have a chance to answer. The future hierophant forces herself ahead.

Mae'e extends her arms, causing our videira to twist to life. Its vines wrench free from the sand. They curl around Zélie's unconscious body, pulling her in.

The videira Emperor Jörah took to the island races to the coast. Vines shoot out and attach to Mae'e's boat. Time slips away as we board the conjoined boats. All around us, the Skulls swarm.

They break from the forest in a craze. Over a hundred arc toward us at once.

"Go!" Amari shouts.

With a push, Mae'e forces us into the seas. The vines whip through the black waters, leaving the Skulls roaring at our backs.

PART IV

CHAPTER FIFTY-FOUR

AMARI

THE TRIP BACK TO New Gaīa feels like it lasts a lifetime. My body still shakes from the horde of Skulls we escaped. Zélie stays unconscious.

There's no life behind her silver eyes.

Tzain cradles his sister to his chest. The blood of every Skull he battled coats his dark skin. Everything in me yearns to comfort him, but I don't know what to say.

I've never seen him act that way.

The only conversation passes between Jörah and Mae'e. Though I'm starting to understand the New Gaīans' tongue, they yell almost too quickly for me to follow.

"You endanger our people——" Jörah starts.

"I followed the Sight!" Mae'e interrupts.

"You endanger yourself——"

"We saved your life!"

The emperor berates Mae'e for leaving the safety of her temple, but Mae'e doesn't back down. I'm left staring at the flickers of blue light around my hands.

It's been so long since I felt the full burn of my magic, all the power at my command. After being imprisoned by the Skulls, I forgot what it was like to bring my enemies to their knees, to connect to their minds, to see what they've seen. . . .

The ground rumbles with the heavy paws of their armor-plated bears. The bronze Skulls create a sea over their barren plains. One cry fills the black night.

"Fyrir Föður Stormanna!"

The chant rings from coast to coast as all six tribes descend on the capital city of Iarlaith. The warriors wait in long lines before their galdrasmiðar. *With waves of their hands, the fur-clad magicworkers carve new runes into the Skulls' chests, preparing them for the Blood Moon in ten days.*

This whole time, I've feared what would happen if we were recaptured. I've felt the threat of being placed back into their chains. Yet in their minds, I felt their resolve, their unwavering worship of their king. Their animalistic rage, primed to rip through every civilization in their way. There's no denying it now. The Skulls are ready to invade.

I have to keep Zélie and Mae'e safe.

When we finally reach the island again, its dense foliage opens up like fans. Our videira zips down the hidden rivers, zooming past the floating lily pads. We travel into the lush forest, greeted once more by its floral symphony and the faint smell of ash. We pass through the woven walls surrounding the city, and the lake air kisses my face. The videira sails down the empty canals, racing for Mount Gaïa.

"Chame Yéva!" Mae'e calls. She's the first to disembark. Her skirts fly as she runs across Mount Gaïa's base.

When I leave the videira, I drop to my knees on Mount Gaïa's black stone. I press my hands together and pray.

"Please," I whisper to Mama Gaïa's spirit. "Please save her!"

The Green Maidens rush out of the temple. Yéva lumbers after them. Six girls take Emperor Jörah and Köa away on woven stretchers. The last two aid Mae'e.

Vines remove Zélie's body from Tzain's bloody arms. Yéva waves her hands, and a tunnel opens in the base of the mountain, revealing a stairwell of pure obsidian glass. Yéva leads the attendants down, and they disappear underground with Zélie's body. Tzain moves to follow, but Mae'e holds him back.

"Men are not permitted beneath Mount Gaīa."

Tzain exhales a heavy breath. I fear he will resist. But he drops his axe and stumbles to his knees.

"Will she be alright?" he asks.

Mae'e stays silent. She is not willing to lie. Tzain turns to me, tears in his mahogany eyes.

"Amari, will you go?"

Mae'e takes my hand and we run. I follow her down the spiral steps. Sweat gathers at my brow. The world beneath Mount Gaīa's surface grows warmer the farther we descend.

Rushing waters flow. Steam fills the air, creating thick walls of white. We reach the bottom and step into a natural spring. The water glistens with emeralds the size of mangoes. Mae'e joins Yéva as they guide Zélie's cot into the pool.

Please. I brace myself. I wait behind the Green Maidens, clutching my chest as the New Gaīans work. Mae'e undoes the braids in Zélie's hair. Her long, textured coils flow free.

Yéva holds out shaking arms. They rise like she lifts the very earth. The stone beneath us begins to hum. The emeralds at their feet light up.

"*Mamãe Gaīa, nós vamos até você.*" Their voices echo around Mount Gaīa's walls. The force lifts the hair on the nape of my neck. The emerald waters grow turbulent, and the air starts to thin. The sacred chant of the New Gaīans fills my ears.

"Ouça-nos agora.
Nós exigimos seus fogos de cura.
Suas águas sagradas precisam de você agora—"

Veins bulge against Yéva's and Mae'e's skin as they chant. The diamond sparkle in their eyes transforms, taking on a new and powerful glow. Yéva's body starts to seize. The mystic falls to her knees.

"Restaure nossas terras.
Traga novos caminhos.
Os antigos reviveram.
Permita que seu Espírito reine."

The mystics shake the walls of the mountain. The rumble travels far above. I barricade myself in a corner as the reverberations pass through my bones. The entire city of New Gaīa quakes at the power the women call forth.

The water glows so bright, I have to look away.

Then a gasp fills the air.

Zélie's silver eyes fly open as Yéva collapses for good.

CHAPTER FIFTY-FIVE

INAN

Silence hangs over our heads.

It crushes like our defeat.

The plans I risked my life to enact run through my mind. I knew we needed an army.

Without Zélie, there would have been no risen Skulls. Emperor Jörah's combined forces could have taken down the other ships. Our war could've ended tonight. Instead we're left waiting to see if Zélie still lives.

I look across the emperor's throne room—Jörah and Köa stand by the doors, awaiting word from Mount Gaīa. When we arrived at the imperial palace, the Green Maidens went straight to work, laying out their herbs and oils on the emerald-brick floors. They ground a mixture together, using the paste to stanch Jörah's and Köa's wounds. When the bleeding finally stopped, they bandaged their leaders' arms with banana leaves covered in woven vines. Their working hands were the only sound to fill the room.

Tzain sits against the far wall, staring at the axe in his hands. When the Green Maidens tried to come to his aid, they discovered none of the blood coating his dark skin was his.

I still don't know what transpired in the cave. Tzain's shoulders seem to slump with shame. And all the while the leader of the Lâminas keeps Tzain under his startling green gaze.

Unable to stay still, I walk to the palace windows. The shouts of New Gaïans travel through the stained glass. In our brief return, the news of our failed attack has flown through the city. The fact that Emperor Jörah was harmed has sent a frenzy through their lands. Palace attendants reeled at the deaths of the emperor's best Lâminas. The very vines seem to hang their heads.

Before, all we had was our word. We were the cruel harbinger of Yéva's prophecy. But now something has shifted. The New Gaïans understand this threat is real.

The Skulls are coming. The Skulls are nearly here. Voices that once cried for our demise now cry out for us to save them.

Three sharp knocks pull me from my thoughts. Tzain rises to his feet. Jörah opens the door to find two Green Maidens. I recognize the faces of the girls who took Zélie.

"*Imperador*," one Maiden starts. I draw closer as they exchange words. Jörah closes the door and turns to us.

"She is alive."

The news hits like a wave. Tzain turns to the wall, hiding from us all. The breath I didn't know I was holding releases from my chest. But the weight of what I discovered on King Baldyr's battleship keeps me on edge. We don't have much time.

According to Amari, the Blood Moon rises in ten days.

"I need to show you something." I reach for the parchments in my waistband. Each is still wet from my plunge into the sea. I take the time to unravel them with care, delicately laying them across the tiled floor.

The men circle around me. Hard lines crease through Jörah's forehead when he sees the map of New Gaïa. It shows the details of the crescent-shaped island, the thick forest covering the land, the volcanic mountains surrounding the floating city, even the temples of the hierophant.

"Where did you get this?" Jörah asks.

"King Baldyr's ship," I respond. I point to the second map, allowing them to see the western borders of Baldeírik. "They intend to strike on the eve of the Blood Moon. In ten days' time. They have a fleet of over a hundred ships prepared to storm both of our shores."

"They will not get through," Köa declares. "Yéva can keep them at bay."

"Yéva is no more." Jörah hangs his head. "She has returned to the Mother Root."

At the revelation, Köa stumbles back. He looks to the window at the faces of his chanting people. For the first time since I've seen the warrior, true fear enters his eyes.

Köa falls to his knees and bows his head. He presses his hand against the floor. Jörah joins him in a moment of prayer. I turn away, allowing them the dignity of space. A long silence passes before Jörah rises back to his feet.

"What can we do?" Jörah asks. "How can we defend my lands? Mae'e is strong, but she is not ready. She cannot keep back a fleet of a hundred by herself."

Everyone looks to me. Staring at the maps, I only see one viable path.

"It's not enough to defend your shores," I decide. "We know of their incoming attack. We have one more chance to strike."

"How?" Köa growls, nearly shaking with the words. His desire to fight the Skulls again runs through me as if it were my own. His need to seek vengeance for Yéva and his fallen men is so strong it burns.

"Their power is in their fleet," I say. "Without it, they're landlocked. They won't be able to sail to Orïsha or New Gaïa. They'll be left vulnerable to *our* attacks."

"We take their ships?" Jörah arches his heavy brow.

"We destroyed one ship tonight." I face the emperor. "What if we could do that to their entire fleet?"

CHAPTER FIFTY-SIX

TZAIN

KÖA DOESN'T SPEAK WHEN we leave the throne room. The warrior charges through the halls, ignoring the limp in his right leg. In all my time in New Gaïa, I've seen his power. His confidence. His ridicule.

This is the first time I've felt the heat of his rage.

All around us, the people of New Gaïa grieve the loss of their warriors and their sacred hierophant. Attendants huddle together to embrace. Servants drop to the vine-covered floor and weep. Even children fall to their knees.

Everything that once felt impenetrable crumbles before my eyes. Inan's attack plan runs through my mind. We have one last chance to stop the Skulls before they come at us with everything they have. But how am I supposed to fight when I can't stay in control?

Shame rips through me at the thought of what I did in the cave. I wait for Köa to retaliate, but he stares straight ahead.

When we make it into the Lâminas' quarters, the entire forces wait in the squares. Köa stumbles to a halt before his warriors. His face twists, and I feel his despair.

"*Saiam!*" he barks.

All at once, his warriors file back into their barracks. I try to follow along, but he shoves me back.

Here we go.

I'm surprised Köa doesn't want an audience. Even if tonight were a victory, I would expect him to retaliate. Green light glows around his bloodstained fingers as he reaches into his skin, pulling out his ivory barong.

"Fight me!" the Lâmina demands. He motions to my axe, but I shake my head.

Köa comes at me so quickly, I don't have time to get out of the way. I cry out as the barong slices my side.

"Fight me," Köa repeats. "Take out your axe."

Something wild dances in the warrior's eyes. Something I haven't seen before. I don't know if it's because he lost his men or because I attacked him and Jörah in the cave. But I won't let him bait me.

I won't activate the power I can't control.

"Köa——"

He lunges and I whip out my axe, catching the blade of his barong. He jumps back and changes form, coming at me again.

The training square rings as his ivory blade connects with the crimson metal of the Skulls. I feel the heavy weight of soldiers watching from the barracks. The trainees' shaved heads peek at our battle from behind the armory. Köa doesn't let up. He hits me with everything he has.

"Where is your strength?" The warrior bares his teeth. "Where is your dignity? You vow to protect your sister with the metal of the enemy?"

He strikes again, and I finally understand the source of his rage—the axe I continue to wield. But he doesn't understand.

I don't know what power I have without it.

"When you have nothing left——" The warrior swipes at me. "When the world has pushed you to your knees, that is when you learn who you really are! That is when you find your true strength!"

Köa lunges and our blades meet in midair. My arms tremble as he tries to cut me down.

"Has the world pushed you to your knees, Tzain?"

Köa strikes again and I see it—that slow, fateful night. The guards who kicked down our door. The agony on Baba's face when they broke his back. Mama's hands reaching out for me, clawing for help. The blood streaming down Zélie's face.

"Has it pushed you to your knees, Tzain!"

I see the moment I lost Baba for good. The arrow that cut through his chest. The warm pool of blood that leaked from his body. The last breaths of life he took in my hands.

"Has it pushed you to your knees, Tzain!"

I swing and I see my sister as the Skulls dragged her away. I feel the way they mutilated her body. I feel all the pain I wish I could take away.

"Ha!" I cry out. The Skull's axe snaps in half as I fall to my knees. The tears I cage inside spill free. My body heaves as they fall.

The pain of my past leaks through me, spilling onto the emerald-brick floor. The realization hits me like a wall.

My life has been an endless war.

Köa walks over to me. The warrior lifts his hand. I expect him to attack, but he places it on my shoulder instead. The warrior bends down, meeting me eye to eye.

"*This* is your strength." He squeezes me. "This is the power you wield."

THE LÂMINAS STEP IN rhythm as we make our way into the jungles outside the city. The thick green canopy hangs overhead. Damp soil flattens under our bare feet.

Köa leads the way of all his men, gait unbroken despite his limp. I don't know where he's taking me. I don't know the weight of what I've done. But for the first time in moons, I don't feel the pull of the bloodmetal.

The hold the Skulls had on me is gone.

"*Um irmão de osso!*" the Lâminas chant as we walk. "*Um irmão de osso!*"

After all the time spent training, I recognize the words.

Um irmão de osso.

A brother of bone.

We reach a clearing with a flattened, weather-beaten boulder at its center. All the Lâminas circle around. I try to join them, but one nudges me into the clearing. Köa stands at the boulder, arms crossed.

"*Um irmão de osso!*"

A shiver travels down my neck as I make my way to the center. A ring of stone torchlights ignites the moment I step in. Flames dance across the warriors' faces. Their shadows loom large behind them.

Köa motions to the boulder, and I lie down. His fingers glow green as he removes his ivory barong. Another Lâmina enters with a tray of supplies. I scan the stone vase filled with molten black ink and the obsidian-glass needle, poised to pierce my skin.

"Really?" I can't hide the hope from my voice as I scan the armory on Köa's own chest. Köa stares back at me, cutting with his green gaze.

"*Você está pronto para lutar com seu próprio poder?*" he questions me.

Are you ready to fight with your own power?

I stare at the ivory barong in his hands, considering the full weight of his question. All I wanted was to keep my sister safe. To keep her out of Baldyr's reach, I was willing to do whatever it took. But the man I became in that cave is someone I never want to be again. I want to fight with all of me.

I want to unleash the might hidden within my own strength.

"*Estou pronto,*" I affirm. The corners of Köa's lips twitch at the sound of New Gaīan. He motions to the Lâminas, and they prepare. Two warriors grab my ankles. Two more grab my wrists. My pulse spikes as Köa stands over me, searching with his ivory barong.

A strange heat passes through my torso like a snake. One of my ribs starts to glow. Köa doesn't give me a chance to brace myself.

My eyes bulge as Köa stabs the obsidian needle straight through the bone.

"*Ah!*"

The Lâminas hold me tight as the black needle digs. The moment the needle hits the rib, the glow intensifies. Köa reaches for the stone vase of molten ink.

"*Um irmão de osso!*" Köa shouts. He lets the stone vase pour free. I can hardly breathe as the molten liquid breaks through me, searing straight through my flesh. My skin molds and remolds before my eyes, revealing my skeleton. The Lâminas struggle to hold me down as a deep crack ripples through the glowing rib.

Köa reaches into my body, and I seize. He pulls the ink-soaked rib free. The other Lâminas shout as Köa shoves the bone into my hand.

"Find your strength!" he speaks in my tongue.

I see myself running after Zélie. I feel Baba's bleeding body in my arms. The weight of my armor when I wanted to protect Amari. The cold rubber of my old agbön ball.

I see every Skull I slayed. Every guard I cut down with my blade. But then I see Mama's smile.

Everything else fades away. . . .

"*My sweet boy!*" *Mama's face lights up as I hand her the black calla lily. Though it pains her, she sits up in her cot. She winces and my smile drops.*

"*I'm sorry.*" *I whisper the words. Her pain is my fault. I drowned in the mountain lake. The blood magic Mama used to bring me back nearly took her own life.*

"*Do not be sorry, my love.*" *Mama motions at me, and I take the flower, putting it behind her ear.* "*You are my heart.*" *She places her hand on my cheeks.* "*You are my strength.*"

The rib's light glows so bright it shines through the entire clearing.

Cracks fill the air as it grows, taking on a new shape. The single rib twists and expands, transforming into a bone axe. Half a meter long, the handle rises like a spine. With its double head, wide, hooked blades shine on both sides.

I squeeze the ivory handle. My chest heaves as my skin remolds. Though no voices fill my head, I feel the might I wielded with the Skull's bloodmetal.

Köa lifts my hand in the air. The Lâminas roar in return.

"*Um irmão de osso!*" they chant in unison.

A thrill runs through me as they all pile into the circle.

CHAPTER FIFTY-SEVEN

ZÉLIE

STANDING ON THE SUMMIT of Mount Gaīa, I feel her heart beat deep below. The world has shifted since I awoke from her sacred spring. I sense the life in the vines around me.

Yéva's loss hangs over the city like storm clouds. Every New Gaīan dresses in white. A never-ending line waits before the Mother Root at the city's center to pay their respects. They whisper words of gratitude into the vines like the fallen hierophant can hear.

Guilt weighs down every breath I take. At times I worry Yéva made a mistake. In her absence, attendants talk to me. At me. They search for answers I can't give. Yéva had been with her people for nearly two hundred years.

She used her last light to keep me here.

If I'd only been strong enough . . .

Regret eats at me. We wouldn't be here if I had been able to stay in control. My gut twists with the golden lightning trapped inside. I hear the words King Baldyr whispered. They shudder down my spine.

Blóðseiðr.

My fingers scrape the medallion in my chest. It's like King Baldyr stands over my shoulder, staring down at the city of New Gaīa.

His presence haunts me though we're oceans apart.

I can still feel the paralysis that hit me when he invoked the blood oath, the sear of the medallion activating at his command. I yearn to take back the magic he ripped from my skin, the powers he used to reanimate his fallen men.

His actions desecrated every sacred Reaper act I've ever known, magic only meant to be used over the spirits caught between this life and the next world. With that power over me, I don't know how to fight back.

I don't know what I'll do if he lands on New Gaīa's shores and attacks.

As the days tick away until the Blood Moon, the city prepares to wage war. The Lâminas train like beasts. The shouts of battle echo from their training squares. Every night they travel into the jungle to activate their newest warriors, tattooing fresh weapons on the trainees' bare skin.

Vineweavers work day and night to create new videiras for the attack, reshaping their boats to add more riders. Their new additions triple the vessels' speed, allowing us to race to King Baldyr's lands.

Other weavers work to erect new fortresses around New Gaīa's borders. Thick vine towers rise from the ocean shores. They take turns practicing their defenses, using elongated vines to snap massive fish from the ocean as if they were the Skulls' ships.

But of all the preparations made, I'm in awe of the Green Maidens'. They work in teams to build an underground network of vines. The maidens move from plot to plot, weaving new escape points throughout the floating city that lead all the way to the black sands.

Watching them work, I want to be strong. I want to keep both our people safe. But every time I think of facing King Baldyr, my throat grows tight.

It feels like I'm the only person in both our lands not prepared for the fight.

"There you are."

I turn to find Mae'e standing at the mountain trail, dressed in all white like the rest of her people. Something has shifted inside her since Yéva's passing. A hardness has entered her diamond gaze.

The new hierophant joins me in the center of the summit. She laces her fingers with mine, overlooking the preparations around her city.

"Jörah's given his word," Mae'e continues. "Their forces set sail in three days' time. They intend for us to stay here."

"You disagree?" I ask.

"I will not leave my people to battle on the front lines. We need to cut King Baldyr down before he has a chance to step into these lands." Mae'e turns to me, and her diamond eyes glitter. "Promise me you will stand by my side."

"You don't understand." I pull away. "You weren't in that cave. I'm the reason Jörah and Köa were injured. The reason those warriors were killed—"

"You are also the reason we struck him," Mae'e pushes me. "When all else failed, *you* were strong enough to attack."

"But what if he takes control?"

"You fight him!" Mae'e says. "You did it before. You can do it again!"

Mae'e opens up her palms, and dozens of vines split through the black rock. They writhe back and forth in the air, commanding a force she didn't wield before.

"What are you doing?" I step back.

Before I can react, the vines lunge at once. I dive to the side as the vines strike the place I was standing like spears. Cracks split through the mountain stone. The vines recoil and head straight for my chest. I nearly tumble off the mountain's edge in my attempt to escape.

"Mae'e, stop!"

The hierophant moves with a ferocity I haven't seen. Before I can dodge again, Mae'e's vines snap around my torso with a vengeance. They raise me into the air and squeeze.

"He seeks to harvest your heart, Zélie!" Mae'e shouts. "Not the other way around."

Mae'e waves her hand again, and the medallion lurches in my chest. I grit my teeth as it burns.

Magic twists from my skin in red streaks, ripping itself free from my veins. King Baldyr stands before me, blood dripping from his golden skull.

"*Fight it!*" Mae'e's voice mutates. Her new powers swell before my eyes. My body starts to ache. The mountain begins to shake.

A flash of anger rises in me, and I push. I claw for the power inside. I think of my people. Of Mae'e's people.

Of King Baldyr and how he must die.

A roar rips from my throat. The medallion lights through my white silks. A current travels down my arms in thin, blinding rays, spilling from my fingertips. Tiny bolts curve from my body like snakes, twisting into the sky as the golden lightning awakens inside. With a rush, bolts of lightning rip through the vines, setting me free.

I look up as the bolts of lightning fade. A fresh coat of sweat covers my skin. With a push, another golden bolt escapes my throat, reaching through the clouds.

"You are not his weapon for the harvest." Mae'e bends down. "You are the force that will bring about his end!"

I push myself back onto my feet and open my arms.

"Hit me again."

CHAPTER FIFTY-EIGHT

ZÉLIE

ON THE EVE BEFORE we leave for Baldeírik, howls of New Gaïans ring through the vines outside the city center. The high pitch shudders through my bones. Plumes of fire shoot into the night, fighting with the stars.

Mae'e and I wait before the waterfall of New Gaïa, preparing to board one of the two videiras that will float through the city's canals. When I catch my reflection in the turquoise water, my breath hitches.

I don't recognize the girl who stares back.

From the moment I left the summit, Mae'e's maidens have prepared me to rally her people under the midnight moon. They doused me in crystal baths, soaking me in their glowing waters. Their nimble fingers wove a collection of white braids through my hair. They threaded in yellow sapphires and golden strings of pearls.

When my hair was done and my body was clean, a girl arrived in my chambers, the oldest Green Maiden I've seen. She spent the soft arc of the night marking my skin: painting pathways of light in shimmering gold. Those same marks shine through my sheer robes, studded with sparkling citrine crystals and glistening suns carved from yellow apatite.

The same girl returns with the final piece. She lays a woven web of canary yellow diamonds over my head like a veil.

"You're a vision."

I recognize the slow steps of the boy I once knew as the little prince. I turn to find Inan behind me, dressed in royal garb. A new mantle shines over his copper skin, decorated with rays like the sun. The New Gaīans have embraced Inan for his service.

Inan offers me his hand and I take it, allowing him to guide me into the second videira. He stares at me as we wait to leave. He opens his mouth to speak, but another horn rings.

Mae'e's videira sets sail. I inhale as mine follows. More plumes of fire shoot into the air.

The war procession begins.

The sight of New Gaīa takes my breath away. Mae'e's people line the canals, dressed from head to toe in red. They match their new sacred hierophant, a vision in deep scarlet skirts. A scarf woven from glittering rubies drapes over her black hair.

The New Gaīans drop to their knees as we pass, heads bowed, lips hushed in prayer. One young girl leaves her mother's side. She takes a doll of Mama Gaīa from her chest and offers it to me.

The New Gaīans follow her lead, extending blessings throughout our trek. Ripe mangoes. Dry rose petals and sticks of cinnamon. Many offer lit tangerine candles.

Every Lâmina follows behind us in the new arsenal of videiras the vineweavers have built as we float through the blessings of thousands. The warriors wear black paint over their faces and bare chests. Crushed ivory marks their skeletons. Thick red lines are painted beneath their eyes.

When we reach the base of Mount Gaīa, Emperor Jörah meets us there. Like his men, tribal paint coats his russet skin. A heavy skeleton mantle sits over his broad shoulders. The emperor shares the unbreakable will in their angular eyes.

Jörah extends his hand to me. Thunder roars above when he takes my palm. I drink in the expanse of his people—the bay of Lâminas, the waters of infinite burning candles, the canals lined with red. Vineweavers hang like spiders, circling above our heads.

Jörah steps forward. He stands firm like the mountain behind him.

"*The day has come.*" His low voice amplifies. "*We face a threat unlike any we have ever known. One that can annihilate our people. Our Mother Root. Our home. Tonight we join together.*" Emperor Jörah raises his arms. "*We pray to Mama Gaīa to bless our lands. Tomorrow, we destroy the enemy! We go! We fight! We win!*"

At Emperor Jörah's mighty cry, the New Gaīans chant. Their voices reverberate through the mountains.

"*We go! We fight! We win! We go! We fight! We win!*"

Mae'e raises her hand, and the entire crowd falls silent. She places a palm on Jörah's shoulder.

"*I wish to speak.*"

The air doesn't dare blow as Mae'e takes center stage. The city is so quiet I can hear the echo of her bare feet walking over the mountain stone.

"*I have witnessed our enemy.*" Her voice is steady. "*I have seen the magic they wield. We face a grave battle. One that may cost more of our sacred lives.*"

Mae'e waits for her words to travel to the farthest stretches of her city. The energy around her shifts. The vines start to curl.

"*But the battle we will wage . . .*" A blaze of passion erupts inside her. "*Will ravage their nation to the ground!*"

Mae'e punches her fist into the air. The New Gaīans roar in return.

"*Let us not forget who we are!*" Her diamond eyes sparkle. "*Let us not forget from whose sacred fire we were forged! We are the daughters and sons of New Gaīa!*"

Mae'e is like the very goddess that watches over her temples. Her divine fire passes through the crowd. Her rally stirs her people into a frenzy. Terror burns to the hunger for blood.

"*She has sent us allies!*" Mae'e grabs my arm. I'm not prepared for her to lift it into the air. "*One who carries the power of the storms in her blood!*"

Mae'e turns to me. Her sparkling eyes dare me to speak. I look out at the crowd, and my chest expands with awe. I can hardly believe where I stand, that people would look to me in a foreign land.

"*We will fight for you, New Gaīa!*" I scream in their tongue. The people shout with such force it shakes through the wind. "*We will give everything we have! We will rip through every Skull!*"

"*Death to the Skulls!*" Mae'e releases a battle cry.

"*Morte aos crânios!*" her people scream back.

Their cries for blood stir the lightning in my veins.

CHAPTER FIFTY-NINE

TZAIN

THE FEAST THAT FOLLOWS the war rally is unlike any I've ever seen. New Gaïans dance to the beat of crimson drums. They howl to the full moon. Golden plates filled to the brim with slow-cooked pork and rice pass from hand to hand. Children nibble on chocolate truffles. People join together in the marketplace, cleared out for the New Gaïans to rally.

"*Vai! Vai! Vai!*"

I pass a crowd that's formed around Mae'e. She dances between twirling skirts, throwing her fists and stomping her feet. Her raven hair flies free. She's almost too beautiful to see.

Amari stares from outside the ring, transfixed by the woman before her. A new glint shines in her amber eyes, and a flush rises in her cheeks.

It's the way she used to look at me.

Watching her now, I think of all we were supposed to be. I see the life I thought we would live. The son of a fisherman with Orïsha's future queen. Somehow, it always felt too perfect to be true.

"Tzain," Amari calls out to me. I join her from the fringes of the crowd. Amari's brows lift at my Lâmina tattoo: a bone axe to replace the Skull's.

"Ready for tomorrow?" she asks.

Despite all we're up against, I nod. Over the past nine days, training with the Lâminas has transformed. No longer on the outside of their pack, the warriors have pushed me past my limits. We've battled from dusk to dawn.

"Are you?" I ask.

Amari flashes me her side, and I catch the obsidian sword attached to her waistband. She flexes a burst of blue magic in her hand, illuminating the carved vines swirling down the black glass. The girl who questioned her place in this fight has disappeared. The valiant warrior I know is here.

"They got her once," she says. "We can't let it happen again."

As we stare out at the sea of New Gaïans, Amari leans her head on my arm. I close my eyes and soak in her soft touch. Her gentle breath. The cinnamon scent of her hair.

I put a hand over her shoulder, and her body softens. The simple gesture takes me back. I still remember the first time I saw her, the moment she pulled the brown cloak from her head after we rescued her from Lagos. Even without her headdress, I could see it in her amber eyes.

The very air she exhaled was rare.

All I wanted was to be enough. To live day after day witnessing the smile on her face. When she told me she loved me, that dream became real.

I felt like I held the entire world.

"Have you seen my sister?" I ask. The crowd that swarmed Zélie after the rally terrified me as much as the Skulls. She couldn't leave for hours. Mae'e's people embraced her like she was their own.

"*Aurelia!*" they shouted. At the time, I didn't know what it meant. Later, Köa shared the translation: *Aurelia. The Golden One.*

"I think she's underground," Amari answers. "The Green Maidens snuck her into the vine bunkers. It was the only place she could be alone."

I nod and start to move, but something holds me back. I push past the way my heart aches.

"You . . ." I clear my throat. It's a struggle to find the right words. "You should tell her." I nod my chin at Mae'e. I force a small smile to my face.

Amari's amber eyes shimmer up at me like stars. She looks at the hierophant before looking back at me.

"Tell her." I kiss her forehead one last time. "You're perfect, Amari. I know she feels the same."

I HOLD THE VINE WALLS as I make my way under the city. Built by the Green Maidens, the new tunnel of vines reaches deep underground. They create a path from the city's floating plots to the safety of New Gaïa's black sands.

A wall of incense greets me when I hit the bottom. My bare feet pass over the warm stone. With time, I reach the canals. Giant lily pads float down the stream, ready to carry people to safety.

My sister glitters at the end of one canal branch. The turquoise waters glow against her dark skin. I can hardly believe I know this girl. That we grew up together in the mountains of Ibadan.

"*Aurelia!*" I whisper.

Zélie turns back to me, a wry smile on her face. Her feet dangle in the waters. I join her at the edge, allowing my feet to slip in as well.

The moment brings me back to when we were young. I see the lake outside our stone hut. Back then, the only enemies I had to face were the boys on the agbön courts.

"You were magnificent." I nudge her. "Baba would be so proud."

At the mention of our father, tears fill Zélie's silver eyes. She takes my hand in hers. We squeeze each other's palms, feeling the void of all we've lost.

"Do you think he'd ever believe we were here?" she whispers.

"Do you think Mama would?" I ask instead. I haven't spoken Mama's name for years, but tonight, her face is all I see.

I couldn't protect her back then. I wasn't strong enough to take down the guards. But this time with Zélie is different. This time I'm not a boy.

I'm a warrior.

I fight with the endurance of the Skulls. I battle with the might of the Lâminas. I'm finally strong enough to protect my sister.

I'll die before I let her get hurt.

"I need you to promise me something. . . ." Zélie's fingers spread over the golden ink on her skin. "If the worst comes to pass—"

"No."

"Tzain—"

"I won't let you talk like that."

Zélie takes away her hand and exhales. Tangerine candles flicker over her silver gaze.

"We're taking them down," I push. "We're going back home."

I know it. I feel it. *Deep* in my chest. This time, we have the nation of New Gaīa behind us. We have all of Inan's plans.

"Look at me." Zélie grabs my clenched fist.

I hate the way my eyes sting.

"Tzain, *look* at me," she whispers. "*Please.*"

She puts her hands on both sides of my face. The tears that shine in her eyes cause mine to fall.

"If the worst comes to pass, you have to defeat them. The Skulls won't stop at New Gaīa. They'll sail for Orïsha, too."

"I won't let anything happen to you."

"But if it does . . ." Zélie releases a shuddered breath. "Promise me you'll fight. Promise me you'll do everything you can."

Though I don't want to speak the words, I force myself to nod.

"I promise."

CHAPTER SIXTY

INAN

MUSIC AND CHATTER ECHO in from the war rally, traveling through the stained glass windows of Emperor Jörah's throne room. I comb over the maps laid across the tiled floors, searching for anything I've missed, anything that will ensure our victory in this war.

In mere hours we sail for Baldyr's shores. Under my orders, we obliterate his fleet. But as the night ticks away, my fingers fall numb.

The fate of both our nations falls to me.

I touch the map of Baldeírik, trying to commit the heart-shaped kingdom to memory. The names of the six territories swim in my mind—*Hlÿr, Faól, Hávar, Vídarr, Dóllyr,* and *Iarlaith.* Each colony holds a main village at its center, surrounded by thick squares that mark grain fields and farmhouses. In the middle of the map lies their sacred forge, no doubt the source of their masks and bloodmetal weapons.

With more resources at my disposal, I know the attack I would mount. I yearn to unleash Orïsha's full wrath. In better times, Burners would lay waste to their food supplies. Cancers would raid their villages. Mother and her Grounders would level their mountains to the earth. The Skulls would pay for every Orïshan life they've taken.

They'd rue the day they ever set foot on our shores.

But with the New Gaïans, I have to focus. The might of the Lâminas and the agility of the vineweavers can only mount one attack. I run my fingers across every name inked into Emperor Jörah's scrolls, feeling the weight of each life at my command. Though I've overseen soldiers before, something about tomorrow feels different. There's no room for error.

I can't afford to lead the New Gaĩans astray.

"I knew I would find you here."

I turn—Mae'e stands in the imposing doorway, a fresh sheen of sweat on her brown skin. Her scarlet skirts swirl around her in the absence of wind. The vines across the floor stretch toward her, magnets finding their way home.

I bow in her presence before gesturing to her gaze. "Because of your Sight?"

Mae'e shakes her head. "Because of *her*."

The hierophant motions me over to the window. I follow just as Zélie and Tzain exit the underground tunnels beneath the imperial palace. At the sight of Zélie, my heart skips a beat. Her beauty shines through her jewel-embroidered veil.

"You are so focused on protecting her," Mae'e says. "I am surprised you tore yourself from these maps to attend the rally at all."

"I couldn't miss it," I remark. "You were formidable. I think Yéva would be proud."

At the mention of Yéva, Mae'e almost smiles, but her lips turn into a frown. "Yéva is a part of the Mother Root now. Every time I visit, I ask for her guidance. I want to know what she would do."

"Have you had success?" I ask.

"Whenever I try to find out about the battle ahead, all I see is the two of you."

"Why?" I arch my brow.

"I do not know," Mae'e answers. She studies me under her diamond gaze. "I was hoping to find out."

We watch as Zélie boards a lily pad back to Mount Gaīa. At the last moment, Tzain wraps Zélie in his arms. Something heavy hangs in the air between them. Zélie seems to fight her own tears as she sails off.

"Zélie shares a connection with the mountain now," Mae'e continues. "Ever since its spirit aided Yéva and me in bringing her back to life. But from the way the two of you stare, I believe Zélie shares a connection with you as well."

As Zélie disappears down the candlelit canal, the dreamscape emerges in my mind's eye. I see the forest and waterfalls that once sprouted at Zélie's feet. I feel the warmth of her body as we tangled through the reeds.

"There is a place," I start slowly. "A space we share in our minds."

"The dreamscape?" Mae'e smiles.

"You know it?"

Mae'e nods. Her fingers rest over her heart.

"It started the day we first met. . . ." My voice trails off as I think back. "The two of us locked eyes, and time froze. A shock like lightning traveled through my veins. Ever since that day, we've been connected. It's like our spirits intertwined."

Mae'e presses her hand to the largest window, opening up the stained glass. The melody of her people blows in with the warm breeze. Mae'e closes her eyes and breathes.

"I am giving you my best soldiers," she says. "My borders will be weakened when we need protection the most. If Yéva is pointing me to the connection you and Zélie share, then I need your word that you will use it. I need you to do whatever it takes to stop the Skulls."

"I give you my word." I extend my hand to Mae'e and bow once more. "No matter what. I will give everything I have to eliminate the Skulls."

CHAPTER SIXTY-ONE

INAN

Waves crash against our videira. The full moon shines above. Jagged bluffs cut through the dark waters like serrated knives. We take cover behind them.

Mists coat the Black Bay of Iarlaith, the port village on the western shores of Baldeírik. The Skulls have been on our lands for so long.

We've finally brought the fight to them.

Jörah hands me a looking glass, and I use it to scan the shores. There isn't one sign of life. Houses built from stacked timber sit on stone foundations. Thick layers of raw earth insulate the roofs. The modest dwellings line the waters, separated from the larger farmsteads. Smaller canoes float in the docks. The tattered blades of a windmill spin through the air.

In the large bay, the fleet of a hundred ships floats before us, vulnerable to our attack. Each ship's silhouette bobs up and down in the water, looming over us like dark shadows. As I scan the shapes of each vessel, I spot familiar lines. The majority of the fleet matches the ship we first escaped. I picture the lower levels full of blast oil, just waiting for us to leak.

This is it.

A flare of determination rushes through me, pulsing through my blood. I think of all the planning that's gone into this moment, the late nights spent studying the different maps and diagrams stolen from the Silver Skull's quarters. Our last chance to stop the Skulls floats before my very eyes. Everything that must be destroyed before King Baldyr can die.

Two separate waves—that's what it will take to decimate the Skulls' fleet. Our own fleet of thirty new videiras surrounds us, each vessel rewoven to triple its speed. The first wave of videiras will launch, tasked with dispersing the blast oil. With only thirty vessels in our forces, each team will have to soak more than three of the Skulls' ships.

That's when Zélie moves in.

Zélie, Amari, and Mae'e float behind us, waiting in a videira specially woven for her to attack. All eight Green Maidens surround her, protecting their hierophant and working the craft. Zélie sits at the center of their octagon-shaped boat, elevated on a pedestal of vines, and dripping with gold. The New Gaïans worked all night to craft her a golden exoskeleton. The gilded armor travels up her arms and down to her legs.

At Mae'e's command, the Green Maidens will set sail. Their single craft will launch the second wave. The other videiras will retreat as Zélie calls the golden lightning from her heart.

All we need is one strike. One strike, and every ship will blow. When it hits, their fleet will go up in ashes.

The Skulls' greatest weapon against us will be rendered useless.

With our lands protected, we'll storm their shores. We'll ravage them with the power of the vineweavers and the wrath of the Lâminas. Their plan for conquests shall die with them.

And you'll live. . . .

I look to Zélie and I think of the vow I made. I picture her setting foot in Orïsha, the new life she'll be able to have.

"Are you ready?" I ask her, and she nods, a hard conviction in her silver gaze. Staring at her, I don't see the girl who entered Lagos that fateful

2222222222

day. I don't see the maji who burned my city to the ground. Tonight, I see Orïsha's greatest fighter.

I see the girl with the blood of the sun.

I hand the emperor back his looking glass.

"We're clear," I say.

A low whistle passes through the vines.

I hold my breath as the first wave sails in.

CHAPTER SIXTY-TWO

TZAIN

MOVING THROUGH THE ENEMY'S waters, I feel the weight of all we're up against. We sail in near silence. The only sounds that rise above the black tides are the faint splashes of water against the shifting vines.

"Slowly." I guide our vineweaver as she brings our videira to a stop. We anchor before the line of ships closest to the black shores. I survey each floating boat. Of the hundred ships we have to soak, I know Köa and I can take out the most.

Our weaver manipulates the sides of our vessel to create a woven ladder. The thick vines twist their way up the ship's hull. The ladder hooks over the railing, and I rise. Köa and I prepare to board.

Sea sprays at my feet as we ascend. Köa takes the lead. My heart starts to hammer as we near the ship. I have to remind myself to breathe.

Köa extends his hand, pulling me silently over the railing. My feet land with a soft thud. The wooden panels creak under our steps.

"This way." Köa follows me as we make our way across the deck. A shiver runs down my spine. Though the ship isn't identical to the one we escaped, the memories of those long nights start to drift back.

We pass through the arched door beyond the lifeboats, moving down the stairs. When I come face-to-face with a row of cages, I freeze.

The sight is too much to bear.

"What is it?" Köa asks.

For a moment, I can't speak. My body falls numb. I see the Skull who grabbed Udo's neck. I hear the bones that snapped.

"Fight through it." Sensation doesn't return until Köa pushes his forehead to mine. "You made it out of the cage. You are here. You are alive."

Köa grips the back of my neck until my shaking subsides.

"Your war is almost over." Köa releases my head. "It is our time to win."

I lead Köa past the second level of cages, past rusted cannons and rooms full of crates. On the third level, we discover four barrels of blast oil below the stairs. Köa carries two to the other side of the ship. I carry the others to the top of the deck.

I hold my breath and focus. The green light tingles as it comes to my fingertips. With it, I reach for the bone axe tattooed across my abdomen. The light sparks as the ivory weapon crackles free.

I still can't get over the rush, the way it feels to wield an actual part of me. With one swift arc, I smash through the barrels. Blast oil leaks onto the deck, soaking its wooden panels.

Köa reunites with me, and we move to the railing. The videira sails underneath. The vineweaver creates a new ladder connecting our railing to the next boat. We move across the ladder with speed, careful not to lose our grip.

Together, Köa and I fall into a steady rhythm. We move from ship to ship, the vineweaver bridging our path. As we work, I see the silhouettes of the other Lâminas across the bay. As the moon shifts in the sky, our collective forces cover all one hundred boats.

I slice through the final barrels of blast oil when Köa whistles for us to retreat. I join the warrior at the railing. Köa slides down the ladder of vines, rocking the videira as he lands. I allow my bone axe to re-enter my skin before doing the same.

As we sail back from their coast, the sulfur scent of all the leaked oil taints the air. I cover my nose and close my eyes, taking in the ocean spray. I brace myself for everything to blow away—

"Tzain."

My eyes snap open. Jörah points me to a vessel in the middle of their fleet. Next to the ship, two Lâminas wait in their videiras. Their vine-weavers flag us over, and our vineweaver sails us in.

When we meet, the New Gaīans speak rapidly in their tongue. My forehead creases as Köa deciphers their words.

"What's wrong?" I ask.

The Lâminas point Köa up the bridge.

"Come along." Köa gestures. "There is something we need to see."

CHAPTER SIXTY-THREE

TZAIN

THE MOMENT I STEP onto the ship, something doesn't feel right. The entire deck is bare. The vessel's masts don't even have sails.

A single light shines on the upper deck. It glimmers from above in red. Köa pulls the cleaver from his left shoulder.

My fingers flash green as I pull free my bone axe.

What is this?

The panels beneath us creak as we rise up the stairs. My insides twist with every step. The hairs rise on the nape of my neck.

A steady scratching grows louder the higher we climb. Something heavy lurks in the air. When we reach the top level, the red door to the captain's quarters sits ajar. I dare to push it open. Moonlight spills across the floor.

My hands fall limp when I see dark brown skin. A young maji lies on the marble tiles. An angry gash sits across her throat. A pool of blood spills from her neck.

Her body is only the first. Dozens of my people line the floors. I follow the trail of corpses to the petite figure standing in the back of the room.

"By the gods . . ."

At the far wall, a *galdrasmiðr* stands, caught in an ecstatic trance. Her skin is pale like ice, and her gray hair is brittle like wire. A horned animal skull covers her face.

I watch as the woman paints with the blood of my people. My soul revolts at the sight. Rectangular runes cover the captain's quarters. They drip from the marble walls.

The runes form a complicated mosaic, creating the image of a man twisting from three streams of magic under a crimson moon. One stream shows lines of blood and metal. The other is made from vines and lava. In the third, I see risen skeletons and storm clouds.

"*O que é isto?!*" Köa roars.

The woman stops. Her stained fingers shake. Köa and I back up as she turns around.

Horror shudders through my bones when she smiles.

"Run!" I try to grab Köa, but the Lâmina runs toward the fight. He whips his cleaver, cracking through the *galdrasmiðr*'s animal skull.

Black paint spreads across the bridge of her nose. White runes fall from her eyes like tears. Köa comes at her again.

The *galdrasmiðr* only raises her hands.

"*Ugh!*" A gash spreads across Köa's abdomen. The warrior stumbles to a stop. He falls to his knees, and the *galdrasmiðr* lunges forward, grabbing him by his hair. Köa cries out as she shoves her hand into his open wound before drifting back to her mosaic.

"*Fyrir Föður Stormanna—*"

I dive forward, throwing Köa's body over my shoulder. I propel myself from the captain's quarters before the magicworker can attack again. Köa's warm blood soaks down my chest.

"Hold on!"

As I sprint across the upper deck, red lights begin to glow all over the bay. A unified chant starts to ring. Shrill voices fill the night.

The *galdrasmiðar* emerge from every ship.

"Fyrir Föður Stormanna, blóð tekit úr öllum áttum——"

The chant builds around us as we fly down the stairs. The *galdrasmiðr* follows close behind. Her feet don't touch the ground.

As I run, the realization dawns. I understand the mosaic painted on the wall.

We haven't launched an attack.

We've walked straight into their ritual.

CHAPTER SIXTY-FOUR

ZÉLIE

WHERE ARE YOU?

Anxiety churns my stomach into knots as I wait for the first wave to return. Slowly, videiras begin to sail back from the fleet.

Tzain and Köa are nowhere in sight.

I climb down from the pedestal of vines and pace the perimeter of our videira as we wait. Nailah sits in the back of the boat, ready for us to hit the coast.

We sit leagues behind the first wave, at the farthest point from the Black Bay. I try to focus on the lightning in my core. I chart the ships I'll need to hit to make the rest explode. But the longer we wait, the more I can't deny what I feel. Too much time has passed.

Something is wrong.

"We need to go after them." I turn to Amari and Mae'e. "Tzain should've been back by now."

"Have faith," Mae'e urges. "Our people are prepared."

I want to believe her, but doubt gnaws at my insides. The medallion pulses in my chest, and I can feel the heat of King Baldyr's breath against my neck. It's as if he stands beside me now, watching his own bay from the enemy's boat.

"Oya, please." I whisper the words. My teeth shudder with my exhale. My goddess saved me once before. I called out to her on those seas. She answered me with her storm.

Let this be the end, I think to her spirit. *Let my brother return*—

"Do you see that?" Amari points.

Out in the Black Bay, a single red light peeks through the mist. It flickers in the distance, on the upper level of one of the ships.

"Do you think it's the Skulls?" Mae'e asks.

I drift to the front of the videira, shaking my head. Another red torch glows from the line of ships closest to Iarlaith's shores. More lights burn throughout the bay. One by one, torches ignite until they burn on every ship.

Then the chanting begins.

"Fyrir Föður Stormanna, blóð tekit úr öllum áttum—"

My hands fly to my temples. The medallion vibrates in my chest. The weight of the air intensifies. It presses down on my body like lead, bringing me to my knees.

"What's wrong?" Amari drops to my side. I struggle to hear her through the noise. Everything shakes inside me as the chanting chorus builds.

"Komið saman á þessari helgu nótt, fyrir rauða tunglið—"

Veins bulge against my skin. Blood rushes to my head. The entire world starts to spin.

When I shut my eyes, all I see is red.

"Retreat!" I gasp. "Tell them to retreat!"

Amari makes the call, and it echoes through the vineweavers. A low whistle sounds, warning the first wave to return. I pray for the signal to reach everyone in time.

Then the black shorelines flicker to life.

No . . .

Heavy drums start to beat from the coast. The Skulls howl like beasts. Horror dawns as thousands of flaming arrows ignite at once.

"Retreat!" I yell, but my words don't travel fast enough.

A long horn blows, and every arrow flies.

CHAPTER SIXTY-FIVE

TZAIN

WHEN THE ARROWS LAUNCH, I'm frozen at the sight. Thousands fly free at once, an army taking to the sky. The burning arrows arc over our heads, poised to strike the Skulls' own fleet.

The chanting *galdrasmiðr* hovers on the top deck. She opens her arms to the attack, a willing sacrifice.

I run for the edge of the ship as the first arrows land.

BOOM!

BOOM!

BOOM!

A jolt like nothing I've experienced quakes through my skeleton. The explosion rips through the panels of the Skull's ship. It blasts through the *galdrasmiðr*'s bones.

Fire erupts all around us. Black smoke fills the night. Köa is ripped from my hands.

The world burns as I fly through the air.

What have we done?

In an instant the entire landscape shifts. The weapon laid out for our enemies strikes against our own. The attack we hoped to wage evaporates before my eyes.

Confusion racks me as I crash into the icy waters. The back of my arm stings with the impact, new wounds raging from the blast. Burning rubble falls into the seas. The tattooed bodies of the Lâminas float past me.

Köa!

I see the leader's bone cleaver before I see him. Severe burns ravage the warrior's body, destroying the armory tattooed across his russet skin. Guilt hits me like an anchor. I force my wounded body to kick, grabbing Köa before he can sink.

Above, videiras sail through the chaos. They race to drag survivors out of the bay. Thick vines wrap tight around my chest, bringing me back up to the surface of the burning waters.

When I set Köa down, the vineweaver pulls the brave warrior to her neck. Her grief threatens to sink the craft. Crimson coats her face as she howls with his death.

The bay is soaked with the blood of the sacrificed maji, the New Gaīans, and the Skulls' *galdrasmiðar.* I can't make sense of the destruction until the waters start to glow.

Hmmmmmmmm!

A dense hum reverberates through the air. The blood in the water joins together, forming a swirling circle in the bay. The circle's glow intensifies as it picks up speed. The seas start to thrash.

All at once, the temperature drops. A dark wave of crimson bleeds above. The night turns red.

My jaw drops as I stare up at the Blood Moon.

CHAPTER SIXTY-SIX

ZÉLIE

IT'S HERE. . . .

The moment I've feared comes to life before my eyes.

At the Blood Moon, Baldyr's medallion ignites. Its golden veins spread to the farthest reaches of my skin. Lightning crackles at my core, stronger than it's ever been.

Foreign chants fill my ears as the waters around us rise. The moon seems to increase in size, looming above the burning bay.

"Secure the hierophant!" a vineweaver shouts. All around us, the vines start to writhe. Panic cuts through me like a knife. Tzain is still locked into the fight.

A single red torch ignites on the Skulls' black shores. Then another. A dozen follow. Torches flicker through the mist, soon by the hundreds, then by the thousands.

The torchlights travel far inland, creating a trail through the darkness. A towering mountain bluff comes to light.

Then I see him.

I feel King Baldyr like the wind. He stands behind the line of burning torches, his skull mask alive in the raging night. The golden veins of the medallion scratch their way up my chin. Mae'e watches in a trance. The red night coats her russet skin.

"No!" I lurch forward. Amari grabs me before I can dive overboard. The vineweavers jump into action. Our boat takes off.

This can't be it. We can't let King Baldyr win. The vision of a burning Orïsha plays behind my eyes. I don't have a choice. I have to give everything to this fight.

We have to stop him here. Here and now. His blood will spill on his shores.

I won't allow him to invade ours!

"Let me go!" I push out of Amari's grasp. I charge at the vineweaver to my left.

"*Please*," I speak in their tongue. "*Take me to the front lines!*"

Despite my pleas, the vineweaver ignores every word. Their vines whip through the water at top speed, dragging us farther away from the fight.

"You have to stop them." I turn to Mae'e. "We need to attack!"

"The safest place for both of you is New Gaïa—" Amari starts.

"No place is safe!" I cut her off. "Not until this king is dead!"

Mae'e looks back and forth between us. Her gaze drifts to the shrinking shoreline. The Skulls howl into the night, praising the Blood Moon.

"Remember what Yéva said," I push. "Remember what you saw!"

Mae'e stares at the medallion in my chest. Amari grabs the hierophant's hands.

"Mae'e, no!" Amari pushes me out of the way. "If you go, you're only giving him what he wants."

"There are two ways this ends." Tears come to Mae'e's eyes. She balls her fists, seeming to call from something inside. "We kill him now, or he kills everyone we love."

"Mae'e—"

"That means *everyone*." Mae'e places her delicate hands on Amari's cheeks, and Amari's face falls as she feels the message behind her words. "You are not the only one at risk of losing those you love."

Without warning, Mae'e pulls Amari into a kiss. My eyes widen as they embrace. Mae'e's fingers dig into Amari's dark curls. When Mae'e pulls back, Amari is in a daze.

"Forgive me," Mae'e whispers.

Amari cocks her head. Her hands fly to her lips. "What are you—"

Mae'e's diamond eyes sparkle. Then thick vines erupt from below.

Each vine strikes like a viper, snapping around every person in our vicinity. Mae'e even grabs the videiras that flank our ship, preventing them from coming after us.

When the vineweavers shout, new vines rise, wrapping around each weaver's mouth. With another wave of Mae'e's hands, the small circle of vines around us detaches from the rest of the videira, creating a boat of our own.

Amari's muffled screams rage out of control. Mae'e gives her one last look before placing her hands into the woven floor.

With a rush, the boat glows, racing toward the Skulls' dark shores.

CHAPTER SIXTY-SEVEN

INAN

WHERE DID I GO WRONG?

The awakened Blood Moon reigns above us. It coats the black night in red. The waters in the bay continue to thrash as the crimson circle spirals below.

The warnings of Yéva's prophecy return. I fear the night we've fought to avoid.

If we can't stop Baldyr as a king, how in the skies will we stop him as a god?

My mind spins in circles as I stare at the burning bay. The few videiras that have endured the blast race back in retreat. The woven vessels carry the injured survivors, bodies ravaged by angry burns.

The corpses of fallen Lâminas float through the waters. I can't bear the graveyard of my mistakes. We were supposed to decimate the Skulls.

This was meant to be the end of their fleet.

How did he know? I shake my head. We've played right into Baldyr's hands. The king already had the maji he needed to sacrifice. I delivered him the New Gaïans, too.

If King Baldyr gets his hands on Zélie and Mae'e, we're finished. There'll be no stopping his onslaught. We need to escape while we still can. We need to make another plan.

"We have to leave!" I run to Emperor Jörah. The flames dance across the leader's square jaw. Jörah stares at the destruction, shark-tooth blade clenched in his shaking hands.

A new wave of guilt weighs down my shoulders. The New Gaïans trusted me with their best. I've not only failed them here.

I've left their nation vulnerable to the Skulls' attack.

"Your people need you," I urge. "There's no time to waste."

Emperor Jörah hangs his head. Anguish twists the creases in his face. But Jörah slides his weapon back into his skin. With a sharp shout, he gives the order and our videira sets sail.

Think. I push myself to restrategize. With the improvements made to the videiras, we propel across the seas with unearthly speeds. The trek back to New Gaïa will only take a few hours. Even Orïsha is within our reach.

I look up to the Blood Moon. In our lands, I know they must see this harbinger of doom. We have to find a way to get back.

We'll need all of us to stop King Baldyr's attack—

"Help!"

The sound of muffled shouts brings us to a stop. In the distance, red moonlight illuminates a tangle of vines. They tie a collection of videiras together. More wrap around vineweavers from head to toe, keeping them locked in place.

Dread numbs my fingers when I recognize the empty pedestal that Zélie sat on. At the first sign of trouble, Zélie and Mae'e were instructed to retreat. But the videira looks like it was attacked by one of our own.

"Quickly!" I say. Emperor Jörah echoes the command. The vineweavers bring us in. Another videira beats us to the confined ship.

Tzain disembarks as I hop on. He starts to cut the hostages free.

"Amari?" My brows lift when I see my sister struggle. I rush to her side. She fights against her restraints, amber eyes wide with worry.

Tzain's quick to slice through her vines. With a gasp, Amari falls into my arms. She pushes me away and stumbles to the edge of the ship, scanning the burning mist.

"Where are they?" Tzain asks.

Amari points back to the Skulls' shores.

"They went to the front." Her voice cracks. "They're taking the fight to the king!"

CHAPTER SIXTY-EIGHT

◄─·•·◇·●◎●·◇·•·─►

ZÉLIE

MAE'E'S CIRCLE OF VINES propels us across the Black Bay. I brace myself for what's ahead. We sail through the thrashing seas. The crimson circle spins beneath us, catching the carnage in its current.

Flames still rage across the boats' decks. Debris flies from the exploding ships. Mae'e's emerald vines rise to whip around us, slapping the rubble away.

The bodies that float before us make me sick. Countless maji fill the bay. They fly through the spiraling waters, eyes empty and throats slit.

Baldyr's sacrificed my people like cattle. All to summon his Blood Moon. I won't let him complete his harvest.

I won't let him win!

The golden lightning I've trained to command builds inside me, a storm prepared to release. Dark clouds swirl on the horizon. A violent force ripples through the wind.

Over a thousand men wait beyond the mist, rabid in their praise. King Baldyr stands behind them. Rage torches through me as I prepare to end him once and for all.

"*Faster!*" I call to Mae'e.

The hierophant pushes herself beyond her limits. Her hands shake and she grits her teeth. Every muscle in her body tenses as we shoot forward. Her vines spiral toward the shoreline.

As we go, I think of the way Baldyr held me down. The way he's poisoned me with his medallion and his majacite crown. I think of the countless maji he's dragged across the seas. Every single sacrifice he's made to harvest the power inside me.

I don't care if his face is the last thing I ever see. I won't let him hurt any more of my people. I will get vengeance for every life he's stolen.

"Launch me!"

Mae'e's vines wrap around my abdomen. With a sharp jolt, they fling me backward before catapulting me through the air. I shoot into the mist, hurtling toward the black beach.

Golden lightning explodes from my hands, cutting through the night in radiant streaks. With the power of the Blood Moon, the lightning answers my command. A warm rush fills me as I ride the crackling bolts across the sky.

Below me, Mae'e lands on the shores. The army of Skulls runs toward her. The hierophant flings out her arms with an ear-shattering cry. Twelve voices shriek at once.

Black vines twist out of the sand en masse, creating a forest of their own. The thick vines unleash their full wrath as they surge. They spiral through the coast, impaling every Skull.

Up ahead, King Baldyr stands defiant. Black marks peek beyond his golden skull. His chestnut hair is pulled back in wild braids. His body carries new scars.

I see the burnt flesh where my lightning hit him last. The sight steadies me as I ready myself for the final blast.

"Blóðseiðr."

My body quivers as King Baldyr invokes the blood oath. His power over me passes in waves. My muscles strain as I fight through his hold.

I fight to stay in control.

Golden lightning rages around my skeleton. A bolt of electricity spreads between my fingertips. Thunder quakes through the air as a red rain begins to pour.

Time runs still as I raise my palms. I align them with King Baldyr's heart.

For Orïsha, I think to the fallen maji.

I set the lightning free—

With a roar, King Baldyr raises one of the medallions. He holds it up to my attack. All at once, my lightning goes haywire. It spreads across the black sands, missing its mark.

Though Skulls are fried below, King Baldyr stands unharmed. The medallion glows in his hand as it takes control of mine.

He whispers the command again, and my eyes bulge. It's like a hand squeezes around my heart.

I seize as I fall through the air.

"*No!*" Mae'e shouts.

Vines reach out from the sands, wrapping around my gut. They save me from full impact as I crash into the dirt. A sharp crack travels through my ribs. I grab my chest, unable to breathe.

Behind me, Mae'e's screams turn shrill. Her vines wither as more Skulls swarm. The world closes in as I'm forced to hear her capture.

Ahead of me, boots crunch over gravel. King Baldyr crouches down until his golden skull is visible.

"*Merle.*" He strokes my face. "*Our time is finally here.*"

PART V

CHAPTER SIXTY-NINE

ZÉLIE

WE LOST. . . .

Everything we fought to stop plays out behind my eyes. I see the flames engulfing Orïsha's coast. The barren land my nation will become. I feel the weight of every skeleton that will lie in the ashes. The magic that will never reign again. A hard numbness leaks from inside.

I've failed everyone I love.

King Baldyr holds me to his chest as we ride across the torchlit plains on a giant beast. The armor-plated white bear gallops with a mighty force. Dirt rips up from its protruding claws.

A wild war party flanks us on both sides. Skulls beat their crimson drums. Their red torches cover us in a garnet haze. Their shrieks echo through my bones.

As we ride, I sense their magic. It fills the lands around us. Towering white trees come to life before my eyes. Faces leer at me through the bark as their leafless branches twist up to the skies.

Massive statues line the main trail, formed from the same blood-metal of their weapons. Moss-covered axes rise from the dirt. Others honor the bears they ride. One statue features a mighty Skull. It hoists a collection of boulders over its tarnished shoulder, creating a pathway for us to ride through.

The voices of their ancients surround us. They pass through the biting winds. Their screams reverberate through the ground beneath us.

Their harsh whispers fill my ears.

"Your storm for his . . ."

As we ride, the warriors chant. A Silver Skull leads their battle cry.

"All hail King Baldyr!"

"All hail King Baldyr!" the Skulls echo.

"Father of the Storms!"

"Father of the Storms!"

The chant spreads from their warriors to the villagers who line the streets. The tribespeople pour out of modest dwellings built from logs. They climb to the tops of their stone wells. Others scale their triangular roofs, thatched with turf and straw.

For the first time, I see the people who make up their tribes. Their hunters. Their tradesmen. Their wives. Each wears a mask made of wood, covering all but their icy eyes.

A young girl runs to the dirt road. She holds on to her mother's skirts. I don't know what to feel when we lock eyes. The girl's red curls blow in the wind as we pass.

King Baldyr rides ahead, unaffected by the worship of his people, the praise of his men. He keeps his focus on the torchlit mountain bluff. On the mountain's side, the sculpture of a giant Skull stretches from the black seas to the bluff's peak. At the top, the silhouettes of crooked statues jut out from under the Blood Moon.

When we reach the bottom, Baldyr comes to a stop. He leaps from his white bear. The king lifts me into the sky like a trophy.

"Prepare the girls!" Baldyr yells.

THE *GALDRASMIÐAR* DESCEND AS ONE. There's nothing Mae'e and I can do to fight them off. Each wears a collection of white furs. They cover their faces with carved-out animal skulls.

The same runes carved into Baldyr's body glisten on their masks. The ancient marks glow red under the Blood Moon.

Chants ring as they remove us from the warriors to drag us into their torchlit caves. Shriveled hands pull at me from every direction. Their fingers hit my skin like ice. They throw the golden exoskeleton into a roaring blaze. They rip through the braids in my hair. They strip me of every item I wear until I'm left shivering, completely naked in the frigid air.

"*For the Father of the Storms . . . ,*" an elder croaks. The woman points, and the *galdrasmiðar* drag me to a wooden bath filled with blood. I choke as they throw me in, holding my head below the murky surface.

The *galdrasmiðar* shove me down again and again. As they chant, the crimson bath boils. They scrub until my white hair is stained red. They scrub to wash away all that I am.

When they finally lift me up, I gasp for relief. My lungs burn. It hurts to breathe. I can hardly see straight through the haze. My head hangs as they throw my body against a stone slab.

Someone uses a rope to tie me down. The rough cords bind my wrists and ankles, forcing me to stay still. An elder approaches me with a whittled bone. She looms over me, bringing me face-to-face with the animal skull.

"*Argh!*" I cry out as she brings the bone down. Someone shoves a strip of animal fur into my mouth. More hands press down on my face, forcing me to stay still.

The elder starts at my temple. She's vicious with every stroke she takes. I seize as she carves rectangular runes into me, the same jagged marks that run through King Baldyr's fair skin.

At my back, Mae'e screams. Her shrieks could break glass. She calls out to Mama Gaīa.

She prays for it all to end.

Help us.

I lift the words to whoever will answer my call. My body twitches against the stone slab. After a while, I can't cry out at all.

With each new rune, more voices enter my head. The medallion glows red. The golden veins that cover my body thicken, growing in strength.

The elder doesn't stop until the runes cover the entire left side of my body—from the black crown in my skull to the very bottom of my feet. When she's done, she releases the whittled bone. I can hardly see beyond the agony, but I follow the bone's path across the stone floor.

By the time they release me from the slab, I no longer exist. They drop me and I crumple into a heap. The whittled bone waits beyond my fingertips. It's all I can do to hold it close. I clutch it in my fingers, hiding it in my hair before they lift me up.

The *galdrasmiðar* dress me in a tattered silk robe. They fix a mask made of golden bones over my nose. When it's over, there's only one item left for each of us: white silk scarves to tie around our throats.

"*Do not do this,*" Mae'e wheezes in their tongue. The hierophant is a shell of the sacred mystic I know. Her entire body shakes. The blood from the new runes carved into her skin falls to the ground.

"*I beg you,*" Mae'e gasps. "*I pray to you. Save us.*"

Every *galdrasmiðr* stares, but the elder breaks from the pack. She removes her animal-skull mask, allowing us to see her own carved-up face. A band of black paint covers the bridge of her nose, accentuating her doll-like eyes.

The elder ties the scarf around Mae'e's neck, staring straight into the hierophant's diamond gaze.

"*Do not pray to be saved.*" Her voice creaks. "*Pray to be reborn.*"

By the time we make it to the shorelines, the dark sands are bare. Skulls lie impaled on black vines. Their blood still leaks into the sand. Jagged glass fragments line the beach, each shaped like a brilliant lightning bolt. Only the dead line the coast.

Zélie and Mae'e are gone.

This can't be happening.

Panic threatens to shut my body down. Every time I picture Mae'e or Zélie in King Baldyr's hands, my throat constricts. I still can't believe the words Mae'e shared. I feel the ghost of her lips against my own, the warm sensation that sent a shiver up my spine.

The way she kissed me . . . I don't know if anything has ever felt so right.

Now I don't know if I'll ever feel that kiss again.

For all I know, Mae'e could already be dead.

No. I remove my obsidian blade. I knock the treacherous thought from my head. There has to be a way.

I won't lose her and Zélie to Baldyr's plans.

"Where are they?" Tzain growls. It's all he can do to keep his head. He clutches his bone axe with shaking hands, ready to cut straight through the enemy's chest.

Inan pulls out the map of Baldeírik and lays it across the sands. His forehead creases as he searches the wrinkled parchment, not knowing which direction to go. I look over the small villages, the Skulls' camps, the capital city of Iarlaith. King Baldyr's commune sits at the nation's center, marked with gated walls.

Think, Amari. I shut my eyes, running through everything Mae'e's ever shared. I remember the connection she has with all of New Gaīa, the way the vines move to greet her.

I rise from the ground, returning to the black vines the sacred hierophant called forth on enemy lands. I run my fingers across the bloodstained stems. The vines are still warm. I call to the Green Maidens along the beach, forcing myself to speak their tongue.

"Mae'e created these." I look between their terrified faces. *"Can we use them to find her?"*

I step back as the maidens close in. They press their palms to the thick trunk. I brace myself as they focus, channeling their Mother Root.

One by one, pain etches through their faces. One maiden falls to her knees. She clutches the left side of her body, touching her skin as if it bleeds.

"There." The maiden points up the main trail. A collection of flickering lights illuminates the long path inland, traveling all the way up a mountain bluff.

The Old Stone. Yéva's prophecy comes back to me. Dread crawls up my spine as I take in Baldyr's sacrificial site. The Blood Moon looms above.

We're running out of time.

Tzain whistles for Nailah, and the lionaire leaps from the ship, bounding across the sands. Tzain hops on and extends me his hand. Inan stops me before I can latch on.

"Wait!" He throws up his arms. "We rush in that way, we become captives, too."

"We don't have time!" Tzain pushes back.

"There's a better way." Inan studies the map once more, and runs his finger around the coast. "Can they use their vines to scale the statue on the mountain's side?"

I do my best to translate Inan's plan to the vineweavers. When they nod, we reboard the videira. The vines spin as we take off.

I lift up a silent prayer as we race to save the girls.

CHAPTER SEVENTY-ONE

ZÉLIE

WHEN THEY LIFT US to the mountaintop, I prepare to meet my end. A stone altar sits on the mountain's summit. Crushed skeletons line its withered columns.

Below us, a sea of Skulls chant. They turn rabid with their praise.

"*All hail King Baldyr!*" Their voices echo through the red night. "*Father of the Storms!*"

The very king they speak of waits at the altar's center, standing between two painted stakes. His golden mask glimmers under the crimson moon. His entire being is marked for the ritual.

Fresh runes are carved into the right side of his body. The blood that drips from his skin hisses as it strikes the stone. Steam rises into the air where it lands, filling the altar with smoke.

Baldyr watches us as we ascend, a different hunger in his stormy eyes. I feel it in my gut.

He's waited for this moment his entire life.

> *A daughter of the Great Mother's storms . . .*
> *A daughter of the Great Mother's forge . . .*
> *A father formed from blood . . .*

Yéva's words return as the *galdrasmiðar* tie me to one of the painted stakes. The prophecy she shared in the town circle of New Gaïa rings through my ears, reigniting every fear.

Before the Blood Moon, all three will unite.
On the Old Stone, the bodies shall be sacrificed.
He will feel the touch of the Great Mother again.
The skies will open once more,
And a new god will be born.

The weight of all that will come presses down on my shoulders. As the *galdrasmiðar* part, I clutch the whittled bone they used to carve their runes into me. I hold on to my people's last hope.

There's only one way to stop King Baldyr's plans.

More *galdrasmiðar* travel up the stairs, their white furs swaying with every step. One pair carries a massive vat of boiling bloodmetal. Others carry the ornate chest Baldyr first brought onto the Skulls' ship.

Baldyr removes the golden key around his neck. He hands it to the *galdrasmiðar*, and they use it to open up the top. The two remaining medallions shine in ancient gold.

Across from me, Mae'e's sparkling eyes go wide. King Baldyr selects the medallion to the left. He raises it to her chest. I have to look away as he lunges forward.

"*No!*" Mae'e's shrill cries pierce the night. King Baldyr shoves the medallion into her sternum. The hierophant thrashes against the painted stake. Violent tremors rock her body, and travel throughout the land.

Veins sprout from the medallion immediately, creating a spiral network that spreads through her brown skin. The medallion starts to pulse. Mae'e's diamond eyes glow red.

King Baldyr drinks in the sight like the finest glass of mead. I feel the smile that spreads beneath his mask. He walks over to Mae'e and grabs her cheeks, inspecting her half-conscious body the same way he inspected me.

Baldyr leaves the altar altogether, moving to the mountain's edge to stand before his men. With a deep laugh, he spreads his arms wide.

"*The time has come!*" Baldyr yells.

His presence turns his men rabid. The Skulls roar in return. Their red torches dance beneath us, creating a sea of burning flames.

King Baldyr returns to the altar. He takes his place at our center. One *galdrasmiðr* pours a circle of oil around us and lights it with a torch, enclosing us in a ring of fire. The heat of the roaring blaze licks my bloodied skin.

The chants from below reach new heights. Feeble prayers spill from Mae'e's lips. Baldyr takes the final medallion in his hands. He raises it to his golden mask. He stares at the ancient metal like it's a newborn, one that will grant him the world.

With one mighty cry, he shoves it into his heart.

Then everything happens at once.

"*HARGH!*" King Baldyr howls with the force he unlocks. The medallion sears through his flesh, clawing on to his skeleton. A dark red light shines through the rectangular runes in his skin. His very being transforms as bloodmetal pours from his body in complex streams.

Mae'e screams as her own medallion activates. New vines twist from her abdomen and pour out of her hands. A dark flame breaks through her russet skin. The stone beneath her starts to heat. Molten rocks spread around her feet.

Her magic twists together like a thread, weaving into Baldyr's mutating skin. My own magic joins, draining me to feed the king.

The medallion in my chest ignites, flooding the mountaintop with golden light. I cry out as its force pulses through my blood. Lightning crackles around my body in a violent storm.

With a sudden jolt, a bolt of lightning shoots into the sky. It splits through the red night. All around me, spirits of the dead rise, their bodies like wisps of silver smoke. The Skulls' dead use the runes carved into my skin like a gateway. My body thrashes as they enter me at once.

King Baldyr roars as his molten body takes to the air. The golden mask merges with his face. The ground beneath us shakes, and the cosmos twist above our heads.

Baldyr becomes a god before our very eyes.

From above, Baldyr positions his shaking hands above our hearts and lifts. Our bodies rip from the painted stakes. Mae'e and I rise into the air, levitating higher and higher as our magic bleeds into the king.

"*All hail King Baldyr!*" The cries of his men rumble through the mountain stone. Lightning and vines swirl around him. Bloodmetal continues to crawl up his skin. Molten rock lifts to coat his feet. The spirits of the dead depart in streams, leaving me to enter their king.

With our magic, there will be no stopping him. No one will be able to oppose the Skulls. If he completes this ritual, it's over for everyone.

Orïsha.

New Gaïa.

The world.

"Zélie!" I hear the shout.

Tzain rides from the eastern mountains, crossing the stone on Nailah's back. A legion of vineweavers reworks their videira like a tank. The hard vines cut through the rock as they catapult their way to us.

Tzain . . .

The last of my heart gives me the courage for what I must do. I won't doom him to live in a world where King Baldyr reigns. I won't allow the maji to suffer that pain.

"Remember what you promised me!" I scream. I have to end this now, while I still have a chance.

I raise the whittled bone in the air.

"Zélie, *no!*" my brother shouts.

I allow myself one final look at the stars before driving the bone through my heart.

CHAPTER SEVENTY-TWO

TZAIN

Time stands still.

Everything I know dissolves at once. The strength I've fought to build evaporates, cut off from its guiding source.

Zélie's silhouette hangs suspended as she stabs the bone into her own heart. Blood leaks from her chest in ribbons. Her silver eyes bulge as she chokes.

I failed you. . . .

All the air in the world evaporates. In a heartbeat, my entire being shifts. I hear the laugh I'll never hear again. I see the day Zélie was first born, the purple blanket Mama wrapped her body in.

The moment Mama first placed her in my hands, I didn't know what to feel. Then Zélie grabbed the collar of my shirt. Her tiny nose wrinkled as she pulled me close. I pressed my forehead against hers and looked into her silver eyes.

I didn't know one day she would become home.

But now . . .

A cavern opens up inside me. Shame rips at what remains of my heart. All the vows I made to protect her crumble into dust.

My little sister is gone.

The lightning that rages around Zélie's body flares out of control.

A giant charge emanates from her medallion as her body falls limp. The blast strikes King Baldyr square in the chest.

"*Vernið Föður Stormanna!*" a Skull yells from the crowd.

Baldyr howls with the pain. His arms fly back from the force. The threads of magic swirling around him come to an abrupt end. The king's mutilated body hangs suspended between god and man.

More yells echo as the ritual falls short. Confusion spreads through the masses below. Baldyr twists through the air, plummeting into the sea of Skulls.

With Baldyr down, Zélie and Mae'e fall to the altar. Their bodies roll against the hard stone. The ring of fire around them dissipates. The fur-clad *galdrasmiðar* descend.

"Leave her alone!" I scream. I snap Nailah's reins. My lionaire gallops as fast as she can. Amari and Inan hold tight behind me as we race.

Nailah leaps from ledge to ledge, bridging the space between us and the altar. Troops of vineweavers flank past us. They use their rolling vines to catapult themselves through the air.

A group of Baldyr's *galdrasmiðar* walks into our path. The rectangular runes on their masks start to glow. With one swift arc, Amari drives her obsidian blade across each *galdrasmiðr*'s chest. Crimson splatters at our feet as Nailah makes her final leap.

When we land on the mountaintop, I jump from Nailah. I fall to my knees, taking my sister in my arms. Her silver eyes hang open. Her body grows colder by the second.

Even as I hold her, it doesn't feel real. I put my hand over the wound in her heart. Her warm blood coats my fingertips. I pull Zélie to my chest.

"I'm sorry," I whisper into her white hair. I feel every single person I've lost.

Mama.

Baba.

Zélie.

I have no one left.

Inan stands over me. He can't bring himself to speak. Around the altar, the battle rages. The Skulls fight to recover the girls. Their vicious yells ring as they charge. The Green Maidens enclose us in a circle of spinning vines. The warriors who try to get through are flung off the mountain.

Within the circle, Amari runs forward. She shuts her eyes and raises her hands. Blue light pours from her palms in waves, bringing the remaining *galdrasmiðar* to their knees. But more Skulls race through the caves with every passing second. Far too many for us to fight.

"We have to go!" Amari shouts at me.

Though everything feels numb, I force myself to rise. I clutch Zélie in my arms and return to Nailah, pulling myself up to her saddle. Inan and Amari follow, both lifting Mae'e's body up.

With a unified twist of their arms, the Green Maidens expel the circle of vines. They clear the way for us to run.

We ride away from Baldyr and his army of Skulls, scaling back down the mountain rock.

CHAPTER SEVENTY-THREE

TZAIN

"There's still a chance." Amari attempts to comfort me as we fly across the seas. New vines cross over our torsos and waists, keeping us strapped to the vessel's side.

The Green Maidens push beyond their natural limits, using their vines to latch onto rock formations and island chains leagues away. Every time they find a new anchor, our videira launches into the sky. We catapult over the ocean waves, hurtling to New Gaïa in record time.

As we soar, I clutch Zélie's body to my chest, unable to loosen my grip. Numbness fights the well of sorrow that threatens to spring forth.

We were supposed to go back home.

My sister was supposed to live.

Please. I close my eyes. I dare to hold on to the shred of hope that lies inside. The New Gaïans were able to save her once before, but that was back when Yéva reigned. Even Mae'e was strong enough to intervene.

Now the sacred hierophant lies unconscious, strapped to the bottom of our vessel in a blanket of woven vines. Her brown skin has turned pale. There's no life in her sparkling gaze.

Zélie may have stopped the ritual, but Baldyr sucked the very life from Mae'e's veins.

The thought of the mutilated king haunts me—the mess of blood-metal and human flesh. I see the twisted golden skull melted to his form, no longer just a mask. Zélie stopped him from becoming a god. But what power does Baldyr still have?

HA-WOOOOOOOOOOOO!

I whip around as a long horn blows. Dozens of black silhouettes appear on the horizon, glowing under the Blood Moon. Crafted from bloodmetal, each carrier is massive. They spread five times the width of any ship I've ever seen. The carriers don't have masts or sails, yet they move with unmatched speed.

Hundreds of Skulls stand at attention on each carrier's flat base. For the first time, I witness their army's collective strength. The hulking men wait in long lines, ready with their axes, their hammers, and their poleaxes.

"What are those?" Amari whispers.

Beside me, Inan reaches for his stolen maps. He looks over the schematics of the Skulls' ships, searching for a match. His hands go limp as realization dawns. He releases the parchments, allowing them to blow in the wind.

"The reason they destroyed their old fleet," he answers.

We watch, silenced by our defeat. Giant runes burn red beneath the vessels' hulls, generating a force that allows them to blast through the seas. Powered by the Blood Moon, the giant crafts traverse entire leagues in minutes. The very ocean quakes beneath them. But one special craft waits in the middle.

Dark clouds crackle overhead.

Baldyr . . .

A mass of storm clouds engulfs the king's carrier, hiding him from view. A whirlpool swirls around the giant craft. The seas around him crackle, open fissures spewing molten rock.

A horn rings, and Baldyr's carrier stops. The two lines on either side of him diverge. Half the crafts sail due west for Orïsha. The other half sail south for New Gaïa.

Promise me you'll fight. Zélie's words return. *Promise me you'll do everything you can. If the worst comes to pass, the Skulls won't stop at New Gaïa. They'll sail for Orïsha, too.*

Tears sting my eyes as I look down at my sister's corpse. I hated her for speaking the words. But watching the carriers fly, I think of everyone left back home—Kenyon, Khani, Nâo; the maji and the kosidán.

The way their crafts move, the Skulls will cross the ocean in mere hours. Their battle for Orïsha will rage before sunrise.

I couldn't save you. . . . I lay a hand on Zélie's mangled cheek. *I couldn't stop their king.*

Something bleeds from deep in my heart. Without my sister, I don't know if it will ever stop.

But I'll keep my promise to you, Zélie.

I hold my sister close for the last time. Vines wrap around her body as I lay her on the videira's floor.

I turn to the Green Maidens and vineweavers, studying how their vines anchor, release, and launch. I point to the carriers heading for Orïsha.

"What will it take to attach to that craft?"

CHAPTER SEVENTY-FOUR

AMARI

My heart races as the island of New Gaïa comes into view. A new ring of vines surrounds the island's borders, creating a floating barrier to keep everyone out.

Every videira that made it back from our failed attack floats in the choppy waters. The New Gaïans wait for the enemy, bone weapons drawn and brown faces grim.

Baldyr's fleet looms in the distance.

It won't be long before the Skulls reach their shores.

"*Limpe o caminho!*" a Green Maiden shouts. The floating wall of vines folds open at once. We sail through the woven walls, heading straight for the main river.

I hold Mae'e's and Zélie's cold hands as we pass through the dense underbrush and the emerald forest. Our videira zips through the lush plains. There isn't a single soul on the surrounding rice fields. Even the elephantaires have been cleared away.

When we crash through the waterfall to enter the city center, all of New Gaïa is up in arms. Hysteria sweeps through the city like a wildfire, spreading from the floating farms to the emperor's palace. New Gaïans flee in every direction, panic powering their every step. Tears stream free. Sharp screams fill the air.

Only a few vineweavers are left to guide their evacuation. They struggle to control the masses. The people crowd one another as they rush to enter the new network of vines. The city of hundreds of thousands moves underground, running away from the approaching Skulls.

And all the while, the crimson moon bleeds overhead. It bathes the city's sacred mountains in red. Dark shadows cover the face of Mama Gaīa. When we pass beneath her, the vines that crawl under her eyes look like tears.

We make it to the base of Mount Gaīa, and the videira we sail unravels at once. Half the Green Maidens lift Mae'e and Zélie in woven stretchers. The others run to the shaking mountain.

In the absence of Yéva, it takes their combined efforts to open the tunnel at the base of the mountain. The stone disks slide apart, revealing the stairwell of obsidian glass.

I turn to Inan—he waits at the mountain's base. He stares after the Green Maidens. I can almost feel the ember of hope that lies in his heart.

All at once, Inan wraps me in his arms. I squeeze my brother tight. Every fear I fight to keep down comes alive.

"I really thought . . ." Inan's voice cracks. "I don't know what I'll do if she doesn't wake up."

"Don't say that." I shake my head. "We have to believe. There's still a chance—"

BOOM!

We pull apart as plumes of black smoke rise in the distance. The air echoes with cannon fire and the faint shouts of the Skulls' brutish tongue.

They've landed. . . .

I drift to the mountain's base. I reach for my obsidian blade—

"Go to them." Inan guides me forward. "We still have time."

I race down the spiral steps, meeting the wall of steam head-on.

When I reach the bottom, Zélie and Mae'e already float in the natural spring. Ribbons of red leak into the glistening waters.

The Green Maidens circle around them. The emeralds flicker at their feet. All at once, they join their hands. I hold my breath as they begin to chant.

"Mama Gaīa, hear us now.
We demand your healing fires.
Your holy waters need you now—"

The waters start to thrash with the maidens' words. The rising steam swirls around their circle. The maidens' pleas echo through the rumbling mountain. A new pressure builds in the air, forcing me to the ground.

The veins bulge along the Green Maidens' arms. Their bodies shake with the power they call forth. But one by one, they start to collapse. They don't wield the force of Yéva or Mae'e.

I don't know if they're strong enough.

Please. I shut my eyes, praying with everything I have. I think back to Mama Gaīa, to her mighty spirit running through these lands. I picture the Skulls amassing on New Gaīa's shores, their leather boots storming through the main waterfall. We can't face this fight alone.

We need Zélie and Mae'e to be reborn—

All at once, a pulse radiates from the mountain's base. The black stone heats beneath me, burning my bare feet. The final Green Maiden collapses from exhaustion. An emerald light rises from the bottom of the natural spring, encasing both Zélie and Mae'e.

I shield my eyes as the bright light travels down their temples and up their feet, meeting at the medallions in both of their chests. It glows through the runes carved into their skin. It threads itself through the gash in Zélie's heart.

Please! I crawl forward. The earth beneath us shakes with new force. Fragments of black glass crash down from overhead. A crack ruptures far above.

"Please!" I cry out loud.

The waters glow so bright they burn.

Then both girls disappear beneath the surface.

Relief hits me like the rays of the sun as Mae'e emerges.

"*Ugh!*" Mae'e inhales a sharp breath, clutching her chest. Her head whips from side to side as she takes in her surroundings, a look of bewilderment in her diamond gaze.

"Mae'e!" I can't stop the tears that fall. I hook my arms around her neck and hold her tight. The medallion in her chest pulses with her reawakened heart.

I move to embrace Zélie, but she doesn't emerge from the waters. I release Mae'e and lunge forward. Panic grips me as I pull Zélie's body above the spring's surface.

"Zélie?" I whisper her name. A world I wasn't ready to face crashes before my eyes. Though her wounds are healed, her body hangs limp.

It didn't work. . . .

Every part of me goes numb at once. Sound muffles in my ears. Bars close around me, trapping me inside a nightmare I can't escape.

I see the first time I ever saw her face, all those moons ago in Lagos's marketplace. I feel the pain of every battle we've fought. Every time I've held her hand in mine.

I don't know what it means to fight without her at my side.

Mae'e moves to me. She places her hand over the medallion in Zélie's chest. Mae'e's forehead creases, and she looks up at the shaking mountain.

"Where is your brother?" the hierophant asks.

CHAPTER SEVENTY-FIVE

INAN

STANDING AT THE BASE of Mount Gaïa, I feel the world closing in. Everything I fought to stop unleashes under the Blood Moon. The woven city unravels before my very eyes.

The New Gaïans continue to clamor underground. Cries ring out as people fight to clear the canals. Villagers leap from plot to plot. The few vineweavers inside the city walls race to usher the youngest to the front.

Outside the city's mountains, the rampage of the Skulls builds. Their collective boots thunder. The sound of clashing iron fills the air. Fire rages through the forest outside the city's center, blazing as the enemy draws near.

I think of Tzain and the vineweavers approaching Orïsha's front. Of Mae'e and Zélie down below.

If she doesn't wake . . .

My mind brings me back to the cage I found Zélie in. The night we shared on the island. I promised to keep her safe.

I promised she would see her homeland again.

Baldyr's onslaught rages, yet I don't know where to fight. I don't know where to go. The weight of my failures threatens to drag me down to the ground—

BOOM!

I whip around. A string of explosions rings beyond New Gaīa's mountain entrance. Another explosion rings, and the roaring waterfall comes to a stop. Plumes of fire shoot into the night.

With one final blast, the mountain crumbles before my eyes. Even from a distance, the heat burns my face. Blazing boulders crash into the canals.

Then hundreds of Skulls charge through the black smoke.

No . . .

Shouts of battle rage as the Skulls descend. They ride longships sculpted from their bloodmetal, using them to sail through the floating civilization.

Red torches set flames to floating plots of vines. Glowing hammers smash through the ornate temples and square huts. Skulls pull the grenades at their belts, setting bombs off throughout the city. Mushroom clouds erupt as a pair of Skulls blast through the red bricks of a schoolhouse.

Horror chokes me as the city of New Gaīa burns. The Skulls take over the canals. A collection of boats moves past the town center, heading toward Mount Gaīa.

My hands tingle as I ignite my magic. I don't know how many Skulls I can take at once. But I won't let them get to the others.

Even if it costs me my life.

A sudden pulse ripples beneath my feet. I'm brought to my knees as the entire mountain quakes. A powerful *crack!* echoes through the red night. My lips part as I look up to the carving of Mama Gaīa. The emeralds light in the sculpture's eyes.

Be okay. My heart thrashes in my chest as I run to the stairwell. Steam rises out of the entrance. New heat sears through the obsidian.

Mae'e and Amari struggle up the black steps, the shaking mountain fighting them as they rise. Each holds one of Zélie's arms around their necks. Zélie's body hangs limp between them.

I move forward, taking Zélie's body into my arms. Every wound has been healed, but she's still cold to the touch.

"Her spirit isn't gone." Mae'e grabs Zélie's hands. "I felt her when I awoke. A piece of her still lies with Mama Gaïa. She's been connected to our Mother Root since Yéva and I brought her back."

"Your vision?" I ask.

Mae'e reaches up to me, grazing my white streak. "When I awoke, I saw you again. I understand the connection that you share!"

I look down to Zélie, knowing this is how it must be. If this is how our battle ends, it's up to her to defeat King Baldyr. Only she can take on his monstrous strength.

"Go." Mae'e points to the winding trail. "Carry her to the mountaintop. Petition Mama Gaïa. Exchange her breath of life for yours!"

Amari's face falls. She grabs on to my arm. "Inan, wait—"

"We don't have time."

I step back, allowing them to take the destruction in. Mae'e drifts to the mountain's edge. The flames of her city reflect in her diamond gaze.

A rage I've yet to see takes hold of the hierophant. Thick vines whir around her like blades. The vines lift her into the air as a current of molten rock spreads beneath Mae'e's feet, ready to release.

Up above, Mount Gaïa roars. A mountain about to blow. Amari looks from me to the approaching Skulls. Tears shine in her amber eyes.

I set Zélie down and pull Amari close as a blue light engulfs both of her hands.

"I'm sorry." I speak the words into her hair. Then I take Zélie's body back into my arms.

I steady myself as I fight my way to the mountain's summit.

CHAPTER SEVENTY-SIX

TZAIN

THE RACING WINDS HIT my body like a battering ram. The force rattles through my bones. I clench my teeth as I grip the vine attaching our small vessel to the Skull's carrier, struggling to hold on.

Two vineweavers sit on either side of me, bound by their hierophant to aid in our attack. The four New Gaïans stare straight ahead, prepared to take on the Skulls.

In mere hours, their carriers have torn through the length of the seas. They split the ocean like an axe. Already, Orïsha's jagged coast looms in the distance.

"Ready?" I look to the vineweavers. The vine attaching us to the carrier pulls us in. Another vine wraps around my torso. With a snap the vine whips forward, flinging me into the air. My arms cycle through the wind as I fly overhead.

For Zélie.

I roll across the ship's deck. My fingers glow green as I retrieve my bone axe. With a cry, I release all I have on the endless line of Skulls. Heartbreak powers my every move.

"*Ha!*" The sensation that used to fill me with the Skull's axe returns, but this time it radiates from my core. Blood rains as my bone axe slices through throats. I drive its cutting edge across the Skulls' bare chests.

Glowing blades come at me at once. Köa's lessons guide my steps. I feel the Lâmina's weight as I roll across the deck. When a group of warriors lunges, I drop to the floor, allowing the Skulls to cut through one another in my stead.

Behind me, vines crawl onto the carrier. They spread like giant spiders, trapping Skulls in an unbreakable web. More vines tangle in the thrashing waters, creating a monster in the seas. Eight legs spin together to form one giant arm, knocking Skulls overboard.

We clear through the carrier before launching ourselves onto another. Masks fall at our feet as we fight. We do everything we can to weaken their fleet. But the moment we enter Orïsha's bays, the first bomb explodes.

"Retreat!" I yell to the vineweavers. The weavers flank me as we race to the carrier's edge. With no time to waste, I leap from the ship. Vines wrap around me, catching me before I land.

The weavers re-form our videira, and we arc around the carriers as floating bombs detonate in Orïsha's bay. Shock waves travel through the ocean. Plumes of water shoot into the night.

Dozens of bombs ignite at once, eviscerating the first carrier. The blasts tear through the glowing bloodmetal. Shrapnel flies with the Skulls.

Alarms ring through Lagos. All at once the forces of Orïsha swarm. A thrill runs through me as maji, tîtáns, and soldiers race through the ports.

"Attack!" Kâmarū yells. The Grounder leads the charge, new armor matching his metal leg. A legion follows him down a freshly erected stone bridge, creating a walkway in the bay.

The maji chant in unison. Green light erupts up their arms. The seabed shakes as hardened spikes rise from the earth. They shoot through the water's surface, impaling the carriers' hulls like fishhooks.

The spikes rise so high, they lift carriers from the seas, far into the air. Skulls tumble from the decks like rocks. The bloodmetal groans as it snaps.

Water flies as broken carriers crash back down to the ocean's surface. I watch in awe as our vessel reaches the docks.

On the shores, Burners lock into special cannons welded to wrap around both their arms. My chest swells when I spot Kenyon at the center.

"Release!" the elder commands.

Blasts of fire shoot forward like comets, piercing through the carriers closest to the docks. Kenyon gives the second order, and the Burners strike again. Fire rages in an endless stream, incinerating the Skulls who line the decks.

"Push them back!" Nâo screams. Behind her, the army of Tiders mounts its attack. Muscles bulge along the elder's arms as she leads a line of Tiders into the waters. They lift their arms in a combined chant.

Teal light gathers around them. The seas thrash at their feet. A mighty wave lifts from the ocean. The seabed reveals itself as the wave reaches its climax, towering a kilometer into the sky.

With a powerful cry, the Tiders release the wave. It crashes over the carriers with a vengeance, twisting the bloodmetal like parchment. The powerful crafts crash into one another like dominoes, colliding as they fall back.

They knock half a dozen carriers out, but they can't stop them all.

"Get ready!" Nâo roars.

I brace myself as the first carrier makes land.

CHAPTER SEVENTY-SEVEN

◄ ⋯ ✕ ⋅ ● ⟩ ● ◎ ● ⟨ ● ⋅ ✕ ⋯ ►

INAN

DETERMINATION POWERS MY EVERY STEP. I don't allow myself to look back. I fight my way up the shaking mountain, clutching Zélie to my chest.

Rumbles travel from far below. Black stone crashes down from the mountain's side. The very ground swells at my feet. Gray steam leaks from the split rock, forming clouds that pile up in the air.

Mount Gaïa wakes with the destruction of her lands. A blaze builds inside her like the fires that rage below. But despite her force, I don't slow. I feel no fear.

Time takes me back, revealing everything that brought me here.

I remember my earliest mornings with Mother, the way we walked through the gilded halls of the palace, hand in hand. There were so many moments spent under the wall of royal portraits, sharing tales of rulers long since passed.

I see the endless days spent training with Admiral Kaea and the soldiers, the alabaster walls of our barracks. I hear the clash of iron against iron as we battled in the training circles. I see the glistening seal of Orïsha, the armor I couldn't wait to don. I remember the quiet moments spent in the palace at night before the throne I used to dream of sitting on.

I reach for the days I used to share with my sister, long before the

Raid. Whenever Mother hosted a gala, I could always find Amari under the table, hoarding platters of plantain and bean cakes.

I remember the old governesses we used to trick, all the distractions caused so we could escape. I hear her high-pitched giggle, the one that stopped the day my sword cut across her back. I think of the brother she should've had.

I think of what our life could've been.

But when I think of Father, all my other memories seem to shrink. I feel the way my shoulders slumped under the eternal weight of his gaze, the burn of the sênet pawn he placed in my hands. The sting of his fist against my cheek. I hear every word he yelled at me, everything he taught me to think. I taste the venom that used to crawl up my throat at the very sight of the maji.

I remember the prince who wanted to wipe them from this world.

And then there was you . . .

I look down at Zélie, taking in her ethereal form. My fingers dig into her white coils, and I feel the night my streak first appeared. The day I was certain my life would end.

I see the day I first saw her in Lagos's marketplace, the moment our paths first crossed. Never had I seen anything more horrible. More beautiful.

More wild.

"You changed me." I whisper the words, praying her spirit can hear. I think back to her dancing at the maji festival, the vision of Orïsha that was born. She was the only reason I thought I could be a different kind of king.

I dreamed of a lifetime spent with her in my arms.

I made her a promise back in that cage. I swore she would live to see our homeland. I can't stop King Baldyr. I can't battle every Skull.

But I can still offer her this.

Petition Mama Gaīa. Mae'e's words return as I reach the mountaintop. *Exchange her breath of life for yours!*

I fight my way to the crater's center. The force of the shaking mountain brings me to my knees. Every breath I take sears down my throat. I choke on the plumes of toxic gas.

"Please!" I gasp through my coughs. I reach for the pulse of Mama Gaīa, for every divine force in Orïsha. The Blood Moon beats down from above, a reminder of all we've lost.

"*Please!*" I scream to the spirits, the very beings I was raised to reject. Tears stream down my face as dark clouds gather overhead.

When lightning crackles, I lift Zélie's body to the skies. I offer her up to the storm.

"Save her. . . ." I whisper the words to whomever will answer my call.

Everything goes white as the mountain explodes.

CHAPTER SEVENTY-EIGHT

ZÉLIE

WHEN I BLINK OPEN my eyes, green is all I see—bright ferns with feathery leaves; the long, narrow stems of sweetgrass. Meadows of mint stretch far, filling the air with their cool, crisp scent. An endless field of reeds spreads out before me, tickling my bare feet as I walk.

It can't be . . .

No sun lies above. A gentle haze surrounds me like a thin layer of fog. Shock pricks my body like needles. I turn in a slow circle, taking everything in.

Though I inhale, I don't breathe in air. I don't feel the brush of wind. I float in walls of white, brought back to a place I never thought I'd see again.

"You're here."

I look beyond my shoulder—Inan stands tall. Dressed in a white silk kaftan, a brilliant smile spreads across his face. A soft peace radiates around him, as tangible as light.

He keeps me under his gentle gaze, beyond fear. Beyond pain.

Under his amber eyes, the weight of the world falls away.

"Are we . . ." The question I'm too afraid to ask hangs on the tip of my tongue. But Inan shakes his head. He runs his fingers through the reeds.

"Mae'e came to me before the battle," he explains. "She kept seeing visions of the two of us. She told me to bring you to the mountaintop. That up here we could exchange the breath of life."

Inan closes the space between us, lacing his fingers with mine. It's then I see our difference—with every exhale Inan releases, his body fades. His skin grows more transparent by the second. Mine only grows more opaque.

"What did you do?" I whisper.

"Kept my promise to you."

I watch, bewildered, as our lives transfer. My connection with Mount Gaïa pulses through me like another heartbeat. The sacred mountain anchors our exchange.

"We still need you." Though his spirit fades, Inan's smile stays. "Baldyr's launched his assault. I can't stop him, but you have a chance."

The bite of tears stings my eyes. I fight the urge to let them fall free. Inan takes my face into his fading fingers. I don't know if he's ever held me with such tenderness. Such grace.

He presses our foreheads together, and I inhale his musky scent. I feel every moment we've ever shared in his caress. Training with him on the mountains outside Gombe. Teaching him how to use his gift. Running through the forest with him in the maji festival.

The very first time we kissed.

The scars he created with his betrayals. The wounds only his touch could erase. We were supposed to bring about a new dawn.

We were supposed to change the fate of Orïsha.

"You still can." Inan squeezes me, breaking through my thoughts. "The Orïsha you will fight for is different than the one we left. It's one where you can reign—" Inan's voice strains, and I feel the pull on my soul. The last of his breath is waning.

Our time is slipping away.

"Find King Baldyr," Inan instructs. "Defeat him once and for all. Take

335

charge of the nation and create the Orïsha we dreamed of. One that can stand against any foreign kingdom."

"What if I'm not strong enough?" I whisper.

"You're the strongest force I know." Inan takes hold of the majacite crown. With a lurch, it breaks free of my temple. Purple light leaks from my head like blood, warming me as it hits my skin.

"Death doesn't destroy you, Zélie," Inan continues. "It frees you. It answers your call."

As the purple light runs down my body, I feel the power once lost. The ability to raise the dead. The magic embedded in my blood.

"I love you," Inan exhales. I look away, unable to take in the words. A sob escapes my throat. The fog around us intensifies, erasing our world.

Despite every time I've come against him, every moment I've held his life in my hands, something sharp tugs at my chest. I'm not ready to say good-bye.

I'm not ready for our story to end.

Inan tucks a lock of hair behind my ear, and my skin starts to glow. His lifeforce kneads through my being. A sharp heat fills my lungs as they expand, beginning to breathe again.

"Inan, I—"

He kisses me, and for one perfect moment, the rest of the universe stands still. His love breaks straight into my heart. It burns through my tears.

The world around us fades as our lips part for the last time.

Though he disappears, I hear him in my soul.

"I know."

CHAPTER SEVENTY-NINE

AMARI

Strike!

There's no end to the Skulls who swarm Mount Gaïa's base. The warriors cut through the waters in their bloodmetal longships, howls of victory echoing from their throats.

The city of New Gaïa burns behind them, creating an orange haze beneath the Blood Moon. Mounds of rubble replace the vibrant temples that used to gleam in the sun. Floating plots of scorched vines sink into the mountain lake.

When the first Skulls land, dark blue light surrounds me. It burns as it tears through my skin. Grief carves at me from inside, propelling me to fight, propelling me to win.

"Ha!" I throw my hands out. Spheres of blue light shoot from my palms like cannons. They strike the Skulls straight in the chest. Cries break free as I force my magic into their heads.

My own mind shakes with the memories that race—the empty eyes of the Skulls' first kills, the blades they use to harvest the bones from their faces. I see the armories where they create their masks. I'm brought back to the stone altar we escaped, the very place they give their blood oaths and receive their weapons.

I rip through the Skulls' heads, tearing apart their memories as if I could tear them limb from limb. My magic leaves the warriors on the stone floor, seizing as they stare up at the Blood Moon.

As I attack, the Green Maidens strike, returning from the natural springs to join the fight. Despite the toll of resurrecting their sacred hierophant, the warriors give everything to defend their homeland.

Vines shoot out like whips, grabbing Skulls by their throats. Maidens snap their necks like twigs. Others lift the Skulls into the air, watching as they choke.

One Skull breaks through the masses, too fast for me to summon my magic. He swings at my head with his battle-axe, the crimson blade aglow with red light. But before I can reach for my obsidian blade, vines snap around his wrists. Others wrap tight around his ankles. The Skull shouts as one of the maidens suspends him, leaving him vulnerable to my attack.

I lunge forward and drive my obsidian blade through his gut. I twist with a vengeance, needing him to feel all the pain that he's caused. But for all our battling, nothing compares to the war Mae'e wages on her own.

The hierophant fights in the bay, vines lifting her into the air. A whirlpool of vines swirls around her at vicious speeds, each wielding massive thorns like serrated fangs.

With a wave of her arms, the lethal plants strike, ripping through the Skulls who attempt to sail past. Bodies fly into the mountain lake, staining the turquoise waters with crimson. More vines pierce straight through the Skulls' guts, collecting corpses on their long stems. Others wrap around the Skulls' abdomens and pull, dragging them from their longships. The vines force their writhing bodies underwater, keeping them down until they drown.

But the vines Mae'e wields are only the first of her attack. Baldyr's medallion still pulses in her chest, granting her new strength. Rivers of molten rock build at her feet, gathering in large heaps. Mae'e's diamond gaze flashes red, and streams of lava shoot out in all directions, incinerating everything they touch. The Skulls she hits burst into flames. Their very bones evaporate.

The sacred hierophant transforms before my eyes, a ferocious beast raging from the skies. Together, we eviscerate the Skulls in waves. We fight beyond our exhaustion, we push through every ounce of pain.

But as we war, the ground shakes beneath us. The stone splits at our feet. Giant rocks crash down the mountain's side, exploding like bombs as they land. When I see the dark clouds move overhead, my hands fall limp.

"*To the shores!*" a maiden shouts.

Before I can react, vines wrap around me, pulling me from the mountain's base. The Green Maidens take to the air, using their vines to swing. I brace myself as I fly.

"Mae'e!" I call out. But the hierophant doesn't stop her rampage. A dense fissure cracks up above, and Mae'e opens up her arms, embracing the impending eruption head-on.

The maidens move past the temples, traversing the rain forests that grow down the mountain's slopes. Their vines snap from trunk to trunk, catapulting us through the dense foliage. Wind rushes at my face as they race for the island's shores.

The entire island quakes as Mount Gaīa explodes.

BOOOOOOOOOOOOOOOM!

The blast rips through the trees. It cleaves through the vines we use to swing. With a rush, I tumble free, crashing into the black sands.

Heat sears the back of my neck. My ears ring with deafening force. I push myself onto my elbows, unable to believe the sight.

Columns of ash shoot high into the sky, darkening the red night.

Vibrant bolts of lightning erupt from the crater, twisting together like a tornado. The lightning gathers in a circle above the mountain's head, falling in brilliant golds, striking purples, and angry reds. Glowing streams of lava run free, raining down the mountain stone.

"*Mama Gaīa* . . ." The Green Maidens around me drop to their knees and bow. A powerful pulse travels through the black sands. More sharp cracks erupt through the air.

Then the very mountains rise.

By the skies . . .

I stare up, unable to speak. Each figure carved into the mountain range surrounding New Gaīa comes to life, creating an army of colossal beings.

Boulders fall from their bodies like rain. Lava passes through their rocks in branching patterns, creating veins. The towering figures crush the Skulls beneath them in mere breaths. The Skulls left in their wake shriek to their deaths.

Deep in the city center, Mae'e's body lifts so high we can see her from the shores. The lava that spread beneath her coats her entire being. Molten vines emerge from the forest, each as thick as their trees.

The molten vines lunge at the fighting Skulls along New Gaīa's beach, searing straight through their flesh. They wrap around the carriers docked in the seas. The vines squeeze so tightly, the mighty vessels crack in half.

Fires rage as they burn through the bloodmetal. The smoldering crafts sink beneath the surface. Mae'e harnesses Mount Gaīa's eruption, wiping the enemy from her native lands.

A hum erupts from the summit. My eyes grow wide as the Reaper I once knew takes to the air. Zélie emerges from the volcanic ash, lightning twisting around her glowing form.

The winds roar beneath her feet. Her white mane crackles free. All at once, the skies rip open. A mighty flood rains down from below.

But if she's here . . .

My hands fly to my heart as the realization dawns. I can't fight the tears that well in my eyes.

"You're gone." I dare to speak the words aloud, and they cut through my heart like glass.

Grief drags me to my knees as Zélie lands on the thrashing seas.

CHAPTER EIGHTY

TZAIN

"Retreat!" Nâo calls.

I join the maji as the Skulls make land. We race down the wooden pathways, heading back to the merchant quarter.

Planks fly as the Skulls' carrier crashes into the docks. The blood-metal tears straight through the port. It barrels through the fortified walls, destroying the specialized cannons and storage houses along the shores. Plumes of dust rise into the air as the carrier razes the port to the ground.

The Skulls leap from the edge of the craft, arms waving as they drop to the ripped earth. They raise their weapons into the air and shout. Red light surrounds their blades, feeding off their blood.

The carrier is only the first to get through. The ten remaining crafts follow in its path. With a mighty roar, thousands of Skulls charge at once.

The ground quakes with the force of their attack.

"Remember the plan!" Nâo yells. The vineweavers and I follow her down the pastel-colored buildings of the merchant quarter. Tamers wait at the end of the dirt path, rose-colored armor sculpted to their bodies. My ears ring with their unified chants. Pink light surrounds their hands.

"*Ọmọ ogun igbó, ẹ dìde báyìí—*"

All at once, wild ryders pour from the empty buildings, the same pink light swirling around their heads. Countless panthenaires lunge forward, their dark coats glistening under the red moon. A sea of rainbow-scaled serpents slides free. Packs of gorillions rage across the dirt path. One-horned cheetanaires bare their ivory fangs. Na'imah leads the stampede, charging on the back of a black-tusked elephantaire.

"Attack!" Na'imah shouts. The animal infantry meets the first wave head-on. Serpents unleash their venom like darts. Panthenaire fangs sink into flesh. White-chested gorillions pummel Skulls into the ground.

At the next divide, Burners stand at the ready, marked by their gleaming red armor. When the retreating maji pass, the Burners strike. Their voices join together in unison.

"Iná jó, iná fónká, iná jó, iná fónká—"

Embers spark at their fingertips, floating through the cracks in the shops' boarded-up windows. One by one, the buildings ignite, exploding like dominoes in a line.

The next wave of Skulls are caught in the blast. Fire rages through the merchant quarter as bodies fly.

"Tzain?" Kenyon calls as I round the corner. In an instant, I'm pulled into his arms. A moment is all we have in the chaos. The Skulls push forward in their assault.

Kenyon takes in the vineweavers, my shaved head, the bone axe tattooed across my abdomen.

"Go on!" He waves us all forward. "Soldiers are waiting in the marketplace!"

My chest heaves as we run through the city, fighting to reach its center. The number of Skulls multiplies at our backs. Maji and tîtáns work together, launching new defenses from every checkpoint.

Grounders open up the earth, swallowing entire legions of Skulls. Welders launch columns covered in gleaming spikes. Bones crunch as they crush the Skulls into building walls.

Winders stand on deserted rooftops, generating powerful blades of air that cut straight through the Skulls. Cancers hit the enemy next, creating orange clouds of toxic gas.

When we finally make it to the marketplace, I find the entire area has been cleared out. Hundreds of soldiers gather together in rows, prepared to take on the remaining Skulls. Each wields new armor and shields carved by Welders to absorb the Skulls' blows.

Metal barricades lie at the soldiers' backs. Collapsed buildings arc around them, closing them in.

"We fight to the death!" a general shouts. "We fight till our last breath!"

Before us, the Skulls' thundering boots crescendo. Their howls ring through the air. Someone tosses me and the vineweavers new shields. I release my bone axe, joining Orïsha's last defense.

"For Orïsha!" The general raises her sword.

"For Orïsha!" The battle cry echoes from every soldier's mouth. We all run forward as the Skulls spill into the alleyway en masse.

The air echoes with our clash. Metal collides with metal. The Welders' armor withstands the brute force of the Skulls, giving my people a fighting chance.

A giant Skull runs at me, battle-axe raised. I lift my shield, absorbing the attack. The force reverberates through the hand-carved metal, sending shock waves through the air.

The Skull strikes again, and I spin out of his range. I grit my teeth as I cut down, chopping off his arm. With another pivot, I swing, slicing my blade across the Skull's neck.

Two more Skulls enter my range. I roll across the floor, bringing myself to the ground. I cry out as I drive my axe through their knees. Blood sprays as they fall to the dirt.

Before me, a New Gaïan moves to restrain a Skull. Her vines snap around his wrists. But the massive Skull reverses the attack, latching onto the vines and dragging the weaver right in front of him.

I sprint across the field as the Skull lifts up his hammer. Before the Skull can attack, I hurl my bone axe in the air, striking him in the center of his chest.

Our battle rages throughout Lagos, from the battered port to the deserted marketplace. We fight with all we have, but no matter how many Skulls we defeat, more pour through the alleyways.

To my left, hammers catch soldiers straight in the chest, sending them flying into the barricades. To my right, a Skull seizes two soldiers by the necks. He squeezes them until they snap.

Another Skull knocks a line of soldiers to the ground. With a vengeful swipe, his glowing blade digs into their abdomens. The massive Skulls strike with no remorse. They cut straight through the seal of Orïsha across our soldiers' breastplates, forcing our soldiers back.

Keep going! I will myself, pushing though my muscles' burn. I don't know how much longer we can keep up the fight. There's no end in sight—

BOOOOOOOOOOOOOOM!

The concussive force blasts through the air. It blows through the deserted buildings before us in a mere breath. I shield myself from the rubble that falls overhead. The clearing smoke reveals a full view of the sea.

The skies split open at the very seams. A rush of rain pelts from above. A string of lightning ripples through the red night from the east. The bolts dance above our heads in a vibrant blaze, golden lines crackling free.

Zélie . . .

I recognize her power. I feel her in the racing winds. My eyes sting as the shorelines of Orïsha transform. It's like a hurricane is released over the seas.

345

Mountainous waves swallow the remaining carriers whole. The Skulls feeding into the alleyway are no more. Their bodies fly as they're carried up, pulled into the raging storm.

I lift my face to the pelting rain, allowing it to wash the blood from my skin. I raise my axe into the air and roar.

The soldiers join me in full force.

CHAPTER EIGHTY-ONE

ZÉLIE

The moment I land on the thrashing seas, the waters start to glow. The white force ripples through the currents. It pulses far below.

My entire body shakes with the strength awakened from deep inside. Electricity rumbles through every vessel. Bolts of lightning shoot from my lips. Chanting voices fill my ears.

I open my arms to the night as I hear the call of my ancestors again. . . .

"Ti ìjì ati òòrùn——"

I shut my eyes, and I'm brought back to the mountaintops of Ibadan. Mama stands before me, head lifted to Oya's storm. The faces of Reapers long passed circle around us, deep purple robes flying in the wind. They spread out their arms, laying their hands on my shoulders, my neck, and my temple.

As they chant, my skeleton shakes. The jolt reverberates through my core. A familiar heat runs through my veins. I inhale as the magic of life and death returns in full strength.

"Òyà, kún mi nínú!" I cry out to my goddess. The air howls in response. Billowing clouds gather above, blocking out the Blood Moon. The clouds spiral above my head, creating the eye of a hurricane. Rain falls in sheets.

Nothing stands in my way as I race across the seas.

This ends here.

The white glow travels through the ocean as I sprint across the surface, spreading far beyond the horizon. I reach for every spirit that has fallen, every body tossed to the seas by the Skulls. I think of every maji we lost on their ships, every New Gaīan left floating in the Black Bay. No life will be lost in vain.

We get our vengeance today.

Baldyr's carrier sails at me at full speed, the largest craft in his annihilated fleet. The force of the hurricane rips through the clouds surrounding his vessel, allowing me to witness the monster he's become.

Nearly double the size he was before, I see the effect of the power Baldyr siphoned from our veins. The beast of a king roars in his place, a mess of blood and iron. Red lightning crackles around his deformed metal skeleton. His twisted mask is smelted to his skin. Molten rock swirls through his body, oozing like an open wound. He stands on an elevated platform above an army of Skulls.

Baldyr opens up his arms, and a fissure splits through the seas. Ocean water pours into the divide as giant plumes of lava fly free. I skid to a halt as the molten wave arcs over my head.

"*Èmí òkú, ẹ gbé mi wò*—"

I throw up my hands, and the spirits of death answer my call. Black shadows shoot forth in twisting arrows, creating an opening through the sizzling red wall. Ash falls before me as the molten wave comes crashing down. Steam rises into the air, creating a dense cloud.

"*You cost me everything!*" Baldyr yells. I grit my teeth as he takes to the sky. Bolts of red lightning crackle in his palms, growing in size.

"*Èmí òkú, ẹ fún mi lágbára yín, ẹ jáde wá nínú òjìji tuntun*—" I chant again, conjuring new shadows of death. The spirits explode from my back, allowing me to fly across the seas.

I twist under the first bolt that Baldyr launches. I spiral to avoid the next. But Baldyr screams into the night. A river of lightning breaks free from his deformed chest.

"*Ha!*" I call forth my own golden lightning, wrapping it around my body in a sphere. The electric wall holds as Baldyr's bolts crackle around my form. When it dissipates, I fight to get to him.

Baldyr throws everything he has, every bit of power stolen from the failed ritual. Bloodmetal vines launch through the air, thorns like blades. Molten spheres shoot at me like cannons. Streams of magma arc through the air like claws.

"You can't stop me!" I shout at the twisted king. With my shadows of death, I repel every attack. There's no way to block my onslaught.

I am the god that's been reborn.

When I reach the carrier, I throw my head back. I scream with the wrath of my gods.

The entire ocean shakes.

Then the first animation breaks through the waves.

Finally!

Silver hands reach through the water. They claw their way above the surface. The watery corpses of maji rise, a legion of souls brought back to life.

Dozens of animations turn to hundreds. In the blink of an eye, there are thousands. The spirits of my people fight through the glowing seas, tearing through the crashing waves.

Animations launch themselves at Baldyr's carrier in droves. They crawl onto the deck, unleashing the full might of their wrath. The Skulls shout as the resurrected souls descend. Their glowing blades do nothing to hold them back. The animations cover the Skulls in their deadly swarm, tearing the foreign warriors limb from limb.

More animations build under me like a mountain, lifting me high into the air. They rise beneath me until I reach Baldyr's plane, level with the source of my despair.

"*Baldyr!*" I scream the old king's name through the building tempest.

Baldyr summons all the power within him. Blood and lightning spiral above his head. Molten metal spews from his chest like throwing knives. They catapult toward me like shooting stars.

"*Demon!*" he roars, unleashing his barrage.

My neck flies back as I raise my hands to the skies. The seas arc around us, closing us into a whirlpool of white.

A thousand bolts of lightning come crashing down, stealing the last of the king's life.

EPILOGUE

"THERE IT IS."

Amari rises from Mae'e's arms to join me at the front of the videira. Fresh tears streak her face. They fall in an endless stream since Inan's sacrifice.

She joins me at the front of the woven vessel as we take in the shorelines of our homeland. The sight makes my throat tight. I can't believe it.

After everything, I've finally returned.

The wreckage of the Skulls' attack lies in the port, remaining carriers half-submerged in the bay. Plumes of smoke rise all over the barren city. The buildings have been blown away.

One figure waits at the edge of the battered port. In an instant, I recognize his powerful build. The axe tattooed across his abdomen shines bright under the sun. The love woven through his rigid stance burns from afar.

"Over there!" I motion to the vineweavers steering our craft. The vessel can't carry me fast enough. We sail through the debris and bodies floating in the murky waters. Countless skull masks stare up at us as we pass.

When I make it to land, I bound from the videira, leaping into my brother's arms. Tzain holds me so tight my body aches, but I don't fight his embrace.

The weight of the ritual hangs between us. The touch I thought I'd never feel again. I hang on to my brother as he sets me down. The magic of my land hums through my skin.

Behind us, a group of maji gathers. My heart swells at the remaining elders and members of the ten clans. Nâo beams at me from the front. Kenyon and Na'imah wait, hand in hand.

"*Jagunjagun!*" Mári bounds forward. My little Reaper runs into my arms. As I dig my head into her curls, I can't stop the tears that spill free. The members of my clan surround me, welcoming me back home.

But the maji aren't the only ones to fill the ruins of Lagos. The surviving soldiers and tîtáns mill through the empty streets. Everyone works together, their union emboldened by the attack.

Nehanda and the Grounders clear the rubble. Burners cremate the remaining Skulls. Khani and the Healers tend to the injured. Maji, tîtán, or soldier—no one gets turned away.

At our arrival, the circle around us builds. The people come together, waiting to hear of the war. The divides between us seem to evaporate. Even Nehanda takes Amari by the hand.

In the building crowd, I see them—the seeds of the dreams I once shared with the little prince. An Orïsha where the maji are safe. A land where we don't have to be afraid. We can rebuild all that we've lost, creating a true nation beyond our brutal wars and raids.

"Is it over?" Mári asks.

I remove King Baldyr's mask from my pack, and lift the golden skull into the air.

A flare of hope runs through me as all of Orïsha cheers.

When we make it back to our lands, we weep.
The tears we cry form rivers through our mountains.
Our heartbreak hollows us from the inside out,
leaving us with nothing but our scars.
But we do not weep for those we have lost,
we do not weep for the horrors we have faced.
We weep because we are warriors.
We weep because, against all odds, we have prevailed.
In our sacred lands, we find the truth——the power no king can erase,
a power carved through the valleys of our hearts,
a force no enemy can bind in chains.
We weep because our magic is eternal.
We weep because our gods reign.
We weep because we feel the ancestors who watch from above,
waiting for the day until we rise to meet our dead.

ACKNOWLEDGMENTS

Writing this book and this entire series has been a journey like no other. Though it's been years since *Children of Blood and Bone* was first published and Zélie, Tzain, Inan, and Amari became characters that existed outside of my head, I still can't really believe all that's happened, or wrap my head around all the love and support you've shown me and this series. Words will never truly be enough to say thank you for allowing me to tell the story of my heart, and embracing the world of Orïsha. Nevertheless, I want to take this moment to share my immense gratitude and love with you now.

To the readers—You will never know the special place you have in my heart. The love, encouragement, creativity, and passion you've shared with me over the last seven years has routinely brought me to tears. I love you, and I am so grateful to each and every one of you. You are a part of my wildest dreams come true.

To the teachers, librarians, and booksellers who have brought Zélie into your classrooms and shared this series with your communities— Thank you for spreading this story and helping it find so many incredible homes. This wouldn't be possible without you, and I am forever grateful for the support you've shown.

To my family—You have been there to celebrate my highest highs, and you have been there to love me through my lowest lows. You more than anyone know how much of a challenge this entire journey has been. Thank you for sticking with me. And thank you for loving me when I was really annoying. I love you, and I'm so grateful that I've gotten to write this series with you cheering me on.

To my Aunty Yemi—You know the special journey this book and I went through. Thank you for walking with me and praying for me until the very end. And to all my aunties, thank you for your prayers and your love.

To my Yoruba Translators—Uncle Segun Sanni, Uncle Oke Champion, and Uncle Abbey Salami—Thank you for the countless hours and late nights you've put into bringing these incantations to life. I couldn't have created the magic in this series without you!

To the entire team at Macmillan—There is no measure for the heart and passion you have put into sharing this story with the world. When I dreamed of publishing a book one day, I never could have imagined working with a team as caring and supportive as yours. To Jean Feiwel, Jen Besser, and Jon Yaged, thank you for taking a giant chance on me and Zélie's story. I will forever be grateful for the journey and the impact we've been able to make on the world. To Tiffany Liao and Christian Trimmer, thank you for all the amazing work you did to bring the first two novels to life. To Mariel Dawson, Molly Ellis, the entire marketing and publicity team, and the Macmillan sales team, thank you for everything you've done to bring these stories to the masses. You've put Zélie's adventures into over a million hands, and you've changed my life forever.

And to Ann Marie Wong and Mark Podesta—Thank you for enthusiastically shepherding this manuscript to the finish line. I feel so lucky to have gotten to complete this journey with you, and I am so grateful for all the passion and dedication you put into bringing this trilogy to a close.

To Margaret Miller—Thank you for nurturing the earliest seeds of this story. You were the first to let me know I had an exciting adventure on my hands, and I'm so grateful for all the thoughts and suggestions you shared.

To Lola Idowu, Samira Iravani, and Keith Thompson—Thank you for the stunning art you created to give Zélie's final chapter the beautiful send-off she deserves.

To Lauren Poyer and Solimar Otero—Thank you for bringing your expertise into shaping the new worlds in this story. The passion and imagination you shared helped to bring New Gaīa and Baldeírik to life.

To my manager, Ronke Champion—I couldn't have done it without you. Thank you for your constant love, support, and belief in me and my dreams. I truly don't know where I or this series would be without your guidance and advocacy.

To my publicists, Marla Farrell, Lauren Gold, and the incredible team at Shelter PR—You are more than fairy godmothers. Thank you for your constant love, support, and care. You have been the most beautiful blessings on this journey.

To my agents, Kevin Huvane, Carlos Segarra and Mollie Glick and Kate Childs, Matt Martin, William Brown, Michelle Weiner, Jesse and Ryan Nord, Humble, Brandon, Elvira, and the entire team at CAA— Thank you for supporting me to the end of this journey! I am grateful for the guidance, and so excited for the adventures to come.

To Roxane, the team at Curtis Brown, and all the international publishers—Thank you for the passion and support you've shown this story. I will never get over the thrill of seeing Zélie's face in foreign languages, and deeply appreciate the ability to have readers from all over the world.

To Alexandra Machinist and Hilary Jacobson—Thank you for advocating for me and this series and starting my publishing career with a bang.

To my friends—You have listened to me neurotically worry about every book in this trilogy for years—I love you, and I couldn't have done this without you. Thank you for making me laugh, thank you for being there when I had to cry, and thank you for cheering me on like no one else could. And to my habibi, my soul sister, my heart——I love you forever and ever.

To Grizzly——My own little Nailah. You stayed by my feet for so many of my long nights. Thank you for being my dog. You were the best friend I ever could have had.

And last, but certainly not least, To God——Thank you for giving me the gift of stories, and blessing me with this chance to share it with the world.